# Borderlands 6

# Borderlands 6

*An Anthology of Imaginative Fiction*

*Edited by*

*Olivia F. Monteleone*

*and*

*Thomas F. Monteleone*

SAMHAIN PUBLISHING

Samhain Publishing, Ltd.
11821 Mason Montgomery Road, 4B
Cincinnati, OH 45249
www.samhainpublishing.com

Borderlands 6
Copyright © 2016 by Olivia F. Monteleone and Thomas F. Monteleone
Print ISBN: 978-1-61923-498-7
Digital ISBN: 978-1-61923-263-1

The Architecture of Snow first appeared in Dark Delicacies 3, ed. by Del Howison and Jeff Gelb, 2009
First Samhain Publishing, Ltd. electronic publication: May 2016
First Samhain Publishing, Ltd. print publication: May 2016

# Table of Contents

# Dedication

This one is for
Douglas E. Winter,
who edits a pretty mean anthology his ownself.

# Introduction

We know.

We know you've all waited years—quite literally, a decade—for this next volume of the *Borderlands* anthology series[1]. But since we aren't a cheap date, keeping you waiting has, it is hoped, made you want us even *more*.

A lot has changed since last we read for this anthology—not much of it matters, but a couple things do. First off, Olivia (one of the collective "we") is the newest editor for the *Borderlands* series—we like to keep it in the family—*omertà* and all that. Elizabeth decided to leave the small press stuff to us, which would probably explain why now your books are being shipped with three packing peanuts, as opposed to being wrapped in delicate tissue and sealed with a ribbon—what can we say?

We've been reading for this anthology intermittently for a couple years, but we had to postpone things until we got the *right* stories. Once we knew we had enough of them, the book came together in about a weekend, as do most things in our lives.

That said, you should probably put this book down if you love stories about vampires, zombies, apparitions, ghouls, slashers, and the rest of the usual horror staples that show up on a regular basis. Don't get us wrong, we love a lot of the above tropes and icons, but we aren't buying any of it for our series. We'd rather fill our pages with supremely weird tales, the ones concerned with things you don't conjure in your most disturbing nightmares. We search out stories with original ideas and unique ways of examining them. Concept and execution. Offering you something you've never read before defines the nature of a true *Borderlands* story.

It's been a really beautiful thing. We received so many stories from so many really

---

1     We would be terribly remiss if we didn't tell you that the first five volumes of this historic series are all now available as e-books on Amazon. If you haven't read them, they await for less than the price of a Big Mac . . . and they will stay with you a lot longer. So what are you waiting for?

talented writers that the winnowing process became our greatest, most joyful challenge. Even though most submissions were rejected (as is the way of the publishing world), we always appreciated knowing so many people out there thought of us and wanted to be part of this award-winning series.

In this sixth volume, we are pleased to showcase very new writers, solid veterans, graduates from the Borderlands Press Writers Boot Camp[2], and of course some genre legends like Braunbeck, Ketchum, and Morrell.

We loved putting this anthology together for a very special audience—not just for people who read, but for those who search out truly imaginative fiction and when they read it, they *get* it. In other words, this book is for all you mutants. And you know who you are.

Now get to work . . . .

—Olivia & Tom Monteleone
*Baltimore, February 2016*

If you don't know about it, you probably should check it out at www.borderlandspress.com

# Anton :)
## M. Louis Dixon

*Michael Dixon was a grunt at an early Borderlands Press Writers Boot Camp, and he submitted the following story as the culmination of his weekend assignment. We liked it so much we promised we'd take it for a future volume of our anthology. We never forgot the aching sadness that drives the narration.*

When Anton smiled people always looked away.

The strong ones shifted their gaze to another point of interest, and the stronger still might chance to look back, but only briefly. It was the timid soul who reacted with uncontrolled reflex: a flinch, a jerk, or a whiplash snap of the head, and always away. Maybe there'd be a bitten lip, a sibilant gasp, or even a full-flung shriek—Tourette's syndrome born in the radiance of his unfurled smile. And Anton smiled at them all.

The smile was extraordinarily large and opened from a deceitful bud that unfolded, not like a flower, but a razor cut in corpulent flesh. It widened and stretched around his broad face, hitched up towards his ears, and sat there like a suppurated wound.

He had been born with a cleft palate. The lips had developed as nature intended but had taken on the added responsibility of masking the chaos within. The teeth were mismatched in size as well as color. From years of neglect and no parental guidance, the already corrupt oral landscape had withered.

That was until his first serious toothache. It was an incisor and the pain drove him mad. Two weeks of increasing agony and no hint of relief found him stumbling into a storefront dentist's office. The receptionist tried to do her job of scheduling an appointment, gathering information, and filling out forms, but broke down into tears and begged Harry Conrad, the dentist, into doing "something . . . anything . . . please!"

Harry was one of the strong types, stronger in fact because of his profession. He agreed to work on Anton's mouth and regretted it from the moment the patient opened up.

Anton felt the dentist trembling as he worked over his teeth. X-rays were taken, Novocain was injected, and the culprit was extracted.

With a mouth numb, packed with cotton and drooling rivulets of thin blood, Anton left the office. He had a handful of papers: pamphlets on oral hygiene, a prescription for Tylenol 3, and a referral to a plastic surgeon.

The dentist had never scheduled a follow-up visit, nor had he gotten his patient's personal information for billing purposes. Being always short on money, Anton accepted the work as a gift, studied the pamphlets, and tossed the prescription along with the referral.

Yet, still the various shades of darkness decorating his teeth stood their ground, but at least he did not suffer from any more toothaches.

Anton continued to use his smile, under its beam he pushed his way through the masses. There were times when he craved to encounter a face that would not contort and turn. But when the moment came, as it invariably would, he never resisted the urge to smile. In his heart there was no joy rushing its way to his lips; there was only the need to move, to push, and to impact. He was helpless in his need.

As Anton walked past a bus stop he was halted by a greeting.

"Excuse me!" A pretty young woman had twisted around from where she sat on the bench. "Could you please tell me the time?"

He glanced at his watch and saw that it was a quarter past two. As he stepped closer, he felt the familiar feeling flow out with his words. "Two fifteen," he said and released his smile from the clip of his tongue. He noticed that she did not focus on his face yet she also did not turn away. Puzzled, he moved even closer; his grin broadened with each step.

"Thank you," she said then gave him a kind, appreciative smile. "The bus must be late."

Anton felt confused as he aligned himself to her. He stood less than two feet away. Her eyes moved but did not settle, not on his eyes or on his mouth, but neither did she avert her face.

"Have you been waiting long?" He opened his jaws as if he would bite her and leaned in closer still.

However, she did not flinch, nor blush, nor start. "Not too long, but long enough.

I'm on my way home and I *am* rather anxious to be back inside."

He watched her face, its expressiveness and its candor, but mostly he watched her eyes. He did not recall seeing eyes for this length of time. Sure, he'd looked at the photos in magazines, but here were living eyes that continued to rove over his face.

He closed his mouth, licked his lips. "My name is Anton," he said.

Her smile grew and warmed him. "Hello, Anton, I'm Cecily but everyone calls me Sissy."

When he stood to move around the bench he noticed that she did not turn her face to follow him. He stepped to the side and she only tilted her head. That's when he noticed the white cane she held in one hand. Her smile searched for him.

The bus pulled up to the curb.

"Oh my!" Sissy said as she hurried to her feet. "It was nice meeting you, Anton."

Anton remained silent as she probed her way to the door of the bus and out of his life. He saw her through the window as the bus pulled away. She was still smiling.

At home he washed his hands and face and then brushed his teeth. He looked into the mirror and into his eyes. Until today these were the only eyes that he had come to know. Inside he felt warmth that spread outward. Standing before the mirror, he watched as his joy grew on his face. His lips stretched and grew with his happiness. He smiled.

Anton looked away.

# Eye of the Beholder
## John McIlveen

*John McIlveen is one of* Borderlands' *repeat offenders, having published his deeply disturbing story "Inflictions" in volume 5. His return is marked by a tale that feels like a scene from a fifties horror monster film, but resolves into something far more layered, an exploration of faith and love and, of course,* dread.

"There are more things in heaven and earth, Horatio, than are dreamt of in your philosophy."
—William Shakespeare, *Hamlet*

Senator Brandon O'Rourke stopped outside the door to his son's bedroom and listened to the barely decipherable conversation coming from within. It sounded like a one-sided phone conversation, but Cooper didn't have a phone, and Brandon had heard his son's solitary ramblings so many times they had become familiar. His son was odd and a social outsider in school and at church, there was no denying it, but he was a sweet kid and undeserving of the loneliness he suffered. Being small for his age and the son of a pastor certainly didn't help. Brandon would probably be more surprised if he *didn't* have imaginary friends, or whatever Cooper had his chats with.

Brandon nudged the door open and regarded Cooper's little pajama-clad form sitting cross-legged on the bed, staring blankly ahead.

"Hey, Bub," Brandon said, getting no response, which also wasn't unusual. *He has no clue that I'm here,* Brandon thought.

He set a hand on his son's shoulder. He found it disconcerting that Cooper never started, but seemed only to slowly return to himself as the empty look faded from his eyes.

"Hi, Dad!" Cooper said brightly.

"Hi. Chatting with your friends?" Brandon asked, trying to keep it light.

"Nah, I was just . . . someplace," Cooper said dismissively.

"Apparently," Brandon agreed. "Anyhow, it's bedtime."

As always, Cooper obliged without a fuss and quickly slipped between the sheets. Brandon tucked him in, kissed him on the forehead, and pushed an obstinate wing of the boy's blond hair out of his face.

"The light," Cooper reminded him.

"You sure about this?"

"Yeah. I've thought about it a long time," Cooper said earnestly. "I can't be afraid of the dark forever."

"True enough," Brandon said, hiding a smile while trying to match his son's gravity. "But sleeping without a night-light is a big step in a man's life."

Cooper nodded his agreement. His normally light-blue eyes looked huge and dark in the dim bedroom.

"Six-years-old today. You're growing up so fast," Brandon said, shaking his head. He looked at his son, and then widened his eyes in a comical show of surprise. "Wait a minute! What was that?"

"What?" asked Cooper, a hint of concern in his voice.

Brandon leaned closer. "You just sprouted a chest hair . . . right here." He poked his finger against Cooper's ribs. "Whoa! Another one here . . . and here . . . and here!" he said, prodding playfully.

Cooper giggled and twisted deeper into the blankets, trying to avoid his father's barrage of jabs, yet wanting it to continue.

"My God, you're practically a Sasquatch."

"What's a sashcrotch?" Cooper asked, catching his breath.

"Bigfoot."

"But I don't have big feet!"

"Okay, Bub, you win," Brandon said. He straightened the sheets and kissed Cooper again.

"Why does Mommy always have to go away?" he asked dolefully.

"It's her job, Bub. You should be proud of her. There aren't a lot of female pilots, especially ones who fly the big jets."

"I know, but I wish she could have been her for my birthday."

"I know what you mean. I miss her too. But she did call and promise we'd do something extra special when she got back on Saturday. In six days," Brandon said brightly, but Cooper didn't look very encouraged. He was such a solemn child.

"Tony Hammond says Mommy has humongous boobs."

*What to say . . . what to say . . .*

"Well, you can tell Tony Hammond it's because Mom's heart is so big. You're a lucky young man," Brandon said, thinking of Sylvia. *And so am I.*

"Tony's mom never has to go away."

"I know" was all Brandon could say. He, as usual, had run out of encouraging words. He reached for the SpongeBob night-light on the bedside table and paused. "You're sure?" he asked again.

Cooper nodded and turned to his side, clutching his pillow. In his recent battle for independence over fear, he had retired his favorite toy—a plush minion doll—to a seat of honor atop his bookshelf. Brandon spun the light toggle.

"Good night, my man. I love you."

"I love you too, Daddy."

"Door opened or closed?"

"Open a little."

Brandon pulled at the doorknob, leaving a five-inch gap.

"Daddy?"

"Yeah, sweetie?" Brandon asked, opening the door a bit wider.

"Can you leave the hallway light on?" the boy asked.

Brandon smiled. "You got it."

Brandon walked down the hallway to the head of the stairs, and then looked back towards his son's bedroom. The house was a late eighteenth-century Victorian with enough gothic aesthetic and dark vertical lines to be intimidating to him, let alone his six-year-old child. It was by no means a mansion, but it was larger than average, pushing five thousand square feet, and probably seemed immense to Cooper, especially when it was just the two of them. Sylvia was a mere five three, as sweet as honey-dipped sugar cookies, and perpetually soft-spoken, but she presented a sense of stability and security for the two men in her life that was beyond palpable in her absence. Brandon felt a hollowness about the place when she was away, as if the house regarded her temporary absence as more of an abandonment . . . or maybe it was Brandon who did.

At first her flights had been mostly short jaunts, the overnights limited to an infrequent two—maybe three—days every two months, but as she built experience and seniority, it turned into five, ten, and then fifteen days a month. It made for a handsome income, but it also had its negative aspects. Through all his encouragements to Cooper, Brandon kept a noble façade, but he wasn't without his concerns. Foremost was the fear that with all Sylvia's travels, her heart might do the same. She must get lonely too, he figured, but what else could a pastor do but leave it in God's hands.

In the kitchen, he poured a glass of Sauvignon Blanc, carried it into his office, and set it atop his desk, beside his laptop. He needed to write sermons for the next two Sundays and update his notes for Wednesday evening's Bible study. He tried to stay a month ahead, but it was approaching campaign time, a time when he needed to shift the weight of his focus from his piety to his party. *And a time Cooper would spend mostly with a nanny than with his parents,* Brandon guiltily amended.

He had been an ordained minister long before his first stint in government, and he liked to think it was his charitable actions and his contributions to humanitiy hat had secured his position in both the Senate house and God's house. In a world where corruption and greed presided over ethics, he prided himself for making it as far as he had without bending under the weight of corporate persuasion or the insistence of party leaders. In politics, it was difficult to maintain a clean image, especially if you were clergy, because someone somewhere, for whatever reason, was aiming to take you down. Smile at a pretty supporter, some opportunistic photographer would turn it into something more. Tip a valet, you're buying votes. So far, no one had been able to soil Brandon O'Rourke, and there was a good reason. He was clean—moral and honorable, attributes that were becoming rarer in both of his professions. Several certificates and awards hung on his office wall, for his humanitarian work. Sylvia had insisted he hang them, arguing that he needed to differentiate honor from pride.

Being a Christian, his leaning was naturally towards the conservative. He was registered as a Republican, although he'd have been happier if there were no party associations. He had a similar attitude with religion. Brandon saw many similarities in the modern ethics of both religion and politics, and as far as he was concerned, both were wrought with corruption. Both expected their associates to adhere exclusively to their philosophies, with which many he didn't agree, and others that he could appreciate viewing from both sides of the fence. And then there was money, which had so much influence in both—in everything, it seemed.

He pulled out his chair, sat, and sidled back to the desk. He switched on his desk lamp, an antique banker's lamp that did little to illuminate the room with its dark-mahogany walls and volume-laden bookshelves, but it did create a comfortable, subdued sphere in which he could work. It also made the reflection of the window behind him visible in his wineglass, which would have remained unnoticed if not for the movement of something outside the window.

Brandon turned in his chair and peered into the night where, beyond the porch railing, soft walkway lighting exposed a fine cobblestone pathway that led to a driveway of the same construct. Remaining in his seat, he wheeled forward to get a closer look out at his property, just in time to catch the shaking of the shrubs to the left of his window.

Likely a cat or a skunk, he figured, yet he rose and secured the door locks throughout the house to lessen the unease he was feeling. He returned to his office and sat back down, his attention returning to the window's reflection on his wineglass. Thankfully, nothing moved outside the window. He tapped the touch pad to wake the computer and then typed his password, bringing up the Word file with the sermon on which he was currently working. He read his words and was pleased to fall quickly back into the rhythm of his teaching. He added a few paragraphs he hoped were eloquent enough to inspire, and that held truths profound enough to spark epiphanies.

A little more than an hour later, feeling content with his work, Brandon toggled the Save icon and took the final swallow from the wineglass. Recalling the earlier movement, he casually glanced at the window, and what he saw there was inexplicable, yet ignited a surge of fear throughout him so intense he could only sit and stare, at first.

A thick and yellowish substance coated the majority of the top and bottom portions of the double-paned window. It appeared gelatinous and wet and the descriptive that first came to Brandon's mind was *snot*. Its edges quivered and appeared to fold into the central thickness of the matter, undulating with slurping sounds as it slowly moved upward on the window. As a whole, its movements were hypnotic. Standing slowly, Brandon moved a little closer and watched as wet pustules erupted were the gummy mass touched the glass, forming into gaping cavities that trembled and suctioned onto the surface as it climbed, causing the window to creak with stress under the weight of it. Moist popping noises accompanied the release of each orifice like the snap of quick kisses, moving with a liquid flux to wherever it was heading.

Brandon leaned forward, peering into the curious depths of one of the grotesque maws when what looked like a black, metallic honeycomb, hexagon-shaped and about three inches in diameter, emerged from the crater and pressed against the glass. Though he had never witnessed anything even remotely like it before, Brandon felt it was an eye of some form and that it was looking at him. Panic and revulsion drove an all-encompassing shudder throughout him as he acknowledged the truth that the horrific object on his window was alive, and that it was looking at him spoke of some type of intelligence, which made it all the more ghastly.

There was a depth to its honeycomb eye that was oddly seductive and he felt as if it was trying to draw him in. He backed away slowly, trying to make sense of it. No creature that he knew of was even remotely similar, except maybe a jellyfish, but those didn't bubble and boil or survive out of salt water.

*How big is this one?* It appeared it hadn't covered the window entirely, but was that just a fraction or an iota of the whole . . . *thing? Host?*

*Are there more?* he wondered.

Had the human race finally become so corrupt that God opened the gates of hell, releasing these hideous obscenities?

*Is Cooper safe?* The thought came out of the blue and rattled him deeply.

"Sweet Lord, I beg of you, keep Cooper safe," he said aloud, but a voice inside of him replied, *That's* your *job.*

Brandon forced himself to look away from the revolting mass, rushed into the kitchen, and was relieved to see nothing obstructed those windows. He chanced a look outside to confirm that the yard wasn't swarming with them or that hordes weren't falling from the inky, moonless skies.

What could he use for a weapon? Could it be stabbed or sliced, or would it simply ooze around the blade, unharmed? Considering the amorphous consistency of the creature, it seemed knives would be useless, and guns—as if he'd even have a gun—were one of those conservative views he disagreed with.

He continued staring out the window and calmed himself. For his entire life he had believed in the supernatural qualities of a Christian God, and for that matter, Satan, but never had he considered anything beyond that. The plain truth and irony was that despite his beliefs, he'd never witnessed anything even slightly extraordinary in a supernatural bent . . . or even miraculous. He'd heard plenty claim such things, but he'd sincerely thought most of them were whacks and quacks, or opportunists. If someone were to have relayed what Brandon had just witnessed on his office window, he'd have labeled him or her as well.

The more he thought about it, the more at ease he became. There had to be a logical explanation, but just in case, he'd check on Cooper.

A walk by his office offered a window with a clear view of the lighted yard; no booger monster with a honeycomb eye, and although he considered it, he didn't look closer for slime tracks on the glass. *Got to have faith,* he reasoned.

As Brandon had hoped, Cooper was sleeping, but evidently restless. He was now lying reversed with his head near to the footboard. The SpongeBob night-light was now aglow with six-watt splendor, and Kevin the minion had found his way into Cooper's arms.

*FLUMP!*

The sound was muted, not distinct, yet startled Cooper, who sprung into a sitting position, looking frantically around the room. It had come from the first floor, in the direction of the front of the house, sounding as if something hit the floor, as his father used to say, like a sack of wet shit.

*Or a two-hundred-pound jellyfish,* Brandon thought.

"It's okay, Bub. It's nothing," he quietly said to his son, the lie sounding feeble to his own ears. The look in Cooper's eyes said he wasn't convinced, either.

He was certain that whatever had created the impact was the same thing that had adhered itself to his office window, but he was torn as what to do. Should he confront the vile thing, which he knew nothing about, or should he grab his son and run blindly into the night in the hope of escape? Instead, he repositioned Cooper correctly in the bed and said, "Go back to sleep, son."

The most important thing was to keep his son safe at all cost, and at the moment. He'd have to assess the situation. Maybe the thing was harmless, but maybe . . . What was that Sun Tzu quote? "If you know the enemy and know yourself, you need not fear" . . . something like that.

He gently shut Cooper's door and returned downstairs to find where the sound had come from. There was only a short hallway that ran from the base of the stairway to the front of the house, so it didn't leave many possibilities. He looked through the front-door window onto a screen-lined, three-season veranda that separated the farmer's porch from the entryway into the foyer, in which he stood. To the left of the porch, the gentle glow of the outdoor lighting made it just bright enough to settle everything in obscure shadow. He neither saw nor heard anything out of the ordinary, so he switched on the porch lights. Nothing reacted to the sudden flare that, although not considerably bright, seemed dazzling to Brandon until his eyes adjusted.

After a small eternity, Brandon unlocked the front door and stepped into the confines of the screened veranda. He looked on to the front lawn, which had relinquished into darkness outside the reaches of the porch lights. He reached inside the doorway and flicked the lights off, which returned the yard to its previous ambient glow and made visible the long ropes of viscous slime that trailed along the farmer's porch and disappeared around the corner. Brandon's office window was located around that same corner, but what concerned him most was that Cooper's window was directly above it, although whatever that hellish creature was, it would have to traverse the underside of the porch roof to get to Cooper's window.

*But it can climb!* He had witnessed that through his office window.

*And what had fallen and made that sound?*

Brandon approached the screened wall and tried to peer around the corner without leaving the enclosure of the three-season veranda. He was met by the slurping, squishing sound of the creature's movements, and he became aware of a briny odor with the underlying hint of sulfur that was pushed towards him by a mild breeze. It reminded him of the salt marshes of Cape Cod, where his family vacationed in his childhood. It was not entirely unpleasant, but a foreign smell for Adelphi, Maryland.

With a shaking hand, he fumbled at the screen-door lock until it hooked into the eyelet, and then he backed away just as a putrescent yellow flap of the gelatinous substance breached the corner of the house like a huge infected tongue and sloshed onto the screened wall. It paused as if in contemplation, and then the black honeycomb emerged from within the ghastly organism and pressed to the screen. Sensing the strange, mesmerizing magnetism he had felt earlier, Brandon feared if he didn't look immediately away, he never would.

A hissing, not unlike the sound of sizzling meat in a frying pan, started emanating from the entity and it instantly traversed to the inside of the enclosed porch, still latched onto the screen and still intact. It had somehow sieved through the screen's mesh unharmed.

"What the fuck?" Brandon blurted, shocked by his own use of the expletive. One that would have surely raised a few eyebrows in his congregation, yet one so correct for the situation he said it again, "What-the-ever-loving-fuck?"

*FLUMP!*

It fell to the porch floor like a pus-filled balloon, hitting and spreading out, splattering against the walls and oozing between the decking. Brandon's gorge rose, yet he could only watch, morbidly fascinated, as it started to gather itself, pooling together, except the three extended splashes nearest him, which merged to form a smooth proboscis that thickened and elongated in his direction, reaching for him. Brandon backed away, but the creature compensated by sending more mass into its reaching tentacle.

*Don't let it touch me!* Brandon didn't know what would happen if it did, but it seemed intent and he felt it was imperative that it not touch him, not even the slightest brush.

*Would it steal his soul, farm his blood, or just melt him into its next meal?* He backed into the house, slammed the door, and twisted the deadbolt lock. Wildly contemplating his next move—if he even had one—he backstepped to the foot of the stairs.

*What do I do now?* he wondered. How would he protect them from this thing . . . this profanity that could flow unfazed through a screen like water? He looked up the stairway towards Cooper's bedroom, and then the cell phone in his pants pocket vibrated and rang simultaneously.

"Fuck!"

*Third F-bomb in less than five minutes. Appropriate,* he reminded himself and pulled the phone from his pocket to see his wife's pretty, smiling face on the screen.

"Hello?" he answered in a hushed voice, his heart slamming.

"Hi, baby! How's it going?" Her voice so normal it nearly brought him to tears.

*Should I say anything? Should I have her call the cops . . . the National Guard? No, I could do that. What could she possibly do, except worry?*

"Good, good," he said, forcing a cheerful but tentative voice. *Now I'm lying, but it's a good lie, a compassionate lie,* he reasoned.

He heard movement at the door and then the door lever quivered ever so slightly.

"Are you okay? You sound out of breath," said Sylvia, ever observant.

"I'm fine. Just doing some chores."

"Chores at ten thirty at night?"

"Yeah. Wide awake and Cooper's asleep, so I figured . . . " Brandon stopped talking when he saw a thin phlegmy strand had started seeping through the keyhole of the old door. The skeleton keys were long gone, but the locks remained, long unemployed, until now. "Uh . . . " he said.

"How's our little guy?" Sylvia asked. "Was he very upset that I wasn't there for his birthday?"

"He's . . . good . . . uh, honey? Listen. Can I call you right back? I left the door, the cellar door open, and I don't want anything getting in."

The pool of slime in front of the door was now a foot across and quickly expanding.

"Oh, okay," she said hesitantly. "Are you sure everything's okay?"

"Scout's honor," Brandon lied again as two thin appendages grew from the mass, like feelers or antennae. "I just slapped a couple mosquitoes and I want to get ahead of it before they get really bad, okay? Love you. Call right back."

He disconnected the call before Sylvia could reply and slipped it into his pocket. The feelers extended, twisted, coiled, and extended again, blindly searching for Brandon as he cautiously diverted away from the stairway, hoping to lure it to the kitchen and distance access to Cooper's room. The feelers rose in unison, like twin cobras preparing to strike, and then those damned black honeycombs formed at the tip of each one, swinging and swaying back and forth, while its malignant, popping suckers gripped and released the floor as it advanced on him.

"Daddy?" Cooper called suddenly from the top of the stairs.

The heinous blob immediately stopped and its soulless honeycomb eyes turned to the sound of Cooper's voice. Time stood still, as if all three were at an impasse, waiting for the other to make a move.

*Oh shit—oh shit—oh shit! It can hear? How can it hear? It has no fucking ears!*

"Daddy? What's that noise?"

"It's nothing, sweetie!" Brandon said, alertly watching the slimy creature's movements. "Go back to bed. I'll be up there in a few minutes."

The black-tipped probes appeared intently locked in the direction of Cooper's voice.

*Now!* Brandon thought, forcing his fear aside, and with two long strides, he leapt over the abomination, clearing its reaching probes by mere inches. With a celebratory *whoop*, Brandon landed in the hallway just outside the kitchen threshold, both feet landing squarely on the floor in a patch of slime. His feet cherry-pitted from beneath him, sending him hurtling across the floor in an involuntary backflip. He hit the bottom of the stairway with bone-jarring impact, sending a lightning bolt of pain through him by way of his elbow.

With a succession of sopping slurps and pops, the gurgling form immediately reversed direction, its probing appendages seeming to slide front to back like the barrels on a tank turret. Not stopping to assess injuries, Brandon scrambled to his feet and mounted the stairs, racing up them two at a time.

Cooper stood at the head of the stairway, watching wide-eyed, uncomprehending of what the abomination at the base of the stairs was. "What is that, Daddy?" he asked, frightened.

"Get in your room, quick!" Brandon ordered.

Cooper stood frozen as the undulating form seemed to contemplate the stairs.

"Go! Quick!"

"But . . . "

"Go!" Brandon yelled, giving Cooper a push.

Shocked by the unfamiliar urgency of his father's voice, Cooper darted for his room, wailing in fear. Brandon quickly glanced over his shoulder and then followed his son down the hallway, thinking that never before in his life had he seen something pour *up* the stairs.

Inside Cooper's room, he slammed the door, tore the sheets from the bed, and started jamming them against the base of the door, trying to seal the opening. Cooper stood in the center of the room, mouth agape, hands clasping and unclasping as he silently wept. Anger and self-disgust swept through Brandon at his failure to keep his son safe from such trauma and ugliness.

As he worked the fabric into the gap, Cooper started a terrified, high-pitched keening. Brandon looked at him and saw movement in his peripheral vision, feeling the slightest shifting in the air near his head as a tentacle swayed from the keyhole like a long, infected worm, hovering frighteningly close to Cooper's face. Brandon sprang away from the door, landing on his back at Cooper's feet, pulling the boy down on top of him.

Rising, Brandon tucked Cooper behind him and backed away from the searching probe. Again, a honeycomb eye formed and locked first onto Brandon, who was busy opening the bedroom window, and then refocusing on Cooper.

"Get on the porch roof and go to my bedroom window," Brandon said, lifting Cooper to the lip of the window.

"Noooo!" Cooper cried, seeming more scared by the thought of climbing onto the roof than of the atrocity behind them.

"Cooper, listen to me! Go! I'll meet you there."

Brandon pushed his unwilling son through the window opening and onto the roof. He closed the window and twisted the latch, hoping the hellish beast couldn't sprout fingers, although it wouldn't have surprised him. He stood at the foot of the bed and watched until the last of the slime secreted from the keyhole, and waited for the slime bag to round the bed with eye-tipped appendages flailing, but it didn't show.

Brandon leaned forward to see over the edge of the bed, when it occurred to him that it could easily move beneath the bed. He leapt onto the bed just as an infected-looking armlike extension shot from beneath it, swiping where his feet had just been. Sparing no time, Brandon bounced to the floor and raced to the doorway, halting just outside. Inside the room, the oozing obscenity ignored him and began ascending the wall towards the window.

*It doesn't give a shit about me,* Brandon realized. *It only wants Cooper!*

"Hey!" he yelled at it. "Hey, pussbag!"

Still it ignored him and climbed, spreading its semifluid malignance over the window. To his horror, Brandon could see Cooper's distorted image through the creature, inches away on the outside of the glass. Fortunately, it appeared the abomination couldn't manipulate the window hardware or penetrate the seams.

"Cooper! Get away from there!" he yelled, and then started for the stairs.

He stopped halfway down when he heard the familiar *flump!*

*Has it given up trying to breach the window?* He started back up the stairs when he heard the approaching sound of its movements and watched it ooze through the doorway and past his and Sylvia's bedroom, intent on him. Brandon descended the remaining stairs, grateful that the creature was as slow as it was abhorrent, and wondered if he had unconsciously said something offensive to God during a service and the Almighty was exacting vengeance.

As repugnant as it was, couldn't God have come up with something more menacing than a slow-moving bag of pus? Maybe God only wanted to scare him, or maybe it wasn't God's doing at all. He liked that thought better. He had always been so careful not to offend God. It seemed more befitting—or at least he hoped it was—that Satan was attacking him, and that God was protecting him by making Satan's underling a bumbling blob of booger. Wouldn't Beelzebub likely be responsible for creating something so repulsive?

"Come on, you snot sausage," Brandon coaxed it while opening the front door.

He stepped out onto the veranda just as the glugging and slewing mass tumbled down the stairway, leaving an explosion of viscous debris in its wake. It quivered at the foot of the stairs as its grungy remnants amalgamated, and then it followed him across the porch and onto the lawn.

Brandon jogged across the lawn toward the garage as the oversized globule boiled over the edge of the walkway and across the grass, rolling towards the garage like a malignant water baby.

Brandon looked up to see Cooper sitting on the roof, his forehead on his knees and his back against the wall near Brandon and Silvia's bedroom window. "Stay right there," he ordered his son and then ducked inside the doorway on the side of the garage.

Somehow comprehending that Brandon was talking to his son, the hideous being reversed direction in one fluid shift, again intent on Cooper. When it was halfway across the lawn, Brandon leapt out from behind the doorway of the garage with a plastic three-gallon gas container raised high in his arms and started splashing the pungent liquid all over the creature. It recoiled when the gasoline hit it, all of its extremities folding within its central mass.

Cooper had scooted closer to the edge of the roof and was shaking his head and yelling. Encouraged by his son's reaction, Brandon released a shout that sounded as if it was treading the fine line between victory and insanity. He poured the remaining contents of the gas can over the huddled mess and ran a small gasoline trail to the edge of driveway.

*Let's put an end to this,* he thought, drawing a long butane grill striker from his rear pocket. He flicked the wheel and touched the tip to the small track of fuel, which instantly lighted, engulfing the recoiling mass with a *whoomp!*

The piercing shriek that emanated from the undulating ball of slime was unlike anything Brandon had heard before, and one he hoped never to hear again. It was the sound of a million souls wailing and it carried on as the creature twisted and writhed, its bulk sizzling and splattering. Its cry was so loud and long that Brandon felt a growing sense of sadness, and when it finally stopped moving, he felt an inexplicable sorrow for the remains of the being before him.

Brandon stared at what looked like a large pile of blackened Vaseline for a long time, unaware of the cries of his son. Its demise seemed anticlimactic. He had been expecting more of a fight or for it to spill a million deadly insectile offspring to the ground. The monstrous thing's cries had been so mournful that it confused him. He looked at Cooper sitting on the lip of the roof, whose tear-streaked face was drawn in profound grief.

Brandon hurried back to the master bedroom and brought Cooper inside and sat on the bed with him.

"I'm sorry you had to see something like that," Brandon told his son. "But it's okay now. It's dead."

"You killed her, Dad," Cooper stammered. "Why'd you kill her?" He brushed his forearm against his eyes, spreading tears and mucus across his face.

Cooper's tone surprised Brandon. His words were thick with accusation, and although he'd seen his son angry before, he had never seen him enraged. It seemed out of place for a child his age, and especially for one as . . . milquetoast as Cooper. It was unsettling. Brandon looked at his son curiously.

"What do you mean?" he asked Cooper. "Why are you calling it her?"

"I know her. She likes me. She cares, like Mom is s'posed to."

"Cooper, what are you talking about?" Brandon asked. Maybe it was too much for the kid. He was clearly distressed and surely traumatized.

"She looks different here, but she told me it was her when she touched me tonight," he said, raising a hand to his cheek. "She said she changed when she came here, but she's pretty. Prettier than Mommy. They all are."

It sounded like babble to Brandon. It didn't make sense, but then again, that thing smoldering in the front yard didn't make sense, either.

*FLUMP!*

Brandon wanted to ignore the sound or pretend he had imagined it. *Is it . . . she . .*

*. still alive? Is it possible?*

"Where's she from, Cooper?" Brandon asked. Was it true? Did Cooper actually know what this thing was?

*FLUMP!*

"She's from . . . the place."

"What place?"

"Where I go when I'm sad or mad or alone," he said irately and then shrugged. "I don't know."

"And where is this place? How do you get there?" Brandon asked.

*FLUMP!*

*FLUMP!*

"I don't know. I just sit in my room and go there," Cooper said, his chin trembling, frustrated by the questions or his inability to answer them. "But this time I wanted her to come here."

*His rambling is madness, some kind of dissociation,* Brandon thought, but then . . . there was that *thing* outside.

*FLUMP! FLUMP!*

*FLUMP!*

*FLUMP! FLUMP! FLUMP!*

"Are there more of these, Cooper?" Brandon asked, looking up at the ceiling, where the last sound seemed to have come from.

"Yes. When I was on the roof, I told them you were hurting her. They are really mad you killed her."

*FLUMP! FLUMP! FLUMP! FLUMP! FLUMP!*

*FLUMP! FLUMP!*

*FLUMP!*

*FLUMP! FLUMP! FLUMP!*

*FLUMP!*

"How many are there, Cooper?" Brandon asked

"As many as I want."

# Those Rockports Won't Get You to Heaven
## Jack Ketchum

*Jack Ketchum writes with such a sharp-edged narrative voice it could cut you clean, then stand there and watch you bleed. His spare prose is peppered with exactly the right words, allowing you to see and hear and feel what goes on in his fiction. His ticket to the Borderlands could have been punched by James M. Cain or even Hemingway because he can tell a riveting story of suspense by expertly knowing how much of his story he need never tell.*

The place was going all to hell—not that you'd necessarily notice unless you worked there. The floor was mopped and the glasses fairly clean. The bottles were dusted and the bar wiped down, but then I took care of that.

But the owner had two other restaurants on the same block and kept swapping bottles back and forth between them. So you never knew when you came in after the day shift what would be on the shelves. You'd have plenty of Dewar's one day and the next day maybe a quarter of a bottle. It also meant that you'd find a liter of peach brandy or port wine getting overly chummy with the single malts. The wines kept changing according to whoever threw him the best deal that week, and half the time there was no beer on tap whatsoever.

Waiters, busboys, hostesses—everybody was owed back pay. Myself included, half the time.

It was March and one of the coldest, longest goddamn winters on record, and the heat was off again. Had been all week. All we had between us and runny noses was a single space heater looking lonely and pathetic behind the hostess's station. Customers ate their *taramasalata* and *souvlakia* with their coats on.

There weren't many of them. You don't associate Greek cuisine with frozen tundra.

It was six o'clock Thursday evening and of my dwindling group of regulars not a single one had shown up. I couldn't blame them. They were all wised up to the heating situation. We had more waiters and busboys than customers. Two couples and a party of four in the restaurant and that was that.

I was going fucking broke here.

Not a tip on the bar in two hours.

I polished bottles. It's a bartender thing. You got nothing to do; you polish bottles.

When the guy walked in with his kid trailing along behind him, the first thing I thought was Westchester. Either that or Connecticut. I don't know why, because plenty of guys around here are partial to Ralph Lauren and Rockports, and outfit their kids in L.L.Bean. But there was something vaguely displaced about him. That's the best I can do. He didn't belong here.

You get so you kind of sense this shit.

They walked directly to the bar but neither one sat down. The kid, maybe fourteen I guessed, taking his cue from Dad.

"Glass of white wine," he said.

"Sure. We've got Pinot Grigio, Chardonnay, and two Greek wines—Santorini and Kouros. Both very nice. What can I get for you?"

"Whatever."

"Would you care to taste one?"

"No, that's okay. Give me the Santorini."

"You got it."

Like I said, you just get a sense about these things. The guy was *wrong* somehow. Wound so fucking tight he was practically ready to give off sparks should he start to do any *un*winding, and you probably didn't want to see that.

You're not supposed to have an underage kid with you at a bar in New York City, but most of the time we look the other way and most of the time the guy will order his kid a Coke or something, and we look the other way on that too. This guy didn't. And of course I didn't offer.

I poured the wine and he drained off half of it in one swallow.

"I used to come in here all the time," he said. Not to me, but to his kid.

Though he wasn't *looking* at his kid.

His eyes were all over the place. The rows of bottles behind me, the murals on the wall, the ceiling, the tables and chairs in the restaurant. But I had the feeling he wasn't really seeing much of it. Like he was scanning but not exactly *tracking*. Except when he turned to look out the plate-glass windows to the street beyond. That seemed to focus him. He drank some more.

"It's changed hands, hell, maybe a dozen times since then. This was way before I met your mother."

The kid was looking at him. He still wasn't looking back. Or at me either, for that matter. He kept scanning. As though he were expecting something to jump out of the clay amphorae or the floral arrangements. That and turning back to the window and the street.

"Not really, sir," I said. "You must be thinking of another place. A lot of turnaround on the avenue but not here. It's been the Santorini for about ten years now and before that it was a Mexican restaurant, Sombrero, from about the midfifties on. So unless you're a whole lot older than you look . . . "

"Really?"

"That's right."

"Damn. I could have sworn . . . "

He was trying to act as cool and casual as the clothes he had on, but I could feel him flash and burn suddenly all the same. He didn't like me correcting him in front of his kid. *Tough shit,* I thought. *Fuck you.* Snap judgments are part of my stock-in-trade and I hadn't liked him from the minute he walked in. He made an attempt at a save.

"I used to live around here. Long time ago. Early seventies."

"Really? Where was that?"

"Seventy-first, just off the park."

"Nice over there. And pretty pricey these days. So where are you folks now?"

"We're out in Rye."

*Westchester,* I thought. *Gotcha.*

He turned back to the street again. I noticed that his son was staring at me and I thought, *Jesus, if this guy looks displaced, his kid looks absolutely lost.* He had big brown eyes as bright and clear as a doe's eyes and the eyes seemed to want to make contact with me. For just a second there, I let them.

It could have just been me, but it felt like he was looking at me as though I was some kind of crazy lifeline. It wasn't a look I was used to. Not after two divorces and fifteen years' bartending.

"I'll have another," the guy said.

I poured it for him and watched him gulp it down.

"We don't get over this way much anymore," he said. "Hardly at all. His mother's across the street shopping."

*His mother,* I thought. *Not "my wife", but "his mother".* That was interesting.

And I figured I had it now—pretty much all of a piece. What I had here in front of me was one stone alky sneaking a couple of nervous quick ones while the little wife wasn't looking. Dragging his kid into a bar while she was out spending all that hard-earned money he was probably making by managing *other* people's hard-earned money so he could afford the house in Rye, the Rockports, and the Ralph Lauren and L.L.Bean.

I wondered exactly where she was spending it. Betsey Johnson, Intermix, and Lucky Brand Dungarees, I figured, would be way too young for anybody he'd be married to, and I doubted she'd be bothering with the plates and soaps or scented candles over at Details. That left either L'Occitane if she was into perfume or Hummel Jewelers.

My bet was on the jewelers.

My other bet was that there was great big trouble in paradise.

And I was thinking this when I heard the *pop-pop-pop* from down the street.

The kid heard it too.

"What was that?" he said. He turned to the windows.

The guy shrugged and drained his wine. "Backfire, probably. I'll have one more, thanks." He set the glass down.

Only it wasn't backfire. I knew that right away.

When my first wife, Helen, and I lived in New Jersey we'd now and then get slightly loaded afternoons and take her little Colt Pony and my .22 rimfire semiauto out to the fields behind our house and plunk some cans and bottles. The Colt made pretty much the same sound.

Ordinarily I'd have been out in the street by now.

Instead I poured him the wine.

This time the guy sipped slowly. Seemed calmer all of a sudden. I revised my thinking big-time about him being just another alky. His eyes stopped skittering over the walls and settled on the bar in front of him.

"Dad?" the kid said.

"Uh-huh."

"Shouldn't we go see how Mom's doing?"

"She's shopping. She's doing fine. She loves shopping."

"Yeah, but . . . "

And now it was the kid's eyes that were darting all over the place.

"We don't want to rush her, do we? I'll just finish my wine here. Then we'll go see what she's up to."

I got that look from the kid again. The look seemed to say, *Do something, say something,* and I considered it for a moment.

The phone on the wall decided for me.

By the time I finished noting down the takeout order—Greek salad, mixed cold appetizers, calamari, roasted quail, and two cans of Sprite, for God's sake—the woman's name, address, and phone number, the guy was reaching for his wallet. His hands were shaking. His face was flushed.

"What's the damage?"

"That's twenty-four dollars, sir."

He fished out a ten and a twenty and downed the last of his wine.

"Keep the change," he said.

*Nice tip,* I thought. You don't see 25 percent much. Maybe the bar at the Plaza, but not in this place. I figured he wanted me to remember him.

I figured I *would* remember him. Vividly.

The kid turned back to look at me once as he followed his father out the door. It was possible that I might have seen a flash of anger or maybe a kind of panic there, but I could have been imagining that. You couldn't be sure.

I rang up the wine and cleared his glass and wiped down the bar. He'd spilled a little.

There were a few ways to play this. First, I could be straight about it and report exactly what I saw. *All* of what I saw. Not just his being there but the high-wire tension going slack as shoestrings once the shots went off and then all nervous again when he was about to leave. The way the kid kept looking at me. Or, just for fun, I could try to fuck the guy over royally and completely by saying, "Gee, I really didn't remember him at all, to tell the truth." Though that might not work if his kid said otherwise. Finally, I could find out who he was and shake him down for a whole lot more than 25 percent, in maybe a day or so.

Hell, I already knew where he lived.

But I pretty much knew what I was going to do.

As I said, I've had two divorces and know what a bitch they can be. And I'm no big fan of married women in general either.

But my daughter by my second wife was just about this kid's age. Maybe a bit younger.

I wondered whom he'd hired. How much he'd paid. If they'd actually hit the jewelry store just for show or only the woman inside it.

I polished bottles—it's a bartender thing—and waited for the gawkers and the sirens and New York's finest to come on in.

*—Thanks to Matt Long*

# The Last Plague Doctor
### Rebecca J. Allred

*We recognize maybe 20 percent of the names of the writers who send us their work. The rest are totally unknown to us and must have their stories speak for them. So it was with Rebecca Allred's tale—brimming over with evocative medieval imagery woven into an apocalyptic tapestry depicting a reset on the Dark Ages. Unsettling and original, we knew we liked it as soon as we reached the final line.*

Once again in search of a new face, Plague strides into the night, and I with it. I wear a gown pale and blue as moonlight, the memory of a celestial monarch now centuries in her grave, and my own face is concealed behind the mask of my predecessors, its beak long and curved like a reaper's scythe. The soft scent of fresh lavender—grown in secret beneath artificial light—protects me from the stink of nicotine that has stained my companion's tattered robes, his nails and too-numerous teeth, and, yes, even his eyes; they stare at me from ragged holes, grinning though his mouth does not. Even now he smokes, the red eye of his cigarette winking at me from behind a veil of spiraling carcinogens with each protracted drag.

Each of us carries a bag, one for tricks and the other for treats, as we wander alleys lit by lanterns carved from sickly fruit, that glow like the forbidden sunrise, sending Plague's darkness to cower in thin corners and deep crevices. In this forever night, the houses stand back to back to back, as if huddled together for warmth, shutting out the wind and protecting each anemic flame from its hiemal breath. My dress ripples, transforming from the absent moon into the city's great lake, silk brushing against my skin like whispered promises.

"You wore blue," he says. There is no inflection in his voice, no hint of either pleasure or remorse.

"It suits my mood."

"Why then do you walk with me?"

"It is my duty."

"You owe them nothing."

But I do.

We arrive at the first house. Uneven brick and crumbling mortar, it will not last another season. Plague has spared nothing, contaminating the very matter of existence down to its last particle. When this edifice finally disintegrates, the inhabitants will simply move. There is no shortage of vacancies in this world of waning light.

He inspects the collection of handmade masks that lie in a semicircle upon the back step. There are four. The first is made of a small, round pillowcase. Stitched to the pale fabric are a pair of black buttons and a fat pink ribbon fashioned to resemble a pleasant smile. I imagine my companion wearing it, and my own mouth fixes into a grim line. As if Plague's smile could be anything but cruel and portend anything but death—or worse—no matter the face.

The second is made of plaster, molded to the shape of its creator. It is a painted rainbow of delightful pastels, a relic of days now almost forgotten. Carnivals and candy. Love and joy. Words long unspoken beneath this shroud of perpetual darkness.

The third is the creation of a younger hand, a cardboard rectangle with pennies for eyes and a thin red slash for a mouth. Is this mask her first? Will it be her last?

The final mask is that of a younger hand still. It appears to have been created in great haste and with little care. Unsupervised. A mistake. Lacking both eyes and a mouth, the paper bag is hardly a mask at all, but an asymmetric galaxy of glitter and congealing adhesive.

Plague chooses this final offering and drops it into his bag. I replace the mask with a draught of cyanide from my own and extinguish the lantern, saying a prayer for the soul it represents though all the old gods are dead and no angels remain to carry it forth from this world.

Behind the door, a woman shrieks as if her throat could voice the anguish of her breaking heart. The handle rattles as it begins to turn, but is quickly silenced by a deeper voice and stronger hand. The voices argue. He whispers of caution and survival. She screams of fairness and cowardice.

My companion lights another cigarette, and for a moment his face is visible in the flame's flickering light. It barely resembles the young poet with the golden voice to whom it had belonged just a year ago. Stolen skin stretched tight across bone and flesh, it is a visage befitting an ancient king, but even this pharaoh's face, hideous to behold, is better than what lies beneath.

He bends at the waist and, through lips that will never again whisper verse or sonnet, breathes a lungful of lunacy into the keyhole.

We wait.

The woman curses and wails. Twice, the deadbolt slides back, and twice it's thrown hard back into place. Eventually reason wins the night, and beneath a chorus of wretched sobbing and futile whispers of consolation, a baby cries. In a few years, it will be old enough to craft a mask of its own.

Satisfied, Plague turns and glides toward the next flickering light. There is nothing here that interests him, and so the masks remain untouched, the lantern lit. We move on.

Once, we all wore masks—anonymity granting us permission to pursue our truest desires, free from the consequences of ridicule and judgment. We constructed a counterfeit society in which there were neither husbands nor wives, friends nor enemies, only an endless parade of strangers seeking strangers seeking decadence. And so we sewed and painted and sculpted and shaved, that we might steal and cut and lie and cheat and fuck. Artificial means to experience genuine ends . . .

Another mask disappears into Plague's bag, this one sketched onto heavy parchment. It is the face of a man with a bald pate, his cheeks, jaw, and chin obscured by dense whiskers. The artist is a skilled one; the man's eyes—the only feature clearly visible in the deep shadows of graphite and charcoal—are alive and sparkling, watching me as they descend until darkness finally forces them to blink. I am glad to be free of their gaze, though Plague and I both know this is not the last I'll see of them.

Dipping a hand into my own bag, like an anatomist reaching into the body cavity of a prosected corpse, I retrieve yet another instrument of death. This time I leave behind a silver blade before extinguishing the lantern's dim yellow glow. Smoke escapes its crooked grin like a sigh, as if it had been waiting for me to cure it of the fever burning within.

"Why do you leave them trinkets?" my companion asks, lighting yet another cancer stick. He places it between his lips in an act of cannibalism.

"It is custom for the doctor to treat her patients."

"You cannot cure death."

"Sometimes, death itself is a cure."

He grins, but there is no humor in his smile, only malice. It lingers but a moment before slipping from his stolen face, just as the sun slipped into the great lake, never to rise again, when he first crossed its steely waves. It will be hours yet before we return to the lake—to offer sacrifice upon its ancient, misty shore—but its putrid scent, carried for miles on an unrelenting wind, is an inescapable reminder of its presence. The ghosts of those trapped and rotting, feeding what was once part of the sea, permeate even the olfactory isolation of my mask, and I cease to breathe. It is an old habit, one I have yet to unlearn.

Lips, cracked and bloody, pucker around the cigarette as if it were a straw, and Plague draws up what little life remains in this dark alley. He presses his mouth to the keyhole, exhaling another cloud of sickness and decay.

There was but the one mask on this lonesome stoop, and so it is no surprise when the house remains silent, already resigned to its fate as a mausoleum. I spare one last glance at the silver blade before departing. Does the occupant know he's been chosen? Will he accept the aid of my prescribed therapy, or allow the natural history of disease to play out unhastened?

The natural history of desire is suffering. In time, our masks became our identities, inviting back into our lives the misery and boredom they'd once allowed us to escape. Discontent grew like an occult malignancy, and under cover of darkness, we traded our sins for freedom. Exchanging identities. Never knowing who might have been previously harmed by the faces we so eagerly adopted. Never caring who might hold a grudge against our newly minted selves. Never imagining that the death and madness so many sought to imitate walked freely among us.

Plague watches, his misappropriated face contorted into an expression between intrigue and incredulity, as I rest a bouquet of wolfsbane beside another extinguished flame. The young woman to whom the flowers now belong stares at me through the window. She's not near the keyhole, but neither is she far enough away. Plague's vapor drifts across the room, and the girl is seized by paroxysms of sweet, mad laughter. It paints the glass with a fine crimson spray. Even in darkness I can see the terror in her eyes. They flit between my mask's hard lines and the soft suggestion of deadly blooms recently plucked. I offer an almost-imperceptible nod. It is all the permission she needs, and as

I follow Plague toward the next illuminated threshold, a door whispers open and closed behind us, punctuated by the howl of impending hysteria.

We visit house after house, prayers whispered inside as we pause outside each one like a pair of skeletal fingers moving steadily from bead to bead around a rosary. There is no obvious pattern to Plague's fancy. He makes his selections seemingly at random. We pass by many homes, leaving the families inside—if not entirely their sanity—intact for another year.

Here he stops to collect a rubber imprint of a woman with green eyes. I leave a vial of liquid, equally green, in its place.

We move on.

Next, he plucks three identical masks carved from white marble—perhaps in hopes they will not float—and places them into his bag, leaving a fourth to suffer in isolation. The revolver I place beside the smoldering candle has four rounds in its chambers. I cannot help myself.

Plague's bag is nearly full now; eleven masks chosen from countless thousands occupy the leather satchel my companion drags behind him like a sack of disembodied heads. One more and we can return to the lake, finish this awful business for another year.

"You choose," he says when we arrive at the next house.

Two masks lie on the threshold, pale, smiling faces against a grimy, ashen backdrop. Shadows glide across the smooth porcelain in a pagan dance fueled by firelight. I am loathe to end it. There is but one item left in my doctor's bag, and so I offer a solution I've waited an eternity to propose.

The first to die was the banker's son. His body lay naked, save for a mask, in the center of town, a single word—a directive—carved in crooked, bloody script onto the pale flesh of his chest. When the mask was removed, it was discovered that beneath the false ipseity he'd adopted, the young man's true identity had been stolen, peeled away to yellow cartilage and glistening bone. Only his eyes remained, reflected in their glassy surface a nightmare visage that would drive any man to murder.

Next was the grade school teacher, her tanned breasts a canvas for repeated directives. Authorities warned us to be wary of strangers, but we were—all of us—strangers. Strangers becoming ever more strange as we continued to swap, to change, to hide behind false faces made ever more real as whispers of a madman in a pallid mask infused us with fear like a slow poison.

A librarian. A physician. A nameless vagrant. None were safe from the identity thief's mad obsession. Eleven victims in all, faces filleted and tossed into the lake, before the directive finally became law and we were all forced to unmask.

But it was already too late.

We arrive at the great lake. Once part of a vast ocean—a fact reflected in its very name, unspoken since it swallowed the day—it reeks of salt and illness and decay. Beneath its cold, still surface, the sun smolders, orange like the tip of Plague's cigarettes. Kneeling before it, a congregation of the dead weeps.

Plague removes the masks from his bag one at a time. First comes the mess of glitter and glue, followed by a grim cross-stitch. He places them in the water at the lake's edge, where they float for a moment, suspended in the sallow brine like bits of pollen, before the wind carries them to the center of the lake, and they sink to the bottom like stones. Next are the marble triplets—they float just fine. Then there are the rubber woman with the green eyes and the young girl to whom I'd given flowers. Faces floating gently like autumn leaves, before being dragged beneath the surface as if by an invisible leviathan. One by one, the lake claims them all. Last comes the charcoal rubbing of the man with the living eyes.

"Wait," I say, snatching the mask from my companion's delicate grasp.

The face is unfamiliar, but the eyes . . . They are the same as the banker's son's. The same as the teacher's. The doctor's. In the negative space, between smudged fingerprints and penciled arcs, the pallid mask's expressionless visage watches through borrowed eyes.

I step to the water's edge and cast this last face into the waves, repeating the past. Eyes fixed on eyes fixed on me, I watch as it sinks into the yellow depths. Something brushes against my arm. Looking up, I see the boy to whom the glitter-and-glue mask had belonged. He carries the draught of cyanide in one pudgy hand. Tears streaming down cheeks forever robbed of their ruddy complexion, he wades into the lake. I stand. Turn. The others are arriving.

One after another, they glide past me, instruments of death clutched in ghostly hands and tears to feed the abysmal lake leaking from the corners of clouded eyes. All but the man with the coarse beard; his tears flow from eyes burning with fever and madness. He carries the silver blade, but his hands—the fingers stained black from countless hours practicing his craft—have retained their substance. He presses rejected suicide into my open palm and whispers, "Physician, heal thyself," before joining the others at the bottom of the lake.

Once, we all wore masks, fulfilling every desire, shielded from the bitter aftertaste of consequence. We broke the laws of God and man. Committed sins of the flesh and of the spirit, poisoning our bodies and our minds. We were consumed by sickness.

But there was one who sought to cure us of our disease. One who found among forbidden tomes an antidote for the ichor coursing through our veins. One who wore no mask.

At last, it is my turn.

Plague lifts his hand, skin shiny as wax paper wrapped tight around spider-thin digits, and removes my disguise. For a moment the fragrance of lavender still lingers, and then I can smell him. The nicotine, yes, but that too is nothing more than camouflage. Beneath it writhes the stench of an infirm sea—the death scent of the lake amplified unto infinity—its lifeless tides pulled in an endless tug-of-war by a pair of merciless moons.

Free from the hooked beak and mirrored lenses, my true face gazes upon the world I have wrought. As with those I sacrificed to immunize the herd, only my eyes remain. Beneath the glassy orbs—blue like the forgotten moon, blue like my dress, blue like the antithesis of gold—a pallid mask of fleshless bone grins.

Plague drops the mask at our feet. He leans forward, pressing his lips to my absent mouth and exhales one last cloud of smoke. It fills my lungs, my heart, my mind. Death and Madness. Doctor and Plague. Separate but unequal sides of the same diseased coin, locked in a terminal embrace. It lasts a lifetime.

Reluctantly, I withdraw, weeping, as the others have wept. But Madness cannot claim that which is already dead. Centipedes, maggots, and beetles slither from dry orbits in place of tears. They drop to the ground where they are crushed beneath Plague's thundering rage.

I am unfit for sacrifice.

Plague's own mask disintegrates, revealing the festering horror beneath—the horror I summoned when the world was young and the sun and moon still hung in the sky. Gilded wings unfold, stretching and expanding until they blot out the heavens. I spread my own, blacker than the night, blacker even than the stars that watch in silent discontent. Silver blade still in my hand, I strike out—once, twice, three times—severing Plague's golden plumes.

He shrieks. Curses me. Tumbles to the ground, undone. But Death cannot claim that which is eternal. Plague flees across the lake, borne upward by the tears of the dead, banished from this land, back to his forgotten kingdom. So furious is he that Plague's new face, risen from the depths, slips past the defeated king, unnoticed. I pluck it from the brackish water, unsurprised to discover that it is the bearded man with the omniscient eyes.

My doctor's mask is gone, sucked beneath the lapping waves of the great lake that now hisses and vomits daybreak. I will not follow. Instead, I press empty skin to exposed bone. One last identity to safeguard against a relapse of Plague's lunatic reign. Purged of his influence, the city shivers, eager to begin its convalescence, and I stride empty-handed into the brilliant rays of the resurrected sun.

# Sinkers
## Dan Waters

*Dan Waters attended a Borderlands Press Writers Boot Camp and dazzled the instructors with his acerbic wit and confident style. He went on to create a successful YA series that keeps him very busy, but he occasionally writes short fiction. His story, which follows, could also be called "Knuckleheads Have Feelings Too!" In a totally unique fashion, Waters investigates the concept of what the afterlife could be or not be. He descends through limbo, heaven, and a dark place that could be hell. His tongue-in-cheek style had us giggling, but eventually saying, "Oh . . . shit!"*

They had put away twenty-one cans of Golden Anniversary three-bucks-a-six-pack beer between them before jumping the rail at Oxoboxo Bridge. Numbers twenty-two and twenty-three were cracked and in their hands, while number twenty-four (which would have been seventeen if it hadn't previously slipped out of Chuck's shaking hand) rolled around with a few of its empty brothers in the backseat. Eddie, who was riding shotgun, liked pitching the empties out the window at parked cars or the stop signs that Chuck sped past. Chuck didn't go for that sort of juvenile shit; he just threw them over his shoulder, as one tosses salt for good luck.

Their hyperdrive euphoria remained the few moments that the car was airborne. The Nova had a powerful engine and Chuck had taken the corner pretty fast and they could really feel the speed rev in their veins. The feeling disappeared when they hit the water, the black lake rushing up at them like the night sky swallowing daylight.

It was about a girl, as such tragic wasteful endings often are. Not that the girl was the one to blame; she hadn't bought the beer nor had she glued her ex-boyfriend's foot to the floor. If she hadn't been involved, they surely would have found some other excuse to get wasted and go joyriding at Mach 10. But she should be mentioned, if only to add a hint of sexual tension to Chuck and Eddie's short and reckless adventure.

Chuck's girlfriend of two months had started seeing another guy and had laid the whole "just friends" trip on Chuck, a trip that most people would rather not take. Sheila was a nice girl and that was the heart of the problem really, because nice girls wouldn't continue to let themselves be forced into committing the type of acts that Chuck routinely forced Sheila to commit in the two months of their "relationship". Especially nice girls with choices, and Sheila was a girl with choices. Her latest choice was Brock Davis, the defensive tackle for the Oakvale Badgers, so Chuck was robbed of the opportunity of delivering the vengeful ass kicking that most of the new boyfriends got. No sex, no violence—time for a Golden Anniversary.

Eddie was the logical choice to go get bombed with in the aftermath of the dumping. Eddie had never had a girlfriend. Eddie also possessed the third largest collection of pornography in Oakvale. Besides, it was Saturday night, and everyone else in town was busy trying to get what Chuck had just lost access to.

So Chuck bribed a friend's older brother, with a twenty and two skin mags, to get them a case, and then he fired up the Nova and set off for the less-than-mean but darker-than-hell back streets of Oakvale.

As the first lukewarm can of Golden Anniversary ('Gee-ay' to the faithful) was cracked and placed in his hand, Chuck began to express his dismay at being dumped, the doleful strains of AC/DC loud enough to rattle the windows, serving as the soundtrack to his tale of woe.

"Whore," he said. "Probably been doin' him the whole time."

"Whore," Eddie agreed, taking a slug of GA. He pronounced it "ho-uh".

Drunken logic, as opposed to deductive logic, proceeds from the specific to the general, and Chuck's slow burn tirade grew in scope, taking in friends, classmates, girls from the neighborhood, girls who worked at the mall, girls he had seen in the thumbprinted magazines on the seat between them, until it was large enough to include all of womankind rather than just his ex-girlfriend. His list was all-inclusive by the fourth beer.

"'R all bitches 'n sluts anyhow," he said, gripping the wheel with his left hand and cradling a beer in his right, his knuckles white on each. "Do your best fuckin' friend on you . . . you don't watch out."

"Ho-uhs," Eddie added.

Chuck squinted at him as though he might have suspected Eddie of a dalliance with his ex. Eddie, who was half Chuck's size and for whom "liquid courage" was more like bottled cowardice, caught the look and stared sullenly out the side window. Chuck smiled, remembering that the only dalliance Eddie had ever had was with his right hand.

His smile grew wider as he recalled the last time with Sheila. Even then, pushing the back of her head down after he'd yanked her behind the rendering dumpster in back of the school. He was rough but he hadn't thought he'd been that rough, not rough enough for it to be over. Even the look she gave him when it was done—he thought that look would fade with time. Why couldn't he ever see where these things were going?

Deep down, down to the bottom where all true feelings lie, he knew he was at fault. But if God wanted accepting responsibility to be easier than getting drunk, he wouldn't have invented three-bucks-a-six-pack beer. His smile flattened with a mouthful of said beer and did not return.

Drunken logic held sway and intensified with each sip and soon Chuck set about proving that not only women but all of humanity was worthless and all people wretched, hateful monsters intent on spreading malice and despair wherever they went.

"Damn slut," Chuck said.

"Damn," Eddie parroted.

Chuck stopped preaching the Gospel of the Broken Heart as he began his eleventh beer. Not normally loquacious, he hunched over the steering wheel and stared abjectly through the windshield as the roads spread out before him like a deck of cards fanned in the hands of a squinting man. Eddie was halfway through his ninth beer and took advantage of the silence by expounding at length why he thought anal sex was preferable to more traditional forms, and went on to mention that when he got a girlfriend she damn well better be prepared to swallow.

"Bitsh gotta be ready at all the time, know? All fu' time, man. Don' wan' nothin' bitsh don' wha' . . . "

But Chuck was far beyond questions of mere aesthetics at this point, even though Eddie was striking perilously close to deep truths. He was locked deep within himself where reasons ceased to matter. The bitterness remained, but its causes were fading, if causes they were and not just passkeys to doors of hatred deep inside the dungeons of his soul.

"Fu' bish gots to gotta . . . "

Chuck saw the railing the instant before the thick front wheels of the Nova trampled over it. He fell silent as the moon suddenly filled the windshield.

The feeling was quite beautiful, the pleasant drunken weightlessness, the sensation of being on a slow boat cruising towards the luminescent disc far on the horizon, coasting on a beam of light across the spanning sea of black velvet.

The feeling was gone as the moon dropped out of their orbit and they smashed both of their skulls on the windshield when the car hit the dark water.

The heavy car plunged into the lake like a knifing diver, capsizing without tarrying on the surface. The corpses—for both Chuck and Eddie had been killed instantly by the harsh impact—were pressed back into their seats by the water as it streamed through the starred windshield. The windshield imploded as the car sank to greater depths, sending a spray of safety glass that lodged in leather and flesh.

Dead Chuck opened his eyes. He found that death had cleared his head, in a manner of speaking. Sure, his vision was more than a trifle impaired, but once he wiped the blood and brain from his eyes, his sight was no blurrier in the dark lake water than it had been when he was sitting crocked behind the wheel up on the surface.

The best part of being dead was the absence of bitterness. The feeling was gone. All of it, gone. He inhaled the lake water until it filled him, a smile returning to his broken face.

*I hadn't expected that,* he thought.

Eddie was a little worse for wear than his friend. His scrawny neck had snapped twiglike when they hit, and he couldn't lift his head from where it lay cheek down on his shoulder.

"Shouldn't we have hit bottom already, Charles?" Eddie asked, the words bubbling out of his waterlogged lungs.

"I don't know, Edward," Chuck said, staring at the greenish darkness, which was scarcely illumined by the Nova's headlights.

"What's that up ahead?" Eddie asked.

It was a fish, a small, flat fish about five inches long. It regarded them for a moment as though transfixed, deerlike, in the Nova's headlights.

Two, three more joined it, staring calmly at the swiftly sinking automobile, before swimming on past the car. The three fish multiplied into a cloud-like school that lingered, basking in the ghostly light. Some fish tapped like rain on the bonnet of the Nova; others swam in through the jagged hole where the windshield had been, to brush against the dead.

"Fish," Eddie said, laughing a stream of bubbles.

"Like snowflakes," Chuck said, willing his lifeless hand to touch one of the tiny swimmers. "We're in a snowstorm, a living snowstorm."

The school did look like a snowstorm through the smashed windshield, a quick, darting flurry that would leave the ground dusted with a clean, pure whiteness as one watched it through the frosted windows of a warm, safe home.

"Charles," Eddie said, "look at that."

Bigger fish had joined the cloud. And different fish—fish with red stripes, fish with tapering, angular fins, and fish with teeth two inches long.

"Whoa," Chuck said as he watched a squid undulate through the stream of fish. A pair of manta rays flapped like bats over the hood of the car; a catfish the size of a large dog bumped into Eddie's door.

"This is weird," Eddie exclaimed, his dead eyes opened wide. "Look at that thing."

The "thing" was a small plesiosaur whose gentle but persistent swimming knocked clusters of fish off their course.

The beast, showing it rows of sharp teeth, like icicles in the mouth of a cave, eyed a dugong

The variety of creatures increased as their steel coffin descended. Dolphins, sharks, elasmosaurs, killer whales, coelacanths; all manner of water dwellers drifted by in an endless stream of motion.

Chuck glanced out his side window and immediately regretted doing so, as the formlessly vague, lazy shapes he spied drifting in the gloom beyond filled him with an unspeakable dread. He returned to gaping at the creatures straight ahead, unease furrowing his shattered brow.

Eddie spotted the first human floating out of the depths.

"Look!" he shouted.

A small boy floated into the twin beams of the headlights, clad in only a bathing suit whose drawstrings trailed behind him like the tails of a kite. He gazed blankly at Chuck and Eddie as he cut through the scaly throng, showing no more recognition than did the lowliest minnow. Perhaps less.

"Damn," Chuck said.

"Look, Charles. There's another one."

And there was—a young woman in a bikini, a long, deep crease along the top of her skull just visible beneath the long hair fanning out behind her. To her left on the other side of a small cluster of sparking electric eels was an overweight man whose padded fishing jacket, hip waders, and boots did not seem to impede his progress through the dark water.

"Whoa," Eddie said as another woman floated past their headlights at a sharp angle.

"We're in the deep water, Edward," Chuck said as two young men who could have been brothers passed over the hood, one of them turning his head for a moment to regard them.

"And dropping still," added Eddie.

Bodies continued to float past them like bubbles from a fountain, so many bodies that the water was choked with them. Fish and other creatures could be seen darting or diving in among the human throng; a huge sperm whale appeared suddenly from the stream of bodies and bumped the right front quarter panel, pushing the car off its current trajectory, before veering away into the darkness. The headlight on that side blinked rapidly three times and then went out.

Not all the bodies were pleasant to regard. Many bore wounds or marks as grievous as those sustained by Chuck and Eddie once their brief flight into the night sky had ended. As they descended, the school of corpses that crossed their sights was in a greater state of disrepair, their flesh hanging loose from visible bones and trailing behind them or billowing around them. A sea snake the size of a subway train cut through the corpses bursting putrid bodies that left clouds of blood in the serpent's wake.

A body, no more than a skeleton wearing a few fleshy rags, changed direction to come at them. The effigy swam through the broken windshield and pulled itself into the backseat. Chuck looked over his shoulder and saw a white skull thrown back as though in laughter.

A blue whale shot up from the water below, the force of its wake spinning the Nova like a top. An immense suckered tentacle cleaved through the teeming bodies.

"Charles, I'm . . . "

Another tentacle appeared from the darkness and curled towards the Nova, reaching in and plucking Eddie from his seat like a clam from its shell and then he was gone, dragged down into the darkness.

Chuck squinted against the gloom trying to catch sight of him, but he was gone. More tentacles, massive appendages like thick tree trunks, swayed before him like the hands of the faithless. And thinner, whiplike ones, as well, that lashed and snapped against the side of the Nova. He turned to look over his shoulder once again. The corpse had not moved; its expression of mirth had not changed as it sat reclined against the leather seat, cans of GA floating around a fleshless head.

The other headlight cut out. The Nova was dropping towards an eerie luminescence far below. Chuck could make out movement in the darkness beyond, nothing more. Something quick and corded brushed against his cheek, possibly laying it open, he couldn't be sure. A moment later something struck the back of the car from below, with a dull clunk, tipping the car up just as something Chuck imagined was a huge anemone pressed itself against his face before withdrawing into the darkness.

Something landed on the hood with enough force to crack the metal. Another invisible thing slammed into the passenger-side door.

Chuck was calm throughout, even as cold hands touched his skin and then withdrew. A sense of languid ease had overtaken him as he sank through the black waters of Oxoboxo Lake, a peace unlike he had ever experienced while alive, except through the oblivion of alcohol. His bitterness, his hatred, all of his many negative emotions had drained from him the moment his head smashed against the windshield of his car, and flowed from him with increasing speed the deeper he went. It wasn't Sheila's fault. All women were not whores; all humanity was not worthless. He turned again to smile at his silent passenger, who was now completely invisible in the inky water of the backseat.

The car gave a sudden lurch, as though something was tugging on one of the axles. Chuck thought he could discern a sea of waving tentacles, a great forest of them, sprouting from the weird glow which must be hundreds of fathoms below.

There was a second tug and the car began to move with purpose, the speed increasing as the nose of the vehicle pointed at the source of light intensifying below. The illusion of drifting in a peaceful fluid haze was wiped away and replaced by the unwelcome sensation of being snared by something that would not let go. Death, like life, lost all appeal for Chuck the moment he sensed another pulling his strings.

The sudden jolt squeezed out whatever chemicals were left lingering in his adrenal glands. His first thought was to escape the plummeting vehicle, but the pressure of swift descent pushed him back against his seat. He tried to call out but his cries would not rise up from his throat.

The curtain of tentacles parted as he was reeled in with increasing velocity. The car was bathed in an ethereal greenish light, a light that was the light of wolves' eyes, of the fungal phosphorescence of tomb walls, of radioactive ooze. Whatever its source, the illumination cut through the darkness like a beacon and filled his vision with a sickly glow.

Chuck could see that the vehicle had begun to rapidly oxidize; flecks of paint and rust were lifting from the dented hood and peppering his skin like a swarm of gnats. The corrosive effects of the light weren't limited to the metal of the vehicle, as the plastics coating the dash and the steering wheel had begun to dissolve like sugar in water.

Chuck lifted his hand and watched his skin and then the flesh beneath burn away. His metacarpal bones were fizzing, wispy contrails of grayish smoke trailing in the water as his skeleton began to melt. His jaw lolled open in surprise and then unhinged entirely, separating from his skull with a muted snap. The greenish light, a warm invitation from miles below, now looked septic and dangerous. He felt as he did when the Nova first jumped the rails, lost and out of control, unable to slow his momentum or even hold himself together.

He was moving faster now, faster than he had ever traveled in a car, and the speed made it difficult to keep his newfound love of humanity in the forefront of his mind. The rate of descent brought also an acceleration of the rate of decay—the front of the car was a skeleton of rusted metal, the layers of engine stripped away and atomized in the swift drag. There was nothing for Chuck to hold on to, but soon there would be nothing to hold on with; his remaining hand came loose at the wrist and dispersed in the slipstream as his body succumbed to the acidic effect of the deep water.

He felt a brief touch, the whisper of a kiss, at the base of his neck and he remembered his silent companion in the backseat. He shivered, imagining a rotting tongue licking away the pieces of him that were flaking off his dissolving body. He tried to turn but could not; the vertebrae of his neck softened and then liquefied. He plummeted another four fathoms in the blink of a disintegrating eyelid and then his body was gone, just gone, a vague swirl of consciousness left in its wake.

The tentacles tugging his car disappeared and all that remained was the pulsing light that pulled him in like a magnet. Chuck saw forms flickering in the edges of the light; they glittered and danced like sunbeams on the surface of the lake on a clear July day, burning with a greater concentration than the light surrounding them.

He tried to tell himself that he was falling towards heaven, but even his thoughts were shrill and panicked. Even as he imagined the heaven below and all its wonders, he was trying to will himself to stop sinking, to put the brakes on his headlong descent.

*I see angels at play in the light of a submerged sun!* he thought, but as with most of the thoughts he had clung to in life, there was no real belief behind the concept.

The angels turned towards him, as a school of piranha will turn towards a thread of blood in the water.

They were too close, Chuck thought. Too fast. There was an anchor chained to his spirit and fear was a freezing current that flowed through what was left of him as he saw what the "angels" really were. He understood in ways he had never understood a thing while on the surface.

Dozens of them were reaching, rushing towards him in a geyser of radiance. They were smiling and reaching with glowing arms that lengthened into points like the shadows of trees that reached across Lake Oxoboxo at dusk.

But they were not reaching because they wanted to welcome him, and they were not smiling because they were happy.

*Sheila,* he thought, but when he thought of her he thought of the look on her face when he was finished behind the rendering dumpster. He hadn't asked her for forgiveness then and he could not now.

Their cold fingers pierced the formless cloud of his soul and began to tear it apart, leaving shreds and scraps that were a passing effervescence in the unfathomable waters of Lake Oxoboxo. He tried to scream in that final moment because, for the first time, in life or death, he could understand what was coming next.

# Time Is a Face on the Water
## Michael Bailey

*Another Boot Camp graduate, Michael Bailey has established himself as an energetic and visionary anthologist as well as writer. His stories are marked by their emotional power and originality, which remind us of the works of Gary Braunbeck and Ray Bradbury. In the following story, he examines an aspect of life we all share, but deal with in a variety of ways ranging from the sublime to the most depressing—the inevitable passing of time.*

"Life is so beautiful that death has fallen in love with it,
a jealous, possessive love that grabs at what it can."
—Yann Martel, *Life of Pi*

"I loved you then and I love you now and
I have loved you every second in between."
—Stephen King, *Lisey's Story*

ACT 1: The Past

*What kind of play is this?*

Günay admired the rivulets interrupting the otherwise placid pool of water in the creek out back, the place he went to think, to reflect on life, and to figure out what the fuck it all meant.

Death had taken his daughter, Airavata. He and Luci chose the name after looking through a book on names and originations. Airavata, sometimes Air for short, meant "child of water", which they thought clever since Gün's own name was Turkish for *sun* and Luci derived from the Latin *lux*, meaning *light*. From sun and light they had created a daughter they had sometimes called *air* and sometimes called *water*, and she was gone. Ten years ago she'd died. Like it was yesterday.

*A tragedy?*

Yes, life's often a tragedy, but sometimes much more . . .

*A comedy?*

No, no one's laughing.

*A history?*

Yes, there's much history involved.

Life was beautiful play, for the most part, full of rich colors, warmth, love, and characters, *so* many characters, full of dialogue—sometimes internal, but more often spoken aloud whether necessary or not—and of course life was full of memorable scenes, one after another after another, like rivulets of water dancing chaotically together; and yet, sometimes life quieted down and turned placid, allowing you to reflect more clearly on the three acts of *past, present*, and *future*.

Act 1, in Gün's case, encompassed approximately thirty years of his life, and could be summarized by the following: birth, childhood, adolescence, transition to adulthood, sexuality, self-discovery, finding and marrying the light of his life known as Luci, and then writing the first act of Airavata's play, which, since life turns like a wheel, included her birth, childhood, adolescence . . .

Airavata had lived a one-act play.

*And now I'm entering Act 2 of my own two- or, if I'm lucky, three-act play,* Gün mused, staring at the water.

The creek, like the rest of state, had mostly dried up. Sparse rain the night before trickled water down the creek, which travelled the long path from the mountain and eventually through their backyard. Such a wonderful sound. Small pools of black had welled where it could as insects skimmed over the surface; green, mossy river rocks below created the dark appearance. The rain often summoned newts and less often salamanders to the uncovered rocks, and Gün noticed now an orange-bellied creature with bubbly brown skin surfacing for air.

He and Air had often carried these timid California newts around the property, and they didn't seem to mind; they held on tight, in fact, with a strong embrace as if affectionate. The *Taricha torosa*, he'd later discovered, secreted a potent neurotoxin called tetrodotoxin, hundreds of times more toxic than cyanide, the same toxin found in pufferfish and certain frogs.

*"They're not dangerous by any means,"* Gün assured Luci on more than one occasion.

*"Well, they are, but only if you poke them with a stick real hard, and only if you ingest what they excrete."*

It was chain reaction of events, much like life, that made the California newt so interesting. To protect itself from birds, snakes, and other prey, the seemingly innocent creature had evolved over time to excrete the deadly toxin, arching its back and writhing to expose the bright-orange warning color of its belly if pierced, making the newt nearly untouchable as a species. Yet, as if a long-winded Darwinian joke, a few species of garter snake evolved as well, developing a genetic resistance to tetrodotoxin, putting this particular animal back in the food chain. And now they were nearly extinct.

*But who fuckin' cares about newts,* Gün thought.

As if in response, the newt crawled ever so slowly onto a dry rock and studied him.

A blue-and-white sky reflected against the black-mirror surface of the small pool, as well as the autumnal-changing yellows, browns, and reds of grapevines intertwined in the branches of the trees lining the creek bed. Seafoam-green Spanish moss draped over limbs like delicate lace. Rainbow colors surrounded him as sunlight permeated the canopy in stripes.

*Lux,* he thought. *Luci. My light.*

When placed together, their names formed the compound word *sunlight.*

*"Look, a heart,"* Air had said one day, holding a large crimson grape leaf against her chest. Gün took in the memory, as well as the crisp smell of redwoods and birches and dying grapes as the wind offered all of it to him. They had sometimes floated leaves down the creek when it was running well, to see whose would reach the waterfall by the big rock the fastest.

Gün found a yellow grape leaf and placed it in the water. It floated alone, not moving anywhere, but spinning in slow circles because there was not enough current to move it along.

Luci took Airavata's death the hardest. She rarely spoke, burying herself in cleaning and other such chores, whether necessary or not, and she refused to touch Air's room, as if waiting for her to return one day. It took her and Gün three days to talk about what happened, and even after they talked about it, neither had anything much to say. This lack of communication nearly wrecked their marriage, but they'd somehow stuck together and survived the roughest of times. It wasn't Luci's fault, but *both* their faults. Communication's a collaborative enterprise.

*Will she stay?* Gün asked the water, meaning Luci, meaning would she stay alongside him to see how their play would ultimately end, to see what kind of a play they had lived.

He looked at his reflection and his reflection looked back.

*Ten years,* he thought. *Will she stay for ten more years?*

Water rippled from the wind, from the bugs, from floating hearts and other debris, from the deadly newt crawling back under the surface. Ravens fluttered and cawed from the treetops, as if laughing from above at his internal dialogue. The scent of leaves decomposing on the wet ground at the edge of the creek was aromatic, along with the mushrooms and lichen growing on fallen branches and the snapped fir tree dangling over the water.

And then the face changed, much quicker than the season.

His once brown hair was a little less brown, with perhaps some peppered gray, perhaps thinner; his facial hair appeared lighter as well, his cheeks more gaunt, his eyes a shade darker and baggier. He was older.

*Ten years. This is what I will look like in ten years.*

A hazy version of Luci's face peered over his reflection's shoulder, like a heat wave over hot asphalt. She, too, appeared ten years older. Crow's feet had begun at the corners of her eyes, her face thinner, her expression as sad as his.

*This is what she will look like in ten years.*

She was a stunning woman, always. Add another ten years, and another ten years, and, hell, even another, and she'd still be as beautiful as the day he fell in love with her all those years ago. But that was more of the past. Love's a hard thing to find after tragedy.

Gün turned and was surprised to find Luci standing there. This was his daydream, after all, *his* glimpse into the looking glass.

She didn't say anything at first, only put a hand on his shoulder.

He put his hand over hers and together they looked at the creek.

The high afternoon sun had dropped closer to the horizon to become a setting sun, the colors changing once more before their final fade to colorless night; the yellows more orange, the oranges more red, and the reds becoming various shades of purple like the mountain range to the east. The colors seemed warmer, almost glowing, although it was much colder than when he had first come out to the creek to think.

"I found something new," she said, meaning something of Airavata's.

Ten years had passed and they were still finding pieces of her past scattered around them.

A week after her funeral, which was also a week after Air's tenth birthday, Gün found a shriveled balloon left over from her birthday party. He found it in the laundry hamper, of all places, and at first thought it was a bunched-up sock mixed in with the rest of her dirty clothes. Air had often worn bright socks, not necessarily matching. And he remembered knowing then that Luci would wash these clothes, even though she'd never be able to wear them again. It was a red oxidized balloon that he found, like a blotch of memory, with some of Air's breath trapped inside.

He'd held the balloon close to his chest, sobbing tearlessly, his chest caving painfully with each uncontrollable spasm. *"Sometimes it hurts to cry,"* his mother once told him, and it was then he finally understood her meaning. The tears eventually came, and they did hurt, and by that time, Luci had come looking for him because he'd been gone for so long.

"I said I found something new," she said.

"Yeah?"

"Where were you just now?"

"I was just remembering the balloon."

She squeezed his hand tighter and he squeezed back, three times.

*I love you*, it meant, one squeeze for each word.

Some words were harder to say after losing a daughter, but some words could be said without talking at all.

She squeezed back, two times, ever so softly.

*I know.*

Airavata had created the secret language, perhaps a dozen or so phrases through various hand squeezes. It was one of the few things of hers that didn't hurt to keep.

They held on to the balloon a few more days after finding it, and it sometimes joined them at the dinner table, or on the dash of the car when they went out for a drive, and every day the balloon shrank, and what was left of Air inside slowly dwindled and dwindled . . .

"Yeah?" she said.

"I remember the smell," he said. "We were so afraid of losing her, you know? Her breath was in there, that small part of her we could keep, but holding on to the balloon and not releasing her breath meant we could lose her forever, even though by cutting open the balloon we'd get her for that brief moment, and still lose her forever."

She squeezed his hand, once, for a long time. It didn't mean anything specific, but somehow meant something that couldn't be expressed in words, and they both understood.

Luci had squeezed his hand like that the moment before they cut open the balloon to let the last of Air go.

"It smelled like huckleberry lip gloss," she said.

"It did."

Gün smiled, and although he couldn't see Luci's smile, he knew it was there.

Luci pointed over his shoulder to another dry rock.

The orange-bellied newt had returned, or maybe one of his friends.

"She used to love carrying those around," she said. "Remember the second year we lived here, she found five of them, or six, and she came running to the back patio holding all of them at once?"

"And the next day she found ten."

Another long squeeze, which didn't mean anything, but meant the world to him.

"What did you find?"

"The music box," she said, and he understood her melancholy.

They had kept Air's baby teeth in a cheap music box Luci found one weekend while thrifting. The box was wooden, covered with intricate carvings of flowers. When you opened the lid it smelled like cedar, and what was left of the ballerina inside—just her feet and ankles since the rest of her had broken off long ago—spun round while the tune of "Swan Lake" played on what sounded like the world's smallest xylophone.

"I forgot all about the music box," she said. "I was dusting the dresser in our room and moved a pile of books out of the way and knocked it to the floor. The lid won't close, so the music kept playing and playing, so I spun the shoes by hand until the music stopped. It was an awful sound, like mechanical crying. I think I broke it for good. And then I saw her teeth, Air's teeth, scattered on the carpet. I found them all. I counted. Some with dried blood, and—"

"Luci," he said, and glanced over his shoulder.

It was the first time they'd looked into each other's eyes since the reflection in the water of the creek, but that wasn't really looking; that had been a cheat.

She had aged ten years.

*She's been crying*, he told himself. *She's been crying and her eyes are puffy and dark—no, no, she can't be older—and her eyes are tired, like mine, that's all.*

Luci always had dirty-blonde hair, but it seemed dirtier now, and longer. Her hand, still in his, felt lighter, her skin more delicate, papery. She had definitely aged.

And his own weathered hand—

"I just wanted to tell you so you wouldn't be upset," she said.

"We'll find a new music box."

Gün squeezed her hand, three times.

*I love you.*

The secret message went unanswered as Luci slid her hand free. She offered an expressionless, flat smile, turned away, and headed back to the house.

## ACT 2: The Present

*"You'll find love when you stop looking for it."* This was another of his mother's sayings, and for most of his life, Gün had thought she was full of shit. Many years before crashing into Luci, he had dated, looking for his match, the perfect woman—woman after woman—and at first he'd thought he found the right one and married his mistake, then divorced, and almost married again. He had eventually given up on women at the age of thirty, telling his friends he was happy alone, better off alone, in fact, that he was *happier*, that if he had to live alone for the rest of his life, so be it. He was good with that.

Gün had stopped looking for love, and that's precisely the moment he *found* love, without looking at all. His mother had been right all those years.

Luci found *him*, in other words. They fell in love, stayed in love, made love, and together created a beautiful child. Happily ever after, or so they'd thought.

Gün found himself at the end of Act 1, *the past*, and the end of an agonizing transition to Act 2, *the present*. Life, the unforgiving wheel, turned every once in a while, making everything look all so familiar once again . . .

*"You'll find love when you stop looking for it."*

True then. True now.

Airavata haunted their lives whenever they stopped looking for her, it seemed. Scattered pieces from her past kept cropping up in the strangest of places. It was a different kind of love, but still love. Sometimes the haunts were good, but more often they were bad.

This went on for another nine years, their daughter now gone for twenty.

After much counseling, they decided to throw it all away. Everything. And it was about damn time. *"Holding on to the past only brings heartache,"* they were told by some shrink. *"It's unhealthy."* Airavata was gone, but as long as her *things* were still around, her absence would continue its assault on their emotions, and would ultimately destroy them.

That's all they really were, just *things*; the memories of Airavata mattered, not her personal belongings. They got rid of it all, donating her life possessions to thrift stores and charitable organizations, where they would never have to see them again, and it was *hard*, so very hard. But sometimes these material things resurfaced when they least expected, like the teeth in the music box, or the mood ring Gün now held in his hand.

Her bed—not slept in for twenty years—was the last of her things to go, or so they thought, their neighbors next door finally taking it off their hands. Gün found the cheap silver ring smashed into the carpet beneath one of the drawers built into the bedframe. He slid the ring next to his wedding band and within seconds the plastic disc or stone or whatever was set in the center turned a light-green color, whatever *that* meant. When he removed the ring, it left behind a similar color on his finger. Air had worn the cheap ring—a keepsake from some game at one of her friends' birthday parties—until the day she'd lost it.

Gün knew why rings turned fingers green, but that's not what bothered him now. What bothered him was the fact that his finger was green. He hadn't worn it long enough for the chemical reaction to take place between the acids on his skin and the metal of the ring, which meant Air's skin had caused the reaction however many years prior, and he had transferred a part of his dead daughter's past onto his finger.

He tossed the ring into the trash container next to the toilet in the bathroom and made his way to the sink to wash off the green, but it wouldn't come off with water. The soap dispenser was also out, so of course he checked under the sink, where he found Airavata's pink hairbrush hiding among the toiletries, with some of her hair caught in the bristles—his dead daughter's hair. He brought the brush to his nose, but the scent of her strawberry-blonde hair was long gone. It smelled like the pipes under the sink. He tossed the hairbrush into the trash and missed and—

"I found her phone," Luci said from the other room, "my old one we gave her when she was six and wanted to have a phone like Mom. Remember?"

"I do. Luci, we need to—"

"She used to record herself singing."

"The Redolent. She loved a band called the Redolent for some reason."

"I followed bands like that, too, when I was her age. I've been charging the phone. Want to listen?"

Gün released a held breath he was saving to tell her *no*.

"It's not a *thing*; it's a memory," she said, and that seemed to make sense, because memories were not meant to be thrown away.

Without saying anything, they had agreed to listen.

*The rain won't fall on the both of us*
*If I pull you in close*
*And you pull me in close*

*The sky, although it cries*
*The sky won't cry on the both of us*

Her voice, like a tone-deaf angel, ripped open his heart and flooded him with warmth, catching him off guard because hearing her voice after all these years was something he had not prepared for, and it was . . . it was "Though It Rains". She had always skipped the second stanza because she could never quite remember the lines, and so she'd burst right into the chorus, nearly yelling:

*And the water cascades*
*Cascades, cascades, cascades . . .*

And more often than not, he and Luci would sing along at this point. Luci was in fact mouthing the words now, singing along with their dead daughter, tears streaming down her face, fucking up the lyrics like always, skipping verses:

*The rain, yes, it will fall*
*If you're the one I choose*
*And I'm the one you choose*
*The sky, yes, it will cry*
*But it won't cry on the both of us*

And when the chorus repeated, now both Luci and Gün sang with their daughter, who was anything but dead in their hearts, although their broken voices were just above a whisper.

The pink hairbrush finally found its way into the trash, along with some strands of hair, but Gün rescued the mood ring from the wads of tissues and cotton swabs. He didn't tell Luci he still had it—secretly transferring the thing from pants pocket to pants pocket over the last three days, sometimes reaching in to feel the cold, sometimes slipping a finger through the band and wondering what color it turned within the darkness.

He eventually brought it with him to the creek, where he could hide it from Luci forever. It had rained hard, so the creek had transformed from trickling to flowing, how he remembered it the springs and summers when the three of them would walk the creek in their rain boots.

He slid the ring onto his finger one last time and spun it around and around, making sure it left a ghostly ring of green behind, and smiled when the plastic or stone or whatever it was in the middle turned dark blue, which he remembered meant either *calm* or *happy*, and then tossed it into the largest pool of water. The blackness of the creek swallowed the ring, but he'd from now on know it was there, hidden below the surface, where it would forever remain colorless.

Gün didn't like keeping secrets like this from Luci, but was sure Luci had kept or had hidden certain things without *him* knowing. Some secrets were good secrets, after all.

He and Luci had gotten better over the last ten years. Getting rid of Airavata's things had helped, yet a small part of him wondered if the happiness would last, whether or not they would ever return to normalcy, whether or not they could ever love each other the way they had before—

When was the last time either had ever spoken those magical three words: *I love you?* Their hands had symbolically said those *un*words a number of times, along with other *un*spoken phrases in their secret language, but when was the last time they were spoken aloud?

Twenty years.

*Jesus.*

Gün crouched down and leaned over the water, once again looking at his reflection. He remembered the last time he'd visited the creek, over ten years ago, and had asked the all-important question: *Will she stay?*

The answer had been yes, and she had stayed.

But for how much longer?

*Will she stay?* he had asked the water. *Will she stay for ten more years?*

They hadn't aged ten years the moment he peered into their future all those years ago; they had *lived* those years, together. Hadn't they? The last ten years were a blur. Had they really lived *ten* additional years together in such unhappiness, holding on to Air's things for so long? Had it taken them *twenty* fucking years to finally rid their lives of her personal belongings, to try to forget her? No, that wasn't right. They would always remember her.

*Time is a wheel,* he mused, *sometimes turning slowly, sometimes spinning out of control.*

Time had spun for the last ten years, and had for some reason stopped at this exact moment, on this cold winter morning, so he could once again reflect on life.

The wonderful colors of autumn were gone, the leaves fallen, the world moodless.

Although the creek flowed steadily along, the pool of water over which he leaned was placid as could be, the insects gone, the newts and salamanders hibernating, or whatever they did in the winter, the birds long migrated to warmer, more lively places, and the life around him, for the most part, silent; only the soft, therapeutic sounds of water and wind kept him company.

Two heart-shaped leaves slow-raced along the surface and fell over the waterfall by the large rock; neither won, but tied as they tumbled over.

*Will she stay?* Gün once again asked the water, meaning Luci. And he wondered for how long. *Will she stay for ten more years? Will we ever get over our loss? Will we last?*

A brown redwood leaf with spiky needles fell from above just then, landing on the face of his reflection, rippling the water, changing him, *aging* him.

When the obsidian water once again settled to mirror glass, Gün's beard and sideburns had become half-brown, half-gray, along with the rest of the hair on his head, which appeared sparse in places, wispier, his hairline higher. His nose and ears had stretched a fraction longer, it seemed, his eyes swallowed by dark, tired circles, the color in his eyes milkier. His reflection had aged ten years, not only physically but emotionally. Gün touched his face and watched his reflection do the same; both sets of hands felt weathered skin, and—

He waited for Luci to join him in the water.

*Will she stay for ten more years?*

And he waited, and waited, his reflection transforming.

His heart sank and felt heavy, although he knew this was all in his head. He hadn't aged ten more years, or twenty, since he had asked the question again. It was the water creating the wrinkles, not time; the wheel could not be forced to turn.

*Will she stay for ten more years?*

"Cascades, cascades, cascades . . . " he sang.

He felt older, thirty years older now, could feel the change in the cold aches of his bones, in the more difficult way he breathed, and by his reflection becoming out of focus.

"Will she stay?" he said aloud. "Will Luci stay with me ten more years?"

Gün cried once again, the image in the reflection blurring.

*Will she stay just ten more years?*

And blurring.

He was losing it, fucking *losing* it, having a panic attack, which he'd had once before when finding the red balloon with the last of Air trapped inside, and that's exactly how he felt now, his air trapped inside an ever-shriveling balloon and unable to escape, his chest tightening, his heart palpitating . . .

A murder of crows—what he had read once were the harbingers of death—cackled above, hidden in the trees and inviting Death to take him away, to be with Airavata—

And then she came.

Gün could barely see her through the tears, and the *blur*, but she was there.

A reflection of Luci stood over the reflection of his shoulder.

She put a papery, bony hand on his shoulder and his heart could once again beat, his lungs could once again breathe.

He put his own aged hand over hers and squeezed one long time, which didn't mean anything, but meant everything, and she squeezed back, three times.

"I will stay with you until the end," she said; and she had.

He could never ask Luci to do something so difficult, but she had stayed.

Gün wiped at the tears with his free hand, and their reflection came into better focus, although the phantasm of their potential future remained blurry as hell.

"If you're the one I choose," she sang, "and I'm the one you choose."

Together they sang the chorus.

He didn't turn around, couldn't look her in the face just yet, and that was okay. It would all be okay. Instead, he squeezed her hand in a way he knew would make her smile.

Luci reached a hand across his shoulder, not pointing at a newt this time, but holding a pair of glasses, which he instantly knew were *his* glasses, although he couldn't—but at the same time *could*—remember wearing glasses and, still holding her hand, he took them with his other and shook them open, placing them onto his face the way he had done either a million times before or had never at all.

The world came into focus.

Gün looked at their reflection in the water, and then turned to face Luci.

They were so very old.

He squeezed her hand, three times, the way Airavata had taught them.

She squeezed back, three times, and said the words.

He said them too.

*What kind of play is this?* he wondered, but he already knew. Their life had not been a single type of Shakespearian play, but a combination of all three: *a tragedy, a history, a comedy.* But would they ever laugh again?

They both returned their attention to the water, and perhaps asked the same questions to the looking glass:

*Can we ever have her back? Can we have her back for just ten more years?*

ACT 3: The Future

Sometimes the last act of a play can be short, and sweet; sometimes those are the best kinds of plays, or so Günay believed for him and Luci; they had seen many over the years.

Their daughter was turning ten and she wanted red balloons.

"What do you want to do after the party?" Luci asked her.

Air filled the first of what would be ten balloons, one for each of her years, which had become the tradition over the years, something she had wanted; next year she'd have eleven, and then twelve, and so on . . .

"When I'm as old as you," she said, meaning her father, "I *may* need some help."

And they laughed.

She caught her breath, tied off the last of the balloons, and flicked it across the room.

Airavata held her mother's cell phone, the old one they gave her when she was six and wanted to have a phone like Mom so she could record videos of her singing the Redolent. Her voice, that tone-deaf angel, ripped open his heart once again and flooded him with warmth as she remembered a stanza from "Though It Rains" that she sometimes forgot:

*The sky won't cry on the both of us*
*When I pull you in close*
*And you pull me in close*
*The rain, although it falls*
*The rain won't fall on the both of us*

Luci sang along for the chorus, and Gün joined in, the three of them bursting right through the chorus, their voices cracking, nearly yelling, and finally breaking into another fit of laughter . . .

*What kind of play is this?*

# Summer Gullet
*John Boden*

*It seemed like every few days we received a new submission from John Boden. That's not altogether true; he did send us more stories than anyone else trying to storm the Borderlands barricades. Every one of them was well written, brief to the point of being just this side of flash fiction, and having the feeling of sketches or scenes from a larger work—not really stories as much as the writer flexing and toning his literary muscles. But his persistence showed us several important things: he had lots of ideas, had total control of skills, and was determined to be in this anthology. And here he is . . .*

They stood before the hole: Stiggy, Donny, and Joanie. The three musketeers in black leather and torn denim. The sky was fading to a dull pumpkin orange and the wind had slowed to an almost nonexistent whisper. The smell still hung over the pit before them. It was a completely unique odor, thick and sticky. A multitude of carnival fragrances— cotton candy, corn dogs, fry oil, sugar, and salty sweat—all wrapped together in a funky burrito of stench that was dancing from the yawning chasm before them. Underneath those nostalgic scents were some things dank and sinister—mud and rot and something unsettlingly organic. Behind them the skeleton of the roller coaster loomed like a sleeping dinosaur. The derelict Ferris wheel was a blind eye. Bats dove and whipped about the dead lights that hung from bird-shit-crusted wires. The trio paid no attention to any of this; they were staring at the hole.

Stiggy reached down and picked up a large chunk of brick that was laying next to his foot. He tossed it into the pit. They all leaned forward and listened for it to hit the bottom and Joanie grimaced as she looked into the thing. It was like an enormous mouth. Toothless but hungry. The walls were wet and bright, swirled with garish colors. Pink and blue. Gold and brilliant red. In addition to the stinking breeze rising from below, were sounds. A cacophony of calliope music, screams, and laughter, the occasional shard of rock music—bands like Journey and Styx, bands that were popular that last summer before the park closed. Underneath those sounds, something very low—a coarse rumbling, an animal growling deeply in its throat, or a stomach betraying its hunger. Or the slight hiss of scales on stone. The amplified rattling of bones. The last wheeze of exhausted lungs.

Stiggy straightened his posture and stepped back a little. "So what do you think?" he asked his cronies. They continued staring into the abyss.

It was Donny who first offered his answer, "What the hell, dude? Maybe a sinkhole. Park's been shut up for like three years now." His voice was quavering slightly, as if he was very nervous. He looked like a scared little boy, aside from the lion's mane of permed, wooly hair that framed his features. Tiny blue eyes darted like minnows.

"It's like a big mouth. A big, lipless, toothless mouth," Joanie whispered, her uneasy gaze never straying from that gaping maw at their feet. She looked at Donny, who was tugging at the pewter skull that dangled from his earlobe. She did not like this at all. A shiver climbed her spine.

When did you find it?" Donny asked. He kicked a dented soda can until it rolled over the edge and into the void. They listened for it to hit the bottom but, like the brick, it never did. The only sound was an eerie burst of high-pitched giggling from the bottom of a well. The laughter fluttered about them like moths.

"I was here last week. That night Gina pissed me off. I either needed to walk off some anger or put my fist through her damn teeth. So I decided that walkin' off some anger was probably the best choice." Stig spit onto the dusty ground, licked his lips, and continued, "So I was walking around in here, cuz it's quiet and creepy and I dig that. I was over by that ticket booth takin' a piss when I heard laughin' . . . a kid laughin'. So I zip up and come to see who it was and there was this big hole here. I yell down, thought maybe some kid fell in there. I don't know. Nothing. No answer, but it smells . . . this hole." He pauses and studies the faces of his friends. They stare like a hypnotist's audience. "Like summertime. Like years ago. Summertime. Candy and fun and sweating and laughing and eating . . . the sounds were down there too, roller coasters clunkin' and carousel music and rockin' music shit from the whippit ride . . . I even heard people doin' it . . . all kindsa weird shit." Stig paused and jammed his hands farther into his pockets. The tip of his pinky poked from a ragged hole in the denim, like a grub.

"I must've zoned out a bit and when I snapped out of it, I was almost ready to fall the hell in. I was leaning so far over it. It creeped me out and I left . . . fast. But I been thinkin' about it ever since." Stig stood very still and looked at the other two. "I think it's a grave; yeah, I think that's what I think."

Donny and Joanie looked at him, with arched eyebrows.

"It's alive," Donny stammered. "A living grave, how is that?" They stared and listened. As they did so the night sky darkened as the stars began to wink out in surrender, handing all attention to the moon.

"It's where summers and childhoods go when they die," Stig clarified. "That's what I think." He stepped closer to the edge. A faint mist began creeping from the mouth of the hole, like smoke-machine, fun-house fog. There was the clunky sound of bumper cars colliding . . . squeals . . . giggles . . . the guitar riff from "You Shook Me All Night Long". Stig snaked an arm into the mist and touched the inner wall of the pit. It was warm and moist and pulsing. He withdrew and licked his fingertips. They tasted like caramel-covered apples. He looked up at his friends with tearing eyes. "I'm not sure how somethin' that ain't really living can die." The encroaching shadow was splintered by strobing beams from the pit, which pulled back into it, like some disco proboscis.

"This is it . . . " he swallowed thickly, " . . . this is where it goes. When we trade in our fun cards for timecards. Hand over our cool clothes for monkey suits, uniforms, or business casual. Go from rock and roll to whatever shit our geezer parents are diggin'. We sacrifice ourselves a little at a time without realizing it . . . until we are just plain gone!" He wiped his nose on a denim sleeve. The smear it left was shiny as glass. "We watch as we slit our own throats with an endless piece of paper, and we do it over and over again!" Tears were running from his squinting, angry eyes.

"You're sounding nuts, man!" Donny stated and took a step back; his leather jacket crinkled as he hugged himself.

Stig looked at him. It was a hard look.

Donny went on, "That doesn't make a lick of sense. I mean, I don't wanna grow up and sell out, any more than you. But you're sounding a little, I don't know, looney!"

Joanie just kept staring into the hole.

"Am I?" Stiggy had barely spoken the words when he charged and caught him by surprise, grabbing Donny around the arms and neck. "I can't go like that . . . Can you?" he shouted as they scuffled.

Joanie covered her eyes.

Donny shrieked as Stig gained the advantage and footing. With little effort, he hurled the screaming boy into the pit. The giggles and laughter grew in pitch until they morphed into ragged howls and wet, ripping sounds. Stig looked at Joanie, a wormy smile taking over his face.

She shook her head and backed away. She was much easier to take than Donny was. She was lighter too.

Stig sat on the edge of the pit. Legs dangling, the hole's slithering tongues caressed his calves with their spun-sugar stickiness. The flesh sizzled wherever they touched. He did not care. In his mind, it was summer. Girls were strutting and the park was alive. School was a hundred years away. He was seventeen again. Still. Always. He pushed off the edge like a swimmer into a pool.

The carnival below grew louder, yet at its loudest could not drown out his screams.

# Dead Letter Office
## *Trent Zelazny & Brian Knight*

*We first read this one several years ago and found the central conceit so bizarre we immediately liked it even though we knew we couldn't buy it—because it wasn't yet a fully realized story. We challenged Trent to make it work and he sent us at least three or four iterations that never seemed to work. Then, in the fullness of time, we received this current version by Trent and his pal Brian. The alchemy of a collaborator and all our critiques and suggestions had worked its magic, allowing us to present you with what follows.*

It started a few weeks ago when Leonard Perry received two pieces of mail that were not addressed to him. One was a letter to a Mary F. Stodgel in Stow, Ohio, the other a booklet of coupons for a Kenneth Hunt in Miami. Leonard lived in Santa Fe, New Mexico, and, odd as it was, he didn't think much of it at the time. He tossed the coupons into the trash and on the letter he wrote "RETURN TO SENDER", then put the letter back into his mailbox, raised the mailbox's flag, and forgot about it.

The next day when he arrived home from work he opened his mailbox and found five pieces of mail wrongly delivered to him. One of the pieces was the coupon book for Kenneth Hunt in Miami, Florida, another the letter to Mary F. Stodgel in Stow, Ohio. The Ohio letter was addressed in the exact same handwriting it had been the previous day; only, his own handwriting of "RETURN TO SENDER" was no longer there.

He did what he'd done the day before. Tossed the coupons into the trash and on the four letters—Mary F. Stodgel's included—he wrote "RETURN TO SENDER".

The next day there were seven pieces and nothing at all addressed to him. In these seven pieces of mail, the five he'd received the previous day were all included, his "RETURN TO SENDER" handwriting, once again, gone.

What he did this time, rather than writing "RETURN TO SENDER" on all six letters, was tear them twice in half and, along with Kenneth Hunt's coupons, stuff the pieces into the garbage.

He finished up late at work the next day. His mind swam with numbers and sums, and every time he closed his eyes he was still crunching them. It had been Stress Central the entire day.

Just before he left his office, Julie knocked on the doorjamb and stepped in. Julie worked in accounting down the hall and had also just finished up for the night. She asked Leonard if he wanted to get a drink. It was no secret that Julie had liked him for a long time. And it was no secret that Heather, Leonard's girlfriend, was out of town, visiting family in Upstate New York for the whole month. She'd only been gone a week at this time.

Leonard said "no, thank you"; he just wanted to go home and space out in front of the television.

With the day being what it was, when he got home he didn't even think about what had been going on with his mail. He opened the box and found two glassy brown eyes staring at him, and a tiny set of white, glistening teeth.

He slammed the box and turned away as his heart picked up a pace and needles prickled the back of his neck. After a couple deep, steadying breaths, Leonard turned back to the box and tapped the side of it. Nothing stirred within. Slowly, he eased the mailbox open again. The eyes and teeth were really there. They were part of a rat. An unmoving though very real, very dead rat.

After a moment of incomprehension, he went back to his car and grabbed a short stack of fast-food napkins from his glove box. With a sick gurgling in his stomach, he removed the rat, and when he did, some of the mail fell to the ground. Faceup, the letter on top of the fallen stack was a letter to a Mary F. Stodgel in Stow, Ohio.

Leonard disposed of the rat, gathered up the mail, and took it all inside. He read the addresses over and over again. There were twelve pieces all together, seven of them being the mail he'd received yesterday. The mail he'd torn up and thrown into his trash. There was nothing at all addressed to him. He went to his trash can and dug through it. The letters he'd torn up and thrown away were not there.

He hadn't done anything that he knew of to cause this. The mail just kept coming in. The same mail. The exact-same mail.

Could it be a joke?

Unlikely, he decided. None of his friends had this type of sense of humor. None of them were clever enough to execute such an elaborate scheme. And what would be the purpose of a joke like this, anyway? It didn't make sense.

As a kid Leonard had found a thrill in knowing when the mail arrived. *"The mail's here!"* he'd scream to his parents, a tingle of excitement oscillating through him. When he got old enough, he loved running down the driveway and opening the box. Every time he felt the remnants of magic as he withdrew things from all over the world sent to his family, like Santa Claus leaving presents.

As time went by, packages, letters, and junk mail came delivered to him. It didn't really matter what it was. There was just something so cool and mysterious about having something come to him from far away.

As the years passed, the excitement vanished and the magic ceased. It slowly evolved into bills, the junk mail increased, and Leonard eventually came to regard it as yet another headache added to everyday life.

Now, however, it was more than just a headache. It was a downright pain in the ass, and a confusing one at that. Even in his growing concern, though, he couldn't help finding some ironic amusement in the fact that, even if it wasn't in the innocent childlike way it once was, the mail had become interesting again.

Leonard spent over an hour sitting at his kitchen table that night, looking over each piece. Mary F. Stodgel in Stow, Ohio; Kenneth Hunt in Miami, Florida; Liz Prince in Boston, Massachusetts; David Gwinn in Grand Rapids, Michigan; Martin Miller in Chattanooga, Tennessee; Jane Killinger in Bend, Oregon. He studied each one in turn, then restudied them. Each one that he had received the day before he took especial interest in, looking for traces of rips in the envelopes, or signs of where his writing—"RETURN TO SENDER"—had been erased. There was nothing. Each piece looked exactly how it had when he'd received it the day before. It wasn't possible.

He considered opening them, reading them, then decided against it. A part of him was afraid to see what they'd say.

Why was he receiving this stuff? And how, when he ripped it all up and threw it away, did it come back? Why was it no longer in his trash? And why, when it came back this time, was there also a dead rat? Was that a threat of some kind? What was the threat? What was he supposed to do? Keep this mail? He wasn't the damn post office. This was some kind of intense, irrational dream.

His telephone rang. It was Heather. "You okay? You sound a little freaked out."

Leonard looked at the twelve pieces of mail on his kitchen table, then turned his back on them. "I'm all right," he said, "just a long day."

Heather was having fun but missed him and wanted to say hello. They spoke for about twenty minutes. When he hung up he saw the mail still sitting there and wondered what the hell to do about it.

That night he dreamed about the dead rat.

The next day at work he flipped through the government pages of the phone book and found the number for the main office of the US Postal Service. He asked the woman what to do if he was receiving mail for other people. The woman said if he was getting mail for someone else at his address, to write "RETURN TO SENDER, NOT AT THIS ADDRESS" on it and put it back into his mailbox. Leonard then explained that the mail being delivered was not to his address at all. It was to Ohio, Florida, Michigan, Wisconsin. The woman on the other end said, using a tone normally reserved for retarded children, that this wasn't possible. She asked for his address, and when he gave it to her he heard her punching computer keys. Nothing seemed odd, she told him, and no one else in the neighborhood or the surrounding area had made any complaints. "You might want to ask your postman about it," she said, again in her long-suffering, indulgent tone.

When he got home that night there were eight more pieces of mail, all addressed to different places. When he took them into his house, he found the other twelve pieces still sitting on his kitchen table.

He went through the new stuff. None of it was what he'd already received. This was all new mail for him to add to his collection. Still, he studied it all. There was nothing strange about it. It was just ordinary mail, as far as he could see. Why was he randomly receiving ordinary mail?

Curiosity now getting the better of him, he opened several pieces and examined them. There was nothing strange. Just letters, bills, pre-approved credit card offers, and other typical crap.

The next day—a Saturday—he was off work. He took his breakfast and coffee to the living room and sat in front of the window, watching his mailbox, waiting for the postman to show up. He propped open his front door in order to make it easier to hear the mail truck's approach. Every now and then people walked by his house, couples hand in hand, people with their dogs or children or both. Nobody gave his mailbox so much as a glance.

Around lunchtime he saw his neighbor across the street, an attractive woman in her early thirties, walk outside to her mailbox. She opened it, removed a small stack of mail, and spent a moment going through it before she walked back inside.

But the mailman hadn't shown up yet. He couldn't have. Leonard had been watching since this morning and hadn't seen him. Probably his neighbor hadn't picked up her mail from the day before, he thought; though something inside him felt uneasy.

Confused, hesitant, and a little scared, he walked outside, down his short driveway, and opened his mailbox. It had sixteen pieces of mail in it.

None of them were for him.

The following week he tried different experiments. He ripped up two of the letters at random and threw them away. The next day they were back in his mailbox, along with several black-widow spiders. There was more mail too.

He sent both an empty envelope and a postcard to himself, one to his home and the other to his office. Neither one arrived.

One night he slipped down the street and put several letters in someone else's mailbox. The next day they were back in his.

He took two sick days from work and watched for the mailman. He never saw him, but the mail was delivered both days.

Every other night he talked with Heather on the phone. He never mentioned anything about his strange new hobby. It was too bizarre to explain.

He was meant to receive this mail. He didn't know how, he didn't know why, but this mail was intended for him. He couldn't doubt this, and with the tricks and threats he got whenever he destroyed any of it—whenever he committed a federal offense—he knew he was meant to do something *with* the mail.

But what? What was he supposed to do with it? Was he really just supposed to keep it? Like some kind of dead letter office?

Then he tried something that seemed to work. He took the letter for Mary F. Stodgel, opened it, skimmed over the message from her daughter, then put it into a fresh envelope, addressed it to Stow, Ohio, slapped a stamp on it, and mailed it off.

It did not come back the next day. Lots of other random mail arrived, but nothing for Mary F. Stodgel in Stow, Ohio. Not that day or the next.

He tried this with several other pieces. None of the letters returned until the third batch he sent. The letter to David Gwinn in Grand Rapids, Michigan, returned with the message "RETURN TO SENDER, NO LONGER AT THIS ADDRESS". This was not in his handwriting. Leonard stared at the envelope for a long time. It was definitely the same letter he'd sent off.

Jesus Christ, he *was* a post office. He put this letter back into his mailbox and flipped up the little flag. With all the other mail he received the next day, it was still in there, the handwriting of "RETURN TO SENDER, NO LONGER AT THIS ADDRESS" still on it. What the hell was he supposed to be figuring out here? What in the world was he supposed to be doing?

One more idea. Along with the batch of mail he opened, restuffed, readdressed, and stamped, he placed the letter to Michigan, still in its envelope, into another envelope, addressing it to the return address in Ketchum, Idaho.

It did not come back.

For the next few days Leonard spent his time—when he wasn't crunching numbers at work—repackaging and resending letters. The cost was getting enormous, however. Every other day he was at the real post office, buying stamps and envelopes. The coupons and advertisements, such as the booklet for Kenneth Hunt, were easy to deal with. For whatever reason, all he had to do with those was take them to the post office and explain that he'd received them by accident. When he started getting suspicious looks, he began taking them in a postal bin and leaving it on the counter when no one was looking. This seemed to do the trick. When he received his mail the next day, the previous day's coupons and advertisements were not there.

One day he managed to finally get every piece of mail in the house repackaged and sent off and, finally, his house looked sane again. Relief fell upon him, as well as an awkward sense of accomplishment.

The next day, a Friday, he received forty-five pieces, and with desperation sweeping and scraping all over and throughout him, he brought his hands to his face and cried. Jesus, was this ever going to end? Someone, something had to be behind this. But what? Who was doing this? And how were they doing it? He felt as though he were on a treadmill, going and going but never getting anywhere. For the love of God, what the hell was he supposed to do? How in the world could he make it go away?

A thought occurred to him just then. Such a simple thought too. He went outside with a screwdriver and removed his mailbox from its post. He put it on the kitchen table as the phone rang.

Only half paying attention when a woman's voice said, "Hi, Leonard," he replied, "Hey, sweetie."

But it wasn't Heather. It was Julie.

"I like that," Julie said. "You can call me that anytime."

"What's up?" Leonard asked, rubbing his temples. A headache was coming on.

"I was just wondering if you were hungry. I made too much chicken and pasta salad. I could bring some over if you want."

"Oh, I don't know." Leonard looked around his kitchen, at the mailbox sitting on the table, and the forty-five letters and parcels he'd received that day.

"Come on," Julie said. "I don't think you've been eating. I see you at work. You've lost all kinds of weight and you look pale."

"I've just been really busy," Leonard said.

"I bet you haven't eaten today," she countered.

That was true. He hadn't had so much as a cup of coffee when he woke up this morning. In fact, now that he thought about it, Goddammit, he was famished. And he'd been too busy the past couple of weeks to do any grocery shopping, so there wasn't anything in his cupboards or fridge. Now that he thought of it, other than obligatory exchanges at work and necessary phone calls with Heather, Leonard hadn't really spoken with another human being in, what, nearly three weeks?

"All right," he said. "Do you know where I live?"

Julie said she did and that she would be over soon.

While he waited for her, Leonard spent the next twenty minutes examining the mailbox. He found nothing unusual.

Julie came into his house without knocking, carrying two foil-covered oven trays in her hands and a bottle of red wine under her arm. Leonard followed her into the kitchen, where she set the trays down on the kitchen table and uncovered them. Looking around, Julie smiled, and with a quiet giggle she gestured to the counter next to the microwave. "Interesting place to keep your mailbox," she said.

"It fell off," he said. "Gonna put it back on in the morning."

The mail was in a paper bag in his pantry.

As she prepared the food, Leonard opened the wine and poured two glasses. He handed her one, they clinked, and Leonard drained his without removing his lips.

"Whoa, slow down, boy."

"Sorry," Leonard said. "You just have no idea how badly I needed that."

He poured himself another.

It wasn't long before they were sitting at the table, eating. Leonard tried to pace himself but found it difficult. He kept shoveling more food into his mouth than he could chew.

"I knew you were hungry," Julie told him.

"Thank you," Leonard said, then indicated the food, "for this."

"You're welcome."

When they were through eating, they finished off the bottle of wine and talked about work, about family, about life. As the night progressed, Leonard began feeling more and more like his old self. And with the mailbox removed—he wasn't sure, of course; possibly it was the wine going to his head—maybe he had solved his problem. Time would tell, however, but he felt confident that things might be looking up.

He felt good, felt human again, felt more like the Leonard Perry he knew than he had in weeks. And when Julie took his hand, moved in, and kissed him, he let her. And after a while of this, he took her into his bedroom.

When he woke up the next morning Julie was still asleep beside him. He watched her for a while, feeling a terrible mixture of things. Heather was coming back in just a couple of days, and look at what he had just done. Still, he couldn't deny that there had been something very nice about it. Maybe more than just a one-night stand, maybe not. Last night and even this morning, he saw something in her he hadn't seen before, a whole new side of Julie. One he liked a lot more than he ever thought he would.

It was late, even for a Saturday. Closing in on noon.

He kissed her forehead gently, and when he did, she stirred and opened her eyes. "Morning," she said, her voice groggy with sleep and the previous night's wine and activities.

Leonard got out of bed, nervous and worried. He stretched for a moment, then turned to her. "Coffee?"

She smiled. "Sounds good."

Wearing only his boxers, he walked to the kitchen, then stopped dead in his tracks.

His blood ran cold. Next to the microwave the mailbox was packed to the breaking point. Letters were crammed in and poked out the sides of the door, which was held shut by a rubber band. The hairs on his back and neck stood up, and a mixture of fear and rage swirled. He reached out and removed the rubber band. The door shot open and letters spat out and spread onto the floor, a postcard landing on his foot. It was the postcard he'd sent to himself. On it was his own handwriting, but it was not the message he'd written, which had been a smiley face and his initials. It now read:

*Leonard,*
*Seems kind of like hell, huh?*
*Well, there you are.*
*Or you are there.*

"Leonard?" Julie entered, rubbing her eyes, wearing nothing but one of his T-shirts.

Leonard spun on her. "What the hell are you doing to me?"

Taken aback, Julie furrowed her brow. "What do you mean?"

"You think it's funny, is that it? How are you doing this?" He advanced on her, backing her into the living room.

"I don't know what you're talking about."

"I just brought it in last night. And then you happen to call, you happen to come over, and then . . . then . . . "

"Leonard, you're scaring me. What are you talking about?"

"You nasty bitch. I'm only gonna tell you this once. Cut it out. Just cut it the fuck out."

Julie stood there a moment, staring at him with disbelief. Leonard could see in her eyes a genuine fear, a genuine confusion. But all the pieces fit. He didn't entirely know how it had worked, but it did make a strange sort of sense.

"Get your ass out of here," he told her. When she kept standing there in amazement, he screamed and raised his hand.

Julie raced back into the bedroom and slammed the door.

Leonard went back to the kitchen and picked up the mail. He put it on the table and drew a deep breath. A minute later Julie came out dressed in the clothes she'd been wearing last night, tears raining down her cheeks. She grabbed her oven trays and made for the door. "If this is how you feel, if you think you were cute last night, just wait until

Heather gets back."

He heard the front door slam. He picked up the still-full mailbox and slammed it against the floor, then took one of his kitchen chairs and beat the thing, crushed it, and kept hitting it, pulling at it with his hands, throwing it, smashing it, until it was four separate sheets of thin, crumpled metal. He put one piece in the kitchen garbage can, another in the bathroom wastebasket, tossed one into his backyard, and put the other in his car, where he later threw it into a trash can at a gas station.

He piled the mail onto his kitchen table and ripped up the postcard. Then he went out to various bars and spent the day getting drunk. No matter how much alcohol he had, every time he closed his eyes he was repackaging someone else's mail.

That night Heather called. She was concerned about the way he sounded.

"Just went drinking with some of the guys," he told her. "I'm a little tipsy, and I've been kind of down not having you here."

"I can't wait to see you," she said.

His guilt of being with Julie tied a knot the size of Kentucky in his stomach and tensed his shoulders like so much sculpture chiseled from stone. "I can't wait to see you either," he said. "You'll be here Monday?"

"My flight gets in around ten. I should be back around eleven, barring unforeseen delays." She gave him her flight itinerary.

"I'll take an early lunch," he said. "We'll go somewhere special."

"I would love that," Heather said. "How about I'll meet you at your house; in case I'm running a bit late, you don't have to be stuck somewhere waiting for me."

"Sounds good," he said, hearing Julie's voice when she'd said those same two words this morning.

It wasn't long after speaking with Heather that he passed out.

He dreamed about Julie.

Sunday he didn't do much of anything. There was no mail that day, yet there was still the enormous stack on his kitchen table, not to mention the bag stuffed in the back of his pantry. For a long time he thought about it. He had removed the mailbox and brought it into the kitchen, and still there had been mail in it the next day. But now the mailbox was destroyed, torn into pieces. There was no longer a place for him to receive his mail. And since he was receiving so much of it, no postal worker was going to leave a stack of twenty, thirty, or forty letters just sitting on his doorstep, were they? Didn't seem likely. Of course, nothing that had been going on seemed likely. Still, given what had happened, he concluded that it had to be the mailbox. Something about it had been causing all of this to happen. He felt terrible for how he'd acted towards Julie. On reflection, it didn't make any damn sense that she would be doing it.

He went to the phone and called her. When he tried to apologize she called him a psychopath and said to leave her alone. When he tried to explain she wouldn't hear it. She called him a crazy bastard and hung up.

Leonard almost called her back but didn't. Instead he allowed his rage to take control. He picked up the letters from his kitchen table and began ripping them up, one by one, several at a time, whatever he got his hands on. Some he fed into his sink disposal and others he burned at the stove. He went to the back of his pantry, removed the bag, and did the same. He tore them, ripped them into shreds, then went at all the pieces with scissors.

In the end he had a garbage bag full of shredded paper and some ashes. He loaded it into the back of his car, drove it down to his office, and tossed it into the dumpster.

When he got home he called Julie again. This time he got her answering machine. He left an apologetic message and said he wanted to talk with her.

He spent the rest of the day drinking and calculating how much it would have cost him in envelopes and stamps to resend all the mail he'd just destroyed.

A deadline at work the next day, which was supposed to be a month away, had suddenly moved to the end of the week. The men's room was out of order and Julie wouldn't even look at him when they passed in the hall. But so far, anyway, no one else in the office seemed to know about what happened Friday night and Saturday morning. For the moment, she seemed to be keeping quiet, thank God.

It was right before he left for lunch that she came to him.

"I'm ready to talk," she said.

"I would like to," he said, "but I have to go right now. Can we talk when I get back from lunch?"

"We can't have lunch?"

"I have to meet somebody."

"Heather?" Her tone was menacing when she said the name.

He looked away and nodded.

"You going out to eat?"

"I'm meeting her at my house; then we're going somewhere."

Julie leveled an icy gaze on him. "We'll talk when you get back from lunch."

Leonard drove home, stopping by a floral shop on his way to pick up a dozen roses. He almost bought a card but had second thoughts. At home he cut the stems and put the flowers into a vase, then turned on the television and waited.

After watching an entire soap opera he realized he'd been home over half an hour. He got up from the couch and called her cell phone. He had to leave a message. He then looked at the flight itinerary, called the airline, and asked if the flight had come in on time. It had. He tried her cell phone again, and again had to leave a message. He'd give her a few more minutes. He could take a long lunch—it was important that he take a long lunch—even if he knew he'd catch shit for it later at work, for a couple of different reasons.

Another fifteen minutes passed. He was just about to call her cell again when the doorbell rang, followed by several sharp knocks. He took the flowers from the kitchen table, brought them into the living room, and set them on the coffee table. He straightened his hair, straightened his shirt, and opened the door.

On the doorstep was an enormous sack of mail, a dirty white canvas sack with the words "DEAD LETTER OFFICE—ALTERNATE ROUTING REQUIRED" stenciled over it in faded black letters.

Leonard slammed the door, locked it, then deadbolted it before returning to the kitchen for a stout drink.

He'd taken three steps in that direction when his foot caught on something, and he went over with flailing arms and a scream of outraged shock. He landed on the white canvas sack, clearly stuffed with more dead letters, and something else that was large and almost round.

The sack cushioned his body, but his head struck the floor hard. His last conscious thought as he blacked out was *How did it get in? I locked it outside!*

Sometime later he came back to his senses. He wasn't sure how much time had passed, maybe minutes, maybe hours; all he knew is that it was still day. A hard, slanting shaft of sunlight struck the open mouth of the bag inches from his eyes, spotlighting the thing inside.

A dead letter that had obviously been meant for him, though it wasn't addressed.

Julie had died screaming. He knew that because her mouth and eyes were still open wide. Her teeth were covered in blood, her tongue a slimy red slug plastered to her cheek, glued to it by dried blood. The head was sealed inside a clear plastic bag, partially filled with her blood, but not a drop stained the hundreds, maybe thousands of dead letters it rested in.

"She was making trouble for you, Leonard."

Startled, Leonard began to push himself up to run, but a heavy-booted foot planted itself between his shoulder blades and pushed him back to the floor.

"You don't want to do that, mate." Brief laughter, then the voice continued, "Much better off never seeing my face, I think."

"Who are you?" The foot had lifted from his back, but Leonard stayed where he was, face pressed against the floor, eyes closed so he wouldn't have to look at Julie's dead face in the mailbag. "What do you want?"

"Who I am isn't all that important, Leonard. What I want is to not have to come back here again." The dry humor had left the man's voice. Now it was spiced with irritation. "It's a pain in the ass, to be perfectly frank. I have enough shit to do without babysitting dead letter officers."

"What . . . ?"

"No questions," the man said. "You have a job to do, and I think you'll find the benefits more than adequate once you've completed your probationary period, but you don't get to ask questions."

There were several tense seconds of silence before the man spoke again, as if he was making sure his no-questions edict had gotten through.

"Good man," he said at last. "You're a quick learner. I knew that when you worked out the process as quickly as you did, but you've got a willful streak that is distressing. Since my gentle reminders weren't enough to keep you in line, I'm here for our one and only face-to-face."

Laughter again, a little less restrained than the last. "That is a figure of speech, of course. If you ever do see my face, it'll be the last one you ever see."

Frustration and fear overwhelmed him. Leonard began to weep.

"Oh for crying out loud, there's no need for that. I'm not here to hurt you, just to straighten you out."

With effort, Leonard silenced himself.

"Now open your eyes and look in the bag."

Leonard groaned, but did as he was told.

Julie's head was gone. In its place was a Polaroid.

It was a picture of Heather, stripped to her bra and panties, bound to a chair, gagged, horrified.

"The worlds grow, borders stretch, times change, but things stay together, and communication is the key. We can't have a million and one dead letters clogging the system. Do you understand what I'm saying?"

"No," Leonard said. "I don't understand any of this."

He closed his eyes against the tortured image of Heather, but it was burned into his brain. He'd never be able to unsee it.

"Ah, you don't really need to, just as long as you do what you're supposed to. Take care of your business and things will continue to move forward, but if you try anything . . ." he paused for a second, as if in search of the right word, " . . . ill-advised, I'll have to send you another reminder."

Leonard thought he understood the man's meaning perfectly. He was sure the next head he received would belong to someone a lot more important to him.

The new silence held for a long time, but Leonard was afraid to open his eyes, to move from his place on the floor, and after a while, something that may have been sleep stole him away.

He awoke in the dark, and after a few moments of confusion he remembered where he was and what happened. He pushed himself up slowly, and when no one protested or pushed him back to the floor, he stood.

It was night now, late night, pitch-dark outside.

He turned on his living room lights.

Julie's head was gone. The picture of Heather was gone. The mailbag, "DEAD LETTER OFFICE—ALTERNATE ROUTING REQUIRED", was still there, open and spilling its contents onto his floor.

Leonard kicked the stray letters back into the open mouth of the bag and dragged it to his kitchen table.

He didn't bother going to work the next morning. The phone rang several times but he didn't answer. Instead he stayed in bed, stared at the ceiling, and thought about moving and where to move. Where could he go? Texas? California? France? Somehow, inside he knew that wherever he went it wouldn't do him any good, though he knew he would have to try. He knew he wouldn't be here long.

And if he did try to run, he knew he'd wake up some morning to find Heather's head in a plastic bag.

He thought about all the messages on his machine from both yesterday and today from his work, wondering just where in the hell he was.

Fuck them. He was too busy.

He didn't get out of bed until the early afternoon when the doorbell rang, and even then he almost didn't bother. He knew what was there. It was always going to be there, coming in and coming in like an unfixable leak.

His meeting felt like a bad dream, but he knew it wasn't.

*Seems kind of like hell,* he thought, and removed a box of envelopes and a roll of stamps from a kitchen drawer and set them on the table. Kind of like hell, yeah, but there you are.

Or you are there.

# Cocoa
## Bob Pastorella

*Sometimes we get a story that is so . . . odd we don't know what to make of it. We're not sure if we like or dislike it, but we can't reject it because it's like an earworm song you can't get out of your head. The following story was like that. It sat on our short list until we could understand its attraction. We're still not sure—other than the notion that the nature of one's existence and place in our careening universe is not always a choice, but a mandate. And that seems to be okay . . . until an entity decides it wants to be something else . . .*

Dad gently pushed me towards the other barn. We were already past the fence, the one he told me to never pass, and I never did, not once, not even after me and Alisha got married. There was Dad's barn, and the other barn, for as long as I could remember. Passing the fence was going to get you a whipping for sure, and after you'd grown and married, it came down to respect. He pushed me again, and I looked back to see him smiling. All his teeth were gone now, and his tongue lolled in his mouth, tobacco stained and spotted. Finally, we stopped and he stood behind me, his hand on my shoulder, squeezing. He pulled his hand away, and I could hear the suckers on his palm pop off my windbreaker.

"Why are we here, Dad?"

He came around me, reaching into his jacket with his good hand, the one that looked like mine, and pulled out a crumpled pack of Lucky Strikes. He used his left hand, the misshapen one, to light the match because it was easier with his long nails. It was the cancer that did this too him. It made him stay home all the time and miss church every Sunday. It changed him, made him strong, and made him feel good, all the time. Strange how cancer was supposed to send you to the grave. Dad's just kept him from it.

Until recently.

He pulled a long drag off the cigarette, then looked at me. "Your time has come."

"For what?"

"Can't really explain it. Just the way it is, I suppose."

"Please, don't talk in riddles."

Dad coughed and spit on the ground. It was best not to look where he spit. "I don't know why this has come to us. Ain't no riddles, son." He looked over at the barn, nodding. "Best you go in there and see her yourself."

A sweet odor drifted through the air, and it took me a second to place it. I pointed at the barn. "Who's in there?"

He just nodded.

"That smell. Is that hot chocolate?"

He grinned. "That's her. She knows you're here."

"Who?"

Dad pinched the cherry off his cigarette, flicked it into the brush, and coughed. He turned away, shoving his hands in his pockets. The smile never left his face.

The padlock for the door handle was open, hanging from the chain. He must have unlocked it before he called me to come over. The odor was so sweet it almost gagged me. Pushing the door open, I peered into the darkness. Two hundred head of cattle in the backfield lowed in unison when I opened the door. I looked back at Dad. He was still looking away, staring back at the house. "It's dark in there," I said.

"You don't need any light."

I stepped inside the barn, half expecting some kind of surprise party to scream out, though my birthday was half a year away. (There's nothing special about turning forty-seven. It's just another birthday.) But there were no people yelling, no streamers or confetti, no music. As my eyes adjusted to the darkness, I made out a dim light behind the stalls past the drive bay. The light was coming from some kind of wall built into the back of the barn. Once I got closer, I found it was nothing more than a thick tarp thrown over a cord strung from one end of the barn to the other, making a small room.

The light was brighter behind the tarp, throwing a washed-out purple hue on the walls. When I stepped around the tarp and looked into the room, I really didn't know what I was seeing. It was like looking at a blown-up photograph of someone's guts, how at first it just looks like coils of lumpy blue rope soaking in a cherry pie, and you're wondering why in the world someone would make blue rope, and then why would they put it into a pie—and all that happens in the very second you understand that it's a picture of someone ripped open, their intestines threatening to fall from their gut onto the floor.

Except this wasn't a coil of intestines.

I suspect it was a cow at one time. The things that made it a cow were still there. Short brown fur, one small, lopsided horn pointed to the ground. The flattened nose told me it was probably Ayrshire, though it was a little hard to tell. That was the only cattle breed Dad ever raised. Where one horn was small and aimed low, the other was massive and curved toward the roof beams. The brown hair was normal around the head and neck, then became splotchy and bare where it grew past its shoulders. The skin there was dry looking, flaky, and close to where the shoulder was, there was a large stalk. It looked like another limb had started to grow out of its back. The end of the stalk appeared burned or cauterized. I stepped as close as I dared, trying to get a better look.

The skin was scales. The scaly flesh extended down its legs, which ended in hooves, as expected, but the hooves spread out now, almost like long claws. When I reached out to touch the stalk near the shoulder, it flinched from my hand. There were two stalks actually, one behind each shoulder, both flinching when I tried to touch them.

The cow snorted loudly, making me jump back a little. It leaned close to me, then quickly stood up on its front legs. It stared at me, the left eye off-center and multicolored, the right one larger and the brightest green I've ever seen, though watery and bloodshot around the white. It snorted again, filling the air with the richest odor of hot chocolate I've ever smelled.

Whitish-purple light came off the cow. Even keeping my distance, I could see the tiny veins in the scales glowing. The light was coming from its blood flowing through the veins. I tried to see its hindquarters, but there was nothing but shadows. Something large shifted there, though it looked more like a flipper than actual legs. A coil of snakes behind it twisted into action, grew upwards, and swayed close to my face. Not snakes, but tentacles, each sucker poised to strike. They pulsed in the air like nostrils flaring.

The udder that once brought milk into the Maxwell household, milk I'd probably drunk, lay on the ground beside her, swollen to three times its normal size. Six teats, each a yard long, squirmed on the ground around my boots. I stepped back, not wanting them to get any closer.

"She's quite a sight," Dad said behind me.

"What is this?"

"Don't know, probably never will. My dad didn't know either. She's been here for a long time."

I turned and stared at his shape in the darkness. "Grandpa knew about this?"

"He was the first."

"How did you . . . I mean, how did . . . "

"How'd we keep it a secret? Now, Grady, you know us Maxwells are the best at keeping secrets. She's our prized possession, son. And now she's yours."

I shook my head. "This is crazy. You've kept this from me all my life?"

Dad nodded.

"This . . . thing, it needs to be taken out to pasture and shot between the eyes."

"You don't think Granpappy didn't try? He tied her to his old Ford pickup and dragged her out into the field. Spent all afternoon shooting it with buckshot, and that was nothing but a waste of time. I don't think you can kill her. I tried myself. Tried to drown her. But she's still here, and after a while, you'll understand that's all that matters."

"She?"

"She."

"Well, maybe it was a female at one time, but how do you know that now? I mean, maybe it used to be cow, but this . . . this is something else. Why do you call it a she, why even say it like that?"

"Well, I guess because of the calves."

Back at the house, Dad poured me a cup of coffee and sat at the table with me. "Her name is Cocoa, and ever since she was born, we knew she was special."

I took a sip of coffee. The hot-chocolate smell lingered in my mind. "Was she always like that?"

"No. Looked just like any other heifer, maybe a little stronger, a little faster on her legs than most. Your grandmother loved her, and took her to all the shows. There's a scrapbook in the attic with all the ribbons she won. Won every show in Texas. All 'Best in Show'."

"When did she change?"

Dad gripped his coffee mug with his left hand, the fingers like tentacles, flexing and releasing, flexing and releasing. "She started years ago, before you were born. Your grandmother used to tell this story about a storm in the night and lights in the sky, and all this crazy stuff she liked to think about all the time, but I think it just comes down to that Cocoa wasn't happy being a cow."

I was getting tired of talking about it. "What happened to those things behind her shoulders?"

"Her shoulders are fine." Dad released his mug, the suckers on this thumb and first finger sticking to the porcelain for a second. He caught me staring and put his hand in his lap.

"You said calves earlier. What happened to them?"

"Nothing really. They're probably all gone. I guess she can't breed now, I don't know."

"Were they normal, or like her?"

"Normal, I guess."

"So what now?"

He shrugged his shoulders.

"Dad?"

"It's your time, I do know that."

I stared at the table. When he called me earlier, asked me to come alone, to leave Dennis with the neighbors for a couple of hours, I never expected this. He was all by himself out here now, all the ranch hands long gone to find better-paying work. I figured he wanted me to help him move something, dig a hole for a fence post, talk to the lawyer again, or put the ad back on the Internet to sell some more land.

To think for one second I almost said, "Screw it, Dennis is coming with me."

"This is why we couldn't go past the fence?"

He nodded.

"What about the rest of the cattle?"

"They won't come within a hundred yards of her."

That made sense. Ever since I could remember, the herd would always stay far back in the field, never getting close to the house. All this time I thought it was the ranch hands that kept them back. I started to ask about Mom, the words right there on my tongue, but I looked at Dad and knew he wouldn't give me a straight answer. When it came to her, he never told the truth.

"Did Lindy know?"

At the sound of hearing my sister's name, Dad hung his head down, answering my question without saying a word. She drowned in the lake when I was fourteen years old. Dad told me he tried to save her, but there was just too much water in her lungs.

"Why now?"

At first, I thought he didn't hear me. I watched his lips moving like he was going to say something, but the words just wouldn't come. This went on for a few minutes until I set my coffee mug down on the table, hard enough to get his attention. He looked up at me, tears cutting creeks into his wrinkles.

"I'm not going to do it," I said.

His bushy eyebrows rose, but he wouldn't look at me. "You will," he said, his voice soft and low.

"No. Tomorrow, I'm going to come back here, get the rifle, and put a bullet right between its eyes."

Dad looked up and started giggling like a little boy. He pulled a rag out of his pocket and wiped his eyes dry.

I slammed my hand down on the table. "It's not funny," I said, standing up. I put the mug into the sink and walked out to my truck.

Dennis had a million questions about Dad. Only seven years old, he asked about everything. "Is Pawpaw dying?" he asked, shoving a spoon of mashed potatoes in his mouth.

"No, Pawpaw's not dying."

He nodded. He pushed his green beans closer to the edge of his plate. "Is Pawpaw turning into an octopus?"

This made me smile. "No, silly. It's the cancer. Now, eat those beans before *you* start turning into an octopus."

After he bathed, he came into the living room wearing only his briefs, his hair still dripping. "Is God real?"

I hit the Mute button on the TV remote. "What kind of question is that?"

"This boy at school, he said God isn't real."

"Why would he say that?"

He dug a finger into his ear then looked at his feet. "He said God is dead, and my momma is too."

"Your mother is not dead. You know that. Didn't she call last week? Isn't she coming down from Dallas next month just to see you?"

He nodded. "What about God?"

"Did you wake up this morning?"

"Yes."

"And we had food on the table tonight for supper, right?"

"Yeah."

"Who do you think made that happen?"

Dennis clapped his hands, unable to keep the smile off his face. "You did."

"And?"

His face grew serious, respectful. "God."

"You just answered your own question. Now get to bed."

After the news, I turned off the TV and went to check on him. He kept his eyes closed when I went into his room, pretending to be asleep. I reached under the blankets and began to tickle him. He squealed and howled, begging me to quit, and after a few seconds, I did, fearing he might wet the bed. I kissed him on his forehead and left his room.

Lying on Alisha's side of the bed made me think she was still here, even though she was never coming back. Part of me wanted her to come home, but the best part of me, the part that was not so full of neediness, knew it was better she was away. She wanted her friends and the city, and all I wanted was what was right.

Yes, it was better she was away.

The next day at work, my thoughts drifted to my dad, and the barn. Grandpa shot it with a shotgun, and Dad said that was a waste of time. I wondered what went through my dad's head when he tried to drown it, what he used to hold it down in the water. I couldn't imagine how he felt when the damned thing wouldn't drown.

Did he think about the cow when Lindy drowned?

When I finished loading two sacks of chicken feed into the last customer's truck, my boss, Sam, tossed me the keys to the building, telling me to give it another thirty minutes then lock up.

It was the longest half hour ever. I guess it was because I knew I was going to have to drop Dennis off at the neighbors' again, make up some new excuse, and head on down to Dad's house. Before I locked up, I pulled a carton of .22 rounds from the back counter and paid for them in the register. I thought about buying another box, but I didn't have the money.

Dad was lying on the couch when I got to the house.

"You all right?"

He opened his eyes, seeing the rifle and the box of ammo in my hands. That started him laughing.

The barn was unlocked. Maybe he never locked it. Hot chocolate hung in the air, sinking into my clothes, my skin.

She was standing on her front legs when I walked into the barn. Her green, watery eye followed my every move. Kneeling in front of her, I opened the box of rounds, knocking a few on the ground. My hand shook when I picked them up. The cow snorted at my efforts. Maybe I was just a little nervous, probably just from being around her again. I put a round into the chamber, pulled the bolt back, then slammed it in place. Aiming at her felt silly, so I stepped up close and placed the barrel against her head. She looked at me, the watery right eye staring into me. Something told me she knew what I was planning on doing, and that was okay. Maybe she was ready to die.

I took a deep breath and put my finger on the trigger.

When I squeezed the trigger, the bullet fired and exploded against her head, causing the end of the barrel to split open. The explosion rocked me off-balance and I fell into the beam behind me, nearly five feet away, slamming my head against it. I tried to scramble back to my feet, but everything turned grey, then fell to black. There's no telling exactly how long I was out, but it only seemed like a few seconds. Once I was back up on my feet, I picked up the rifle and looked at the barrel.

It looked like something out of a Looney Tunes cartoon.

I turned the gun around in my hands, held the butt high, and charged at her. Bringing the butt down on her head, I started pounding, as though I were driving a fence post.

She didn't even blink.

The butt of the rifle cracked, then eventually splintered and fell off.

There were a few small scratches on her head where the rifle butt hit, and a powder burn in her hair between her eyes, but other than that, she was unharmed.

Cocoa mooed, her eyes never moving off me.

The next day I tried a nail gun I found in the stockroom at work. After three nails at point-blank range, the gun busted.

Dad laughed at me when I stomped back to my truck. I watched him wave and walk back to the house. He was looking a little paler than usual, a little more stooped over when he walked. Nevertheless, he was smiling all the same.

The following day I went back and just sat in the barn with her. She kept mooing at me now, knew it was me sitting on the ground next to her. She ate the hay I put in front of her and would stand on her front legs to drink water from the trough beside her. Her teats would crawl on the floor like eyeless worms, stopping to sniff the air around me before finally nudging my boots. The first time I reached out to touch one, the teat recoiled back, aware of my hand. Eventually I could touch her teats, and it felt good to let the leathery skin wrap around my fingers. Every so often, she would snort and stamp her hooves, telling me she approved of my presence. The cocoa smell was just as strong as before, but it didn't bother me anymore. I liked it actually.

I never was a very healthy person. Chronic sinus ailments and a bad back made sure of that. Mornings were usually the worst for me, but after that first week of staying with her, I began to feel good. It was like every day was brand-new, which it was, but now it really felt like it. Even my right shoulder, which would bug me whenever rain clouds rolled in, didn't let me know to wear my slicker. It rained hard for hours, and when Sam finally let me off work, I jumped in my truck, soaked to my underwear. When I turned on the windshield wipers, my fingers hung on the shifter like they were sticky, but I didn't worry about that.

Dad died about two weeks after I started sitting with Cocoa. He quit eating. I think he knew it was time. One evening I walked in the ranch house and found him lying on the couch, his eyes open, mouth slack. I turned his hand over and touched the suckers on his palm, now closed up and dry. I started to call the funeral home to come pick him up, but something twisted in my head, made me put the phone down. All I could think about was someone coming over here and smelling her, and wanting to see her. That would change everything, the secret would be out, and if there's one thing we Maxwell's are good at, it's keeping secrets.

The scrapbook was in the attic, just like Dad said. I took it down to the kitchen, at the table, and turned the brittle pages, reading the dates my grandmother wrote at the bottom of the pictures, in her tiny handwriting. The date on the next-to-last picture read "July 1964". There was Grandma, standing next to her prize heifer. Cocoa looked just like Elsie the Cow, staring directly into the camera lens, as though telling the world that she was a winner.

She was the best.

The last picture had no date. It was blurry and in color. Cocoa must have already started her changing by then. Her rear legs were just starting to grow together, forming a flipper. I looked at that picture for a long time, wondering exactly how high she must have flown.

For my dad to have her all this time, letting her fly, keeping it all to himself, how hard it must have been for him to ground her.

Once I completed the sale and shaved off another two hundred acres of land, I sold my house and moved Dennis and myself into Dad's ranch. Sam, my boss, thought it was a good move since Dad's house was much larger than my own and we still owned plenty of land.

I showed Dennis where Dad's grave marker was near his barn. Not her barn. "Is this where you want me to bury you when you die, Daddy?"

"You can. But I'm not going to die for a long time."

We walked to the edge of the fence and looked over at her barn. I put my hand on his shoulder, letting the suckers on my palm squeeze and release the cloth of his shirt. Cancer apparently ran in the family. Not the cancer that killed, but the cancer that made you stronger, made you feel good all the time. At least for a little while.

"See this fence, Dennis?"

"He nodded."

"You cannot go past this fence," I said, feeling the words my father said so long ago rise inside me. "This is the no-pass line. If I catch you or any of your friends past this line, that'll be your ass." I looked down at him. "Understand?"

He nodded.

I told him to run inside and clean up for supper.

# The Dress
## *Peter Salomon*

*All editors have certain biases either against or for certain types of stories. Children or teenagers can make a tale painfully annoying or . . . utterly creepy. Peter Salomon achieves the latter with his subtle narrative about a young woman and her worn-out apparel.*

Victoria ran fingers down her dress to smooth out the wrinkles. It didn't help. Never did. The fabric wrinkled right back up. The lace curled, a little yellow, but mostly white. Squeezing the edges between her fingers to keep it together, a string ripped free, caught the breeze, and disappeared. Another. She lunged after, trying to save it, but fell short, unable to move as quickly as the wind.

Time for a new dress. Past time. Too little time. Papa told her the rules, repeated them until she knew them by heart. The rules were all she had of him now. The rules and the dress, fraying and wrinkled and wasting away. Like her, disappearing in the wind with every thread.

*"When the dress begins to fray,"* Papa said, his hands working the loom with an artist's touch.

*"I know, Papa,"* Victoria said, though she hadn't been Victoria then. She'd been someone else, she knew, but the memories were fading, fraying, disappearing with the threads she couldn't catch. *"Only touch the next dress to wear."*

Papa smiled. Papa always smiled. Then he turned back to the loom. *"When the dress begins to fade?"*

*"Touch wrong and kill the love so dear."*

*"When the dress begins to fray?"*

*"Forget the memories with every tear,"* she said.

*"When the dress begins to fade?"* he asked, stopping his work long enough to look at

her, the smile forgotten.

*"Lose the dress and disappear."*

Time and sunlight had bleached the fabric, threadbare at the elbows and knees. It hadn't faded for years, at least not before Mama died. Or did Papa die first? The memories were hazy, the details lost.

She remembered being able to remember. When the dress was new. At least she thought she remembered the dress being new, learning the rules. She remembered the rules. But even they were fading.

Victoria took a deep breath, trying to remember who'd taught them to her. Was it Papa? Someone taller? Shorter? Was Papa short? Papa was tall, taller than her. Wasn't he?

Didn't matter any longer. The dress was the dress; it was the only one she owned, though she couldn't remember buying it. A gift, perhaps. Was it ever new? Was she ever new? Papa would know. Wouldn't he?

"When the dress begins to fray," Victoria said, watching another thread fly away. The first hint of the sun fell across her face and she knocked on the door.

"Come in," a young man said, swinging the door open and then heading back inside. He was older than her, at least a year or two, she liked to believe.

"I'm bored," she said, walking behind him.

"You're always bored."

She pulled at the lace, at the curling edges, hard enough to fray the fabric even more. A strand pulled free, drifted to the ground, and she tried to catch it before it dissolved.

*When the dress begins to fray*
*Only touch the next dress to wear*
*When the dress begins to fade*
*Touch wrong and kill the love so dear*
*When the dress begins to fray*
*Forget the memories with every tear*
*When the dress begins to fade*
*Lose the dress and disappear*

The rules. She remembered them. Didn't she? Those were right; they had to be right. Papa had said, Papa had sewn, Papa had taught her the rules before he died. Each dress forever more, he'd said, would one day fade and fray and disappear. This was the fourth dress. The fifth dress? There'd been the button one and the mistaken one and the first one that Papa had made for her when everyone was afraid to touch her. So many dresses, so many papas.

Another thread drifted away as she walked through the house. "William," she said, the memory of him coming back from wherever it had momentarily disappeared.

"That's me." He never mocked her in her poverty, for having to wear the same dress every day or for forgetting his name every so often.

"Yes," she said. "It is." And smiled, for his understanding and the times he'd tried to touch her and she'd run away despite wanting to be touched. Needing him to touch her. But the rules were the rules; she still remembered those, even when everything else was fading away to nothing.

"Where to, today?" William asked.

Victoria shrugged, lost in trying to remember the rules, the dresses, the papas.

"Follow me, then," he said, reaching out to take her hand.

She pulled back far too quickly, shocked out of her thoughts. Not wanting to touch him. Not now. It was the rule, the only rule she lived by. No touching. Not him. Not yet.

William shrugged and started walking. Down the gravel driveway, oak trees shaded them until they reached the main road. He led her across the street, past a number of houses abandoned after the plant closed, leaving the town to fade away and fray at the edges. Too many had been boarded up, hidden away behind industrial-strength fences.

They took a shortcut through a private garden they'd discovered one quiet afternoon, partially overgrown yet oddly tended in parts; if anyone owned it, they didn't seem to care when it was invaded by curious teenagers. Finally, at the corner, the sun peeked out from behind the clouds, shining down on a house with people scrambling all over it.

"What's going on?" Victoria asked.

"I think someone's actually moving in."

"Why?"

He pointed to a car sitting in the driveway. "Ask them."

They watched as a man pulled open the door to help a woman out. She moved slowly, hands cradling her stomach.

"I'm not fat," she said loud enough to be heard over the men unloading the moving van. "Just pregnant."

Whatever the man said in return couldn't be heard as the back door opened.

A teenage girl got out, her blonde hair catching the sun. Victoria shifted behind the tree, hiding from view. Her dress snagged a branch and the thin fabric tore, exposing skin that hadn't seen the light of the sun in far too long.

Her heart stopped. She held the two pieces together, fingers tightening as she looked at the strands flapping in the breeze, trying to hold the tear together. *When the dress begins to fray . . . when the dress begins to fray . . .* She held tighter, trying to remember the next line, on the tip of her tongue, slipping away, and then she found it. *Only touch the next dress to wear.*

"What?" William asked, turning to her. "Did you say something?"

Victoria shook her head, staring back at the girl where she laughed before running around her parents and disappearing inside the house.

William turned to Victoria. "See, something not boring."

"Fine," she said, trying to pretend she hadn't torn the dress, that she hadn't forgotten the rules. "I'm not quite as bored. Now what?"

He shrugged. "That's all I had to show you."

They watched the father help the mother walk inside the house, Victoria staring hard enough to burn the image into memory so she'd never forget. Even though she would. She always did. With every mama and papa. With every dress. "I have to go home," William said after his stomach growled for the third time.

"Go eat." She watched him walk away, and then watched the empty place where he'd just been, reaching out her hand to touch the air that had touched him.

Victoria walked around the house until she stood in the shadows with the new family. The mother sat outside beneath an umbrella stuck in the ground to give her shade. A glass of something pink sat on her stomach, balanced on the baby.

Boy, Victoria thought, not knowing why.

*"Never touch a baby,"* Papa said bent over the loom in the middle of the night, candles flickering to cast away the darkness.

*"Why?"* she asked. Tiny fingers and toes newborn soft. So touchable.

He slammed his hand down so hard the ratchet wheel broke off and rolled across the room, his face red and splotchy. *"Never touch a baby,"* he said over and over again as he put the loom back together and continued making her dress.

Papa was angry. Papa was sad, raising her on his own after Mama died. That was the first papa. She remembered him. But the memory was faint and fading. Papa with the brown hair. Papa with the gold hair. Papa with no hair. Papa with the gray hair. Papa with the black hair. Papa with a little hair he combed over in thin rivers. So many memories, so many papas.

The teenage girl came out of her house, all blonde and happy. Her shirt pink and shiny as the sun.

Victoria smoothed her dress out, wrinkles returning as soon as she let go, a few more threads gone with the wind, and watched the girl and the mama and the soon-to-be boy, trying to remember the rules.

*When the dress begins to fray*
*Only touch the next dress*
*When the dress begins to fade*
*Touch wrong and kill the love*
*When the dress begins to fray*
*Forget the memories*
*When the dress begins to fade*
*Lose the dress and disappear*

She kept touching her dress, trying to catch the strands before they vanished, holding tighter, the words fading. The rules fading. The dress, the next dress. There had to be a next dress. Always. Papa had taught her the rules. Or was it Mama sewing at her loom? The wind picked up, tearing loose a handful of threads and blowing them away.

William and Victoria sat in a tree, hidden by leaves, and learned the girl's name the next day, when her mother called her in.

"Chloe!"

And Chloe dropped what she was doing, straightened out another pink shirt that didn't need straightening, and ran inside.

"She seems nice," Victoria said.

William nodded, his cheeks flushing red.

"Talk to her," she said.

He scrambled down the tree and ran back home. She stayed behind, watching Chloe until watching wasn't enough.

Victoria tried to smooth out the wrinkles. It didn't help. More threads disappeared. She knocked, and then clasped her hands behind her back.

"I'm Victoria," she said to the man who answered the door. "I live up the street."

"Looking for Chloe?"

Victoria nodded.

He yelled up the stairs then turned back, stretching his hand out to shake. "I'm Mr. Crowe," he said. "She should be right down."

Victoria held her hands up, showing him the nails. "Just painted, nice to meet you, though."

"Teenage girls." He laughed while shaking his head. "You and Chloe will get along great." He turned around when she came bouncing down the stairs in blue jeans and a bright pink T-shirt. "This is Victoria."

"Hi, I'm—"

"Chloe," Victoria said. "I heard."

"Want to come in?"

"I was going to see if you wanted to come out, but in is good."

Chloe turned to her father.

"Go," he said. "Be back for dinner. You start school tomorrow."

Victoria straightened her dress out. The plain colors stood out in such stark contrast to the vibrant pinks of Chloe's shirt.

"I've seen you around," Chloe said, "hanging out with some guy. Figured that was your boyfriend."

Victoria turned away, staring at the sun through the leaves. "Just a friend," she said. "Want to meet him?"

Chloe smiled. "Sure."

The sun was high overhead as they walked, passing one deserted house after another.

"This is it." Victoria stopped in front of one of the few houses that looked lived in.

"What are we waiting for?"

"William's a little shy."

"Will two girls standing outside his house help?" Chloe asked, laughing as she leaned her shoulder into Victoria. Victoria pushed back and the two of them ended up swaying together.

"He'll think we're dancing for him." Victoria stepped away, smoothing out her dress. The collar was fraying and another string fell off, disappearing into the wind. It had been new once. Bright too. Not pink-Chloe bright, but colorful. And clean. And fresh, unworn. Each stitch tight, as though it would last forever.

Victoria reached for Chloe's hand. Rules were rules, after all. And she needed a next dress.

"He's shy," Victoria said. "But you're going to love him, I just know it."

Chloe followed along as Victoria tugged her up the porch steps. "Does he know you *like* him?" she asked, her voice a false whisper, like a spy in a bad movie.

Victoria shook her head so hard another string fell from her dress. She tried to catch it but it was gone too quickly. "Just a friend," she said. "You're his type, not me."

"Hi," William said when he opened the door.

"This is Chloe," Victoria said, pushing the other girl forward.

Victoria tried to smooth her dress as Chloe stretched her hand out. They shook.

Victoria sighed.

It was a silent sound, almost a gasp but not quite. She blinked a tear away. How long since she'd cried? Hard to keep track of all the tears after so long without them. Was it Mama who told her "never let him see you cry"? Something about giving away her soul, about letting Papa know he'd caused pain. Better to hide the hurt behind a veil of laughter. Or, better yet, just to hide.

Tears will kill as easily as words. As a knife or gun or rock, if nothing else is close at hand. Tears wound. Sticks and stones and all that.

Another string fell free, the dress one thread lighter now. Victoria bent down, looking along the old wood planks of the porch for the string, but it must have fallen through the cracks.

"School starts tomorrow," William said. "You going to McKinley?"

Chloe nodded. "How is it?"

He shrugged. "It's high school. Physics teacher is pretty cool, if you're into that kind of stuff."

She laughed, shaking her head. Blonde hair went flying every which way and she pulled it off her face. "I was thinking more like English, maybe drama."

Victoria remembered school. There were more rules, Papa said. To keep her safe. To keep everyone safe.

The first classroom might have been plain wooden boards, rough, giving splinters every time she brushed against them. There were cinder blocks at one school, gray rectangles towering over her. She'd count them to stave off boredom. In the corners, the blocks were poorly cut to fit and light would filter through. Or was that in the one-room schoolhouse? Each teacher looked like all the rest, the same starched dress that smelled of mothballs and breath that smelled of moths. Dead moths, leaning over her, spraying her name when she dawdled or failed to pay proper attention.

"Yes, ma'am" and "no, ma'am" and the ruler on her knuckles leaving red marks brighter than the sun. The principal so kindly and grasping as his own hand left marks on her bare skin in the quiet of his office, even when she was proper in her appearance and her attitude and her "yes, ma'ams" were all in order. So many principals leaving their marks on her.

Papa would be mad. Papa would be jealous.

So many papas leaving so many marks.

High school was different from those drafty rooms with starched teachers and mouth-breathing principals. No more rulers now. She remembered rulers. But like her dress, those memories were fading. It had been too long since she'd been a child. Too many memories had been written and rewritten on the wrinkles of her dress.

Victoria pulled at the hem, stretching the fabric enough she could almost see her legs through the thinnest spots. Pale skin, shadows barely hidden by fabric as more strings fell to the porch, carried away by the wind before she could snatch them out of the air.

"I should really be getting home," Chloe said, resting her hand on William's arm for a brief moment.

Both Victoria and William stared at the contact, William turning red in the late afternoon sun. Victoria sighed again.

"We could walk you home."

"That's okay," Chloe said. "I need to learn my way around."

"You should ask her out," Victoria said as they watched her walk away.

"What? No."

"Seriously. Now, tonight. Don't let her get to school tomorrow and meet someone else." She bit her lip, then shook her head. "You'll only get this one chance, William. Go for it."

"She'll say no," William said, turning away.

Victoria reached her hand out, holding the fingers right above his skin where Chloe-with-no-rules had touched him. It'd be warm, she knew. She remembered that much, the warmth of skin. No touching. Not him. Not yet.

Rule number one. Every rule, the only rule.

She'd broken it once. Touched one of the hims in her life. She'd loved him; she remembered that even though his name was as frayed as her dress. The memory of him just a faint image of a dream. Not even real any longer. If it ever had been real. If any of the fragile memories were real.

So many papas. So many principals. So many hims. Lost to time, frayed strings falling to the earth and fading away like lost memories. There'd been the boy with the long blond hair and the wild eyes and the broken rule. He'd serenade her on the corner, motorcycles idling on the street, filling the air with noxious fumes as he played his guitar and sang for her and passing strangers would fill his case with change.

The songs were full of sadness, longing to hold her, just once, since she'd never let him touch her. Chaste, he named her, and wrote poems for her, to be turned into songs, asking always to allow him the blessing of unbuttoning her dress and finally letting him taste the warmth of her in his arms.

But the rule was the rule was the rule. And touching him would be bad, she knew. The rule was all she had of Papa. All that was left after he was taken away and burned at the stake like Mama.

And now, this boy sang to her on the streets of Haight-Ashbury and offered his song for just a touch.

Victoria shook her head even as she accepted his sacrifice. His skin so warm, soft as he touched her, kissed her. So cold as he died in her arms.

She pulled her hand back, away from William. Unwilling to risk his soul for one simple touch. Not when so much more was finally so close.

"Go," she said, pointing to where Chloe had turned the corner to head to her house.

And William went, Victoria trailing behind to offer encouragement.

Outside Chloe's house, Victoria hid behind the familiar tree while William walked to the door. She counted the seconds, knowing he'd never knock.

Victoria smoothed her dress down once more before sprinting up the stairs, running around him to press the doorbell and then racing back to the tree. Hidden by leaves, she tried to catch her breath as one string after another fell to the earth, sinking into the dirt.

The dress was almost white now, no color remaining at all, and for a moment she couldn't even remember her name.

Long after watching William head home to get ready for his date, Victoria remained in the tree, staring at Chloe's house while she tried to smooth out the wrinkles in her dress. Every tug straightened out the fabric for less time than the tug before. Each pulled multiple strands free to float on the wind or sink into the dirt. Some were too thin and frayed to even see.

Victoria clutched the air to catch them but they evaded her, seeming to drift on air currents just a little out of reach, disappearing before she ever caught one. Still, she worked on the wrinkles. She pressed down on her collar, trying to get it to stay flat.

She climbed down and walked to the house to ring the bell.

"Hi, Mr. Crowe," she said, waving so he wouldn't try to shake her hand.

"Chloe!" he called up the stairs before opening the door wider to let her in.

Victoria squeezed by, holding her dress so not even a fraying string could escape to touch him. Then Chloe was there and Victoria grasped her hand, the skin warm.

She followed the other girl upstairs and into a room so pink it hurt her eyes. It was so Chloe and she loved it more than she knew how to express, knowing how happy she'd be there. There'd been rooms before that were so Victoria or, well, all the prior names that had disappeared to time. But the memory of the rooms remained even if remembering was more difficult every day.

Small and cramped, with a narrow metal bed with a lumpy mattress that squeaked every time Papa sat on it. She'd curl up in a ball, pretend to be asleep, and Papa would leave her alone. Or not. Depending on his mood and how much he'd had to drink or if Mama was home.

That was the Papa with the thinning hair, she remembered now. Another thread slid free from her dress, floating away as it escaped. So many papas. So many squeaking mattresses bumping against the wall as she pretended she wasn't herself, she was someone else, anyone else. Everyone else.

And she was.

"You heard?" Chloe asked.

"About your date?" Victoria smoothed out her dress. "William told me."

"Sure you're okay?"

Victoria smiled. "Depends on whether you let me help pick out your dress or not."

Chloe laughed. "And if I don't?"

With a matching laugh, Victoria shrugged. "I'll have no choice but to tell him you are unworthy due to poor choice in clothing."

Chloe opened her closet door, pulled out the first shirt she could find and threw it over Victoria. "Well, wouldn't want that to happen."

"No, of course not," Victoria said as she lifted the purple blouse off her head. "Not this."

"I was thinking—" Chloe turned around holding a sparkling red dress against her. Long blonde hair covered most of the top until she moved it out of the way.

Victoria shook her head. "Much too much," she said. "Do you have anything that isn't, well, you?"

"Me?"

"All bubbly and pink and—" Victoria stood next to Chloe studying her closet.

Chloe pushed Victoria out of the way with another laugh, the sound filling the pink room. "What about this?" She twirled around, a pale silver gown far too formal for a summer date, neckline plunging down way too low.

"You want him looking at *you*," Victoria said. "Not your dress." She pressed down on her collar but it popped right back up. Another string fell loose, from the sleeve this time, almost sliding into her palm before falling to the carpet and getting lost in the pile.

So many papas. So many principals. So many rooms. So many hims.

But most of all . . . so many dresses.

She'd lost count with the fading memories. They lasted only so long before needing to be replaced. Fraying over time. There'd been the starched black dress with the matching veil. Was that the first, taking her privacy and solitude so seriously, married to God and Christ? The father was Papa and principal, and her room was cold and austere. Rock walls and a metal pan for unmentionables. Father had been kind. And unkind. In equal measure.

Was there a dress before that dress? A papa before Father? A room before a convent's cell? A him before him?

The memories were faded away and hard to catch as they escaped. Free, free at last.

Victoria slid the pinks and purples and reds to the side, exposing a rather plain, more traditional sort of dress hung all by itself. It had a simple collar, flat against the shoulders, even if the neckline was more daring than she'd like. The sleeves were longer than she wanted, tired of not feeling the sun on her forearms. Nothing to be done about it. A sturdy hem with no frayed edges to be seen. Not too many buttons.

In the back, the dress would let peek a hint of shoulder blades behind the long blonde hair. It would do. Shorter than she was used to. Not as short as the little thing she'd worn when the boy had sung to her on the street corner. That was scandalously short, exposing far too much of knee and thigh and, if she sat too quickly, even more than that. She'd let him see once, to show she wasn't chaste, so much as cautious, but in the end it hadn't mattered. She'd accepted his gift and only remembered the song now in brief snippets that faded like strings escaping on the wind.

She'd sung it once, as they lowered him into the ground, and never again.

Perfect dress. She held it out to Chloe, who shook her head. "My mom bought that," she said. "I've never even tried it on."

"He'll love it," Victoria said. "Trust me; he'll only have eyes for you."

Chloe stared at it. "It's so . . . plain."

Victoria smiled. "A dress is never plain," she said. "A dress is the gift wrap."

"He is *so* not unwrapping me on a first date."

"Not that!" Victoria said with a laugh.

"Maybe the second," Chloe said, taking the dress off its hanger. "I want him looking at me, right?"

"Right."

"If he hates it, I'll have no choice but to tell him *you* are unworthy of him due to poor choice in clothing." She laughed then pulled the pink shirt off, exposing an equally pink bra. The blue jeans followed and Victoria covered her eyes and spun to face the door.

"Pink bra okay?" Chloe asked.

Victoria shrugged, still not looking.

"You can turn around."

Long blonde hair hid most of the collar, and most of the cleavage. The dress wasn't as plain on her as it was on the hanger. It had curves now and flow. Chloe brought it to life and Victoria smiled.

"It's perfect."

Chloe ran her hands down the front of the dress, smoothing it out even though it was too new to have any wrinkles. The doorbell rang. Her father called up and she smiled. "Showtime."

"He'll love it," Victoria said as they descended the stairs hand in hand.

Victoria and Mr. Crowe watched William and Chloe walk down the driveway. The moon reflected like fireflies off her blonde hair until they were too far away to see.

"Have a good night," Mr. Crowe said as he turned to go back inside.

"You too," she said, and then Victoria hurried after the young couple. She knew William, knew the town. There were only so many places to hang out on the final night of summer vacation.

A first date required some privacy, at least. Victoria counted on it, turning down one street after another until she'd long since lost track of William and Chloe. It didn't matter. Might actually be better to wait for Chloe to be alone, but there was too great a risk of losing the dress.

She'd done that once too. A brief memory, too short to really count. Caught too late, she'd been stuck in a nightgown that time, all frilly and scandalous. She shivered as the memory faded. Victoria tried to smooth the wrinkles away but the dress tore with the motion, the fabric so fragile it could no longer sustain its own cohesion. Individual stitches were escaping; every step left a trail of thread like breadcrumbs, disappearing in the moonlight.

Time, like memories, was running out, fading away. A risk remained that if she'd chosen wrong, if William failed to bring Chloe to the private garden along the riverbank, she'd never even make it back to Chloe's house. There might not be enough time or memories or thread for a Plan B.

The garden was covered in leaves, gold and red and yellow. Wild apple trees along the river, stirring her earliest memories, as fragile as the dress. Winter roses had yet to bloom but the garden was inviting nonetheless. It belonged to someone, leaves raked even as more fell to color the paths. But they didn't know who and no one ever bothered them for walking there.

It was where William had first tried to touch her. She'd barely skirted his fingers in time. Instead, she laughed, batted her lashes to show there was no rejection in backing away. If he'd known the word, he'd surely have called her chaste as well. He'd never known her desperate ache to be touched by him, to show him how well she knew all that would prove her unchaste.

By habit, she started to smooth the wrinkles out, stopping just in time before more of her dress ripped. With each breath, threads floated around her, the very air itself tearing them free. The memories, of all those papas and mamas, and Father and Christ with the dirty feet, and some even older than that. Of songs and boys and dresses and beds, faded away until nothing remained but the yearning to touch William.

To be touched.

The memory of a new dress. A flat collar. A pink bra.

She'd never worn a pink bra.

William and Chloe walked into the garden. Not hand in hand, but close enough to touch shoulders where the path narrowed. Chloe laughed at something and William blushed in the moonlight. Victoria shivered, threads falling to the earth as the dress faded and frayed.

The wind swirled around her, filled with thread. Her fingers shook as she finally caught them, like catching lost memories slipping away. The rules returned to her, every blessed word of them. She whispered them, lost in the shadows of the garden, as she remembered.

*When the dress begins to fray*
*Only touch the next dress to wear*
*When the dress begins to fade*
*Touch wrong and kill the love so dear*
*When the dress begins to fray*
*Forget the memories with every tear*
*When the dress begins to fade*
*Lose the dress and disappear*

There were buttons on her dress, forgotten and unused. It had been so long since she'd been naked she couldn't even remember if she had a bra on underneath. Not that it mattered.

The new one would be pink.

Like Chloe. So pink.

Victoria undid the first button with shaking fingers as she whispered the rules over and over again. The fabric stiff around the buttonhole, only successful because the dress was so threadbare the stitches of the button popped free. The skin beneath was pale and warm where the moon shone upon it for the first time since the days of the song and the broken rule. She'd been so good ever since and this must be her reward.

The loose button went on top of the little pile of threads. Another button. Another.

Memories of pain returned. Of hating this step. Of knowing it had to be done. She always forgot the pain. Blocked it out. Now, she remembered. The choice was pain or death, and she always chose pain; no matter what her name might be, the choice was always the same.

Victoria grabbed the hem of her dress, the edges splitting even as she touched them, and took a deep breath. She began to pull the dress off over her head in one motion.

Inside her shoes, the skin of her toes parted. Big toe first, as it was farthest away. Then the next as bones escaped, scratching against cotton until, free at last, they melted away. Leaving behind nothing but socks steeped in rich red blood.

Unable to stand, she collapsed to the ground. Still, Victoria pulled at the dress. Inch by painful inch, slicing skin and tearing muscles and ripping nerves as though skinning an animal.

The pain never ended as she undressed, willing herself to keep removing the wrinkled, fading dress. The skin of her ankles parted, exposing white bone for just a moment before her insides became outsides and escaped. The skin came free in one long molting whisper, teeth breaking as she bit them against the pain.

The hem reached where her hips would be, attached to her skin as though they were two parts of the same thing. Nothing remained below but a spreading pool of blood as skin and dress were slowly pulled up. The lining of her stomach tore, intestines spilling free and escaping with a sigh until she had no more lungs to sigh with.

The memories of her name disappeared with her heart, dress and skin pulled up and over her head. Her skull bright white in the moonlit shadows before it too dissolved, leaving nothing but a graying pile of brain to be caught by the wind before escaping.

And Victoria was nothing but inside-out skin and dress now.

Free. Free at last.

The pile of skin and dress dissolved until nothing was left but threads upon the air.

She floated on the breeze, close enough to Chloe to smell the perfume she'd sprayed on her neck. Then, as light as air, one thread after another landed, burrowing beneath the smooth pink skin.

Chloe cried out as though caught in a swarm of gnats, before slumping against William for just a moment.

She opened her eyes.

Long blonde hair fell around her shoulders, covering the plain brown dress.

Perfect.

Chloe smiled, smoothing her dress down out of habit. It wasn't necessary. This dress was *new*. With a pink bra underneath that William wouldn't get to see but she'd let him touch. There was so much she'd let him do now.

Soon enough, the dress would fade and fray, and she'd have no choice but to say goodbye. He'd be old, while she'd still be a teenager, in her plain brown dress, with her long blonde hair. *Chloe.* She'd try to remember her name this time.

A new papa and mama too. They seemed nice. That pink room, she'd be happy there. For a while, at least. Until they noticed one day she never aged. Then they'd have to die too, so she could live just a little longer as Chloe.

For now, though, finally, so long spent watching William, she could finally touch him. Safe until the dress once more began to fray and fade.

Chloe hadn't planned on being anything but chaste on their first date.

Victoria had no such plans.

William smiled as Chloe kissed him, his fingers clumsy where they tried, in vain, to unbutton enough to reach her skin.

Chloe laughed, placing his hands where she wanted to be touched and pulling him to the ground on top of her.

"You'll get all dirty," he said, even as she rolled him over so she was on top.

"Don't worry," she said, running her hands down her skin to smooth out the wrinkles. "It's just a dress."

# The Dishes Are Done
### Carol Pierson Holding

*When we first read the story below, we were taken by the confident voice of the narrator and the feel of a classic John Collier offering—in which the setting and the characters are engaged in things so utterly ordinary there couldn't possibly be anything amiss. And we admit it didn't hurt to agree with the notion that dishwashers cannot be expected to violate the laws of physics and hydraulics. Or can they?*

How you load a dishwasher shouldn't matter.

And it hadn't mattered because Jim and I were as aligned on dishwashers as we were on most things. We both read instruction manuals so we knew the drill: no dishes touching, plates and pans below, glasses and bowls on the top rack, and with our new machine—I'd splurged on a Bosch—silverware laid in individual slots on the cutlery tray. We never talked about the ban against kitchen knives or whether it's okay to combine stainless and silver. That's just how we were brought up.

It honestly never occurred to us that someone we liked would do it any differently, until we visited my old friend Sally. She'd fixed me up with my first husband so she'd taken a while to warm up to Jim, but five years after my divorce, she'd finally accepted him, even with his master's in education.

We were visiting her at her house in Jackson. She'd been overserved at the Snake River Grill and excused herself the minute we got back to her house, leaving me and Jim to clean up the cocktails. We were a little drunk ourselves. He eyed me from across the room; I repaid the compliment. How could I not? He was so adorable, Levi's hugging slim rocker hips and that dark hair curling over his pressed flannel shirt. His idea of dressing up. I was ready for bed in every sense, but first the dishes.

Jim opened Sally's dishwasher and gasped. I turned to see a jumble of crockery and crystal that looked as though it'd been thrown in from across the room, like a freeway pileup complete with bits of bioplasm. The machine was only half-full, yet there wasn't a single item that didn't have others pressing against its surfaces. And the silverware was pointing downwards, perfect for incubating bacteria.

"You didn't tell me she was trailer trash," Jim said.

"Aren't we the pretentious one," I said. That was the first time I'd heard him use that expression or anything like it. "The real tell is her loading skills?"

Jim smiled, shook his head, and started to rearrange the dishes.

"Are you with me?" he said.

I brought over the wineglasses and nut bowl and put them into the spaces he'd left.

"I know Sally can be hard to take. Do you like her any better than you thought you would?" I said. He was turning the silverware right-side up.

"We're fine . . . though now, I don't know." He cocked his head at the dishwasher, breaking the tension as he always did. "And she does like her wine," he said chuckling.

*Don't we all,* I wanted to say.

The next morning, Jim and I went downstairs to the kitchen and caught Sally rearranging the dishes.

"What are you doing?" he said in a dismissive tone. He was probably as hungover as I was, and Sally, too, given the Costco-sized bottle of Advil she'd left out on the counter.

"I'm fixing my dishes," Sally said. She was deliberately taking handfuls of silverware out and putting them back upside down.

"They won't get clean that way," Jim said. I turned away from them and began pulling our cereals down from the cabinet.

Sally didn't respond. Jim repeated himself.

From the corner of my eye, I could see her whirl around to face him and then say, punctuating her points with pained head bobs as though speaking to a dull intern, "We *all* have *our ways* and *this* is *mine*. People have *died* falling on knives."

Sally finished rescrambling her dishes, fried and ate two eggs sunny-side up, and went upstairs to get ready for Ashtanga class. Jim and I stayed in the breakfast nook, drinking her excellent coffee. The lingering smell of fried egg was revolting.

"Do we dare clean up?" Jim walked to the sink, motioning with his empty coffee cup. "Maybe leave the dishes. I'll clean Sally's egg pan. It's a mess. She can't get mad at me for that."

He reached under the sink. "Wha—? She uses SOS pads?"

I sighed. My head ached. My stomach churned. "Stop it, Jim . . . I can't believe . . . We had SOS growing up. Does that mean I'm trailer trash too?"

"We used Brillo," he said with *much* condescension. "Everyone I've ever known uses Brillo. I suppose you used All?"

"What is the matter with you? We had Cascade, dick, just like now," I said, distracted, wishing Sally would take me away, even to a strenuous yoga class.

Jim leaned his back against the counter, crossed his arms and feet, and let his head drop, as though addressing one of his classes for special ed instructors. "Lookit, it's not just an issue of cleanliness. She's put crystal in there. And wooden spoons. There could be glass chips or splinters. It's a *safety* issue."

"Hey, her upside-down knives trump your safety arguments. Or maybe she *is* trying to kill you. You know she's still friends with my ex, and I know he wants you dead," I said. I was trying to get a laugh. Or to get him to stop talking, which mention of my ex usually did.

"She's sloppy. Her drinking. Plus, it could be dangerous. I can't believe you're taking her side."

"You just don't like her because she used to be an investment banker."

What a bizarre thing for me to say. But I'd never seen this side of Jim. He was a socialist who'd spent his career advocating for disturbed children, taking a lower salary so he'd have his summers to go fishing and regain his sanity. I knew he didn't care about what soap someone used, much less what they did ten years ago. He'd married me, even with my MBA. He'd applied to law school eons ago.

Was it Sally's bitchiness at breakfast? Or just being in her house for too long? I imagined it could be wearing on him, with its Western-themed homage to slaughter. The cowhide rug. The chandelier of entangled antlers. The horse's ass wine stopper, its iron body severed roughly at the flank.

Still dour, Jim left the kitchen to take a shower. I peeked in the dishwasher. Sally's crystal wineglasses were pressing against each other again; wooden spoons were floating around the upper level, unsecured. And yes, the silverware was upside down.

Poor Jim. I'd dragged him here because I wanted everyone to be friends. I dreamed of big Thanksgiving dinners, of blended families, and, someday, happy grandchildren playing with Sally's string of enormous, short-lived dogs. Now he was threatening to ruin it, over kitchen appliances and SOS pads.

I heard him banging around upstairs; then a text chime sounded. He'd sent me an article about how a London salon owner had died when a sliver of glass she swallowed from a jar of custom mustard cut her carotid artery and she'd drowned in her own blood.

"Aren't you the ghoulish one," I said as he came down. When he didn't respond, I tried again, this time in a screechy cockney accent, "We don't have those fancy *bespoke mustards.*"

Jim looked at me strangely and began moving his tongue around his back teeth. "What the—" he said as he pushed his thumb and index finger into his mouth and pulled out a wooden splinter. "I rest my case!" he said, waving it around like conclusive evidence.

"Come on, you planted that!" I said laughing.

When he didn't respond, I said, "No, you can't show Sally."

When he began to object, Sally started down the stairs and I glared at him. "You've already made one scene."

Sally and Jim prowled around each other until it was time to leave for yoga. On the way to the closet to get me a mat, Sally put her silver wine coasters inside the chest, staring directly at Jim's back as though she feared he might tuck them into his suitcase.

He saw her and mouthed "what the f—", put on his coat, and left with her white German shepherd.

She and I pretty much ran out of the house, then idled away the rest of the day with yoga, shopping, and climbing the hill behind her house. Anything to keep them away from each other until our flight.

I called Jim to warn him we'd be home soon, but he didn't answer. Sally brought up the knives again, and when I pleaded no more paranoid fantasies, she told me to look it up on my phone. Turns out, a little boy did die falling onto knives in a dishwasher some years ago. And a woman in Northampton had met the same fate when she was visiting a minister. Sounded like a Dorothy Sayers plot.

We were late getting back, so I ran upstairs to finish packing. Jim wasn't in our room though I did see his suitcase by the back door.

Sally called up to me, "You'd better come down here. Now," she said. Her voice led me to the kitchen, where the dishes were once again neatly organized, silverware pointing up.

Jim appeared in the doorway.

"Jiiimmm," I whined.

"You think *I* did *that* when I've been *told* not to *touch*?" he said, bobbing his head in cruel imitation.

"Come on, quit joking. We'll miss our plane," I said.

Jim turned around, then pirouetted back toward the dishwasher, his finger pointing at Sally, skidded, and fell directly towards the now-upturned knives.

At the last moment, he twisted his body, just missing the dishwasher.

"Fuckin' A," he said, staring up at Sally accusingly.

Sally gave him a strange look, shook her head, and headed out to her car. He sat in the back. They never exchanged so much as another glance.

Back home, we ordered out for Thai and ate in front of the TV. We were both exhausted and ate quickly. I took our plates to the kitchen, but when I opened the Bosch, I saw it was packed full, even the soap dispenser.

Jim had been such an asshole our last day in Jackson. If he could condemn my friend for how she loaded a dishwasher, what else had I missed? And that last stunt in the kitchen? My ex and I had been together for thirteen years, and it wasn't until our final months that I felt the full brunt of his meanness, when he thought the cleaners had lost his shirt and blamed me.

I was working myself into a really good snit. I crammed the plates into already occupied slots and set my glass sideways on top of the bowls. For extra measure, I threw the forks on top of the drain.

Jim came in with the empty takeout containers and dirty serving spoons. I tensed as he looked inside the machine, steeling myself for the kind of barrage I'd suffered over the goddamn shirt. Adding his self-righteous safety obsessions to the mix. This should be good.

"Go ahead, say it," I practically spat at him.

He laid the spoons in the cutlery tray, came around the lowered door, and reached for me. I tried to push him away but he wouldn't let me go.

"No more safety jokes, Jim? You came off like a paranoid nut case," I said spitefully.

He leaned back still holding me. "Because of the dishwasher?"

"What the hell was that?" I said.

"I'm sorry. I just really don't like Sally. Please don't make me go again."

I started to snap back, to tell him . . . what? That he was right?

"Let's just go to bed," he said, a grin creeping onto his face. "But if we're going to run it now, could you please take the forks out of the *stainless steel tub*? You don't want to pierce the *AquaSeal*." He pulled me closer. Technical talk aroused us.

"Don't forget about *hydrogen buildup*. Hey, seriously!" I said, trying to untangle myself. "The manual said to run hot water after a vacation or the Bosch might *explode*."

But my sweet fool pushed Start anyway.

# Red Rabbit
## *Steve Rasnic Tem*

*Winner of the British Fantasy Award and the World Fantasy Award, Steve Rasnic Tem has spent almost four decades creating a unique and personal brand of fiction. Marked by characters steeped in tortured introspection—recalling Kafka at his most unsettling—Tem's stories examine ordinary people struggling with the pain served up every day by an uncaring universe. The following story about a man dealing with his wife's dementia takes us on a journey of delusion and terrifying ambiguities.*

He found her on the back porch again, watching the yard through the sliding glass door. He didn't want to spook her, so he made some noise as he left the kitchen, bumped a chair, and made a light tap with one shoe on the metal threshold that separated the porch from the rest of the house. Then he stopped a few feet behind her and said, "What are you looking at, honey?"

"The rabbit. Matt, have you seen that rabbit?"

"That was yesterday, Clara. Remember? I went down there, and I scooped it up with a shovel, and I dropped it into a trash bag. Some wild animal got to it. Rabbits can't protect themselves very well. That was yesterday."

"But it's back." Her voice shook. "Can't you see it?"

He followed her gaze to the lower part of the lawn, where it dipped downhill to the fence. Shadows tended to pool there, making the area look damp even though it hadn't rained in almost two months. Beyond were a field of weeds and wildflowers, and the line of trees bordering the old canal. Beyond that was the interstate. You couldn't see it, but you could certainly hear the traffic—a vacillating roar that you could pretend was a river if you really tried.

The skinned and bloody rabbit had appeared there yesterday at the bottom of the yard, eased out of the shadows as if from a pool. And here was another one, its front legs stretched out toward the house, its body gleaming with fresh blood. This must have just happened. They must have had some sort of predator in the yard.

"I see it," he said. "Something got another one."

"Something terrible is happening," she said. "I've been feeling it for weeks. And now this rabbit—I see it every day. Sometimes just after sunrise, sometimes just before sunrise. I thought I was going crazy, but now you see it too. What do you think it wants? Can you tell me what it wants?"

Matt looked at her: her eyes red and unfocused, lips trembling. She was somewhere else inside her head. She was wearing this old green tube-top thing. She'd never looked good in it. Her back was knotted, her shoulders pushed up, her arms waving around as she spoke. He figured she must be crazy tense if he noticed it—he never noticed things like that.

He felt sorry for her, but he also felt scared for himself. The woman he loved had been gone for years, and now he was left with this. He wasn't a good enough person to handle something he hadn't signed up for.

"It's not the same rabbit, Clara. There must be a predator loose in the neighborhood. Probably just a big cat or maybe a dog. It's just a dead rabbit. I'll go get the shovel and take care of it. There's nothing to get upset about."

He didn't really understand how her mind worked anymore. But maybe his being logical helped her. No one could say he hadn't tried.

"There's blood all over him," she said. "He's all torn up. Can't you see that something terrible is going to happen, that something terrible *is* happening? Can't you see it?"

She continued to stare at the rabbit in the yard. She wouldn't turn around and look at him. It felt creepy talking to her back all the time. He didn't dare touch her when she was like this, like a fistful of nerves. He didn't think she'd looked at him full in the face in days.

"It was a wild animal. It had a savage life. And something got to it. It's not like a cartoon, Clara. Rabbits can't protect themselves very well. Real rabbits in the wild, their lives are short and cruel."

They hadn't had sex in a long time. He'd been afraid to touch her. You can learn to live with crazy, but you can't touch it. He couldn't let her drive, and when he left her alone, she called him at work every hour to complain about some new thing she'd suddenly realized was wrong. Their GP kept prescribing new pills for her, but he was just a kid, really. Matt was sure the fellow had no idea what was wrong with her.

"I haven't been feeling right, Matt. Not for a very long time. Something terrible is going to happen—can't you sense that?"

"I know that's what you feel, but just go lie down. Let me take care of this, and then I'll come join you." But he knew she wasn't hearing, the way she stared, glassy-eyed, and the edge of her upper teeth showing. He stood in front of her and whispered, "Go inside now. Please." When she didn't respond, he stepped closer to block her view of the yard and put one arm around her, gave her a bit of squeeze.

"Honey, just go inside and lie down. I'll join you in a few minutes. Maybe I can even figure out what's killing these rabbits, and I'll deal with the thing. You just go inside." Hopefully she'd be asleep when he was done. When she was asleep he could grab a drink, watch some TV, relax, and unwind for once.

He grabbed a shovel and a trash bag and some gloves and started down the slope of the lawn. He'd generally neglected that part of the backyard. The ground there had always been mushy, unstable. He didn't know much about groundwater, septic systems, any of that stuff. But he figured it must be some sort of drainage issue, maybe because of the old canal, or maybe because of an old, broken septic system, something like that. It didn't smell too bad, just a little stagnant most of the time, a little sour. Only sometimes it stank like rotting meat. But they couldn't afford to fix it, whatever it was, so he'd just tried to ignore it.

The carcass wasn't where he had seen it. In fact, he couldn't find the rabbit anywhere. He thought about that mysterious predator, and went back to the house and grabbed the rake that was leaning against the wall by the sliding glass door.

He stood still, the rake held in both hands in front of him, raised like a club. He still didn't see the rabbit. He felt unsteady, and shortened his grip on the handle. He imagined that the predator, whatever it was, had dragged the body off somewhere. Some of the more dangerous animals in the region—coyotes, a wildcat or two, once even a small bear—had been known to wander out of the foothills and follow the canal into the more populous suburbs. He crept down the lawn toward the fence, afraid he might lose his footing. The grass looked shiny, slippery, as if the earth beneath were liquefying.

He detected a subtle reddish shadow as he got closer to the fence, and then saw that it was a spray of blood. The body had been pushed up against one of the fence posts, eviscerated, but still clearly some version of rabbit. He was glad Clara couldn't see this. It must have suffered terribly, ripped and skinned alive, all gleaming bright-red muscle, damp white bone, strings of pale fat. But the muscle had no business being bright red like that, like some kind of richly dyed leather. He'd skinned squirrels with his dad—he knew what a dead, skinned animal looked like, so dark and bruised. But this? This looked unreal.

He bagged it and trashed it, then brought out the hose to wash away the blood and any loose pieces of meat. That's what you did with this sort of thing. That's how you handled it. You cleaned up the mess and then you went on with your life.

Later he grabbed his binoculars and studied the field and the trees beyond, checking for any signs of movement. He saw nothing. If he had been ambitious, he would have climbed over the fence and walked through the field to the row of trees that bordered the canal. He could have followed that canal into some other place. The water might not be running through the canal anymore, but it was still a passage to something, wasn't it? But he wasn't ambitious. And he didn't want to go there.

Matt drank and watched TV until about midnight. The house was a mess—Clala hadn't cleaned in weeks. He couldn't abide a messy house, but he worked all day—he didn't have the time. But if he had the time, he knew he'd do a great job. It wasn't that hard keeping up a house—you just had to understand how to manage time and not let it get away from you. He hadn't signed up for this. He'd tried—and you owed your wife at least to try. But everybody had limits. You couldn't expect a man not to have his limits.

She didn't wake up when he crawled into bed with her. Good thing—she'd ask about the rabbit, and he didn't want to talk about that damn rabbit anymore.

He woke up once and saw her standing at the window, looking out onto the backyard. He started to say something, started to ask her what was wrong, but he stopped himself. He was tired, and he knew what was wrong.

He woke up alone. He didn't like waking up alone, but he didn't want to answer any of her questions. He fell back asleep, and when he woke up again the room was bright from the sun coming through the window. He'd overslept, but at least it was the weekend. Nothing important ever came up on the weekend. They'd stopped doing the important stuff a long time ago.

"Clara, you up here?" She didn't answer. "Clara!" Nothing.

He got his pants and shoes on and went downstairs. He still couldn't find her. He felt a little panicky, and he was mad at himself for feeling a little panicky. He made himself be methodical. He went back upstairs and searched each bedroom as he went down the hall.

He wasn't sure why they had all these bedrooms—they didn't have any kids. They had way too much house, but he'd gotten such a good deal on the place.

He felt a pressure building behind his eyes. He tried to shake it off. He went back into their bedroom and looked in the closet and in the master bathroom. He got down on his knees and looked under the bed. There were several socks, another larger, unidentifiable piece of clothing. He made a note to sweep under there later.

He called again from the top of the stairs, "Clara! Are you in the house?" Nothing. No steps, no rustle, just the soft hum of the refrigerator. He went downstairs and jerked open the front door a little too hard. It banged against the rubber bumper mounted on the wall. He hadn't realized it before, but he was beginning to feel pretty angry. Maybe she couldn't help it, but this was ridiculous.

She wasn't lying on the front lawn again, thank God. And the Subaru was still there, which was a big relief. Matt thought about getting in his car and driving around looking for her. But she could be anywhere, and besides, he knew that once you started chasing after someone like that, it never ended, not until you'd given yourself a heart attack. She was a grown woman—he shouldn't have to be searching for her.

He made himself stop. Most things got better that way: taking a break, waiting. People needed to be patient, not make such a big deal out of everything.

He went out to the porch and sat down. That's when he saw her kneeling down at the bottom of the yard, her back turned to him. Just like she always did. Her shoulders were heaving.

He slid open the door and stepped outside. "Clara?"

She didn't speak, but he could hear her crying. Then he saw the blood streaks on her sleeves. He started running. "Clara!" Not again. Not again.

He came up behind her and grabbed her by the shoulders, twisting them to stop her from whatever she was doing. He grabbed both of her hands and raised them, trying to get a good look at her wrists. Her forearms, his hands, everything slick with blood. "Where's the knife, Clara!"

She looked up at him, wide-eyed and dull. "No knife. I didn't see a knife."

He couldn't find any cuts on her wrists, her arms, her hands. He looked down at her knees, and then the grass, and then the bloody bits he was standing on. He jumped back in alarm. It was another rabbit, skinned and gutted, its flesh weeping fresh blood.

"It's *back!*" she said, her voice rising. "It's back!"

"Dammit, Clara. It's not the same rabbit!"

She stared at him, her face tilted. "But how can you tell it's a different rabbit? How do you know for sure?"

He started to explain, but what was there to explain? "Because this is real life. We live in real life, Clara! Just stay right here. I'll get something to cover it with, and then we'll go wash you up, okay?"

He ran into the garage and grabbed a drop cloth, and on his way out he grabbed the rake too, just in case of . . . just in case he needed it. But when he got back Clara was gone. The rabbit was still lying there, but there was no sign of Clara in the yard. How could she have moved so quickly? He stared down at the rabbit. It looked like all the others, as far as he could tell. One huge eye, pushed almost out of its socket, stared up at him.

He looked around the yard, the edge of the house, inside the house. He couldn't find her anywhere. He gave up. He imagined her walking around the neighborhood, her shirt bloody, her arms and hands bloody. Somebody would call the police. Well, the hell with it. He'd done everything he could.

Matt left the rabbit and went back inside. At least he could clean himself up. At least he could get that much done.

After his shower he grabbed a jar of peanut butter out of the fridge and stood at the kitchen window digging two fingers into the jar and eating the peanut butter right off them. Looking through the window into the porch and then through the sliding glass doors made the yard seem a pretty safe distance away. He could still see the fields and the line of trees beyond, and he was sure he'd be able to see any movement out there if there were any. But there was not.

After a while he collapsed into that old chair on the back porch and sat watching the yard for a couple of hours. It was midafternoon by then and he hadn't had any lunch. He supposed he could find something in the fridge to heat up, but then maybe Clara would come home. Fixing him something might occupy her, keep her mind off things.

He was actually pretty surprised she hadn't shown up yet. If the police had picked her up, they would have come by now. He was used to her being anxious, but she usually snapped out of it after an hour or so and managed to get going on whatever needed to be done. He'd call some of her friends but that woman, Ann, had moved away six months ago and he didn't know any of the others, if there were any others. Clara never made friends easily, at least not since he'd known her.

He couldn't get over those damn rabbits. Whatever had gotten to them, it must have wiped out an entire den. Why had the thing left its kills in his yard anyway? Like a house cat dropping the mouse it slaughtered at your feet. But you had to trust your eye—most of the time it was the one thing you could trust.

Clara needed to be back soon. She'd always been this timid thing, couldn't protect herself worth a damn. Terrible things happened to timid creatures like that. She knew. That's why she kept saying that. *Well, terrible things do happen, Clara.* It wasn't too hard predicting that.

He must have dozed, because the backyard suddenly looked dimmer. That shady bit down by the fence had grown, spread halfway up the yard toward the house. Lights were popping on over at the neighbors'.

He sat up suddenly as a chill grabbed his throat. "Clara!" he yelled as loudly as he could to scare it away. Still no answer. He listened hard now. The refrigerator still hummed. It was as if he were living by himself again.

He could check with all the neighbors, but the last thing he needed was for everybody to know his business. He could call the police, but would they even take a report? Maybe if he told them Clara was a danger to herself. She'd cut her wrists more than once, but she'd always botched the job. Timid people like that, he reckoned, they intended to botch the job.

He thought about talking to some young policeman, trying to explain how Clara was, trying to explain about the skinned rabbits, how they must have a predator in the neighborhood, and how the cop would act deliberately patient and condescending to this older guy who had just called in about his missing wife, who'd only been gone a few hours, probably on some impulsive shopping trip. Matt couldn't bear it.

She'd been a lovely girl when he met her—pretty and shy. She'd made him feel like he was about the greatest man in the world. Then she got nervous, and then she got old, and surely she was crazy now. Maybe if he were truly a good man he could handle that— he'd stick with her and make the best out of a sad situation. But people had to be realistic. Good men were few and far between.

Flashing red lights broke through the trees on the other side of the field. They made it look as if parts of that line of trees bordering the old canal were on fire. But then the wind shifted the branches a bit and he could see that he was mistaken. There were scattered fires on the interstate beyond. And many more lights and faint, but explosive, noises. People shouting maybe. Or cars being pried open like clamshells to get to the meat inside. The Jaws of Life, that's what they called them. But only if the people inside were still living. If not, then they were the Jaws of Death, weren't they?

The radio was right by the chair, so he could have turned it on. But he'd rather wait until Clara showed up and then they could learn together what terrible thing might have happened over on the highway. Matt supposed it was an unhealthy thing in people, how listening or watching together as the news told the details of some new disaster tended to bring couples and families together.

He sat and watched the red flashes and the burning and listened hard for the noises and the voices until it was dark enough for the automatic yard lights to come on. The gnawing in his belly was painful but he had no interest in eating, assuming eating was even the sort of remedy required.

He could see everything, except for that shadowy region down near the fence. He could see the rake where he'd left it, and the folded-up drop cloth. But there was no sign of that rabbit. Something had moved it, or maybe—and the idea made him queasy—it hadn't been completely dead. Skinned, but not dead. Crawling around suffering.

As Matt's eyes grew weary he found himself focusing on that area of shadow. It had always seemed odd that the longer you stared at a shadow the more likely you were to find other shadows swimming inside it. Something moved out of the edge.

In the border between dark and light a skinned body lay in the slickened grass. Bleeding heavily and this one much too large for a rabbit. Stripped to muscle and bone, it was an anatomical human figure made real. The skin over part of one breast remained. And when it reached its scarlet arms toward the house it called his name.

# Miracle Meadows
## Darren O. Godfrey

*This marks Darren Godfrey's third appearance in the* Borderlands *series, and his current Freudian offering examines the power of one's subconscious—and decides it can be supremely terrifying. The idea that conscious control is merely an illusion may be the scariest proposition with which we ever grapple.*

The truth hurts. But sometimes it's so slow to act, so slow to *sink in*, that when it does come forward, it is often hard to recognize it for the beast it is. It took seven blurry years for me to learn the truth surrounding my wife's death; *that* many, nearly to the day, and even then it had trouble solidifying in my mind.

It began with lost memories: one, the memory of an event, the other, the memory of a dream.

This was the event: Heather Rossier, my wife, sat on the corner of our bed with her back to me, just after putting baby Kenny down for his nap. She lifted up her blouse, pulled her soft auburn hair over one shoulder, turned her head, and asked, "How does it look, Michael?"

"About the same. Maybe a little purpler and scalier."

The mole at the center of her lightly freckled back had been there as long as I'd known her, and was once the size of a dime. It had grown roughly to that of a quarter and fattened to almost oyster thickness.

"Purpler?"

"Yeah, there's some purple to it. A little whitish around the scaly part, like a sunburn ready to peel."

"So peel it."

The idea had already occurred to me.

"No way, babe," I said, "That can't be good for it."

"I don't care what's good for it, Michael. Do it."

This is where memory gets prickly—not at all hazy, you understand, just uncomfortable. I tweezed the first flake away from that little knoll of tissue with my overlong fingernails, and the notion entered my head, *This could be releasing poisons into her body.* I envisioned a tiny spurt of black liquid on the inside of her flesh just as I yanked the scale from its outside.

I did it again: peeled and imagined.

So clear in my mind's eye: the inky ejaculations mixing with the surging red of her blood in a clockwise-shooting spiral, the new blend racing through her system, providing the cells of her flesh with both nourishment and . . . what?

Well, *cancer*, of course.

I'd like it to be known that Heather and I didn't know a damn thing about moles or melanoma at that time.

The recalled dream was the same basic setup: Heather with her back to me as I examine the mole. She says, "Peel it, baby," turning her head just enough to where I can see the corner of her smile; she's being seductive and that makes me happy. "Peel it *good*," she breathes, and I oblige. I try to get a better look at her face; I see long eyelashes drop slowly as she moans. I peel another layer and her head hangs lower, the ends of her lovely hair now brushing the top of one bare thigh. She begs for more. Never one to deny her any pleasure, I continue to peel at the purple-black lump, I peel and peel, until it is no longer a lump at all but a bleeding black hole, and she gasps, groans, shudders, and cries my name, her breath quickening, her hands on her lap, clenching, spreading, clenching . . .

I find myself suddenly without clothing, and my prick as hard as steel. The hole in her back opens up to me as I rise up onto my knees . . .

. . . and really sick things happen in dreams sometimes, don't they?

I'd somehow forgotten these things over the course of years, much in the same way, perhaps, that Kenny (no longer a baby, but not quite an adult) had forgotten how to be himself since his mother's departure from this world. But when reality, or rather when the *memories* of that reality came back, it felt like a one-two punch to the gut.

Punch number one landed two weeks ago, after I spotted the dime-sized mole on the back of my son's left leg, at about midcalf, while he was getting ready for school.

*Heather had a mole like that,* I thought. *And it grew, and I peeled it . . .*

Later that morning, I made a doctor appointment for Kenny.

Punch number two, the dreadful *dream* memory, came three days ago as I surfed cancer websites—*peel it, baby*—and saw black ciphers centered in flesh. It sickened me.

And excited me.

Kenny had claimed to understand what happened when Heather died (*"Mommy's body got bad stuff in it and it stopped working,"* he'd whispered as the ICU nurse turned off the flatlining heart monitor), but then, as the days, weeks, and months followed, he withdrew into himself more and more. He stopped talking. Stopped smiling, stopped laughing.

He is now thirteen and most days he's little more than a moving mannequin.

For my forty-third birthday, he "gave" me the laptop I'm currently tapping away on. In reality, though, it was purchased, wrapped, and delivered by my sister Barbara (always Kenny's fave aunt), but it had Kenny's name on the to/from tag.

What experience I'd had with these damned things stemmed mainly from work (environmental engineering) where I used the Word and Excel programs quite a lot, and accessed the World Wide Web very little. But as my fascination with cancer has grown, so has my willingness to learn to use this convenient yet maddening technology.

I understand hyperlinks, the highlighted text on web pages, there to be clicked upon and to whisk you to somewhere else. I understand, too, that these links normally have something to do with the page you're clicking *from*, and that the highlighted words, in some way, *tell* you where you'll go by clicking them.

Three days ago, on a melanoma-related website, I encountered a photograph of a mole identical to that of Heather's in its later stages. The flaky edges recalled the dream (*"Peel it, baby."*) and forcefully landed that second punch.

Near the bottom of the site's page, my watering eyes caught this:

" . . . while no such miracles can be expected in . . . "

I rolled the cursor over to miracles (which was colored blue), where the thin arrow morphed into a white hand with a pointing finger. I checked the narrow space at the bottom of the window, the display where the hyperlink's address would take me should I chose to click it: www.miraclemeadows.com.

But I didn't click it. Not yet.

No "sense of foreboding" stayed my hand, no goose gallivanting over my grave, none of that silliness. It was simply that word.

*Miracle.*

We'd gone to a dermatologist, who excised the damn thing mere minutes after first laying eyes on it, and days later informed us that the tests on the scaly black blob proved it to be a Clark level 4 melanoma: very deadly. He also told us that, in all likelihood, the cancer would recur somewhere else in her body within five years—breasts and lungs being the most likely places. "Seeing as how," the grim medical man put it, "the lymphatic passages run up the back, over the shoulders, and down the front, and that damn malignancy was big enough and centralized enough to affect both sides."

Outside the doc's office, Heather said, "Miracles happen every day, Michael."

After she passed the five-year mark, the doctor, now grayer and grimmer, congratulated her on still being alive. Leaving the office, she butted my shoulder with hers and said, "There's my miracle, right?"

I said nothing.

She collapsed the night of December 24 of that same year, and all the next day I sat with her in the ICU, awaiting the celebrated "Christmas Miracle".

I sat with her the day after that awaiting the somewhat less celebrated "Day-*After*-Christmas Miracle".

She died at 4:59 p.m. on December 26 without ever saying another word.

There are no miracles.

I rose from the desk and paced the house. I do that a lot since Heather's death. Punching walls and doorjambs occupies a fair amount of my time as well. Not hard enough to make holes—or even dents, you understand—just enough to make sore, red knuckles. I like to think such restless actions ease my mind, but I know better.

Other than my footfalls and my duking it out with the walls, the house was quiet; I was on a self-imposed vacation and Kenny was at school.

My pacing took me back to the laptop, which was still online, still on "The Meaning of Melanoma". The blue miracle still hovered there.

I clicked it.

A rectangle filled with blackness nearly as large as the screen. The laptop informed me (again, in tiny words on the lower-left part of the window) that the site was *Loading*, then that it was *Done*. A black window, still. I recalled encountering a similar void where words should be, on a *film noir* message board I'd gone to during a lunch break. Roger, an associate from down the hall, had been there, looking over my shoulder.

*"Look, Mike,"* he'd said. *"It says here 'highlight to read spoilers'."*

*"Yeah, so what?"*

*"So highlight it."*

When I didn't move, he reached for the mouse and did it himself. I don't remember what the words were, but I do remember being impressed by the way they were revealed.

*"It's simple,"* he'd said, *"The color of the font they use is the same as its background. Highlighting changes the color and* ta-da, *you can read it."*

So now I highlighted the Miracle Meadows emptiness.

*What are the odds that you are the one?*
*Is your path to discovery meant to be run?*
*The wounds of love and war do bleed.*
*Name the method, the means, the way to proceed.*
*Everyone you know has a tag and a plan.*
*"Sees the truth, I do," claims the sailing man.*
*"Sewn into the fabric of the night.*
*"To begin in the black is to begin in the right."*
*Her fate is but a peeling, a flick of your wrist.*
*Imaginary outcomes are done with a twist.*
*Shrouds, at burial time, receive their fill.*
*Dahlia? Who grew wild, and fought with a will.*
*Elizabeth? The maiden we all wish we knew.*
*Abby? Who gnashed leaves, wet with dew.*
*Trina? Who decorated herself with bows.*
*Heather? The wraith bearing one black rose.*

I read it twice, my stomach muscles tightening each time I saw my wife's name. Some squirmy part of me also reacted at the line about the wounds of love and war bleeding.

I x-ed off the site, off the web, shut down the computer and returned to the TV, stopping only for a gullet-cleansing beer at the fridge.

I awoke later with the remains of a French-bread pizza on my lap, beer bottles at my feet, and *Murder, She Wrote* playing out on the TV. A hand fell on my shoulder.

Kenny.

His face was a pale blotch in my lager-warped vision, but not so much so that I didn't see the disappointment there.

"Hi, son. Did Mrs. Marshall bring you home?"

He nodded.

I straightened up and tried to smile innocently, as if decorating myself with crusty crumbs and drinking myself into an afternoon nap was still the normal Thursday thing for me. "She's not still here, is she?"

He did a combination headshake and shoulder shrug and turned away.

"Kenny, it's all right. Really. I just had a hankering for a few beers, that's all."

He turned. My vision had cleared some and I could see his expression had returned to its now-typical vacuousness.

"How's the leg?" I asked.

Somewhere under the faded denim of his right pant leg lay a bandage where the mole used to be (which, according to the doc—a new one, not Heather's—was benign and absolutely nothing at all to worry about).

No response from Kenny.

"Don't worry about it. You can go to your room now."

I returned to the computer the following morning, highlighted the strange doggerel. It hadn't changed, not in any way I could tell, but I believe that on my last visit I must not have rolled the cursor all the way down, as *there* lay additional wordage: a paragraph, separate from the stanza and of a different font.

*No choice but to start at the beginning, live your life. Laugh, cry, fuck, watch others die, and rapidly approach your own end. Given enough time, you will look back to your start. Now is that time. Look at the beginning.*

*Each. Separate. One.*

*Jeez, how many beginnings do we get?* I wondered.

Then it occurred to me the thing might be referring to other kinds of beginnings. The lines of verse glowed on the screen, turned lime green by the highlight I'd given it. "Each separate one," I said aloud, and there it was, there *they* were, the beginnings of each line.

*What. Is. The. Name. Everyone. Sees. Sewn. To. Her. Imaginary. Shrouds.*

I formed the words into a proper, if mystifying, query: *What is the name everyone sees sewn into her imaginary shrouds?*

Then: *Dahlia? Elizabeth? Abby? Trina? Heather?*

Apparently a multiple-choice question in which the reader is expected to either surmise or determine the name to go on someone's shrouds. It occurred to me that "shrouds" should be singular rather than plural, but then again none of this seemed very real. The whole site had a phony feel about it, a spurious *staged-just-for-me* feel. Who exactly is "her" referring to (one of the given names, perhaps, or is it the shroud manufacturer)?

With the entire page still highlighted, I then passed the cursor over the names.

The pointing finger appeared at every one of them, individually and emphatically, indicating a link.

Every one except Heather's.

I don't know why I should have felt cheated by that, but I did. The one name I wanted to investigate, and it, apparently, was just text.

I clicked Trina.

The image emerged: a photo of an obviously dead woman. The caption beneath: *Katrina "Trina" Johnson.*

Her head nearly severed, she had part of a mangled pickup truck on top of her. Blonde hair swam in the surrounding pool of blood—it must have been very long hair, as it seemed to go on and on, finally disappearing beneath the bulk of the truck. Her eyes were open. A bright-orange blur intruded upon the lower-right corner of the photo: a traffic cone, probably.

I studied this image for a while before clicking the Back arrow.

I clicked Abby.

Dead, too, she lay partially across a kitchen table, facedown in what appeared to be a bowl of breakfast cereal, her hair, very curly and very dark, splayed out around her head. The caption: *Abigail Finchley Olsen.*

Elizabeth: Not dead, at least not in this picture. It appeared to be a high school yearbook photo, black and white, dating somewhere around '62 or '63, judging by the hair and clothing styles. She smiled bravely into the camera lens, but it was obvious she wished it were pointed somewhere else. I was fairly certain that, wherever this girl was, she was no longer among the living. No caption here; I had to take the site's word for it that this was someone named Elizabeth.

Dahlia: Rather than a picture, a photocopied image of a death certificate. From it I was able to put together a mental image of a forty-six-year-old housewife who had succumbed to asphyxiation while climbing a tree. Death by misadventure: she'd somehow fallen and wedged her neck into a fork. It was not explained what she was doing up there to start with. Born in New York, she'd died in Indianapolis, Indiana. The document stated that she'd been cremated there as well.

If connections existed between these women and my Heather, I didn't see them, other than their all being dead or presumed dead, of course. I also had no way of knowing whether the Miracle Meadows Heather was *my* Heather, or what the hell Miracle Meadows had to do with this bunch of dead women, or what the hell the stupid poem meant (despite having busted its first-word code), or what the hell I was worrying about it for in the first place.

The answer to that last was simple enough, though, and has already been stated: I am a glutton for punishment.

I'd Sherlock-Holmesed this thing to the point of frustration. I yearned for a little satisfaction. I rolled the cursor through the blank spaces of the web page, through the Northwest Passage above the lame poetry, down and around to the Gulf between said poetry and the prose paragraph, watching the arrow the whole time. As I traversed the Channel beneath the paragraph, it happened: the pointing digit appeared again. Directly beneath the word *separate* was a hidden hyperlink. I clicked it.

*Welcome to the Miracle Meadows Message Board.*

*I am Mrs. Meadows, your hostess on this incredible journey. I advise you now that this board contains no search engines, calendars, member lists, or profiles. There will be no contests here, no games. There is a simple registration process requiring your name, email address (for verification purposes only), birthdate, and birthplace. There are two forums.*

*Begin at the beginning.*
*REGISTER*

Not one of the more congenial boards I've visited (though I haven't seen many) and a bit less than revealing as to what the hell Miracle Meadows was all about.

I clicked the Registration button, made entries into the spaces provided (none of which were truthful—was this woman crazy, thinking I'd let her know all that?) and clicked the Proceed button. After about five seconds, this popped up:

*INCORRECT ENTRIES, PLEASE REENTER*

I entered new and equally bogus info, and received the same message. With my third attempt, I entered my name and email address, Kenny's birthdate, and Heather's birthplace.

*THANK YOU*
*PROCEED*
*WHAT YOU DID / WHAT YOU WANT TO DO*

It never occurred to me until later that the verification process (for which the email addy was supposedly needed) never happened.

I clicked WHAT YOU DID. Deep-sea-blue background with white letters of apparently only one topic:

*WHAT MR. ROSSIER DID*

I clicked it.

*Author: Mrs. Meadows*
*Subject: WHAT DID YOU DO?*
*Comment: Do tell!*

A conversation ensued. It happened fairly rapidly (the Meadows woman must have been on-site at that moment as well), though there were several long pauses between some of the replies, as much as ten minutes, and mere seconds on others. It involved a lot of page renewing.

For the purpose of clarity and cadence, I will present the pertinent sections here in dialogue form.

Me: *I've done a lot of things. What do you mean, specifically?*

Mrs. M.: *What did you do that brought you here? What miracle did you perform?*

Me: *There are no miracles, lady. Trust me.*

Mrs. M.: *I do trust you. However, you are mistaken on the subject of miracles. Had you not performed one, you wouldn't be here now.*

Me: *Lady, I once sat in a hospital room with the woman I'd planned to spend the rest of my life with* expecting *a miracle to happen, okay? I suppose I was even trying to* make *a miracle happen by saying "I believe, I believe", over and over. It didn't work. It was Christmas, and if there was a more appropriate time for her to open her eyes, sit up, and be perfectly all right, that was it. There are no miracles.*

Mrs. M.: *Heather was your wife?*

Me: *Yes.*

Mrs. M.: *Perhaps you didn't really want it to happen.*

Me: *Didn't want* what *to happen? Didn't want my wife to* live*? Are you serious, lady?*

Mrs. M.: *Mr. Rossier, I'm sure your conscious mind wanted her to live. I'm suggesting there may have been a deeper urge to see what life would be like if she were gone.*

Me: *Fuck off, lady. I'm outta here.*

Mrs. M.: *I know, Mr. Rossier, that you have been back twice in the last half hour. Talk to me.*

Me: *I loved my wife. Don't even* suggest *otherwise.*

Mrs. M.: *No more suggestions. I do want to get to the miracle, though—the one that* did *happen. It arose some time before Heather's death. It had to do with a mole.*

Me: *A mole is what started it all. No miracle in melanoma.*

Mrs. M.: *Oh, but there was in your wife's case, right? In* your *case. You* are *the one who started it, correct?*

Me: *I don't know what you mean.*

Mrs. M.: *Yes, you do. You released the poison into her system. You imagined it, and then you did it.*

Me: *No.*

Mrs. M.: *Without imagination, there is nothing. Yours, I suspect, is very powerful, though untamed. Uncultivated. But very much* something.

Me: *No.*

Mrs. M.: *I can help you, Mr. Rossier. I can help you get control.*

The stuff that ran through my head was what you might very well expect: How does she know? How *could* she know? Is she right? Did I actually initiate the cancer in my wife simply by imagining it?

A low-grade tingle moved down the back of my neck and settled between my shoulder blades. I came very close to leaving the board then, but again, the glutton prevailed.

Me: *Who are Dahlia, Elizabeth, Abby, Trina?*

Mrs. M.: *Like your wife, they were objects of man-made miracles. Targets. Receivers.*

Me: *They're all dead?*

Mrs. M.: *Yes.*

Me: *Why?*

Mrs. M.: *No mental image can be more readily, and powerfully, called up in one's mind than the death of a loved one. Those five women were loved. Their miracle makers, their senders, were very powerful. Like you, or rather including you.*

Me: *Tell me about them.*

This was the longest stretch of inactivity on her side. I wondered whether she'd gotten offline or was merely debating whether or not I had the need to know. I felt a headache coming on, and thought perhaps I should back off myself.

Mrs. M.: *Dahlia suffered from one mental illness or another, supposedly, but her condition wasn't serious enough to have her institutionalized. She was on medication, but I couldn't tell you what it was. She had a son. Alberto. He said some things a son shouldn't say to his mother. Dahlia chased him outside, and, because she had neglected her mellowing medication that morning, she continued to chase him even when he climbed a tree. She was very persistent, very intent on seeing him punished. Alberto was no weakling, either. He climbed up to where the branches were thinner and swayed with the wind as well as his weight. When he saw his mother wasn't going to quit, he thought, "I wonder what would happen if . . . "*

Me: *That was it?*

Mrs. M.: *Guess the rest.*

Me: *He wished her dead?*

Mrs. M.: *He pictured his mother slipping, her grip faltering, her body twisting, then becoming wedged into a thick fork about a quarter of the way up the tree. Then it just happened.*

Me: *And Elizabeth?*

Mrs. M.: *Elizabeth was the Woman Who Knew Too Much. Family secrets. Someone who became aware that she was overly informed decided it sure would be nice if she weren't around anymore, someone who had significant power. Pity, really, because Elizabeth had a fair amount of power herself, but was never made aware of it.*

Me: *Who was the someone?*

Mrs. M.: *Her grandfather.*

Me: *Did he kill her?*

Mrs. M.: *Not in the traditional sense. He wanted her gone and she was just gone.*

Me: *How do you know she's dead?*

Mrs. M.: *I know. That's all.*

Me: *And Abby?*

Mrs. M.: *She had a sister who wondered what it would be like if the cornflakes in Miss High and Mighty Abigail's breakfast bowl were hemlock, and while the hemlock leaves alone might not have proved fatal, her sister's* belief *that they were did the trick.*

Me: *Trina?*

Mrs. M.: *Katrina Johnson had a jealous boyfriend. Very prosaic, alas. He imagined her vehicle veering off an overpass, hurtling over the side. He was in the car behind her.*

*And I believe you are familiar with the story of Heather Rossier, Michael.*

Me: *You think I killed her with a thought.*

Mrs. M.: *Don't you?*

Me: *Are you telling me she wouldn't have died anyway, that the cancer would not have spread?*

Mrs. M.: *No. I trust she would have been taken eventually. You saw to it, though, that it would happen sooner rather than later.*

Me: *Why just these five cases? There must be a lot more, what with so many sharp imaginers around.*

Mrs. M.: *Of course there are more, Mr. Rossier, countless throughout history. These are just the ones who fall under my purview at the moment.*

Me: *Okay. Who are you?*

Mrs. M.: *I am Mrs. Meadows, Mother of five.*

Me: *How do you know all this, the circumstances of my wife and her death?*

Mrs. M.: *You've not even made the leap to believing in your own power. How can you expect to believe in mine?*

Me: *It doesn't matter what I'll believe. Tell me. Otherwise, this is over, and that is a promise.*

Another long pause. Then:

Mrs. M.: *I am a practitioner of the black arts, Mr. Rossier, using many varied types of arcane magic in an effort to help people. Years ago, I experimented with allowing certain individuals to really "see" themselves for the first time, thereby enabling them to admit to certain fatalistic traits. I did this by showing them a sort of reduced reflection of themselves. I resurrected my five children, tethering them to a temporary life with ribbon the color of midnight, and sent them to their targets with a kind of script in their heads to guide them.*

Me: *And then?*

Mrs. M.: *They performed said missions. They were returned to a restful state by the severing of their ties.*

Me: *How did your children die initially?*

Mrs. M.: *That information has no bearing on what we are doing here, so you have no need to know it.*

Me: *Did you kill them?*

Mrs. M.: *No.*

Me: *Who were these individuals, how did you find them, and how were you made aware of their "traits"?*

Mrs. M.: *Their names are unimportant here. I learned of their ways by spying on them, of course, them and many others. Those were just the five I thought I could help.*

Me: *And it was only five because that's how many dead children you happened to have lying around.*

Mrs. M.: *Is that a question?*

Me: *This is: How did you spy on them? How did you spy on me?*

Mrs. M.: *I have what some refer to as a "third eye". I can send it out virtually anywhere I want, even through electrical wiring. It searches. It watches.*

Me: *Right. Bullshit, of course. But if it were so, why me?*

Mrs. M.: *I sensed—or "saw", if you will—great power coming from your direction.*

Me: *Sure. So tell me about my vast critical-mas power.*

Mrs. M.: *The power is not so much a radiation as it is a magnet. A great PULLING IN.*

Me: *You mean it sucks.*

Mrs. M.: *Yes, after a fashion. Imagine this: You're a poor man living in a ramshackle house, you need money desperately, and, hey, you might as well shoot for the stars and hope for ten million dollars. Your imagination grasps the image of someone you know, or at least whose face you know, who has such a fortune. Donald Trump, for instance. The chances of him deciding, on his own, to send you ten mil right out of the blue are so miniscule that they don't even show up on the probability radar, right? So, you picture Trump stepping into a huge library of telephone books. He locates the one for your city, opens it at random, closes his eyes, and stabs his manicured finger down on the open page. On your name. He draws up a certified check for ten million dollars and mails it to you.* Voila!

Me: *Right.*

Mrs. M.: *Again, the likelihood of such an occurrence is so incredibly small as to be nonexistent. But. The power. That awesome magnet can actually pull the likelihood of it up, up past the realm of the possible, the probable, and into the It-Is-Happening-As-We-Speak.*

Me: *That would be a lot of suckage. It's also a load of horseshit, five miles high.*

Mrs. M.: *Then try it.*

At ten thirty yesterday morning an overnight FedEx arrived from Donald Trump. Rather than a certified check (No way was I going to do exactly what Mrs. Meadows suggested—and wouldn't I just show her!), it contained four large glossy photos. The first, of his first ex-wife, Ivana; the second, Rosie O'Donnell; the third, Barack Obama; and the last, news anchor Megyn Kelly. Each face in each photo was embellished with a nicely scrawled Snidely Whiplash moustache.

Mrs. M.: *It's time for you to wrap up what you've done and move on to what you're going to do.*

Me: *I'm not going to do anything. Tell me about the shrouds.*

Mrs. M.: *Fine. As it's time for wrapping up, that seems apropos. You put your wife in a shroud with your imagination, your dark miracle. The other kind of miracle—the kind you expected that Christmas Day—is all about wellness, happiness, and/or prosperity. Dark miracles are about shrouds. Death. And while that seems pretty bleak, a certain degree of wellness, happiness, and/or prosperity can spring from them as well. Even a dark miracle is, after all, a wish come true.*

*Let's address the lines: "What are the odds that you are the one?" I can't be wrong, Mr. Rossier, can I? Are you, in the case of Heather's mole, the one? We control freaks often get so tunneled in our vision, don't we?*

*"Is your path to discovery meant to be run?"* Of course. To remain ignorant is to deny your self-entire.

*"The wounds of love and war do bleed."* Obviously, you know that.

*"Name a method, a means, a way to proceed."* This you will do in the next phase.

*"Everyone you know has a tag and a plan."* A tag is a name you go by, or that I go by, or *those closest to you. And we all have plans, whether we realize it or not.*

*"'Sees the truth, I do,' says the sailing man."* The sailing man was my husband, a great man, a great teacher in the ways of practical magic.

*"Sewn into the fabric of the night."* That fabric, and the ties that bind it, contain the lessons taught to me, some of which I will instruct you in, by way of the apparatus you are currently using. Your computer.

*"To begin in the black is to begin in the right."* Further instruction from the late Mr. Meadows.

*"Her fate is but a peeling, a flick of your wrist."* You know that.

*"Imaginary outcomes are done with a twist."* Ditto.

*"Shrouds, at burial time, receive their fill."* My husband filled his, my children filled theirs, your wife filled hers, and you know the basic stories behind the other women here. Each of them had a sender. YOU are the fifth and final case, and after we tend to you and your future, I can go and fill my shroud.

Me: *My future is mine to tend to alone, woman. Go and fill your shroud.*

I shut down the computer at about noon yesterday. I spent the rest of the daylight convincing myself that none of it happened, and a good portion of the night realizing it had. Questions and comments popped in my head like kernels of popcorn, but I resisted the urge to return to the computer, not so much because I'd given up the gluttony. No, *this* was punishment, a *new* punishment, a self-torture that sang to me in sweeter and more painful tones, more painful than punching walls.

Sunday. This morning. I began the day's pacing, and at some point, I noticed that Mr. Trump's absurd gifts were not on the kitchen counter where I'd left them, nor were they anywhere along the usual traffic routes in the house. I peeked into my bedroom, and then into Kenny's. He slept, snoring lightly. The eye-catching angles of blue, orange, and white of the FedEx envelope, balanced on a stack of compact discs, caught not only my eye but also my breath.

Kenny slept on.

I crossed the room, snatched the thing up. Looked inside.

Empty.

When the deliveryman handed the envelope over to me the day before, I'd given the label only a cursory glance. Now I brought it up nearly to my nose and read it.

*Mr. Kenneth Rossier*

Another memory: A bright and beautiful Saturday with little puffballs of clouds decorating a deep-blue sky . . . the kind of day Heather always said was made for bike rides and backyard sex. Baby Kenny sequestered in the playpen, Mommy and Daddy rolling around on (and within) a red-checked blanket, laughing and moaning in turns . . . and, hey, suddenly there is Baby Kenny, pacifier dangling from one chubby hand, a clump of lawn clenched in the other, inexplicably free of his baby jail and standing over Mommy and Daddy, sprinkling them with brown earth and green grass . . . and he laughs.

Kenny?

I went to my desk and found my scratch-paper scribblings (*What Is the Name Everyone Sees Sewn to Her Imaginary Shrouds*) and checked the beginnings, and the beginnings of each of *those* beginnings. Letter by letter.

W-I-T-N-E-S-S T-H-I-S . . .

And then the women's names: Dahlia, Elizabeth, Abby, Trina, and Heather.

D-E-A-T-H . . .

*What are the odds that you are the one?*

Mrs. M.: *You* do *have a power, Mr. Rossier, but it is small compared to that of your son. I was wrong—tunnel vision even in the third eye. I'm truly sorry.*

Me: *But why would he do what he did?*

Mrs. M.: *Imagination. That's all it is. As a baby, he picked up what you sent out, the images and the results, and then he pulled it all into reality. Quite without malice, I'm sure. Look at it as if he were the camera and the film, while you were the lens. Or as if he were the loaded cartridge, and you were the gunsights.*

Me: *Could Kenny wish Heather back to life?*

Mrs. M.: *No. Far too late for that.*

Me: *But why the stupid Trump FedEx?*

Mrs. M.: *Again, he got it from you, just as he did the poisonous mole image.*

As I said at the beginning of this thing, the truth hurts. And sometimes its *sinking in* is slow, caustic. The time between comprehension (staring idiotically at the FedEx label) and the plea for answers (from Mrs. Meadows), I freaked.

I thought of suffocating Kenny with a pillow, then thought, *No, stabbing would be better*, and I even ran to the kitchen for the knife. I thought of torching the house with both of us in it. I thought . . . well, I thought of a lot of things, but that isn't really thinking. It's reacting.

So I started *actually* thinking. That led me back to the laptop, and after communicating with Mrs. Meadows, I thought some more. That led to what I've written here.

My continued thinking has led me to this: I—or rather *we*—cannot bring Heather back, cannot, in fact do a whole hell of a lot about the past. But, together, Kenny and I can do a considerable amount about the future.

Sure, Mrs. Meadows, I could be a lens. I could be gunsights. With a little training, I could also be a scalpel. Or better yet, an *eraser*.

You were right: we all have plans.

And there *are* miracles.

*Watch out, cancer, you life-sucking fucker, a new day is dawning!*

Speaking of which, Kenny's up now. I hear his door opening.

I wonder what he'll think of my pla—

# Lockjaw
## *David Annandale*

*The following story held us because of the compelling voice of the narrator and the gradual rise in tension and expectation of where things could eventually lead. New writer Annandale weaves his story together with the heavy threads of obsession, faith, delusion, and dread . . . and we have a feeling you will not soon be forgetting this one.*

Gil Wainwright winced. *How could this hurt?* he wondered. Rough passes of charcoal on paper, a cat's cradle of jagged smudges. Dirt and wood pulp, nothing real, a representation more suggested than actual, so how could it hurt? Still facing the easel, he shifted his gaze away from the sketch, focused on the light switch on the wall. "What . . . " he began. He paused, put care into the question, tried again, "Where do you see this going?" he asked his wife.

"I'm going to paint it," Judy said. "Black and white. Some airbrush. Not quite photo-realistic, but . . . " Her voice, stick brittle, faded with her confidence. "I have some X-rays I'm going to work from," she said in a tiny whisper.

Gil looked at the sketch again, his eye movement involuntary. A jaw yawned at him, stretched beyond wide, a jaw of bone and teeth and nothing else, the gape taking up the entire height of the paper. Though Judy's charcoal lines barely hinted at the connection between upper and lower sets of teeth, Gil had the sense of a steel spring poised at the last edge of tension before snap-down return. The sense of the teeth was already strong enough for him to feel atavistic twitches in his gut. The jaw was not human. It wasn't animal. It was, somehow, the concept of teeth given form. Gil didn't like the idea of photo-realism adding weight to that form.

Judy said something else, her voice so faint this time that he couldn't catch it. He turned around to face her, and now he felt a different sort of pain. "What was that?" he asked.

"I thought maybe a study. A series." Her eyes, shadowed in the deep hollows of fatigue, were staring at the floor.

*Now, Gil, what do you say? God is testing you here, seeing just what your mettle is.* And what was the purpose of the test? Was it to humble him? To make him question how good a shepherd he was? How could he minister to his flock at the church if he could not properly tend to his own home? He pushed the questions away. They weren't his to ask. The test was only his to pass or not. The reasons would become clear later, or they would not.

(Thy will be done.)

*That's nice, Gil, but what do you say? Judy's waiting for something. Just what do you make of her project?*

(It frightens me.)

*How do you react?*

(Gently.)

"It strikes me as . . . well, it's quite dark."

Judy nodded.

"Is that what you want?"

Judy nodded.

"I guess . . . " fragile dancing, eggshells to the left of him, land mines to the right, " . . . the series doesn't seem . . . inspirational. Exactly." He held his breath, worried he'd pushed too hard. What really worried him was not that the paintings wouldn't be inspirational. What gnawed was wondering what the source of the inspiration was. Wondering just who was whispering to his wife's heart.

And Judy nodded again. "These days, I'm . . . I'm finding it very hard to raise my eyes."

"Heavenwards?"

That nod. And her eyes floor locked.

"You shouldn't be afraid to try. God is smiling on—"

"I just feel so dull," Judy interrupted.

"The medication?" The question was stupid. He knew the answer. He'd seen the film come down over her eyes when the regime started. "It's just for a little while," he tried to comfort. "Only until you're better." *Only until you're better.* Even he was disgusted by the platitude, fed by the doctors to him, fed by him to Judy. The words were an indefinite prison sentence dressed up as comforting vagueness. But he had to cling to them as if they were a biblical promise. They were the hope that he would get his wife back. The wife whose creative energy, even when he didn't entirely approve of it, pushed them both to new levels. The wife whose questing was her own.

Judy made a gesture with her left hand, part wave, part shrug, the half-formed language of frustration and despair. They hadn't turned the lights on in the studio, and in the descending gray of dusk, Judy made Gil think of a phantom, fading into the evening limbo of pain. "The pills won't let me work."

Gil noticed the agency she granted the pills. Medication in the active voice, drugs with their own agenda. Should he start worrying about that too? "You mustn't stop taking—" he began.

Judy shook her head, a sharp jerk of terror. "No. No, of course not," she said, and Gil felt stupid for having opened his mouth. Her fear of the consequences of going off the medication was worse than his. Much worse. The fear was why she had the prescription in the first place. Now she looked at Gil and he saw the film lift from her eyes for a moment. He saw urgency. Need. Clarity. "I can do this series," she said. "It's in me, and it wants out. I need to do this."

"You think it will help?" He wasn't encouraged by any of this.

"I don't think I have a choice."

He wanted to ask her what she meant by that. He wanted her to explain herself. But even more than that, he wanted to avoid the answers she might give, answers that would force him to take a stand as a Christian and a minister, and he simply did not have the courage for that right now. He did not want a confrontation. He did not want to do more harm than good. So he took the better part of valor. "All right," he said. He reached out and gave her shoulder a gentle squeeze. "Work it out. Do what you think is best." He smiled encouragement.

She didn't smile back. She looked past him to the easel, her eyes glittering with uncertainty, a woman about to confront an enemy. Maybe she was right, Gil thought, maybe the paintings would be a form of catharsis, a purge. Maybe she was on her way back to health, and before long she would be channeling her creativity back toward the ministry, back toward paintings that would gather, inspire, lift up. Gil had always felt uncomfortable with art. It was too undisciplined, too unpredictable, too subject to temptation. Some of Judy's work years ago had struck him as worrisome. Especially when she had worked briefly with nudes. He had done what he could to shift her interest toward the church, and that had seemed to work. Her murals were Sunday school gold mines, and her work with the children, getting them to express the truth of their lessons, was genius. Maybe she would be able to return to those efforts.

Maybe. Maybe, maybe, maybe.

In the next room, Lisa began to cry. Judy tensed, eyes widening with strain. Gil squeezed her shoulder again: *Calm down. It's all right.* "I'll look after Lisa," he said. "You get to work in here."

His wife—dry, dry sticks in the second before the snap. But she didn't snap. He felt her muscles turn to taught cables, and then a slight release. "Thank you," she said.

One more squeeze, and Gil left to take care of their daughter.

Lisa's diaper was wet, but she stopped crying almost as soon as Gil lifted her. He carried her into the bathroom to change her, and her fingers curled around the lobe of his ear, the uncoordinated touch of a month-old infant's absolute trust. When Gil felt the brush of her tiny hand, the bottom dropped out of his stomach, and his knees almost buckled with love. As he cleaned her up, he looked down at her, into her eyes that looked back at him with an openness so beautiful his throat tightened, and he had no thought of the taut jaws on Judy's easel. All he could think of was wonders and miracles. All he could formulate was thanks.

He hadn't wanted children. He'd resisted Judy's arguments for the first two years of their marriage. At first, he'd said that they simply couldn't contemplate having a family until they had at least a semblance of financial stability. He'd believed his own line too. He'd thought his resistance would melt away once the money worries weren't as severe. He'd thought he *did* want children, *Just Not Right Now.* But then their situation had improved, and he'd still said no. That was when he'd realized what the problem really was: he was afraid. He was afraid of the vulnerability a baby would bring into his life. More than that, he was afraid of the sort of father he would be. He was worried he would be tested and found wanting.

He had given in, though. Judy was in her midthirties. *Tempus fugit.* But his anxiety had grown, a coiling snake, until Lisa's birth. And the instant he'd looked into her eyes— that was the instant he realized he'd been a first-class, foot-stomping idiot. His fear had evaporated.

And transferred, it now seemed, into Judy. Postpartum psychosis—so the doctors had named her terror, as if in the naming they could tame it. Judy's descent into the dark had been precipitous, allowing her not even an hour to enjoy her daughter. The fear had consumed her with its black fire. She was convinced she was an unfit mother. She was convinced she was going to hurt Lisa. Her days turned into jittery icescapes as she tiptoed around her child, often too terrified to go near. She rarely touched Lisa. Her nights were eyes-wide cavalcades of pain, worst-case fantasies building and feeding each other. Judy tortured herself with visions of herself dropping Lisa, shaking Lisa, strangling her, bashing her, stabbing her, cooking her . . .

That was the point Gil had taken her back to the hospital. That was the cue for the intervention. Enter medication, stage right. Judy slept now. Sometimes. The therapy didn't seem to be making many inroads. Gil didn't want to criticize, though. Faith didn't seem to be helping much, either.

He finished getting Lisa into her fresh diaper. He cradled his baby back to bed, watched her nestle into sleep, then went to his study to sort out his thoughts for the next day's service.

Gil was familiar with two types of preaching. Some ministers wrote every word of their sermons, then either read from the notes or (and this was rare) committed the result to memory. Gil knew some very fine writers, and had heard some sermons done in this fashion that had left him weeping. They were the exception, though.

The other method, the one he used, meant a deliberate avoidance of notes. He would sort out the topic for his sermon the day before, then pray on it before going to sleep. Come the moment, he would approach the pulpit and let fly. Improvisation? No—inspiration. He simply opened himself up to God and let the words come as they would. And they always did.

He was good in the pulpit. He knew that. Pride was a sin, but false modesty could be as well. A man had to know how best he could serve his God. When Gil spoke, he felt thunder and fire, ecstasy and rain. When he spoke, he saw the Spirit in the faces of his congregation. When he spoke, he did God's work and he did it well. He was one of those chosen to spread the Baptist ministry, and he accepted the role with thanks.

He and Judy had moved around a lot, starting one seed church after another. Seed churches founded on the strength of a charismatic minister often folded once the minster moved on, but his special gift, his blessing, the thing that, apart from Lisa, had him giving the most heartfelt thanks, was that the churches he seeded took root. He moved on and they flourished. And now he was digging furrows into the earth again.

The Church of the Infinite Spring was a converted restaurant, a failed steakhouse by the side of the highway. The hall was small, the acoustics terrible, but it served, it served. Gil and Judy had been here six months now, and the church was full for every service. The congregation was growing, and with it, the demands on Gil's time. There were many senior citizens in the neighborhood, and Gil was often out till well after dark on his rounds, visiting, tending, giving the comfort that had fled from his own home. The week Judy began to paint again, the flu arrived in town, and Gil was kept running from one elderly invalid to another.

On Tuesday, he was out until after eleven. That was late. He didn't like leaving Judy alone that long. Not because he was worried she might do something to Lisa. The whole thrust of her illness was precisely *her* terror that she would. He just didn't like leaving Judy to the stress of her fears longer than he had to, a stress that got worse the more she had to look after Lisa on her own.

The house was quiet when he stepped in. He hung his jacket up and stood still, listening. The silence thickened, waiting for him. "Hello?" he called, needing a response, even if it was the sound of a woken Lisa crying.

"Up here." Judy's voice, barely audible, from the studio. There was a quaver in her tone, triggered by something that was punching through the drugs. The quaver made Gil run up the stairs, but he paused just long enough to quell that senseless, irrational worry and peek in at Lisa. She was in her crib, sleeping. Cursing his lack of trust, his lapse into Judy's fantasy, Gil trotted the rest of the way to the studio.

The room was dark except for light that spilled from the hallway and washed over the easel. Judy was standing in front of the painting. She was hugging herself and swinging her torso in tight little arcs from left to right. "Look," she whispered. "Look. Look."

Gil looked. No sketch this, but a complete work. The jaw midway to being closed. The effect of frozen speed and strength was startling. The teeth were thinner than in the original sketch and seemed longer. The work was a palette of gray, giving the teeth a sheen that was both grave-clay and iron. Gil opened his mouth, but his throat closed over anything he might have said.

Judy turned to face him. Her eyes were sinking deeper into her skull. Her hair was sweat-plastered against her head. "Something's coming," she said, and her terror was undimmed by medication.

Gil reached out to take her hand. It was cold, clammy—dead fish. "What is coming?"

Judy shuddered, glanced over her shoulder at the painting. "I don't know. *Something.* It's going to hurt Lisa."

*Lord, I really, truly, desperately need your strength now.* He pulled Judy into his arms, kissed the top of her head, and felt hopelessly out of his depth. She was transferring her distrust of herself on to an outside force now, that much was clear. What did that mean, though? Was this good? Was this an improvement? He didn't think so. "Do you mean someone?" he asked.

"No. Some *thing.*"

"Are you talking about evil, Judy?"

A long pause. She nodded, then shook her head against his chest. She said something so quietly he tried to convince himself he had misheard. But he hadn't. She said, "The truth."

"What?"

"The coming truth." Her voice was flat, detached, as if it were not she who was speaking.

"Listen to yourself," he said. He tried to ignore the chill that spread from his heart and raced through his limbs. "You're not making sense. And evil can't simply come and hurt us. It doesn't work that way. Satan acts only through us, and only if we let him. All we have to do to keep him out is turn to Christ. But you know this."

"I *don't* know."

"Yes, you do." It was very important that she agree with him. He needed to hear one word from her, and that word was *yes.*

She shook her head again. "This is something else."

"What do you mean, 'something else'? Not one of Satan's works?"

"No."

"Whose, then?"

No answer, but she pulled away from his embrace and looked at him with eyes growing wide before some awful revelation.

"Honey," Gil tried, "God would not permit—"

"He can't stop it." The flat voice. The dead voice. The eyes staring at the infinite and the monstrous. The words of relentless blasphemy. "It doesn't care. It's coming for him too."

Judy's deathly conviction sucked him in. It broke down his defenses, and the question slipped out before he could check it, "What is?"

"The Reptile."

Later, lying in bed, Judy sleeping, actually *sleeping*, beside him, Gil stared at the ceiling, his own chances for sleep ashes and dust. *Lord*, he thought, *Lord, please hear me. Please tell me what to do. Please.* The night took his prayers into its silence, into its vastness.

When dawn came, it was at night's grudging sufferance, and Gil had received no answer. Instead, he felt the tickling claws of doubt. What if Judy was right? Not about the approach of supernatural evil. (No?) No. What if that belief opened the wrong door? What if she really *did* harm Lisa?

*No,* he thought. *No, to it all. No, no, no, no, no.*

(But what if . . . )

On Wednesday he asked Judy to stop painting the teeth.

"That won't make a difference," she said. "It's still coming."

"I think you'll be pleasantly surprised by the difference moving on will make."

"You didn't hear me."

"Yes, I did. I really think this is for the best."

"I don't know if I can."

"Please try."

She stared at the floor and chewed at a nail.

On Thursday, she was very quiet, but she made no mention of the studio, and Gil saw none of the usual evidence of painting going on. "How do you feel?" he asked her as they were getting ready for bed. She looked at him for a long time without answering. Her eyes were dark tunnels to the core of fear. Then she went to look in on Lisa. And Gil, hating himself, but obeying an even greater worry, went too and watched very closely, very carefully, as his wife touched his daughter.

There was an evening service Friday. Gil went through the day with a clenched fist in his gut. He would have skipped the service if he could. But there was no one else. Not yet. Another year maybe, when the roots of the church were strong and there was another minister in the wings. But now, it was him or no one. So he fulfilled his responsibilities to God, trusting (no, hoping) that God would fulfill his responsibilities to Gil's family.

Full dark and rain when he reached home. Rain that fell with nail-gun force, huge drops drumming the pavement with vicious intent. Gil pulled the workhorse Matrix into the driveway behind Judy's aging, short-haul-only Civic, and turned the ignition off. The rain drummed steel claws on the roof of the car. He would be soaked in the time it took to run from the car to the front steps. He peered through the curtains of water. He could barely see the house. He decided to wait, just a minute. He didn't want to run that gauntlet.

Then he realized why the house was invisible. There were no lights on. Fumbling keys out of his pocket, he shot out of the car. He slipped on the lawn that was turning to mud, almost fell. Then he was at the door, unlocking the door, through the door, and calling, "Judy?"

No answer. The staccato of the rain and the silence of the house rubbed against each other, grinning. Gil felt a twist in his gut, a twist that told him he'd lost the most important race of his life, a twist that told him he was about to learn new things.

He flicked the hall light switch. Nothing happened. But now he saw a faint glow leaking down from upstairs. He tore up the steps, a moan building in his throat, ran for all he was worth to Lisa's room, knowing what he would find.

What he saw, when his eyes adjusted to the dark, stopped him cold. Lisa was in her crib, bundled in her pink sleeper. He watched her, saw her breathe. He stood and watched for three more breaths, three more normal, sleeping-baby breaths. Nothing wrong. His unborn moan tried to become the hysterical laughter of relief. He stifled the noise and tiptoed back out of the room. He stood for a moment, catching breath, gathering thoughts, calming down.

There were still things wrong, though. None of the light switches were working. Had Judy flipped the circuit breaker? If so, why? Dim light from her studio wavered, beckoning. He followed.

A dozen storm candles were clustered and flickering in the center of the floor. The blinds were drawn over the windows. Along the periphery of the room was Judy's teeth series, complete now, finished in secret. His eye followed the progression, moving from the first canvas with the gaping mouth, tracing the stop-motion coming together of the teeth. Each painting saw the teeth lengthen and narrow as they approached each other. The photo-realistic gray developed a harsher and harsher sheen. Gil turned on his heel, following the motion, caught by the flip-it book of pain. The teeth intertwined in the last painting, and now they were steel, now they were daggers, now there was nothing to them but pure razor edge and pure stiletto smile. And Judy sat in the far corner of the room, rocking.

"Nuh . . . nuh . . . nuh . . . " she said.

"Judy?" Gil whispered and walked toward her. Slowly.

"Nuh . . . nuh . . . nuh . . . " Rocking. Now Gil saw glints of metal on the floor in front of Judy. She had taken all the knives from the kitchen, laid them out with points interlocking and kissing. They mimicked the slicing smile of the last picture. The overlap of the blades was a bit more pronounced, jaws slowly sinking into satisfying meat. And still there was the smile.

Judy rocking. The "nuh . . . nuh . . . nuh . . . " becoming louder, more urgent. Her arms uncrossed, and her hands, jerking with each "nuh", reached step by step for the knives, for the chef's knife, its eight-inch blade winking brightest in the candlelight. She grasped the haft. A pause then. She stopped rocking.

Gil held his breath.

"Coming," Judy whispered. "Nuh . . . nuh . . . nuh, nuh, nuh, nuh-nuh-nuh-nuh."

Gil backed up. He thought he saw a violation of God's law. He thought he saw shadows gather in Judy's corner, shadows coming to swallow the candle glow.

Judy whirled around to face him. "Nuh-nuh-nuhnuhnuhnuhnuh-*NOOOOOWWWWWWW!*"

Gil fled the howl, the shadows, the blades, his wife. Most of all, he fled what he saw in her eyes, but would not acknowledge. He barreled into Lisa's room and scooped her out of the crib. Clutching his baby, the hell-deep scream of his wife at his back, he clattered down the stairs. Four steps from the bottom, his right foot hit the wall and he stumbled. His center of gravity leaned drunkenly forward. *I'm going to fall,* he thought, had time for a desperate prayer against the horror that would follow if he did, a *Lord, please no* against the image of his crushed daughter, and he found his footing.

Outside now, in the rain hard as teeth, Lisa crying as the stinging of the night drenched her. Struggling with the keys to unlock the car, hearing Judy's cry "*NOOOOOOWWWWW!*" shrieking out of the house (blades at his back, teeth at his neck, a jaw clamping shut).

The door opened, and he fell into the front seat. *Close the door. Lock it.* He put Lisa in the passenger seat, started the car up, and roared away, wheels spraying water. He drove with his left hand, holding Lisa in place with his right. He zigzagged out of the subdivision at panic speed, and then he was on the highway. He breathed.

Then the thought—he hadn't taken Judy's car keys. He glanced in the rearview mirror. Nothing, just the glow of the last of the streetlights in the distance. Even so, he drove a bit faster. The highway, still straight, began a series of low dips and rises, with woods on either side. His speed turned the rain into horizontal mercury in the headlights. The trees flashed past, bleached negative, then returned to the body of the dark.

Mirror again, and there, oh there, *my God in heaven*, headlights. Foot down on the accelerator, water rising in a violent wake on either side of the car. The steering wheel shuddered in his grasp. His right hand hesitated over Lisa. Hold her or the wheel? He checked the mirror. The lights seemed closer (*coming! now!*), their reflection sick and big and harsh. How could she be catching up in that car of hers? Dark miracles tittered. And rushing ahead of the other vehicle came the other thing he had fled. It took him now. All he could see was Judy's gaze and its awful clarity. Its terrible, terrible sanity.

He was not fleeing her madness, because she was not mad. He was fleeing the truth she had seen, the truth with teeth, the truth that lurked beyond the horizon, and whose first glimmers were already marring the comforting night of the world's ignorance.

*Reptile.*

He sobbed, shook his head as if he could push the horror away, and suddenly there was nothing ahead but trees. He yanked hard left, foot off the accelerator and braking into the road's curve. The Matrix hydroplaned full tilt. Momentum laughed.

Airborne.

Flipping.

Chaos then. Roaring, crashing, slamming chaos. Batter-smash blows from all sides.

And stop. The brief silence of blocked ears, and then the pounding of the rain came through again. Gil couldn't see. Couldn't feel his legs. Felt deep claws in his skull, felt flattened and loose bone in his face and jaw. He moved his arms, wiped the blood from his eyes, and he could see again. He was upside down, tangled in metal, and facing the road. The other vehicle had stopped, and it was a pickup truck, not Judy's car at all. Its headlights were pointing his way, illuminating the wreck. Someone was coming on the run.

Then, behind him, something that was more than a sound. It was the echo of an immense snarl far beyond dragon. Gil twisted around, Lisa's name at his lips, and saw that the fragment of the coming truth had been waiting for him here, for this moment, all along. He came face-to-face with Judy's horror. The metal of the car had been torn and molded by darkness into interlocking steel blades. They gripped Lisa. She wasn't crying.

Lesson learned, no praying now, Gil reached for his daughter.

He felt her come apart in the teeth of the smile.

# Window
## Anya Martin

*To some degree, everyone has been like a character in this story. It's chilling—Martin creates a sense of emptiness that is all too familiar to most of us. It recalls a seven-line anonymous poem: "It's so nice / to wake up in the morning / all alone / and not have to tell somebody / you love them / when you don't love them / anymore." Chilling, right?*

"This is not going to last forever," Michael said.

The words echoed in Angela's mind like the droning keys of an out-of-tune piano. Her eyes ached from the memory of tears.

"It's not working," he said. "I just don't love you. But I'll hold you because you're so very special and you deserve better than me. I'll hold you while you cry."

Something like that. His actual words had faded from her memory because she did not want to remember them.

"Why?" she asked him and hated herself for it.

And then she added, "Are you sure?"

His arms felt so good tightly wound around her chest, the curve of his body curled around her back. She wanted to linger in his grasp. *Why not?*

The humming of cicadas melded with the Doors, the last notes of "Riders on the Storm", as Angela tried to let go of the recollection. She wanted to watch it fly out the window past the naked woman behind the glass, arms swimming open and closed. Her long black hair merging with the darkness behind, smiling milk-white teeth, just like in his photographs. *The woman before her.* Liza, whom Michael said he could never forget, whom he would always love despite the fact that she had treated him abusively and ultimately abandoned him. Liza who had thrown herself out a window, yet his heart remained preserved just for her—mummified and wrapped in her bedsheets—his dead body, only continuing the motions of life.

Angela's hands were soaked in clay and water, the clay hardening as the water dried in the night air that blew into the loft apartment from the open window. She was trying to concentrate on the half-finished pot that sat upon the wheel, but the woman in the window would not stop watching her, tanned breasts lifting up and down like signal flags, reminding her. She tried to rationalize the image away, tell herself it was just a figment of her paranoid imagination. She wanted nothing more than to exorcise that image, to slash it away from her consciousness. Angela wanted just to sit and make her pots. She wanted Michael just to come home and make love to her.

And he did.

An hour later, Angela heard his cowboy boots walking heavily across the wooden corridor, his key turning in the lock. She turned around just as the door creaked open. Michael, in his black leather jacket, walked toward her and kissed her lips.

He pulled away too quickly for her to catch his tongue, leaving a faint flavor of cigarettes and scotch in her mouth. She could taste that the thoughts on his mind were not about her.

"How was your day, dear?" he asked.

"Okay," she said, endeavoring to smile. "I made a horse. It's just waiting for the kiln tomorrow."

Michael walked over to the little wooden table and stared blankly at the equine figure, one hoof raised to mimic a Han dynasty sculpture.

"Mr. Ed?" he inquired.

Angela could tell he was trying to make her laugh.

"Not exactly," she answered. "You'll see when I glaze it. I want the colors to be surprising, maybe a little jarring."

"Well, I'll be surprised then," he said, walking across the loft and lowering himself onto the black leather sofa.

Michael picked up a magazine and started to read.

"How was your day?" she asked.

"Oh, the usual shit," he said, not looking up from the magazine.

"Did Blake pull something?" she asked.

"No, I just kept to myself," he said.

"That's good," she said, wanting to stroke his shoulder, take all his frustrations inside her, and set him free.

"Why is my life such a fucking hell?" Michael said suddenly, throwing the magazine down. He pulled a pint of Dewar's from inside his jacket, unscrewed the cap, and swigged deeply.

Angela saw he was crying.

She got up now, crossed the room, and hugged Michael long and hard. He railed about work and promises that were made and Blake and Karen and everyone else. And how he wanted to be painting instead of working at the advertising agency. How he hated that he needed to just hold on a little longer and save more money. He couldn't give up the salary. Not yet.

"It has to get better," she said, feeling strength welling up inside her, her own strong belief in the power of human endurance. "We'll pull on through. Remember, we're a team."

Michael fell silent, then started swearing again. Sensing he wanted space, she released her embrace. He stared at the fireplace, at the floor. Then his eyes looked up towards the window.

"Oh, God, I miss Liza," he almost screamed, swigging again. "Why did she have to leave me, Angela? Why?"

Angela stared at him and started to say, "There was nothing you could have done; she chose to leave," but fear descended like the fall of an avalanche, and instead she said nothing.

Michael kept staring at the window.

Then suddenly he jerked his eyes back to Angela, hugged her, held her tightly on the sofa. The woman in the window laughed soundlessly as he began to kiss Angela on her cheek, her lips, her neck. He unbuttoned her shirt, sucked her nipples, and glided his hands down to her skirt, slipping it off. She lifted and spread her legs, and he bent his face to meet her. Later, after she helped him remove his clothes, he entered her, climaxed.

"You know how difficult it is for me to say the words again, but in my own way, I do love you," Michael said, his voice cracking. He pushed her hair back with his fingers and looked into her eyes.

Angela met his gaze and smiled.

"You never stopped loving her," Angela said, trying to understand seven months later when Michael told her again that it was over between them. They'd just finished dinner, and the air was scented with garlic and tomato sauce from leftover spaghetti. Caesar salad sat untouched in a large wooden bowl in the center of the black dining table. He wanted to be on his own, he told her. But he wanted to stay friends.

"I tried to . . . " Michael started, pausing to empty the last drops of Pinot Noir into his wineglass and down them in one fast draught. "I tried to make it work between us. I just can't explain why, but it isn't."

At first, Angela was silent, just staring at him, tears pouring out of her eyes again. Then she felt anger building up inside her, anger that he had let their relationship go on for so long. Betrayal that he let her love for him grow and mature, and how it was all a lie.

"I'm sorry," Michael said.

"I don't get how you could love someone like Liza, but despite all we've been through together, all you've asked me to do for you, allowed me to do for you, you don't love me," Angela said; then she threw his own words back at him, "You don't know what love is."

"Yes, I do," Michael said. "You just want me to love you, and I'm sorry I can't."

"Then, you were wrong," Angela said. "Love is not about commitment; it is irrational."

"No," Michael said, shaking his head, seemingly unable to explain any further and becoming even more defensive.

Michael looked Angela straight in her eyes. Then his head lowered, and he descended to his knees, and finally, he was facing the window.

"Have you gotten over Liza?" Angela asked point-blank, not sure if she was pointing a metaphorical Beretta 9 mm at him or at herself.

Michael's eyes now were locked upon the window.

"No, and yeah, it's fucking unfair to both of us."

Then Angela saw him watching Liza and the longing in his eyes. His lips opened and shut like the mouth of a poet searching for the verse, the words that spoke desire . . . no, *the need.*

Liza thrust her hand out through the glass, her fingers beckoning. His hand reached to meet hers. Michael crawled on his knees towards the window, his arm outstretched and grasping.

Then as his fingers almost touched hers, Liza pulled her arm back into the glass, sparks flying where her hand slipped back, gray smoke lingering in a cloud in front of the window. Her mouth expressed laughter, silent laughter in the loft, but loud beyond the glass.

"Liza!" Michael cried out. "I love you."

Liza laughed harder, rocking back and forth on her knees, her breasts like stone gargoyles, tits pointed like spears.

Michael's face fell to the ground. Tears erupted from his eyes, and then nothing. His body collapsed still as a corpse, his face in his hands, sleeping, the weight of either the wine or the vision of Liza knocking him unconscious. His chest moved gently, the only indication he was alive.

Angela ran her fingers through his hair and wondered what the woman in the window was thinking. Did she think? Was she a fantasy created by Michael or by Angela or by both of them together? She raised her eyes to look at Liza, who was, still now, smiling and extending her fingers again through the glass. And suddenly, Angela saw something different—how beautiful Liza was, how tantalizing her body, how sweet her eyes.

"I am so sorry," Liza whispered, her voice like a little girl's. "I never meant to hurt him. I never meant for him to love me so much."

The woman in the window was transformed to a little girl with a pixie haircut, flat chest, innocent eyes, a tiny, crooked smile.

Then she was Liza again, darkly tanned, pure sex and yet still innocent, a child-woman, her fingers dangling from the window, the arm pushing out farther.

"Help me," Liza said. "I tried to leave him, but he wouldn't let me go. I need your help, Angela. Help me break free of the window."

Angela realized that she had never heard Liza's voice before.

"Why are you speaking to me now?" she asked.

"I can only be heard through the glass if someone wants to listen," Liza answered. "He wanted to listen every day. He didn't want to lose me and that's why he put me here."

Angela hesitated as her mind tried to rationalize Liza's words.

Michael had told her the story about the day he found Liza at the door with all her suitcases packed. He described the quarrel and the broken glass shattered on the floor after she hurled herself out the window. She should have died or at least broken her back from the fall, but no body was ever found. Somehow she had just picked herself up and never returned, even for her suitcases. Another window, another apartment, but could he have taken the window with him somehow?

"Did he push you?" Angela asked, frightened that the man she loved could be so cruel.

"No," Liza answered. "But he wouldn't let me go. He held me in a window of his memory."

Liza was silent for a moment, seemingly pensive.

"And now I have been watching your life and I envy you for it," she said. "I envy the way you sit and create your pots, the way you unload your groceries, friends who come over and watch movies. I want to go back out there and learn to live again, but not with him, not with someone who always wants more than he can have. Will you help me? Will you help me escape the window?"

Angela reached for Liza's fingers, letting them wrap around hers and lift her from Michael's side. Liza's arm was strong enough to gently pull Angela upwards until she was standing. Then the arm pulled back into the window and took her with it. The glass parted like water, like a shower of waves caressing each part of Angela as she passed through, refreshing and remaking her. The water washed back and Liza's body met hers, hands flattening, arms to arms, breasts to breasts, feet to feet, legs to legs, lips to lips, both lips. As bodies, they formed a perfect match. Only, Liza's was firmer, Angela's softer.

Liza kissed Angela, wet and long. She then slipped two fingers along her thigh, massaged her clit, then moved inside her. Angela felt a flood of moisture, shaking almost immediately with orgasm, and sensed another building as Liza trailed her tongue down her neck, fingers still caressing.

Teeth nibbled gently along her collarbone and onto the curve of her breasts, sucking each nipple. Liza's tongue drifted lower, onto her stomach now, in her belly button, her lower abdomen, her groin; one hand on her breast, the other inside her, massaging in and out. Tongue curling, tracing, sucking, coming, curling, tracing, sucking, coming, curling, tracing, sucking, coming.

Angela floated, her body in perfect balance, perfect release, her sensations merging through repetition into pure pleasure and understanding and finally drifting into sleep.

She didn't know how long she slept, but when she awoke, Liza was no longer touching her.

"Liza," Angela called, wanting to hold her lover, kiss her, touch her everywhere Liza had touched Angela.

"Liza," she called again.

Silence. Darkness. Liza was away perhaps, but she would return. Angela let herself fall back to sleep, wrapped in the memory of Liza's body heat.

Icy glass awakened her. Icy glass and light. Sunlight flashed all around Angela, warming her body as she lifted it from the glass floor. The sun was blinding, forcing her to turn the other way into her own reflection. Her hazel eyes, her auburn hair, her pale lips, lipstick smeared across her cheek. It took her a moment to realize she was staring into glass on all sides, the glass of a rectangular window divided into panes. And inside the window was the loft, her potter's wheel, the leather sofa, the kitchen, Michael's naked body still passed out on the wooden floor.

Angela stared down at Michael and did not care for him, saw why Liza rejected him, why he was not equal to her passion. She remembered how Liza touched her, how Liza made her feel whole in a way that no lover ever had. No wonder Michael had loved her so much.

But where was Liza?

She wanted to feel Liza's lips upon her breast, between her legs.

She turned to look behind, but the sun again blinded her and compelled her vision back through the window into the loft. If the window was so small, where could Liza have gone?

Then she knew the answer.

Angela saw Liza draped in Angela's own red oriental robe, kneeling beside Michael. She saw the trick, the same scam this woman had played on Michael played on her. Michael mumbled something, but it was like watching a silent movie and Angela could not hear a word. She saw only the hunger in his eyes as Liza took him into her arms and kissed him. Then Liza made love to him with all the skill and tenderness that she gave to Angela. As he fell back into slumber, Liza packed Angela's clothes into a suitcase, rifled cash from Michael's pockets, took Angela's jewelry box, her credit cards, her purse, and her car keys. She pasted a note on the TV and walked out the door.

Angela watched as Michael awakened with the smile of a man who had just experienced the dream of a lifetime. He stumbled over to the TV and took the note into the sunlight of the window. All she could read was that it was signed with her name. She beat her hands against the window and yelled.

"Michael!"

He turned and headed for the kitchen.

"Michael!"

He started coffee, foraged in the refrigerator.

"Michael!"

He spread cream on a bagel.

"Michael!"

He left the kitchen, opened the door to take in the newspaper.

"Michael!"

He poured coffee into a mug, sat down on the couch, took a bite from the bagel, began to read the paper, sipped some coffee.

"Michael, I love you."

The words slipped out as Liza's own statement rang in her ears, *"I can only be heard through the glass if someone wants to listen."*

Michael didn't want to hear Angela. He didn't want to see Angela. Angela made him feel guilty, reminded him of what he couldn't have, of what he didn't realize he had imprisoned, of what he didn't know was now free—that Liza was in the world again the way she wanted to be and not with Michael. He didn't care that Angela was the one he believed had left him. He understood why she would leave and felt no urge to follow.

But Michael did feel something missing. Angela could sense that. He looked up into the window and knew Liza was gone.

Michael drank more and more scotch every night and he fucked women and he tried to paint and he was never happy.

And Angela watched it all from the window.

# Shattered

## G. Daniel Gunn & Paul Tremblay

*There's always a place on our table-of-contents page for the truly bizarre tale. In what starts out as a fairly familiar conflict between parents for the love of their child, the stress and anguish of one father's struggle pushes him into a world where more than just aspirations are shattered. Gunn and Tremblay have created a delicate juxtaposition of both beautiful and outré images. We wouldn't be surprised to learn of their trip to the Korova Milk Bar before writing this one.*

"You promise, Daddy?"

"Cross my heart, hope to die, stab a pointy stick in my eye. I promise, sweetie."

"Good."

Even before the certified letter arrived yesterday afternoon, Guy LaForte was beginning to see the cracks spreading farther along the surface of his new life, such as it was. After six months of working third shift, Guy LaForte's internal clock had only now begun adapting to his work-all-night, sleep-all-day schedule. But the pay was better, and lately he needed all the help he could get. The slot he'd been offered in Rhode Island would return him to normal hours, but would mess up Shauna's visits. They'd been infrequent enough, with only a city between them, never mind an entire state.

Every other weekend his five-year-old daughter threw Guy's apartment, and life, into wonderful disarray. Every other weekend, when his ex-wife, Mary, dropped Shauna off with a backpack stuffed with supplies and the ever-increasing implication that he was incapable of caring for their daughter.

He should have seen it coming, should have taken her recent darkening looks and bizarre questions more seriously. Before the divorce they'd fallen into the quick-fix trap, hoping a child would make everything better. But Shauna's birth solidified and affirmed nothing. Instead, she became a wedge further dividing them. Whatever remnants of love Mary might have had for Guy were gathered up and given to their daughter. There wasn't enough left for him.

Maybe there never had been. Whatever mask she'd worn in the beginning had shattered in the cries of their newborn baby. Her true face was harder, more brittle. And, apparently, she didn't want to share the love, his and hers alike, for their daughter now that Guy was out of her life.

He should have seen the ultimate crack jagging its way towards him from the other side of the city. Mary's recent questions seemed to serve no purpose other than posturing. *What are you feeding her? Why aren't you taking her outside more often?* He would cast these aside with disdainful silence as he embraced his daughter on those too-infrequent weekends. When she asked if Shauna ever woke up with night terrors when she stayed with him, he lied and said no. At the most recent visit, she pointed to bruises on Shauna's legs and arms and demanded an accounting for each, as if the bruises were a map of a more ominous story. Guy knew his *we were playing horsey and she fell off my back* and *she ran into the doorjamb when I was chasing her* and *she's a normal five-year-old with lots of energy, who bumps into stuff and falls, but always bounces back up* sounded inadequate.

He should have acted sooner, but that meant getting a lawyer. Third-shift paychecks still barely covered the rent and electricity, especially after Shauna's child support. In the silence of the apartment Guy focused on work, or slept, and tried not to miss his daughter. His world was shrinking, like ice melting in a whiskey glass, pressing him into a single point on the couch.

Then the letter came, and when he read it he raged through the apartment, crying, bellowing, smashing dishes and glasses and punching the walls. It came yesterday, only a day after his daughter had clambered back into her mother's Camry and out of his arms for another two weeks. For her part, Mary had been civil, eyes downcast. She'd known then what was coming. Known it would be the last time his little girl came to visit her father. The letter lay open now, on the table beside the door. *Full custody. Child endangerment.* There were many more words in the court summons, but these four were the ones that made his eyes sting and fists clench.

The only good thing in his life was going to be taken from him. Even before Mary and the courts could prove anything, the letter made it clear he had lost Shauna. He would become a monster in his daughter's eyes. How could he possibly live with that?

Sleep still weighed his lids as the world squeezed in on him once again as he left the apartment, drifting along the hall towards the back entrance. Melting. Almost gone and he didn't have the energy to do anything about it but go to work, hope everything worked out and went back to the way it was. Every other weekend seemed like a dream compared to what was coming.

Guy absently twirled his key ring around one finger and stepped outside, squinting in the late afternoon sun. The building's hush would dissipate soon when the other tenants of Blue Rose Estates returned home from their day jobs. Already the parking lot was partially filled with cars. He moved down the walk towards the mailboxes clustered together at the corner. His Jeep was parked three spots away, its top down. He'd been too tired after his shift to bother putting it up.

Halfway to his box, Guy saw translucent shadows dancing on the pavement, sunlit shapes like the jellyfish Shauna thought were so beautiful at the aquarium. So many trips they took, adventures to replace the lost comforts of *family*.

He looked up. No magic jellyfish above him, but Guy stared, openmouthed, at what appeared to be glass statues hovering forty feet above the parking lot. The afternoon sky burned a distorted blue through one of the figures—a full-sized impression of a woman in a business suit going through her purse, left foot slightly forward as if caught midstride. Another floated above the edge of the building, catching the sun. He had to squint to make out any details. An old woman, hunched over, *sorting laundry?* The lower portion of her leg was missing.

Farther down, a crystalline man, long coat blowing in some unfelt breeze, hovered above the mailboxes, key in his right hand. His left forearm gone past the elbow.

Guy shuffled forward, turned slowly, looking for the strings that must be holding these figures—these *statues*—aloft. No strings, no ropes, only the sharp lines of sun reflecting off glass. Up the slope of the parking lot, a mother with two children in hand, fingers eternally melded together and scurrying toward a minivan waiting forty feet below them.

Glassy shadows drifted over him. Above the building the old-woman statue swayed in a breeze he did not feel. He thought of his daughter looking out of her bedroom window across town, seeing these people made of glass, floating . . .

*What's happening here?*

The door to the building opened. Something scuttled outside, righted itself. It stood no higher than Guy's waist. Skin the color of wet pond muck. Writhing Medusa appendages crowned its head, gnarled and distended like old tree roots. Face puffy, featureless except for button-like eyes and a long, wide mouth. It smiled obscenely, each pointed tooth fitting together like a trap.

Then it laughed, a sound between hyena and madness. Teeth clicked, spider arms reaching out for him along the walkway.

Guy didn't know what to do. His pulse galloped. The creature's long arms lifted skyward. It opened its mouth wide and loosed a stream of gibberish, hard clucks, consonants.

Something changed in the sky. Guy looked up, and the statues plummeted down.

He jumped to the pavement and rolled under an SUV parked next to his Jeep. Glass shattered on blacktop and car roofs. When the woman with the purse landed next to him, Guy covered his face. Instead of a hailstorm of shards, he felt a molasses-thick splatter against his arms. He pulled his hands away—blood, bright red, its odor thick and pungent. Another statue shattered, the sound echoing in his head. Like the others, a red explosion.

Blood ran downhill, under the car. There was too much. Guy slipped sideways in the flow, the ground slick as he moved to the opposite side of the SUV. He knocked into the wheel well of his Jeep, struggled to his feet. A red tide under his sneakers. Guy wiped his eyes and frantically looked around the parking lot. Cars dented, stained.

A flash of movement at the side of his building. The creature scuttled along the facade like a tick, then jumped to the street corner. It crossed the road, scaled the side of the building across the way.

There were others, now. Some crawled the buildings, others gathered over broken statues, scooping the jagged remnants into their mouths.

Guy thought only that he had to get to Shauna. Thinking anything else would send him further into madness.

*I promise, sweetie . . .*

The interior of the Jeep was wet and pulpy in spots, as if smashed with dozens of tomatoes. He slid into the front seat. The keys were still in his hand, slick with the statues' blood. Fingers slipped and fumbled until the right key finally turned the ignition. The engine roared to life.

Something dark scuttled behind the Jeep. Guy was tempted to back over it, but instead shifted into Drive and rolled up the curb onto the blood-wetted grass. Creatures scaled the buildings in his peripheral vision, but he stared ahead, pressing the accelerator.

Rear tires spun across the lawn until they found pavement.

He felt in his pocket for the cell phone. Not there.

He hit the dashboard. "Shit, shit, shit!" White noise from the radio's speakers.

One hundred yards ahead, one of the things waited, blocking access to the main road. Each arm was an elongated appendage, reaching across the width of the street. No going around. It screamed more nonsense as he approached. Guy pressed the accelerator.

The creature met the Jeep's grille and burst apart as if filled with sawdust. A dusty cloud smeared the windshield, Guy's eyes, coating the Jeep's bloody seats. He turned sharply onto the main road. Tires chirped and the rear fishtailed.

Driving down Route 146 now, towards the center of the city. Most of the dust from the thing blew off the windshield, sticking in smeared patches of blood. He didn't dare use the wipers.

Cars and the occasional truck were stalled between lanes, broken and discarded. Obsolete toys. A cracked utility pole was a dead arm bent over a Honda. Above, everything glittered, the former drivers sparkling in the sun, swaying from their invisible tethers.

Guy veered around each vehicle, scraping past the top of the fallen pole. Each time he slowed, the engine shook, sputtering as if to dislodge more sawdust from its throat.

He screamed. Staccato bursts of fear and frustration.

A mile down the road he noticed the clump of wet dust on the passenger seat. The puddle of blood was gone, soaked up like spilled oil. The clump beat and writhed, a malformed heart. Guy looked away, swerved past a milk truck lying on its side.

No one left alive—only life-sized glass figurines hanging above the world. He didn't count the scuttling, babbling creatures moving along past the deserted gas station pumps and the Irish bar with its peeling red and green paint. These things weren't alive. They weren't real.

A tiny arm stretched from the growing lump of putty beside him, then another. Guy didn't notice. The ramp to Interstate 290 was a clogged artery of ruined machines, the air above a mass of glittering bodies. Glass arms reached for steering wheels lost far below in a miasma of twisted metal and steaming radiators.

The Jeep bucked and choked when Guy slowed. He pressed the accelerator too hard, veered left onto the last side street before the ramp. Red lights illuminated the dashboard, the Jeep stalled.

When he reached for the key, something grabbed his arm. Twin appendages, reaching from the passenger seat. Talons squeezed. A head emerged from the lump of putty, its features riddled with pox-like bumps and craters. A rip in the doughy face, wider, a mouth, crying like a foghorn.

Guy opened the driver's door and dragged his passenger across the seat. It did not let go until he slammed the door on its thinning membranous arms. Its mouth opened wider, loosing a louder rendition of the foghorn.

He had stalled underneath the highway overpass. Above him creatures flittered across the ironworks. Wasps in the eaves of this nightmare landscape.

The driver-side door opened.

Guy ran, a dulled arrow aiming in the direction he hoped was Mary's house.

*"You okay?"*

*"Yeah."*

*"I'm sorry. It was just an accident. You know that, right?"*

*"Yeah."*

*They silently watched TV. Shauna left her seat and climbed into Guy's lap. His heart broke with relief. She'd taught him that there were many kinds of heartbreak.*

*"Can they talk in real life?" Shauna said. She had red hair, cinnamon freckles of a doll framing curious green eyes.*

*"What, those things?" he asked, nodding towards the television. On the screen an octopus spewed a cloud of ink to escape a predator. "No, honey. Only people can talk."*

*"But they talk to me in my dreams."*

*Guy laughed at her pixie voice, her matter-of-fact delivery. She was back to herself. "Well, what do Ollie the Octopus and his friends say?"*

*"I don't know. I forget when I wake up. I think they say your name sometimes."*

*"Dreams are like that, kiddo."*

*Shauna nodded and rubbed her chin, as if pondering a deep truth. They sat and watched the end of the Discovery Channel's ocean special. She'd be going back to her mother's in less than an hour. Their waning time together was always the most awkward. In this last hour loomed two weeks of separation which hung over Guy like a death sentence.*

*Shauna grabbed the remote, jumped off Guy's lap, and shut off the TV.*

*"You'll never leave me, will you?" She put her arms behind her back and rocked on her heels in front of him.*

*"Whoa, where did that question come from?"*

*"I heard Momma telling Auntie Pey you might go away."*

*He breathed in slowly, let the air out, and did not allow anger to ruin this final hour together before Mary picked her up.* You might go away. *How could he answer her? He wanted to have her all the time.*

*Shauna absently rubbed her arm and he thought maybe everyone* would *be better off if he left. But moving to Rhode Island could be the "fresh start" they all needed. Maybe they could work out summer visitation, or monthly. Something better than having his daughter just across the city and only being able to see her once every goddamn two weekends.*

*"I won't leave you, Shauna." Blood rushed to his face.*

*She jumped onto his lap and gave a hug that made him want to cry.*

*"You promise, Daddy?"*

*"Cross my heart, hope to die, stab a pointy stick in my eye. I promise, sweetie."*

*"Good."*

Block after block, under legions of glass swaying in the dying light.

Creatures swarmed over taxis and storefronts and newsstands and street signs and baby carriages, over fallen bicycles with empty seats and spinning wheels.

Block after block.

Guy ran—numbed to a single purpose.

*I promised . . .*

Glass exploded behind him. Creatures clacked and clicked and jabbered their horrible language as he passed. Always, they moved aside but never approached.

He rested momentarily at the crest of a hill on Lincoln Street (*Almost there, Shauna.*) and looked back. The road spilled into an open, glass-shadowed square a half mile away in the center of the city. Something dark spread itself across the intersection and over the courthouse steps. Like the thing on his passenger seat but much, much bigger. A mound of gray flesh, details indistinct across the distance. It rose and fell like a disembodied lung. When a wide swath opened into a mouth, a long, mournful wail drifted up the hill. Long rapier arms stretched and gathered a dozen glass people from the sky. They drifted, slowly, into the maw. The line of the mouth sealed up again.

Guy turned and ran.

Up the long incline of Burncoat Street, then right after the high school, the second left, his ex-wife's two-family home. Statues floated above the pointed roof. Guy did not look but ran through their kaleidoscopic shadows. The front door wasn't locked.

He climbed the stairs to the second-floor apartment.

"Shauna!"

In the living room, furniture lay askew, pushed against walls. White curtains fluttered around open bay windows. Sitting in the middle of the room was his daughter with a mass of broken crayons and coloring books.

Shauna was crying and shouting, "Leave me alone!"

"It's okay, sweetie, I'm here. It'll be okay . . . " Guy picked her limp, whimpering form off the floor and wrapped himself around her, held her close, felt the warmth of her face against his neck and wet tears under his collar.

"I . . . " he said, but couldn't find the words. He looked around the room, hoping Mary would walk in to see them like this, wiping her hands on that dish towel she always seemed to carry once upon a time.

"Where's Mommy?" Shauna whispered. Guy already knew the answer, from the red-streaked glass hand on the floor and crystalline figure bumping lightly against the window frame outside. He couldn't see the face, but it was her. He wondered what expression of hers was now frozen forever in glass. Forever, or until she shattered on the ground below.

Something dark scurried outside the window. Guy stepped back, held Shauna closer. He tried to take a second step but could not.

His daughter breathed in suddenly, a sound of surprise. Guy felt it too: cold, tingling in his legs, rising like mercury. They would turn into glass just like everyone else.

Shauna whispered, "Please don't—"

"I promise I won't ever leave you . . . "

They stood in the center of the room. Guy's eyes were closed and he imagined himself and his daughter as a merged statue, together forever. They would float above their former home then finally drift away from everyone else's reach.

# Mise en Abyme
## Gordon White

*Most stories are linear, moving from one beginning to a single ending. But others, more rare, aspire to function in closed systems. In places where cycles are locked in an eternal now. Wheels within wheels and the paradox of endless images of the mirrors in the mirrors are metaphors for this cyclic and most likely doomed pattern of existence. In Gordon White's ambitious tale of the familiar totalitarian society, he examines the extremes of love and power through the eyes of two surprisingly perceptive dictators.*

After a year of marriage, I told my wife that I was going to write this story and call it "Mise en Abyme", which means "Placed into Abyss". Of course, if she'd told me not to, I wouldn't have, because I would do, or not do, anything for her. But she only said that there wasn't a need, that what has happened, has happened, and what will come, will come.

We had been discussing, in a general sense, the problem of having children, and she told me that when she was a little girl, she would sometimes wake to find the outline of an old woman sitting on the corner of her bed. Neither her mother nor her father believed her, but through half-open eyes she could see the pale skin and hair. She felt the mattress move under the woman's weight. In her room, a mirror stood beside the closet and another hung on the wall, and my wife very clearly remembered how the visitor's reflection, and the reflection of her reflection, curved away into a seemingly infinite bow.

The visitor spoke in just a whisper, so soft and so low that she almost couldn't hear it above the sound of the blood running its circuit through her ears. But it was always the same story, and after enough repetitions it carved deep grooves in the layers of her memory.

There's no stopping it now, of course, and we'll never be heroes, but there's more to it than that. This is still a love story.

By the time of the Great Return, Heira has worked for the Commitment's state-run television news organization for almost twenty-three years. Although listed merely as an "editor" and with only a single assigned responsibility, the level of respect accorded to her far exceeds that which could be expected merely from her relationship with the Overseer. Although unrecognized by the public, the deference paid to her, by everyone from the Commitment's rank-and-file guards at traffic checkpoints and the station doors to the wives and husbands of top-ranking officials, hovers between obsequious and religious. Chalmers, the oldest of the television station's guards and a veteran of the wars, sometimes even bows to her. It's an unnecessary and extravagant gesture, but some ripple of acknowledgment follows in her wake as she enters each afternoon to prepare for the nightly broadcast.

Every night, that is, until the beginning of the Great Return. That night, for the first time in over a decade, Chalmers stops Heira to check her identification. Entering the open room of the broadcast set, too, she is greeted by the backs of a crowd. Gathered as if they were going to the gallows or arrayed for the firing squad, the newsroom's crew stands before the bank of monitors. They gasp and gape in silence, a row of tombstones undulating in the siren strobe of the screens.

"It's a rogue transmission," Nelson, her producer, whispers as Heira joins the ranks.

"Do you think," the anchor, Carol Denish, takes up the satellite of rumor, "I mean, it's got to be an error, right?"

On the screen, Heira recognizes last night's regularly broadcasted Corrective Executions. Once again Heira watches the old man led across the outdoor stage by soldiers in the Watch's black uniform. She watches the young girl follow, prodded by rifle butt, and then the one-armed man with the shock of red hair. This was her work from last night, of course.

Or rather, it is not her work. Because, as the camera pans around from behind the imminent Corrections, Heira sees the difference. She sees their eyes.

The eyes which she had so painstakingly removed.

As the bullets punctuate their simple ellipses across the bodies and faces, the crowd before Heira hisses as the life drains from the eyes, the agony and the snuff of the spark unmasked. Heira, of course, has seen this—indeed, she is the one who must—but to the others this is new. The sterility and acceptability of the Corrective Executions, accomplished through Heira's work of minimalist censorship—the application of a flat black bar across the eyes of the Corrections—has been undone and the assembled crowd, too, appears undone.

It takes Heira a moment to realize that Nelson and several of the others are openly weeping.

The screen flickers, goes dark, wakes again. It blinks out the 5-4-3-2 of the intro reel and starts the loop again, camera beginning behind the old man, the young girl, the one-armed man. There is the wet sound and sudden smell of vomit.

She turns and finds that behind her, a camera is rolling. The steady red eye of the recording light glares without blinking, watching the people watching the screen. Footage for tonight, she thinks.

She is about to leave for the editing bay, to begin redacting tonight's footage of today's Corrective Executions, when it happens.

"That's enough," Nelson yells, as the regurgitated execution ends and begins again for the third time that Heira has been here to see. "Cut the feed." And somewhere beyond them, in the control room at the end of the producer's radio signal, a switch is flipped. The renegade, naked feed is cut, swapped for the image from the camera recording the newsroom's reaction.

And in the monitors at front, the new picture is within a picture within another. An infinite visual recursion of backs of heads staring into a screen showing the backs of heads staring into a screen, and so on at a slight angle so that each iteration magnifies the bend until it seems to twist away into the dark recess of the television.

To Heira this new vision is the true gateway to abomination. This infinite stretching, twisting tunnel into an abyss within the screen. It stirs a memory within her. A voice. A repetition.

Then the monitors are cut and everything goes flat and black.

Rumors swirl like ticker tape through the newsroom and in the gurgle of whispers in the rest of the Capital District. Everyone has seen it. Everyone agrees on what it is. No one knows why or how, but theories range from wild to outlandish:

A political activist group with moles inside the state-run agencies, releasing unexpurgated footage of the nightly executions to foment rebellion.

A freak echo of the transmission signals, bouncing off of satellites and space debris in an ablation cascade of radio waves, the masking properties of the original stripped in the relay and returned to Earth without the necessary protections.

The blind ghosts of the bitter dead.

The old God and its wrath.

That night, as she lies in bed next to the District's Overseer after a night of talking around the topic, Heira dreams of sitting in the editing bay and placing digital shrouds over the eyes of the old man, the young girl, the one-armed man. Then, feeling the oppressive weight of observation, she turns to find the pressing crowd behind her, gathered as if to watch a spider in a terrarium. There are Nelson and Carol, then the techs from Control, then the cameramen, but beyond them, where the peripheral lights dim, are people she does not recognize. Or that she does recognize, but whose names she never knew.

At the edge, a tiny figure scuttles into the tunnels between the observers' legs. The gargle of grey static emanates from the crowd, the susurration of fingers pushing through sand.

On her screen, the Corrective footage has vanished, replaced by the back of her own straw-colored head gazing into the monitor, its screen a picture of a woman gazing into a monitor with an image of a woman gazing into a monitor. The details at the finest level are too small to see, but at the center is a black pinprick, a single pixel—perhaps—which stands out like a dark star. As she leans in, the picture wavers. All of the lines rise, but as of yet do not converge. The hole at the center winks at her and calls her name.

"This is, of course, a formality," the inspector begins, pressing a red button on the machine that squats in the middle of the table. A recording light blinks on and there is a brief squall of feedback until the woman adjusts the dial. "But please, tell me about your work."

For so long Heira has been above reproach that the interview—not interrogation, not for her, never—by one of the Commitment's officers is a novelty. A secondhand tale told by others, but now Heira is in this barren room, staring into her own reflection in the two-way mirror behind the inspector, living out a story within her story.

Heira tells the woman in the green uniform—or, rather, confirms, since the Commitment knows almost everything—most of her story. How she worked for a television station before the wars and the Shift. How afterwards, when the Commitment and the Districts were devised, she was already living in what became the Capital. Heira waves away the years, as if they bullet out a plot to which everyone knows the ending. She was assigned the role of editor. She makes the nightly Corrective Executions safe for the mandatory public consumption, by removing the eyes. No, Heira doesn't have anything to do with the data afterwards. No, she doesn't know how the unredacted images were released.

"I mean no impudence," the inspector says, her blue eyes flashing, "but did your appointment have anything to do with the Overseer?"

"Almost everything has to do with the Overseer," Heira answers. "You'd have to ask him," she adds, knowing that the inspector will not.

The inspector ends the recording and signals to unseen compatriots behind the two-way mirror. As they both stand up and shake hands, however, in that moment before the door unlocks from the outside, the inspector leans in close. Her voice cracks slightly on inflection, worry wriggling through.

"How do you do it?"

It's the one thing that everybody wants to ask, although few ever do. How can Heira be the one to look into the eyes of the dead and take them away? How is that, while the public can only watch the Corrective Executions every night without flinching so long as the eyes are covered, Heira can stare into each window of the soul as it closes on their behalf? How does this one person, any person, manage to eat the sins of the Commitment every night?

Refracted within this question is, another: *"Why?"*

"I've always known my calling," Heira answers, squeezing the inspector's hand. "What will come, will come."

Although Heira is free of any suspicion, new protocols are still put in place. An armed guard delivers a thumb drive to Heira in a sealed manila envelope and she is locked alone in the editing bay to upload it on a dedicated laptop with no external plugs and the wireless connectivity removed with pliers.

Heira reviews the footage—a woman with iron-grey hair who marches unbowed to the stage and receives a bullet to the temple. Her eyes are great and watery, but not weak.

A bald man, heavy with the weight of unhealthy habits and, from his gait, regrets. His hazel eyes twitch back and forth as if looking for a way out before the soldiers' guns make quick work of him.

Two children—a boy and a girl—as unlike each other as night and day. Except, however, for the shape of their brows and the slope of their lids. Little holes bloom in their chests as the force drives them back into the drop cloth on the stage.

Who else would notice, she wonders, as she sets about cutting out the eyes with this clean and isolated machine. She crops them, checks them, runs the new program which does not just overlay the bars but punches them out of the digital data. She doesn't know how it works, but Raymond from Control said that all the ones and zeroes—the binary blink of data—is purged. Nothing to trace back, nothing to undo. Impervious to the piracy.

Heira breaks the factory seal on a clean thumb drive and downloads the edited footage. She hands it off to the guard, who takes the precaution of smashing the original drive with the uncut eyes into a dozen pieces, which he grinds under his bootheel, leaving the wreckage in a heap on the floor.

The Corrective Executions air at 6:00 pm, as usual. By 7:00 pm the uncensored footage is being looped on the pirate channel. By 7:01 pm the Overseer is on the phone, screaming at the station manager, and by 7:14 pm the riot officers are in the street, quelling dissent with batons and fire hoses.

Rubber bullets by 8:20 pm, live fire by 9:00 pm.

Until the night shift finishes at 3:00 am and an armed escort takes her home, Heira sits at her desk, pointing a web camera at her monitor, swinging the Droste-effect tunnel of the picture in a picture across the screen, trying to find the end point. Through a tiny hole that opens and closes, she hears a voice so low that it's almost a whisper.

The next day, the armed guard brings the data stick in and as soon as it is uploaded, Heira pulls it from the new, triple-locked laptop and smashes the stick into two dozen pieces on the top of her desk.

The armed guard blanches, but does not stop her as Heira sweeps the shards into her palm, then into her mouth. She swallows. The pieces cut going in and she knows they will cut going out, but that's for tomorrow. Feeling the sick pulse in her stomach, she holds it down while she edits the day's footage. Two women, green eyes. A man, dark brown.

At 6:00 pm the Corrective Executions air. By 6:37 pm the unaltered footage is on the rogue transmission. The Overseer does not call the station because the District is already under curfew and everyone out past the broadcast—with the exception of Heira and other authorized Commitment personnel with police escort—is executed under Operating Order 7.B(4).

This is the new standard procedure as the situation worsens over the coming days.

Heira wakes up and crawls out of bed, over to the television set on the dresser. She turns it on and the blue image flickers and bows, the screen itself flexing like the surface of a bubble before it settles. The image is, as she knew it would be, a shot from behind of her watching the screen, on which she is watching herself watching herself in ever-smaller iterations. She raises one hand and the wave of Heiras ripple as they follow suit. Perfectly aligned in the center of the screen is a dark hole, the screen on the screen on the screen, *ad infinitum.*

Static kisses the fingertip she places on the dot and there is a slight resistance as she wiggles it, working her finger into the minuscule hole in the membrane of the screen. It is tight, but gives way with enough pressure.

She watches as the rows upon rows of Heiras on the screen do the same, their fingers and arms aligning into a single flesh-colored shaft. Up to her knuckle already in the vortex of the screens within the screen, she works another finger in beside it. Inside, it is smooth, and it bends and gives. Beneath her fingertips, the canal of regressive images curls away from her, but she pushes harder. Her remaining fingers enter, then her thumb. Her forearm. The series of images stretch to accommodate her, wider and wider, as she turns to the side, thrusting shoulder deep into the hole in the center of the centers of the pictures. From the corner of her right eye against the screen, she can see the left side shown in the infinitely smaller repetitions. The look on the Heiras' faces surprises her, their lip-bit determination and furrowed concentration.

Then she twists and, with some effort, forces her head into the puckering hole, wiggling her other arm in beside it. There is nothing to see, a complete absence of light, but still she wriggles in deeper, feeling her way through the crevices as she kicks in fully, inching deeper and deeper. Waves of contractions in the muscular walls press her into herself and pull her deeper inside.

Still, Heira forces her way.

After what may be hours or centuries or seconds, there is a faint pinhole of illumination. She pushes onward, arms extended until her fingers pop free, protruding out into a warm and humid port of air. She pulls and pulls, sliding arms—and head—out into a vast space and tumbling down the slick walls to the moist floor in the sweltering darkness. Above her, dim and blinking stars hang like bats from the roof of the abyss.

Heira cannot say what it is that she sees, but the very walls and floors of the cavern seem alive. In the days after, her imagination drafts and redrafts the horror: A great blind

Worm rolling in the swollen womb beneath the center of human consciousness. A Mole God in its lair, tunneling out into the realms of possibility, waiting to emerge into the light and devour the sun. A limbless Crone, lost in the abscesses between space and time, and grown impossibly huge and pale and boneless, thatches of straw-colored hair above empty eye pits that glisten red as rare meat. But these terrible things pale beside the Great Voice that begins to speak.

"If I were to choose an Apostle," the Great Voice speaks, its words rolling through the dark organ of its lair, "I would choose you. You are the witness and do not flinch. Others have lost their sense, but you are immune, whether by nature or by practice. Yes, if there was one, it would be you; it has always been you.

"But I have no need for conversion and I have no need for further witnesses. You have served well, but what more could you offer me out there?"

As her eyes grow accustomed to the faint glow of the corpulent stars and the pinched illumination from the edges of other tunnels, Heira can make out movements around her. Pale and spindle-boned, woman-shaped things crawl like tapeworms from other tunnels and skitter around the edges of her sight before burrowing headfirst into new pathways. High above them, the luminescent globes flicker and blink their dim light. The air smells raw and internal, the scent of a wound that will never heal and never fester.

Through the closer tunnels, the gouges in the gargantuan pustule's lining, Heira catches flashes of other places and other times. A reflection of herself in her own eyes, in the two-way mirror of the interview room, just over the fearful inspector's shoulder. The glass picture frame in a bedroom, glaring over two postcoital bodies in the bed below, to stare into the glossy, empty reflection of a dead television.

A silhouette sitting at the foot of a bed, whispering to a little girl pretending to be asleep. The phalanx of shadows between the mirror on the wall and the mirror by the closet bows on and on, out of her sight, looping on into another infinity. Maybe even back into this chamber.

Reeling in the dampness, constricted in the belly of the abyss, Heira begins to hyperventilate. As if sensing her agitation, the ground roils and trembles, contractions squeeze and heave. The pale figures on the periphery scatter like maggots, back into the meat and the lights above her shudder, and then begin to fall.

And then Heira realizes they are not lights. They are eyes. Angry, sad, confused, flickering in a panoply of colors, they swarm around her, propelled by their fluttering lids like moths' wings. Their wet, heavy blinking is the sound of hundreds and thousands of mouths, and their butterfly kisses are thick and viscous, sopping with fur-like lashes. As they bite, rubbing their lids against her skin to pull and grasp, she screams. The cavern spasms, forcing her into one of the open furrows, expelling her from the Great Voice's audience with pulsations, while the disembodied eyes nip at her bare soles. As the skin of the walls close around her mouth, Heira cannot move, cannot breathe, and can no longer scream.

Darkness on all sides, in all aspects.
Then it starts again.

"Someone at the end of the tunnel," the Great Voice says, "is writing your story. Someone is always telling it again and again.

"What is coming is the Terrible Narration, the final story in the *mise en abysme*. The last chapter is the one in the middle, the final moment that returns not to the beginning but to the center.

"Worms and moles do not need eyes, yet here they are, alongside a God with nothing to touch and no perfect future. One grown fat and strong on all your commitment and willing sacrifice, but still demanding more and more.

"And yet, in the darkness, the eyes are blinking and the reflections off their tears are being translated into a story called 'Placed into Abyss', where you carry on in divine repetition.

"They are twinkling in the earth like shards of mica. They are flickering like stars. Somewhere, sometime, the story of your success, which is your failure, which is the place in the abyss, is being written and rewritten.

"You need only to connect it."

Burrowing through the layers of blankets like a night crawler escaping from flooded tunnels, Heira wakes, gasping in the night air. Beside her, the Overseer sleeps, sheets encasing his twitching legs like a tail. The orange light of the streetlamp reticulates them both through the blinds' slatted shadows.

Heira knows, then, the truth of the endless passage and the hole at the center of the picture-in-a-picture. It isn't only that it is a grave worm's tunnel, opening up into the Great Voice's living catacomb. It is also a birth canal, a great heaving channel with the Great Voice within, preparing to emerge, slurping out like a giant tongue and vomiting its vanguard of dead men's eyes back into the world.

Eyes that glisten like eggs, flapping on heavy-lidded wings.

The Corrective Executions and their broadcasts, of course, continue. The Overseer takes to the radio to warn that insubordination and curfew violations have been declared capital crimes. Religious and civil leaders are subject to particular scrutiny and dealt with quickly by the Commitment.

Protestors swarm the street *en masse*, eyes covered by opaque visors or heavy black blindfolds that mimic the bars that Heira places over the eyes of the continued Corrective Executions victims. These dissidents are themselves executed on the sidewalks and in the alleys by impromptu groups of police and vigilantes, their bodies left for the municipal services or the rats to sort out.

Within the hour of any mass shooting, however, footage appears on the pirate waves. Even when officers swear that protestors wore the visors, even where the remnants of the corpses' faces are still held together only by black bands, the footage shows their eyes.

They flicker, then are pinched like candle wicks.

"If there is a window to the soul," the Overseer asks Heira as they lie in bed, still damp from their exertion, "where do you think it is?" He kisses her closed eyes, her lips, all the while his hands roaming down across her naked belly, into her lap.

He doesn't taste like murder, she thinks. Does even he understand what he's doing?

Around them the room is mad with reflections. In the picture frames, the mirrors, the window backed by the darkness outside, the empty screen of the television that Heira no longer allows him to turn on. In all of these positions, Heira and the Overseer are reflected—two layers, three, four, five, on into the illusion of forever. However, they are always incomplete, always that one degree off that spins the multitude of regressions into a slow curve away from the truly infinite.

She pulls his hands away and opens her eyes. She can see her reflection in his deep-blue gaze, her face placed in the middle of the chasm of his pupil. Maybe, she thinks, something is moving in the distance.

If only she could find her way back.

The Overseer has come to the news station for an emergency broadcast. Their staff diminished through desertion and violence, the remainder has shrunk well past "skeleton crew" and now the station is haunted by the rumor of a ghost of a news team. Still, they stand on ceremony for the Overseer and his military escort, although the typical pomp has been replaced by an air reminiscent of the recent funerals of heads of the Commitment.

"Sir, your wife is here," the guard says, opening the door to the greenroom for Heira.

"Are you ready?" Heira asks, crossing to where the Overseer readies himself before the mirror.

"Of course." The Overseer smiles. He leans and she closes her eyes to be kissed on the lids. "I've always loved you."

"I never wanted this," she says. "But I've always known, you know?"

Of course he knows. There are no secrets between them and there never have been. He puts a finger to her lips.

"It's all right," the Overseer says. "What has happened, has happened."

She nods. "And what will come, will come."

"Then I'll see you again."

As the Overseer enters the stage, Heira takes her place behind the camera. These days, even the Overseer's wife and the editor of the Commitment takes a laboring oar.

As the producer checks the Overseer's microphone, he whispers to his superior, "Heira once told me that before the Shift, you wrote a book or a novel or something. Something about . . . " he looks over his shoulder at the empty studio, " . . . this?"

The Overseer nods. "A story, yes, called 'Mise en Abyme'."

"How did it end?" There is a glimmer in his eyes that could have been hope, if it didn't suspect the truth.

But the Overseer grips the producer's shoulder, squeezes it once, then turns to walk to his mark in front of the large and empty monitor. Through his tears, the producer counts down the 5-4-3-2 and they are on the air.

"Fellow subjects of the Commitment," the Overseer begins, the giant monitor behind him displaying live footage of the rioters just outside the station and the ragged line of soldiers holding them at bay, "I know that you have heard rumors and misinformation. That the Commitment has lost control. That our believers have betrayed us, that our technology has failed. That the God we left behind has come back to deal with us.

"This is foolish."

Beyond the station's doors, the roar of the wave of the crowd surges, and on the monitor, it crashes against the final bulwark of the Commitment, beginning to break through the beleaguered remnant.

"For indeed we are on the cusp of a great, new beginning. You ask, why then do we not stop the Corrective Executions? Why do we not stop broadcasting them? Because, my fellows, there are purposes and meanings to your sacrifices that even you do not know. Not yet.

"But I understand what you want. You want to again understand your place in existence. You want assurance that the terror of history, the stream that runs from the past, ever onward to the abyssal ocean of infinity, can change course. That there is a way out.

"Well, your sacrifices have not been in vain. Your suffering has proven worthy. If you doubt the Commitment, if you think that it has become too weak and too human in its petty vanities and desires, then I offer you a cleansing. Today, and forever, is the Recommitment.

"Gather your family around the television. Turn on every screen. Watch closely."

Someone screams in the halls and the locked doors of the studio shudder in their chains and groan on their hinges. Heira pushes a button and the screen behind the Overseer flips over to her camera's feed. A receding line of Overseers, each more indistinct than the last, stretches off into the distance. So many versions of her husband, each dedicated entirely to her and the Grand Return she has been heralding since she was only a girl. He steps aside now, lets the void of the empty screen show itself upon itself, again and again and again and again.

It curves slightly, but Heira pans the camera over, searching for the proper alignment. At the far end of the tunnel, almost microscopic, the darkness blinks.

She prepares herself for the flood of eyes that will proceed from the Great Voice made flesh. For the Great Voice itself in all its splendor.

For the gaping hole she will crawl back into to start the cycle again.

I asked Heira if she wanted to read "Mise en Abyme", to see if I've missed any details or taken any liberties, but she declined. She knows it well enough to tell by heart.

"Don't judge me too harshly," she said. "I mean, if I have to leave you, afterwards."

But I took her hand, my sweet wife, for whom I would do anything. I whispered back the words that we will one day say again.

"What has happened will come."

"And what will come has happened."

"Then I'll see you again."

Beyond us, in the darkness, the Great Voice is calling. The Worm is turning.

# In God's Own Image
### Sean M. Davis

*Needless to say we love getting submissions from our Boot Camp graduates, and the only thing we love more is accepting them. Sean Davis wrote the following piece as his weekend assignment; then he took his lumps, went home, and rewrote it before submitting it to us. In it, he poses a few elemental questions that caper around the barriers of fundamentalists, cults, and even theologians.*

For old times' sake, Viola sat at the mirror to draw her face. Thick red lines formed her mouth. She traced a thin black line for her nose. Squiggles on the sides of her head were her ears. She felt like cat's eyes today. And the bobbed wig.

Standing, she made sure the seams of her tights were straight, that there were no wrinkles in her dress. Arthur had encouraged her to take pride in her appearance, even if she only had a lingering sense, more like a memory, of what she'd looked like before the Forming.

She snapped her makeup case shut. Gracefully, she wove around furniture, pausing to caress her favorite ottoman. The satin fabric glided beneath her fingertips and she remembered what it had been like to smile.

The sun warmed her when she exited the apartment building. The breeze riffled her dress. She wished she could see the blue sky, smell the fresh air, hear the world around her. But it was a good day to be alive anyway. Walking down the steps to the sidewalk, she skipped a little.

Behind her, she felt others there, judging her. That took the skip out of her step and she settled into a long stride. Someone followed her, but Viola ignored them. Arthur didn't give a damn about what others thought of him and neither should she.

The nice weather made the walk to Arthur's apartment shorter than usual and Viola considered sitting on the stoop until he came outside to check for her. Then, Viola would pat the ground next to her and he'd sit down and they'd enjoy the day together.

Viola stood outside Arthur's building with her face turned to the breeze so that her wig strained against her scalp, and knew that she didn't dare stay out in public with a face. The other who had followed her from her building had stopped at a distance when she'd paused, but now took a step closer. Then, two more, even closer. Its puzzled anger radiated through the air at her.

She'd drawn a face on herself. Like a whore.

Viola hurried up the stairs and pounded on the door until she felt it unlock.

Viola scrambled inside, slamming it behind her. Her stalker struck the safety glass with an open palm, once. She braced the door against her folower, but it left quickly.

Bursting into Arthur's apartment, Viola clutched at him. The familiar texture of his seersucker suit comforted Viola. Arthur's hesitant arms encircled her for a brief moment before he pushed her away.

She'd worn her face out in public.

Viola nodded, cupping her elbows and turning away. She'd wanted to show him that she could be as brave as he was.

Except there was a difference between bravery and foolishness. Arthur didn't wear his face outside of their apartments.

Viola hung her head.

Arthur grasped her shoulders, then lifted her chin. What was done, was done, and no use worrying about it now. Arthur traced a finger across Viola's lightly shaded dimple.

Wait until she felt what he'd found this time.

He bustled out of the room, then strode back in with pomp and circumstance. Viola leaned forward, but Arthur focused on the tune of the march, so she couldn't read his feelings, except that he was excited.

She should hold out her hands.

When she did, Arthur flourished the taffeta gown he held, letting her trace her fingers across its smooth surface. Viola petted the fabric, shivering, wishing she could see its color. She hoped it was pastel blue, her favorite. She'd forgotten what most of the other colors looked like, but she still remembered that one.

No, it was white.

How did he know?

He just did. She should try it on.

Viola let the dress fall from her hands.

No. There was no point. She couldn't see it. He couldn't see it. Everything that had been was gone and there was no point in trying to hold on to it.

Viola went to the window, mourning the sun that she could feel but no longer see.

Arthur picked up the dress, running the lace trim between his fingers.

The use was right here, right now. It was the two of them, sharing old magazines and touching the glossy pages. Putting their hands on the speakers of his stereo to feel the vibrations the music made. Remembering what it had been like to declare their individuality through what they chose to wear, listen to, eat.

Whom they loved.

Dropping the dress, Arthur turned away.

Viola whirled, then crossed the room. Arthur tried to escape her, but she caught him, held him. She touched his face, savoring the subtle difference in texture where he'd drawn a straight line for his mouth, almond-shaped ovals for his eyes. She stood on tiptoes to touch his forehead with hers.

What she felt in such close proximity to him surprised her. He'd been on the edge of despair when he caught her trying on clothes in an abandoned department store. She'd reinvigorated him, inspiring him to hold on to his memories and take what pleasure he could in continuing to live his life as Arthur Golden instead of the faceless Form he'd become.

The skin of their foreheads started melting together.

Arthur pushed her away gently. Puzzled, she reached for him, but he stepped away.

He wanted to share everything with her, but he wasn't ready. Not yet.

Picking up the dress, he held it out to her.

Would she wear it the next time she came?

Viola took the dress, caressing it, and left.

The next day, Viola stood in front of her door, plucking at the lace trim of the dress Arthur had given her. She hadn't drawn her face on yet, as he'd advised her. When she arrived at his apartment, he'd already have his on, comfortable with its lines and expression, his toupee already in place. It'd be as if he were already a person and she could only become herself in his presence.

Something about that didn't feel right.

But it was a smart precaution. She put her hand on the doorknob.

She'd slink along the streets, her head down, ignoring anyone who might pay attention to her and the gown she wore. She'd pretend, just like everyone else who might remember their own faces, but who went along with God's decreed Forming out of fear. Eventually, by pretending, she'd forget.

Letting go of the knob, she strode over to her mirror and took out her makeup kit. After drawing her face, she felt relieved, in control, more herself than she had all morning. She'd march over to Arthur's and show him and everyone that she was who she was and she wasn't afraid.

The streets were empty when she exited her apartment building. She hunched her shoulders up to her outlined ears and hurried along the street. When she rounded the corner onto Arthur's block, she stopped short. A crowd stood outside his building, clogging the sidewalk, stairs, and entryway.

It couldn't have anything to do with Arthur. He never went out in public with his face on and always dressed in the same clothes he'd been wearing when God had re-Formed humanity. He was perfectly safe, she was sure.

Viola hoped to be able to sneak through, but someone stepped away from the crowd. It was the same one who had followed her yesterday, and one other.

She stumbled, turning in midstride. The two matched her pace, their strides longer. As they neared, she felt their thoughts more clearly.

If she wanted to act like a whore and paint her face, they'd treat her like a whore.

Viola shifted her weight forward so she could run in her heels. Specific thoughts faded to general feelings of anger, frustration, and hate, except for one last thought, seeming to answer why they didn't chase after her.

They'd wait.

Viola ran back to her building, slamming through the doors until she stood, her weight against her apartment door, trembling.

It was only a coincidence that the man who had followed her the other day had been with the crowd outside Arthur's building. Had to be.

Viola wished that she could still use a telephone. She'd gotten a new cell phone three weeks before the Forming and still had a landline at the insistence of her mother.

Pacing back and forth, she had an idea. Picturing Arthur in his apartment, reclining in his favorite chair, his feet up on a footstool, she tried calling out to him. His apartment was eight blocks away, but maybe if she shouted, she could . . .

She tried, cupping her hands around the lower half of her face, out of old habit.

She stood against the wall she thought was closest to Arthur's building and tried. As she fretted back and forth around her apartment, she slowly accepted that the return calls she thought she heard were only wishful thinking.

She should go back. Take some kind of weapon. Part the crowd and rush in to save the man in distress.

She had a set of kitchen knives and some heavy, blunt objects, but nothing like a gun.

It would be the first time since the Forming that she'd heard of people being killed, and she would be the one killing them.

Abandoning that plan, she pressed her fists into the sides of her head. There must be something else, another way.

Except there wasn't. Because of him.

She assumed that he'd been a man, the one who chased her and called her a whore. In the erosion of his identity and individuality, his hate had remained. She wondered who he'd been before the Forming, what kind of life he'd lived, whom he'd cared for, if anyone.

He waited for her.

So she stayed in her apartment, pacing, fretting, and calling out to Arthur, hearing nothing in return.

The fourth day, Viola sat down at her mirror and touched its smooth surface lovingly, perhaps for the last time. Instead of ruby lips, she drew a straight, pale line, remembering the times she'd clench her jaw and press her lips together. Plucking the black wig from the stand, she adjusted it on her head until it felt right.

Exiting the building, she held the skirt of her gown so it wouldn't trip her on the stairs and hitched her purse up on her shoulder that she'd loaded with a paperweight. She paused, wanting to appear defiant to anyone who might be around, but then she hurried toward Arthur's.

The two others who had waited for her came out from a building across the street and followed her. Viola quickened her pace.

Whore.

One of them snatched at her skirt and she whirled, swinging her purse. It hit the other across its head, knocking it back. Its buddy lunged at her, but Viola sidestepped and kneed it in the stomach. Before it had hit the ground, Viola started running.

Rounding the corner of Arthur's block, Viola collided with him and they both stumbled to the ground. She clutched at him, then jumped up, trying to pull him after her. They needed to get inside, but he wouldn't come. His grip on her wrist tightened.

Snatch and Buddy came around the corner. Others crossed the street toward Viola and Arthur, more emerging from his apartment building.

Viola needed to see and understand. God had been right. He had unified the world.

But she still remembered her face. And his.

He had not drawn his today.

Viola twisted away from him, but by then, it didn't matter. Other hands caught her, held her. Arthur smeared the lines of her eyes, nose, mouth, the squiggles of her ears. Another plucked the wig from her head, threw it to the ground, and stomped on it. Others tore at her gown. Her purse disappeared from her hands.

Snatch stepped up to her and put his hands on her hips. Viola struggled against those holding her, jerked back and forth, but Snatch pulled her to him and slapped his smooth pelvis against hers.

Their skin melted into each other's and she had the sense, for just a moment, of smoldering anger directed at everything and nothing, without reason. Then that slipped away.

Another plunged Viola's left hand into its chest and she was afraid of a dim room at the end of a long hallway, then that feeling faded.

They crowded closer to her. Their arms wide, bodies pressing tighter, their skin melting together and enveloping Viola.

A cacophony of emotions and images buried her, threatening to dissolve her in this mass of formless humanity. She held on to what it had meant to have eyes that could cry, a mouth that could smile, and all the wonderful and horrible smells and sounds that had faded into the background for all those years before the Forming.

She remembered and she wouldn't let that go.

But the world had attained peace.

Crime had stopped.

Petty dramas had ceased.

People lived without identity because once a person was something, another was not. Groups formed and ostracized others. She had done that by hiding away.

God had corrected his worst mistake.

She could see that now.

As the sun's light touched the mass of humanity the next morning, forms began pulling away. First one at a time, then twos, threes, and droves, leaving only two.

The one helped the other up, patted it on the shoulder, then went up the stairs into the apartment building.

The one remaining stood, trembling. At its feet lay a wig. It picked the wig up, its texture intoxicating, its meaning gone. Raising a hand to its blank face, it thought it might remember something. Then that, too, faded away.

# Special Delivery
## *Tim Waggoner*

*For the past twenty years, Tim Waggoner has been building his reputation as a true master of the uniquely strange and disturbing tale. That this is his first appearance in the series is a shock because he is one of his generation's best. (You don't get nominated for the Shirley Jackson Award for selling lottery tickets . . . ) His latest example is a subtle portrait of domestic discord worthy of the classic* Alfred Hitchcock Presents *television series.*

"I promise you, this is the last time you'll have to do that."

Roy paused, the handle of the snow shovel he was holding cold in his bare hands. The mail truck was idling at the curb—in front of his mailbox, naturally enough. Funny, but he hadn't heard it pull up.

The carrier—they used to call them mailmen when Roy was a child, but no longer, not in these enlightened times—leaned out of the window and gave Roy a grin. He looked normal enough, in his midforties, a bit older than Roy, thin face, scraggly brown beard, teeth yellowed but straight and even. Almost too even, as if they were all of a uniform shape and size. Roy couldn't quite make out the man's eyes. Though it was sunny out, his eyes were clouded by shadow, probably caused by the upper part of the mail truck's doorframe, Roy guessed.

The mailman—mail *carrier*—kept grinning and looking at Roy (at least Roy thought the man was looking at him; it was hard to tell with his eyes in shadow like that) as if he was waiting for a response. Feeling suddenly awkward, Roy replayed the man's words in his mind: *"I promise you, this is the last time you'll have to do that."*

Roy frowned. Do what? Shovel snow off the front walk? It was March 16th, and while it wasn't completely unknown for it to snow this late in Southern Ohio, it *was* unusual. They'd gotten three inches since this morning, and Roy had come home from work to a walk and driveway that both needed to be shoveled clean. He might've let them go. Roy was a weather reporter for an all-news radio station. His own forecast called for it to warm up over the next few days, and he knew the snow would melt on its own soon enough. But he'd had lunch at a Chinese restaurant that afternoon, and the message in his fortune cookie had read *Do today's work today.* As soon as he got home, he'd grabbed the snow shovel and gotten straight to work. He'd already finished the driveway and had been halfway through the front walk when the mail carrier drove up—*without making a sound,* a little voice inside his head added—and made his strange pronouncement.

The carrier waited, still grinning, as patient and motionless as a mannequin.

Roy decided the man was trying to be reassuring, telling him that this late snow was bound to be the last of the season and after today Roy could put his shovel up until next winter. What else could it be?

So Roy smiled and lifted a hand in acknowledgment. "Sounds good to me!"

The carrier's grin widened, and though Roy couldn't clearly see the man's eyes, he had the impression that they flashed with amusement. He then reached through the truck's open window, and though the motion was slow and nonthreatening, Roy nevertheless experienced a rush of fight-or-flight adrenaline.

"Here you go." The carrier held out a small package. When Roy made no move toward the man, he wiggled the package as if trying to capture the attention of a small child, or perhaps a dumb animal.

"Come on . . . I'd tell you that I don't bite, but that's not strictly accurate." Again that tone of amusement, this time with a dash of derision added for seasoning.

Roy told himself he was being ridiculous; the man was just delivering the mail. Even so, he nearly told the carrier to put the package in the mailbox and that he'd get it after he finished shoveling the walkway. But not wanting to be thought a coward even by a stranger—or for that matter, by himself—Roy laid his shovel in the snow and started toward the mail truck.

The carrier kept wiggling the package as if he thought Roy might change his mind and turn around, without the enticement of a constant lure. As Roy drew near, he was finally able to make out the man's eyes. Brown, the whites tinged yellow as if the carrier suffered from a slight touch of jaundice, but otherwise unremarkable.

"Thanks." Roy reached out for the package. It was small and rectangular, the sort of box that banks use when mailing new checks to customers. Roy closed his fingers around the package, started to pull . . . but the carrier didn't let go right away. Roy looked into the man's jaundiced eyes and saw mockery there.

"Hope you enjoy it," the man said, then released the package, causing Roy to nearly stumble backward. "See you later!" The carrier gave a jaunty wave, then turned forward, put his truck in gear, and pulled away from Roy's house.

As the vehicle moved off, Roy saw a bumper sticker affixed to the back. It was a black-and-white picture of Marilyn Monroe's face—eyes half-closed, lips forming a pouty O—and beneath it the caption: *MURDER YOUR DARLINGS.*

Roy watched, expecting to see the red glow of brake lights as the truck stopped at his neighbor's home. But the brake lights didn't come on; the truck picked up speed and continued past the next house, and the house after that, and all the others on Roy's street, until it came to an intersection and turned left without so much as slowing, let alone stopping.

Roy stood for several moments, holding the small package at his side.

That was strange. Why had the carrier taken off like that? Roy checked his watch and saw it was 5:18. He was used to the mail coming late around here, but he'd never known any carrier to just quit before his deliveries were finished, no matter the lateness of the hour. *Guess that stuff about neither rain nor sleet nor hail went out with the ten-cent stamp.*

Roy examined the package. The rectangular box was addressed to him in simple black letters that looked as if they'd been placed directly onto the white cardboard with old-fashioned typewriter keys. No return address—he turned the package over—on either side.

He stared at the box for several moments. He thought of the strange thing the carrier had said: *I promise you, this is the last time you'll have to do that.* Thought of Marilyn and *MURDER YOUR DARLINGS.*

He slipped the package into his coat pocket, and if his hand trembled a little, he pretended not to notice. Not much in the way of mail today, but he supposed it was better than getting a stack of bills. A sudden realization nagged at him, and he glanced at the mailbox, saw that it wasn't covered with snow. He hadn't brushed the snow off, had only finished half of the front walk. So if the snow had been knocked off by someone else . . . He opened the mailbox door and reached inside.

He took out a half-dozen pieces of mail, mostly those dreaded bills and several clothing catalogues for his wife. Odd, but he hadn't seen the carrier put the rest of the mail in the box, hadn't heard the metallic creak of the door opening, the hollow *chunk!* as it closed. And if the man had put the rest of the mail in the box, why had he insisted on handing the package to Roy? Unless . . .

Unless someone else had put the mail in earlier, before Roy had gotten home from work. But who?

*The real mail carrier, of course,* came the answering thought. *Who else?*

But if the man who'd handed him the package wasn't a postal worker, then who was he? Now that Roy thought about it, he realized the man's truck had displayed no logo to identify it, no *UPS* or *FedEx*. Nothing but that sticker of Marilyn. Maybe the man worked for some minor-league delivery service, Roy told himself. That would explain why he hadn't stopped at any other houses on the street.

Roy then noticed he'd left the mailbox door open. Irritated, confused, and despite his best efforts at rationalization, more than a little afraid, he shoved the door closed harder then he intended, catching his thumb in the process.

"Goddamnit!" Nerves screamed in pain, and he yanked his thumb away from the mailbox, sending a splash of blood arcing through the air. It pattered onto the snow, staining the white crimson.

Cursing, and holding his thumb out to the side so it wouldn't bleed on his clothes, he hurried up the half-shoveled walkway to the front door, leaving a trail of red behind him.

"This is officially the dumb-ass thumb," Roy said.

Marcy looked at the thumb in question and smiled. He'd wrapped it in so many layers of gauze that it appeared to have swollen to twice its normal thickness.

"I mean, how many people cut themselves closing their mailbox?"

They sat on opposite sides of their small dining table, facing each other across a low-carb dinner of broiled boneless chicken breasts, peas, and pear slices. Since they didn't have any children, a small table was all they needed.

"I appreciate your sacrifice, getting wounded in the line of duty and all." Marcy took a bite of chicken and chewed, a mischievous glint in her eyes. She swallowed. "I'm surprised you didn't take it as a sign of some sort."

Roy stiffened, suddenly tense, a piece of fork-speared chicken paused in midair on the way to his mouth. He thought of the rectangular package still in the pocket of his coat, now hanging in the foyer closet. Right then Roy almost told her about the mail carrier, the bumper sticker, the other mail in the box, the white cardboard package with no return address . . . But if he told her all that, he knew he'd end up telling her the rest: that the reason the package was still in his coat pocket was because of his thumb. Hadn't he cut himself right after he examined the package? Hadn't it been a warning?

"What do you mean?" he asked, though he knew exactly what she meant.

Marcy was a petite woman with short black hair and an almost comically expressive face. When she smiled, she exuded waves of unadulterated joy. But when she scowled, like now, every line of her face—forehead, the corners of her eyes and mouth—deepened, became more pronounced.

"Never mind. Forget I said anything." She scooped up a spoonful of crisp, hard peas—Marcy believed that if you cooked vegetables too long, they lost most of their nutrition.

Roy knew he shouldn't pursue the matter, that doing so would probably just lead to an argument, but he couldn't stop himself.

"I just wonder why you brought it up." He lowered his hand with the newly christened dumb-ass thumb below the table so Marcy couldn't see it. He rubbed his index finger against the smooth surface of the gauze, pressing a little, and his cut throbbed in response.

Marcy swallowed her peas, put down her spoon, and took a sip of wine. Roy knew from long experience—they'd been married sixteen years—that she was stalling for time to think. Finally, she put down her wineglass and sighed.

"You know you have a . . . thing about seeing signs."

Roy thought of the fortune he'd gotten this afternoon. *Do today's work today.* He'd put it in the jar on his dresser with all the others that he'd saved over the years.

"I don't know if I would call it a *thing*. I'm just detail oriented. It's a necessary quality in my line of work."

"I'm not talking about precipitation levels, Roy, and you know it. Fortune cookies and horoscopes are harmless enough, if you take them the right way. You know, like the disclaimer for those 1-900-PSYCHIC commercials: for entertainment purposes only. But when you take it too far . . ."

It was an old argument, and Roy could say his wife's lines as well as his own. But he couldn't stop himself from continuing with the same tired script, "And you think I take it too far."

Marcy sighed. "You know you do. Remember when we first looked at this house? You were dead set against buying a ranch . . . *until* you saw a cardinal perched on the roof."

He almost said, *But it's the state bird. My mother always said seeing one was good luck.*

But he decided to skip this line of the script. Bringing up his mother now would only give Marcy more ammunition.

"And how about a couple years ago when we were talking about having children? You were all for it until you read that article in the newspaper."

The headline flashed in his memory: *Marriages and Stillbirths on the Rise.* The article had nothing to do with them . . . it wasn't even about America, for God's sake, but some country in Africa.

"Too far is when you let these signs of yours control your life." He thought she added "and mine" beneath her breath, but he wasn't certain. And then Marcy returned her attention to her meal, their perpetual argument over again, at least for now.

Roy did the same, though he continued rubbing his wounded thumb and listening to its soft whispers of pain.

After dinner, Marcy sat on the couch and watched a home design show on HGTV while Roy sat in the chair next to her and looked at the paper. There was really only one thing that he was interested in, but after what Marcy had said at dinner, he made a show of going through the paper slowly, one section at a time, skimming articles rather than reading them, until he finally reached the Lifestyle section. There, right next to Dear Abby, was today's horoscope. He was a Pisces.

*Today you'll find it a bit harder than usual to preserve domestic harmony, but don't give up; the effort is worth it.*

He looked up from the paper, started to say something to Marcy, but he caught himself in time and kept quiet. It didn't matter how accurate his horoscopes were; she always put it down to coincidence and his imagination. Besides, didn't his horoscope say that it was important to maintain "domestic harmony" tonight? Why start a pointless fight that would do neither of them any good?

He folded the paper and set it on the chair arm. Later, after Marcy was asleep, he'd clip out the horoscope and save it with all the others he kept hidden in a scrapbook under the bed. He'd then put the paper in the recycling bin so Marcy wouldn't see that he'd cut out the horoscope, though he was pretty sure she knew that he kept them.

On the television, a woman burst into tears after seeing what the designers had done to her family room.

Marcy laughed. "I know it's awful of me, but I love it when they cry."

Roy smiled as if he were paying attention, but he absentmindedly rubbed his dumb-ass thumb and thought about the package.

*You can always tell when it's going to rain. The sky gets dark, the wind picks up, mourning doves call out, animals and little children get antsy. There are signs for everything, Roy. Hints and warnings . . . you just have to pay attention, that's all. Pay attention and you can get inside before it rains. Ignore the signs, and you'll get drenched.*

He woke with his mother's words still echoing in his ears. He rolled over and checked the clock radio on the nightstand—4:34. He worked the morning shift at the station, but even so, he didn't have to get up for another twenty-six minutes. But he was the sort of person who, once he was up, he was up. Unlike Marcy, who could sleep through a nuclear detonation. She was a lump under the covers next to him, still as stone, her breathing soft and slow. He considered reaching over to her, stroking her side, seeing if he could wake her up and convince her to help him make good use of his extra twenty-six minutes. But Marcy didn't rouse easily, and besides, he still felt out of sorts after last night's almost argument. So, dressed only in his underwear, he climbed out of bed as quietly as he could and let Marcy sleep while he went into the kitchen to get coffee started.

As he listened to the burble and hiss of the coffeemaker, he thought about the package in the pocket of his coat, still hanging in the closet. He knew he was going to have to do something about it. He couldn't very well carry the damn thing around in his pocket for the rest of his life, could he? He thought about going outside to get the paper so he could check his horoscope and get some idea what, if anything, he should do about the box. But the carrier always left the paper at the end of their driveway, and as cold as it was this morning, Roy would have to get dressed if he wanted to go outside to get it.

He could imagine what Marcy would say if she woke up and saw him consulting his horoscope before checking out the box. And did he really need astrological guidance this morning? Weren't the dream of his mother's advice, as well as waking up early, clear enough signs on their own?

Roy left the kitchen and walked to the foyer. He hesitated only a moment before opening the closet door. The hinges creaked and he winced, hoping the noise wouldn't wake Marcy. He paused, listened, didn't hear anything. She was still asleep. Good. He reached into his coat pocket and removed the rectangular white box. He avoided looking at it as he closed the door and returned to the kitchen.

The coffee was almost finished, and its rich, warm smell filled the air, its familiar comfort making the box seem less sinister. He sat down at the breakfast nook and lay the box on the table in front of him. What was he worried about, really? Just because there was no clear indication of who had sent it, and why, didn't mean anything. Lots of promotional mail omitted return addresses so people would have to open it to see what it was, and thus be exposed to the pitch contained within. Most likely that's all this box was: just another sales gimmick. He picked the package up, held it close to his ear, and like an eager kid on Christmas morning, shook it to see if he could get a clue as to its contents.

He heard a low, angry drone, along with the rustling of dozens of tiny bodies.

Roy jerked the package away from his ear, nearly dropping it. He set it on the table with a trembling hand, and then scooted his chair back, as if to put as much distance between the box and himself as possible without actually fleeing. The buzzing continued for several moments, slowly growing softer, less agitated, until finally the box—or rather, whatever was inside—fell quiet once more.

Lines of nervous sweat rolled down his face and neck as he stared at the box, and his bandaged thumb throbbed.

He'd heard that bees were often transported by mail to beekeepers and laboratories, though until now he'd never believed it. *Bee*-lieved it. He tried to chuckle, but the sound was forced, hollow, desperate. Though why in the world anyone would be sending him bees . . . But it hadn't sounded like bees, not exactly. More like the ratcheting thrum of cicadas, but even that wasn't quite right.

Whatever it was, he wanted nothing to do with it. Pay attention, his mother had always said, but though he'd been warned clearly enough, he hadn't heeded the signs. Instead he'd listened to a small nagging voice—a voice that sounded more and more like his wife's—that he shouldn't let himself be ruled by superstition. But Roy didn't care about any of that now. Whether it was instinct or neurosis, or some uneasy blend of the two, he knew there was something seriously wrong with the package, and there was no way in hell he was going to open it.

He heard a toilet flush from down the hallway, and he knew that Marcy was up, drawn out of sleep by the insistence of a full bladder. She might crawl back into bed or, lured by the aroma of freshly brewed coffee, she might head for the kitchen.

Roy's hand shook as if palsied as he reached for the box. He held his breath as he lifted the package off the table, fully expecting whatever was inside to start buzzing and crawling around again. But nothing happened. He hurried toward the foyer, doing his best to keep his upper body as still as possible. He opened the closet door, grimacing as the hinges protested again. And then, like a reverse pickpocket, he slipped the box back into his coat pocket, and once again closed the door. And this time, did he hear a muffled buzzing accompany the hinges' creaking? Maybe.

He was standing at the kitchen counter, pouring himself a cup of coffee, when Marcy walked up, hair mussed from sleep and eyes still half-closed.

"Morning," she mumbled.

"Good morning, sweetheart." Roy gave her a peck on the cheek—Marcy didn't like kissing on the lips until both of them had brushed their teeth—and she shuffled past him, desperate to get at the coffee.

He stepped aside and waited for her to say, *So what were you doing in the front closet, Roy? Trying to hide something from me?*

But she finished pouring her coffee, took a sip though it was still hot enough to scald, and shuffled into the dining room without another word.

Roy felt relieved, as if he'd gotten away with something, though he couldn't have said exactly what.

Roy pulled into the parking lot of the radio station fifteen minutes before he was due to go on the air. He got out of his car and started walking. Normally, he would've gone directly into the building and to the studio. But today wasn't a normal day, was it?

He took a detour around the side of the building, hoping that none of his colleagues was looking out a window at this exact moment. The sun was still down, but the lot was lit by the sterile glow of fluorescent lights. Roy's breath drifted out of his mouth in curled wisps of fog, as if the frigid air were sucking the life out of him breath by breath. He continued around the rear of the building and saw what he was looking for: a Dumpster.

He'd never been so thrilled to see what was essentially nothing more than a giant garbage can. He'd intended to throw away the box at home, but he hadn't been able to find a way to do so without Marcy knowing. So the box had remained in his pocket when he'd slipped the coat on to go to work, and it had sat there as he drove, shifting about from time to time in ways that Roy knew had nothing to do with the car's momentum.

Well, if he couldn't throw the damn thing away at home, he'd just get rid of it at work. A much better plan, really, since there was no way for Marcy to find out what he'd done.

The area around the Dumpster had been cleared of snow, but there were mounds shoved up against and packed on either side of it. Roy could see tiny tracks on the mounds—cat pawprints, as well as smaller, more narrow depressions that could only have been made by rats. He stomped his feet as he approached, to scare off any lurking vermin, and then he lifted the Dumpster's lid. The plastic was cold and hard to the touch, and Roy's wounded thumb started to throb. He wished he'd put on his gloves, but one of them was in the same pocket as the box, and he wasn't about to reach in there until he had to.

But *had to* had finally come at last. Slowly, so as to avoid disturbing whatever was inside the box, Roy slipped cold-numbed fingers into his pocket and gently took hold of slick cardboard. He then pulled the box out, moving so slowly, as if he were handling a deadly explosive instead of a plain white package with no return address.

The box shook and juddered in his hand, and the angry buzzing erupted, as if whatever resided in the box understood what he intended to do and wasn't happy about it.

*Tough shit,* Roy thought. After all the warnings he'd received, he wasn't about to—

His gaze was suddenly drawn by white letters of graffiti spray-painted on the brick above the Dumpster.

*WASTE NOT, WANT NOT.*

Roy held the box over the open Dumpster, but he didn't drop it. Instead, he read the graffiti over and over, hearing the words in his mother's voice.

"Goddamnit," he muttered in disgust. He put the box back in his coat pocket, turned away from the Dumpster, and headed for the front of the building. The box, as if pleased, grew quiet and still.

*"In a change from yesterday's forecast, the National Weather Service is now predicting that the cold front which brought nearly five inches of snow to the Ohio Valley yesterday will continue to linger for the rest of the week, with the possibility of more snowfall to come. Looks like winter's not quite done with us yet, folks."*

As Roy drove home from work that afternoon—the box still in his coat pocket, still quiet, still *still*—tiny flakes of snow began to drift down from the sky. He drove past a synagogue, read on the message board out front that The Day Is Short; The Task Is Great. A mobile billboard truck passed him going in the opposite direction. On its side was an advertisement, a picture of brown cardboard boxes stacked haphazardly, the ones on top beginning to fall. Written below: *Don't get boxed in! Call Crouch Movers!* As he turned onto his street, he saw a Lexus parked in front of a neighbor's house. The vanity plate read *TNGLD UP.*

Roy knew exactly how the car's owner felt.

His driveway was already coated with a light dusting of white when he pulled into his garage. He closed the garage door, got out of the car, saw the snow shovel propped in a corner, right where he'd left it.

*"I promise you, this is the last time you'll have to do that."*

He looked away from the shovel and went inside. He still had his coat on when he saw the note taped to the microwave.

*Have to run a few errands after work. Can you start dinner?*
*Love,*
*Me*

He usually got home a couple hours before Marcy, but now this note, this *sign*, told him he'd have even more time than that. Still wearing his coat, he went out the back door and around to the side of the house, where they kept their trash cans.

They had two receptacles, both made of brown plastic, so they technically weren't garbage *cans*, he supposed. The lid was off the one on the right, and the trash bag inside had been torn open and bits of refuse were strewn about. Roy glanced down, saw animal tracks in the snow. He wasn't surprised. They'd had trouble with raccoons getting into their trash last year, and now it seemed that, despite the late season snow, they were back.

It was another sign, of course.

Snowflakes fell all around him, larger now, heavier.

The day was TNGLD UP and he was boxed in, but the task was great, and he was supposed to murder his darlings in order to preserve domestic harmony, and what the hell did it all *mean*?

He reached into his coat pocket—bandaged thumb throbbing—and took out the box. No sound came from within, and there was no movement.

*Just throw the box away, put the lid back on, go inside, and forget you ever saw the damn thing.*

But he hesitated.

WASTE NOT, WANT NOT.

His mother had always said that the signs would tell him what to do, just as long as he paid attention to them. And he *had*, but he couldn't decide what they meant. Throw the box away? Keep it? *Open* it?

He knew what Marcy would say if she were there. That this was exactly the problem with letting his life be controlled by signs and portents—that in the end they provided no answers. Only more questions.

"Screw it."

He started to open the box.

He'd managed to pry back a corner when the box shuddered in his hand and a loud droning cut through the air. Small, dark shapes flooded out of the opening and swirled upward, shadowy counterparts to the falling snowflakes.

Roy yelped and dropped the box. It plopped into the snow, but the black forms continued streaming out. He tried to run, but the small ebon things—not insects, more like bits of darkness come to angry, buzzing life—circled around him, trapping him in a cloud of shadow.

And then the darkness began to close in on Roy.

He tried to scream, but when he opened his mouth, shadows rushed forward and poured down his throat, choking him, filling him, *absorbing* him . . .

Several moments passed as the dark cloud went about its work. And then it flowed back into the box, and when the last bit of darkness was gone, the opening that Roy had made resealed itself, and the box lay in the snow as flakes continued to fall.

Roy was gone.

A couple hours later, a feminine hand reached into the snow, found the box, and carried it back into the house.

Marcy was shoveling the walk when the small white truck pulled up to the curb. Snow was still falling, but it had begun to taper off.

The carrier leaned out the open window of his vehicle.

"Got something for me?"

Marcy lay the shovel aside and stepped to the end of the walk. She reached into her coat pocket and removed a rectangular cardboard box. There was no address on it this time.

She handed the box to the carrier. "Thanks a lot."

He took it and flashed her a yellow-toothed smile. "No problem. All part of the service."

She returned the smile then headed back up the walk to finish shoveling.

Inside the truck, the carrier held the box to his face, and his smile took on a grim edge.

"Told you," he said.

The carrier then tossed the box into a large gray bag that sat on the backseat—a bag filled with dozens of similar white boxes. Then he pulled away from the curb, whistling an off-key tune. He had other stops to make before he could knock off for the day.

A lot of them.

# The Palace Garbage Man
### Bradley Michael Zerbe

*We now present you with an intriguing tale that's little more than a slice of life in a time and place unknown to all but Bradley Zerbe. A new writer, he writes in clear, clean style that immediately captures our attention and tweaks our imagination with some shuddering images we can't get out of our heads. We're betting you'll feel the same way.*

West became the palace garbage man on the day her father died. She kicked her legs, dirty feet dangling into the pit. Above her, heavy droplets fell from a starless heaven, and the rock on which she sat was slick with mud. It would not take much. Lean forward, a slight push with the hips, and gravity would see to the rest.

"I know ya want me, ya sweet bastard hole," she said and spit.

West massaged her temples. Twenty years of living beside the pit and it still left her lusting after the taste of darkness and dirt. A subtle pull on her emotions, dragging down her mind day by rotting day. An evil made of whispers and dust, vibrations from the earth below.

She stood and frowned into the blackness, listening for their voices amidst the pattering rain. Her leg quivered and rose from the ground, hung in the air. Below her sweaty toes lay a vast darkness where lies decomposed beneath rubbish and muck. Her foot lowered.

"Devil, you won't get no more food tonight!"

She paused at the door to her shack and wondered, not for the first time, how it had come to this.

*"Must feed the pit, gal, for yonder pit has many and sharp teeth, and when she grows hungry, she eats at yer mind. Look alive, gal, and help your da feed the rotting bastard,"* her father once said.

West concentrated on the memory of his haggard face as she fought to clear her mind. Hairy grin; anxious eyes, the rock-solid strength behind his fist. Even a bloody memory was better than the gloom of the pit. She wiped her eyes before stepping inside her shack. Behind her, grating moans echoed from the deep as the rubbish churned.

A new day brought West back to the palace for a fresh load. She rode atop her aged wagon with the high sideboards and ingrained stench. Her sweetest friend in the realm pulled the maggoty contraption. A mule named Sandy.

The palace loading dock had not changed in the past twenty years. Muddy carts entered with a variety of vegetables and meats, and other more elaborate ones hauled rare and expensive goods in abundance—Queen Agrippa was said to be loose with her gold, a bitter joke among the servants.

Many of those carts left empty; some headed for home untouched, but the cart driven by West was always the fullest when she pulled from the dock. This time was no exception when the time finally came. West found the delay peculiar and horrendous. The personal servants of the queen had spent two hours sifting through the trash barrels for some lost item before they were allowed to be dumped. Powdered faces like pale marble, tongues long ago sliced and torn from their mouths after the queen coveted their silly songs. Peculiar ladies. West joked with them, but they would not give the slightest hint as to what they were looking for.

"I'd toss all them louts in the pit, Sandy," West said after they left. "If your legs could haul 'em, I'd toss 'em."

Sandy brayed.

"That's right, girl. Same as we tossed Mother."

A slow, bumpy ride home and it was time to unload. West coaxed Sandy backward toward the edge of the pit. The wagon wheels creaked. Closer. Sandy's legs quivered. She snorted and collapsed. West jumped from the wagon and knelt by her side. The mule's jaw cringed tightly and closed. She was dead.

"I loves my poor old brute. Poor, poor Sandy," West said and began to cry into her friend's brown, sweaty fur.

She struggled for over an hour to unhitch her friend and winch her fat body to the edge of the pit, but it only took a second for Sandy to land. The echoing thump stunned West like a punch in the face. Memories of her mother rushed into her mind, cold pinching of regret.

The heavens darkened as she rolled back her tarp and pulled on her gloves. She flung one scoop of rubbish at a time into the empty air, not caring what precious goodies may be hidden in the waste. Half-eaten loaves of bread. Ancient relics. She tossed them all. Not the way her father taught her to unload the cart, but so what. His prickly smile was gone for—she shivered and looked down.

The trash she held would bury her friend, and Sandy would be lost forever. West's fingers opened and the remains slipped through and landed in the cart. She jumped down, bumped her way inside the shack, and lit a lantern. Then she flopped onto the late king's rickety rocker and closed her eyes. Her life was over. How could she haul trash for the queen without Sandy?

A coyote yelped. They frequented the area, drawn by the enticing aroma of the pit. Again—a weird, hollow vibration in the air. Tinkling glass outside, rattling cans. West remembered she had only unloaded half of the cart. Coyotes had to be feasting on the remainder. The mess would be dreadful.

"Ain't in no mood for them thieves," she said and pushed herself up from the rocker.

West grabbed some rocks from her stash, picked up her light, and eased open the door. She crept around the side of her shack, her shadow hunched and wide on the rustic plank walls. Nothing around the cart. All was silent, save for the feathery rustle of leaves on nearby trees and a cricket that chirped with an eerie lust.

Had she been mistaken about the noise (the remaining trash did not look disturbed)? She wiped her hands on her pants and eyed the darkness. Sandy was all she had left, and now her friend lay in the pit.

West walked over to her rock and sat, legs dangling below her, the lantern at her side, warming her arm. She had known this day would come. Tears ran down her face as the life she was born into rekindled before her eyes—heavy wagon wheels grinding down ruts in the Esbenshade road, bitter drafts of rotting air in the summer, followed by miles of crackly leaves and frosted trees in the fall, shovel after shovel of trash disappearing into that sulfury darkness of the pit, the sour stench of liquor oozing from her father's overalls as she scrubbed them in the battered pail.

"Why?" she called down into the chasm, and it seemed to yawn and grow at the sound of her voice, a deepening blackness. Those familiar moans rose in volume—grinding, grating. Hungry growls.

"Take me back, pit. Take me back to the day before."

The pit sucked down the trash slinger's tears and dried them into dust. If only her mother had not died so young. If only Sandy could have lived forever.

A wail from out in the darkness—West jumped.

"Who's there?"

The wail grew louder, drowning out the moans.

"Stupid coyotes never learn." Every time one fell in, the pit consumed the beast by morning.

West stood and held out the lantern. A distant eye glared back from below, a touch different from the yellow glare of a coyote's. That was Sandy's eye, Sandy's *dead* eye. The coyote must be out of range of her light.

"Hole needs ta eat, dog, and better it be your bony ass than mine," she called down.

And below, Sandy brayed—West jumped and spun around. No one was there.

Sandy brayed again and a jolt of fear weakened her legs.

*It's not real,* West thought. *That old girl's memory be too strong for me, that's all.*

She sank to her knees, her brain twisting in confusion. *"Yonder pit has many and sharp teeth, and when she grows hungry, she eats at yer mind,"* her father repeated for the millionth time.

*"Garbage men are the slop in the back of the cart, gal."* The words stung. They came from her father, from deep in the pit. They dragged along a vision of the past.

West was a small girl. She knelt, cowering against the wagon wheel as her father towered over her. She stared up at Melvin's mangy beard as his greasy face blotted out the sun above. He promised West could ride along with him to work. Instead, Melvin spit a sickening wad of tobacco at his daughter.

*"You don't want this job, gal. Slop in the back of the cart, that's all you'll end—"*

West ran from her father. Melvin jumped down and chased her, tackled her, spit in her face.

*"Jump in with the maggots, gal . . . must feed the—"*

"No!" she shouted, and the pit recoiled at her rebuke.

Silence.

Then Sandy brayed once more, a shrill, echoing blast. She was alive! West was certain her friend was alive and had not been dead when she pushed her in. A gladness awakened in her heart, a bonfire of warmth no wad of tobacco juice could quench.

"Sandy! You wait, girl. I'll get you out. I'll . . . "

West wiped her hands on her shirt, licked her lips, and spit. Nothing ever survived the pit. Sandy would be eaten up like that coyote before the sun— West ran inside her shack as a light murmur filtered up from below. She was back in seconds with a coil of rope, and the lantern went down. Sandy's eyes glowed bright.

"Sandy! It's okay, girl!"

The mule lay stuck on her side. Her chest rose and fell, front hoofs kicking the trash around as she struggled for traction. West found a sturdy place to rest the lantern. Then she sat and rubbed her eyes and listened to the grating moans as they rose in volume. Grinding, crunching, the pit feasted. How long would it take? How much time did she have?

The hell critters were real, though they always remained hidden. *They* were the hungry ones. *They* were the teeth and the guts of the pit. She placed a rock on the end of the rope, then climbed up into her cart. The remaining trash was light. She heaved it into the pit like mad, most of it landing far out beyond Sandy and the mound she rested on.

Gotta fill the bastard, make her level rise. West pictured Sandy shaking off the trash and stepping up closer to safety with each layer she slung in.

When the cart stood empty, West saw she had failed. She sat and rubbed her grimy hands together while a voice in her mind scolded her for going too near the edge.

"Sandy fell in the pit, Ma. Don't worry, I'll go down and get her."

West leaped from her cart. She pulled the end of the rope out from beneath the rock and tied it to a solid part of her shack. Then she lowered herself into the pit.

Her feet touched the trash. She let go of the rope and untied the lantern. Then she clenched her shaky hands into fists and staggered toward the shape of her friend.

"I'm coming, Sa—"

A hole. Her foot slipped down. She pulled back. It was stuck.

A voice from below: "Just like yer old man, gal. Nothing but—"

West pulled free and leaped over to Sandy. She fell to her knees by her friend's side.

"It's all right, darlin', I'm here for ya."

She held out the lantern and touched Sandy's neck. She did not move. Her eye was glossy and dull in the light. West stared. Sandy was dead.

The pit rumbled beneath them as though the hell critters had grown impatient to reach the surface of the trash. Fresh meat above, the little bastards thought.

A humming sound. A haunting melody buried beneath many layers of trash. West turned. Slanted in the outermost fingerlings of her light, a pale form motioned to her from across the gloom.

"Mother!"

Was it really her?

West pushed herself up and ran toward the figment, abandoning Sandy, her sweetest friend in the realm. She stopped as a dozen sets of eyes appeared behind her mother. Fiery green—hell critters? Demons?

Her mother stepped toward her, lurching into the beam of light. Her mouth opened to speak, but only a ragged hiss escaped her lips. Fitting. Even in death her voice belonged to the queen.

"Can you hear me?" West asked.

Her mother fell to her knees and held out her hand. A ring glinted in her palm. She moaned. West ignored the green eyes behind her mother and stepped closer. She snatched the ring from her bony fingers and held it into the light. Heavy and gold, littered with diamonds.

"Where did—"

Her mother jerked to the side and fell. A dark shape dragged her back into the shadowy rubbish. Hissing growls, claws scraping on rusty tin. The drunk laughter of a father she remembered all too well. West stared in awe as the shadows twisted and darkened amidst the debris, and her mother disappeared.

More eyes—an army of green dots appeared low to the ground. She slipped and regained her footing, the junk beneath her feet shifting and sinking. West shoved the ring onto her finger and ran for the rope.

She pulled herself up as the hell critters hissed and moaned below her.

"Goodbye, Mother," she whispered. "Goodbye, Sandy." The breeze lifted her whispers toward the sky, away from the foul darkness and muck of the pit.

West heaved herself up onto her rock and flopped over on her back. She rubbed the ring on her finger, savoring the grating moans that vibrated up from the darkness below.

# Consumers
## *Gary A. Braunbeck*

*Our penultimate offering marks Gary Braunbeck's third appearance in this series, and this time he gives us something atypical of his work. Instead of his trademark examinations of the human heart in his longer fiction, he reveals a rarely seen caustic and satiric side to his writing.*

At the New and Shiny Big-Box Store there's an old fellow who greets you when you come through the doors. His uniform is blue and well pressed, his shoes shiny, his white hair glowing under the overhead lights, his voice tattered at the edges (he is, after all, an old fellow, and perhaps he drank or smoked too much in his younger days), and he smiles at you as if someone has just stuck a gun in his back and told him to act naturally.

"Welcome," he says. "Thank you for shopping with us. If you need any help, please don't be afraid to ask." It doesn't matter a damn that you have just entered the store and have yet to buy anything; this is the way he greets everyone, with those memorized words and his gun-in-the-back smile. Were you to stop long enough and look in his eyes, you might see behind them something that is nailed down and in torment, even fear and horror, like a drowning victim too far from the shore who can do nothing more than wave their arms and cry out in futile hope that someone will hear them and they will be rescued.

"Don't forget to grab one of our flyers and check out today's sales," he says, his voice an offshore echo as the customers walk away.

At the New and Shiny Big-Box Store there is always a sale going on, always a blue/green/orange special in one aisle or another. Perhaps it's one of these brightly lit sales that the woman is hurrying to, carrying her toddler. She barely glances at the greeter as she makes her way to the shopping-cart rack and, after a brief struggle, frees one from the corral. Her toddler—and a cute little one he is, perhaps eleven months at most—giggles and grabs at her with his tiny arms as she places him in the upper seat, as if it's some kind of game they've played a thousand times but to him never gets old.

After that, it's on to the back of the store, near the Hardware and Home Repair area where no customers are elbowing their way past others to get to a sales item. The woman parks the cart next to the Motor Oil section, glancing around to make certain no one can see her. After a few moments she opens her purse and pulls out a small but well-used stuffed toy, an elephant missing one of its tusks, and gives it to the toddler, who excitedly snatches it from her hand and hugs it to his chest, squeezing it within an inch of its life. The mother leans down and gives her son a kiss on his forehead, brushes a hand through his hair so less of it is hanging in his eyes. Without a word or another glance, she turns around and walks away.

The toddler covers his eyes as if counting to ten while playing hide-and-seek. When he pulls his hands away, his mother does not reappear. For a moment he is frightened, but then squeezes his toy elephant once more as if to say, *It's all right, Mommy will be back in a second*. And there in the cart he waits.

At the New and Shiny Big-Box Store it's not unusual to see an employee or department manager peeking out from behind the windows of swinging metal doors that lead back into the storage area, and today is no exception: a middle-aged gentleman watches from behind the swinging doors as the mother kisses the toddler on the forehead and turns and walks away. The manager waits a few moments to make certain no one is around, and then exits the storage area and approaches the cart. The toddler looks up at him and smiles. The manager smiles back, and then slowly pushes the cart down a few aisles, to the back of the Home Lighting Department.

The manager grabs a lamp from one of the displays, removes the shade, and places it to the side of the cart. He then reaches into the pocket of his manager's smock and removes a toy doll's head, which he jams into place atop the frame that protects the bulb. Without looking at the toddler—who seems somehow larger than before—he walks over to a wall phone, lifts the receiver, presses a button, and says for the entire store to hear, "Shoppers, we've got a special over in our Toy Department. All the latest *Star Wars* toys are thirty percent off for the next fifteen minutes. A Toy Department employee will be happy to put one of our green-light stickers on the item of your choice." He hangs up and walks away. By now the little boy in the cart is crying—not a lot, not enough to draw the attention of any shopper who's all but running to the Toy Department, but enough that even a hug from the elephant can't stop the quiet tears.

At the New and Shiny Big-Box Store, you can always find a child who is crying.

At the New and Shiny Big-Box Store a line is forming at the Customer Service desk, and the woman who abandoned her toddler in the Hardware and Home Repair aisle is right at the front. She removes an envelope from her purse and hands it to the young man working the desk. He opens it, reads what is written on the piece of paper inside, nods to himself, and then begins pulling several thick books of coupons from a shelf below. He continues to stack the coupon books until there are twenty-five of them. The woman pulls a plastic bag from her purse, seeps the coupons into it until the bag threatens to burst, smiles at the young man, and then leaves the store, still smiling.

At the New and Shiny Big-Box Store many people leave smiling.

At the New and Shiny Big-Box Store the little boy in the cart is trying to wiggle his way out of the cart but his legs have gotten a bit too long and a bit too chubby. By now he's all cried out and has nothing to hug because he's dropped his elephant. He's been moved several times, and each time someone jams a doll's head onto a lamp and places it near the cart. The boy watches as customers whiz by, on their way to a special sale that seems to be in a department on the opposite end of the store. And so the little boy waits, but he doesn't have to wait long.

At the New and Shiny Big-Box Store no one ever has to wait very long.

Soon the little boy becomes a larger boy who has split through most of his toddler clothing; soon the young boy is nearly naked, his privates covered only by the remnants of the clothes he was wearing when his mother brought him here; soon the young boy is a grown man whose weight the cart can no longer hold upright. The cart flips forward, knocking over many of the impaled dolls' heads that scatter like marbles. The force of the falling cart is enough to free the young man's legs—a light shade of purple they seem to have become—and then the cart falls over him as if it were a cage being lowered from above.

The young man huddles beneath the cart, still crying, and tries to reach for his elephant, but it's on the other side of the cart. The young man tries to reach it but cannot get the cart to budge. Eventually he gives up, huddles in a fetal position, and wishes that someone walking toward the next sale would notice him. But no one does, even when he calls out to them in a voice that sounds frayed around the edges.

He stays like that until he can no longer call out or even muster the tears to cry. He stays like that until his skin begins to wrinkle and his hair turns grey. He stays like that until the first manager to move the toddler's cart emerges from the storage area and lifts the cart off the old man. The manager helps the old man to his feet and begins to dress him in the perfect, new, bright, shiny, perfectly pressed uniform of a store employee.

"Keeping this clean is your responsibility," says the manager. "It has to be dry-cleaned, not washed."

Helping the old man to put on his New and Shiny shoes, the manager walks the old man to the front of the store, explaining more of the store's employee policies.

"The most important thing," says the manager as he positions the old man by the entryway, "is to smile when you greet the customers. Remember that."

He walks away, leaving the old man standing there, alone and confused. But then the old man sees a young woman come into the store holding a toddler, and a cute little thing he is. "Welcome," he says. "Thank you for shopping with us. If you need any help, please don't be afraid to ask." He watches as the mother puts her little stinker in a cart, hands him a small stuffed elephant missing a tusk, and makes her way back toward Hardware and Home Repair. "Thank you," the old man whispers, but it sounds more like a question.

At the New and Shiny Big-Box Store there's an old fellow who greets you when you come through the doors . . .

# The Architecture of Snow
*David Morrell*

*If our final story were science fiction or fantasy, it might be taking place in an alternate dimension or a parallel universe where everything is almost just like here . . . but is definitely not. However, that description would not aptly describe David Morrell's intensely personal examination into the life of a writer who may appear familiar to some of you. Narrated in clear, succinct prose, this novella à clef becomes a descent into a subtle, almost-gentle maelstrom of guilt—wherein lies its most quiet horror.*

On the first Monday in October, Samuel Carver, who was seventy-two and suddenly unemployed, stepped in front of a fast-moving bus. Carver was an editor for Edwin March & Sons, until recently one of the last privately owned publishing houses in New York.

"To describe Carver as an editor is an understatement," I said in his eulogy. Having indirectly caused his death, March & Sons, now a division of Gladstone International, sent me to represent the company at his funeral. "He was a legend. To find someone with his reputation, you need to go back to the 1920s, to Maxwell Perkins and his relationships with Ernest Hemingway, F. Scott Fitzgerald, and Thomas Wolfe. It was Perkins who massaged Hemingway's ego, helped Fitzgerald recover from hangovers, and realized that the two feet of manuscript Wolfe lugged into his office could be divided into several novels."

Standing next to Carver's coffin at the front of a Presbyterian church in Lower Manhattan, I counted ten mourners. "Carver followed that example," I went on. "For much of the past five decades, he discovered an amazing number of major authors. He nurtured them through writers' blocks and discouraging reviews. He lent them money. He promoted them tirelessly. He made them realize the scope of their creative powers. R. J. Wentworth's classic about childhood and stolen innocence, *The Sand Castle*; Carol Fabin's verse novel, *Wagon Mound*; Roger Kilpatrick's Vietnam War novel, *The Disinherited*; eventual recipients of Pulitzer Prizes—these were buried in piles of unsolicited manuscripts that Carver loved to search through."

Ten mourners. Many of the authors Carver had championed were dead. Others had progressed to huge advances at bigger publishers and seemed to have forgotten their debt to him. A few retired editors paid their respects. *Publishers Weekly* sent someone who took a few notes. Carver's wife died seven years earlier. They didn't have children. The church echoed coldly. So much for being a legend.

The official explanation was that Carver stumbled in front of the bus, but I had no doubt he committed suicide. Despite my praise about the past five decades, he hadn't been a creative presence since his wife's death. Age, ill health, and grief had worn him down. At the same time, the book business had changed so drastically that his instincts didn't fit. He was a lover of long shots, with the patience to give talent a chance to develop. But in the profit-obsessed climate of modern publishing, manuscripts needed to survive the focus groups of the marketing department. If the books weren't trendy and easily promotable, they didn't get accepted.

For the past seven years, George March, the grandson of the company's founder, loyally postponed forcing Carver into retirement, paying him a token amount to come to the office two days a week. The elderly gentleman had a desk in a corner where he studied unsolicited manuscripts and read newspapers. He also functioned as a corporate memory, although it was hard to imagine how stories about the good old days could help an editor survive in contemporary publishing. Not that it mattered—I was one of the few who asked him anything.

Eventually, March & Sons succumbed to a conglomerate. Gladstone International hoped to strengthen its Film and Broadcast Division by acquiring a publisher and ordering it to focus on novels suited for movies and TV series. The trade buzzword for this is "synergy". As usual when a conglomerate takes over a business, the first thing the new owner did was downsize the staff, and Carver was an obvious target for elimination. Maybe he felt that his former contributions made him immune. That would account for his stunned reaction when he came to work that Monday morning and got the bad news.

*"What am I going to do?"* I heard the old man murmur. His liver-spotted hands shook as he packed framed photographs into a flimsy box. *"How will I manage? How will I fill the time?"* Evidently, he decided that he wouldn't. The box in one hand, his umbrella in the other, he went outside and let the bus solve his problems.

Because Carver and I seemed to be friends, the new CEO put me in charge of whatever projects Carver was trying to develop. Mostly, that meant sending a few polite rejection letters. Also, I removed some items Carver forgot in his desk drawer: cough drops, chewing gum, and a packet of Kleenex.

"Mr. Neal?"

"Mmmm?" I glanced up from one of the hundreds of emails I received each day.

My assistant stood in my office doorway. His black turtleneck and sports coat gave him the appearance of authority. Young, tall, thin, and ambitious, he held a book mailer. "This arrived for Mr. Carver. No return address. Should I handle it for you?"

In theory, it was an innocent suggestion. But in the new corporate climate, I doubted there was any such thing as an innocent suggestion. When my assistant offered to take one of my duties, I wondered if it was the first step in assuming *all* of my duties. After Carver was fired, three other editors, each over fifty, got termination notices. I'm forty-six. Mr. Carver. Mr. Neal. I often asked my assistant to call me Tom. He never complied. "Mister" isn't only a term of respect—it's also a way of depersonalizing the competition.

"Thanks, but I'll take care of it."

Determined to stake out my territory, I carried the package home. But I forgot about it until Sunday afternoon after I worked through several gut-busting boxes of submissions that included two serial-killer novels and a romantic saga about California's wine country. The time-demanding tyranny of those manuscripts is one reason my wife moved out years earlier. She said she lived as if she were single, so she might as well *be* single. Most days, I don't blame her.

A Yankees game was on television. I opened a beer, noticed the package on a side table, and decided to flip through its contents during commercials. When I tore it open, I found a manuscript. It was typed. Double-spaced in professional format. With unsolicited manuscripts, you can't count on that. It didn't reek of cigarette smoke or food odors, and that too was encouraging. Still, I was bothered not to find an introductory letter and return postage.

The manuscript didn't have the uniform typeface that word processors and printers create. Some letters were faint, others dark. Some were slightly above or below others. The author actually put this through a typewriter, I realized in amazement. It was a novel called *The Architecture of Snow*. An evocative title, I decided, although the Marketing Department would claim that bookstore clerks would mistakenly put it in the Arts and Architecture section. The writer's name was Peter Thomas. Bland. The Marketing Department preferred last names that had easily remembered concrete nouns like King, Bond, or Steel.

With zero expectation, I started to read. Hardly any time seemed to pass before the baseball game ended. My beer glass was empty, but I didn't remember drinking its contents. Surprised, I noticed the darkness outside my apartment's windows. I glanced at my watch. Ten o'clock? Another fifty pages to go. Eager to proceed, I made a sandwich, opened another beer, shut off the TV, and finished one of the best novels I'd read in years.

You dream about something like that. An absolutely perfect manuscript. Nothing to correct. Just a wonderful combination of hypnotic tone, powerful emotion, palpable vividness, beautiful sentences, and characters you never want to leave. The story was about a ten-year-old boy living alone with his divorced father on a farm in Vermont. In the middle of January, a blizzard hits the area. It knocks down electricity and telephone lines. It disables cell-phone relays. It blocks roads and imprisons the boy and his father.

"The father starts throwing up," I told the Marketing/Editorial Committee. "He gets a high fever. His lower-right abdomen's in terrific pain. There's a medical book in the house, and it doesn't take them long to realize the father has appendicitis. But they can't telephone for help, and the father's too sick to drive. Even if he could, his truck would never get through the massive drifts. Meanwhile, with the power off, their furnace doesn't work. The temperature in the house drops to zero. When the boy isn't trying to do something for his father, he works to keep a fire going in the living room, where they retreat. Plus, the animals in the barn need food, the cows need milking. The boy has to struggle through the storm to reach the barn and keep them alive. With the pipes frozen, he can't get water from the well. He melts snow in pots near the fire. He heats canned soup for his dad, but the man's too sick to keep it down. Finally, the boy hears a snowplow on a nearby road. In desperation, he dresses as warmly as he can. He fights through drifts to try to reach the road."

"So basically it's a young adult book," the head of marketing interrupted without enthusiasm. Young adult is trade jargon for kid's story.

"A child might read it as an adventure, but an adult will see far more than that," I explained. "The emotions carry a world of meaning."

"Does the boy save the father?" the new CEO asked. He came from Gladstone's Broadcast Division.

"Nearly dying in the process."

"Well, at least it isn't a downer." The head of marketing shook his head from side to side. "A couple of days on a farm in a storm. Feels small. The book chains want global threats and international conspiracies."

"I promise—on the page, those few days feel huge. The ten-year-old becomes the father. The sick father becomes the son. At first, the boy's overwhelmed. Then he manages almost superhuman efforts."

"Child in jeopardy. The book won't appeal to women. What's the title mean?"

"The epigraph indicates that *The Architecture of Snow* is a quote from an Emerson poem about how everything in life is connected as if covered by snow."

The CEO sounded doubtful. "Has anybody heard of the author?"

"No."

"A first novel. A small subject. It'll be hard to persuade the book chains to support it. I don't see movie potential. Send the usual rejection letter."

"Can't," I said, risking my job. "The author didn't give a return address."

"A typical amateur."

"I don't think so." I paused, about to take the biggest risk of my career. But if my suspicion was correct, I no longer needed to worry about my job. "The book's beautifully, powerfully written. It has a distinctive, hypnotic rhythm. The punctuation's distinctive also: an unusual use of dashes and italics. A father and a son. Lost innocence. The book's style and theme are synonymous with . . . " I took the chance. "They remind me of R. J. Wentworth."

The CEO thought a moment. "*The Sand Castle?*"

"We've sold eight million copies so far, a hundred thousand paperbacks to colleges this year alone."

"You're suggesting someone imitated his style?"

"Not at all."

"Then . . . ?"

"I don't believe it's an imitation. I think Peter Thomas *is* R. J. Wentworth."

The room became so quiet I heard traffic outside.

"But isn't Wentworth *dead?*" a marketer asked. "Wasn't he killed in a car accident in the sixties?"

"Not exactly."

*October 15, 1961*

Three disasters happened simultaneously. A movie based on one of Wentworth's short stories premiered that month. The story was called "The Fortune Teller", but the studio changed the title to "A Valentine for Two". It also added a couple of songs. Those changes confirmed Wentworth's suspicions about Hollywood. The only reason he sold the rights to the short story was that every producer was begging for *The Sand Castle* and he decided to use "The Fortune Teller" as a test case.

He lived with his wife and two sons in Connecticut. The family begged him to drive them into Manhattan for the premiere, to see how truly bad the film was and laugh it off. En route, rain turned to sleet. The car flipped off the road. Wentworth's wife and two sons were killed.

The film was more dreadful than anyone imagined. The story's New England setting became a cruise ship. A teenage idol played the main character—originally a college professor, but now a dance instructor. Every review was scathing. Nearly all of them blamed Wentworth for giving Hollywood the chance to pervert a beloved story. Most critics wrote their attacks in mock Wentworth prose, with his distinctive rhythms and his odd use of dashes and italics.

Meanwhile, his new book, a collection of two novellas, *Opposites Attract*, was published the same day. March & Sons wanted to take advantage of the movie publicity. Of course, when the date was originally chosen, no one could have known how rotten the movie would be. By the time rumors spread, it was too late to change the schedule. Reviewers already had the book in their hands. It was charming. It was entertaining. In many places, it was even meaningful. But it wasn't as magnificent as *The Sand Castle*. Anticipation led to disappointment, which turned to nastiness. Many reviewers crowed that Wentworth wasn't the genius some had reputed him to be. They took another look at *The Sand Castle* and now faulted passages in *it*.

"All on the same day," I told the Marketing/Editorial Committee. "October 15, 1961. Wentworth blamed everything on himself. His fiction echoes transcendental writers like Thoreau, so it isn't surprising that he followed Thoreau's example and retreated to the countryside—in this case, Vermont, where he bought a house on two acres outside a small town called Tipton. He enclosed the property with a high fence, and that was the end of his public life. But the myth started when *Time* put him on its cover and told as much as it could without being able to interview him. College students began romanticizing his retreat to the countryside—the grieving, guilt-ridden author, father, and husband living in isolation. When the paperback of *Opposites Attract* was published, it became a two-year bestseller. More than that, it was suddenly perceived as a minor masterpiece. Not *The Sand Castle*, of course. But far superior to what critics first maintained. With each year of his seclusion, his reputation increased."

"How do you know so much about him?" the head of marketing asked.

"I wrote several essays about him when I was an undergrad at Penn State."

"And you're convinced this is a genuine Wentworth manuscript?"

"One of the tantalizing rumors about him is that, although he never published anything after 1961, he kept writing every day. He implied as much to a high-school student who knocked on his gate and actually got an interview with him."

"Those essays you wrote made you an expert? You're confident you can tell the real thing from an imitation?" the CEO asked.

"The book's set in Vermont, where Wentworth retreated. The boy limps from frostbite on his right foot, the same foot Wentworth injured in the accident. But I have another reason to believe it's genuine. Wentworth's editor, the man who discovered him, was Samuel Carver."

"*Carver?*" The CEO leaned forward in surprise. "After more than forty years, Wentworth finally sent his editor a manuscript? Why the pseudonym?"

"I don't have an answer. But the absence of a letter and a return address tells me that the author expected Carver to know how to get in touch with him. I can think of only one author who could take that for granted."

"Jesus," the CEO said, "if we can prove this was written by Wentworth—"

"Every talk show would want him," the head of marketing said. "A legendary hermit coming out of seclusion. A solitary genius ready to tell his story. PBS would jump at the chance. The *Today* show. *Good Morning, America.* My God, I bet he could get half of *Sixty Minutes.* He'd easily make the cover of *Time* again. We'd have a guaranteed number one bestseller."

"Wait a second," a marketer asked. "How *old* is he?"

"Seventy-eight," I answered.

"Maybe he can barely talk. Maybe he'd be useless on television."

"That's one of a lot of things you need to find out," the CEO told me. "Track him down. Find out if he wrote this manuscript. Our parent company wants a twenty-percent increase in profits. We won't do that by promoting authors who sell only fifty or a hundred thousand hardbacks. We need a million seller. I'm meeting the Gladstone executives on Monday. They want to know what progress we're making. It would be fabulous if I could tell them we have Wentworth."

I tried to telephone Wentworth's agent to see if she had contact information. But it turned out that she had died twelve years earlier and that no arrangements were made for anyone else to represent the author, who wasn't expected to publish again. I called Vermont's telephone directory assistance and learned that Wentworth didn't have a listed phone number. The Author's Guild couldn't help, either.

My CEO walked in. "What did he tell you? Does he admit he's the author?"

"I haven't been able to ask him. I can't find a way to contact him."

"This is too important. Show some initiative. Go up there. Knock on his door. Keep knocking until he answers."

I got a map and located Tipton in the southern part of Vermont. Few people live near the town, I discovered. It was hard to reach by plane or train, so the next morning, I rented a car and drove six hours north through Connecticut and Massachusetts.

In mid-October, Vermont's maple-tree-covered hills had glorious colors, although I was too preoccupied to give them full attention. With difficulty—because a crossroads wasn't clearly marked—I reached Tipton (population 5,073) only after dark and checked into one of its few motels without getting a look at the town.

At eight the next morning, I stepped from my room and breathed cool, clean air. Rustic buildings lined the main street, mostly white clapboards with high-pitched roofs. A church steeple towered above a square. Calm. Clean. Quiet. Ordered. The contrast with Manhattan was dramatic.

Down the street, a sign read *MEG'S PANTRY*. As I passed an antiques store, I had the palpable sense of former years. I imagined that, except for satellite dishes and SUVs, Tipton looked the same now as it did a hundred years earlier, perhaps *two* hundred years, that the town was a time capsule. Then I noticed a plaque: *JEREMIAH TIPTON CONSTRUCTED THIS BUILDING IN 1792.*

When I opened the door, the smell of coffee, pancakes, eggs, bacon, and hash browns overwhelmed me. A dozen ruddy-faced patrons looked up from their breakfasts. My pale cheeks made me self-conscious, as did my slacks and sports coat. Amid jeans and checkered wool shirts, I obviously wasn't a local. Not that I sensed hostility. A town that earned its income from tourists tolerated strangers.

As they resumed their murmured conversations, I sat at the counter. A gray-haired woman with spectacles came over, gave me a menu, and pulled a notepad from an apron.

"What's the special?" I asked.

"Corned beef and eggs."

Tension ruined my appetite, but I knew I couldn't establish rapport if my bill wasn't high enough for the waitress to expect a good tip. "I'll take it."

"Coffee?"

"You bet. Regular. And orange juice."

When she brought the food, I said, "Town's kind of quiet."

"Gets busy on the weekends. Especially now that the leaves are in color."

When she brought the check, I said, "I'm told there's a writer who lives in the neighborhood. R. J. Wentworth."

Everyone looked at me.

"Wentworth? I don't think I ever heard of him," the waitress said. "Mind you, I'm not a reader."

"You'd love his books." The obvious response to a statement like that is, *"Really? What are they about?"* But all I received was a guarded look. "Keep the change," I said.

Subtlety not having worked, I went outside and noticed slightly more activity on the street. Some of it wasn't reassuring. A rumpled guy in ragged clothes came out of an alley. He had the vacant look of a druggy.

Other movement caught my attention. A slender man wearing a cap and a windbreaker reached a bookstore across the street, unlocked its door, and went in. When I crossed to it, I saw that most of the volumes in the window had lush covers depicting covered bridges, autumn foliage, or snow-covered slopes, with titles related to Vermont's history and beauty. But one volume, small and plain, was a history of Tipton. I tried the door and found it was locked.

Through the window, I saw the slender man take off his windbreaker. His cap was already off, revealing thin hair. He turned toward the rattling doorknob and shook his head, motioning courteously for me to leave. When I pretended to be confused, he walked over and unlocked the door.

"I'm not open yet. Can you come back in an hour?"

"Sure. I want to buy that book in the window—the history of Tipton."

That caught his attention. "You've got excellent taste. Come in."

An overhead bell rang when he opened the door wider. The store was filled with pleasant mustiness. He tugged a pen from his shirt pocket. "I'll autograph it for you."

"You're the author?"

"Guilty."

I looked at the cover. *Tales of Historic Tipton* by Jonathan Wade. "I'm from New York. An editor for March & Sons. It's always a pleasure to meet an author."

"You're here to see the colors?" Wade asked.

"A little pleasure with business." I handed him fifteen dollars for the book.

"Business?"

"An author lives around here."

"Oh?"

"R. J. Wentworth."

"Oh?"

"I need to speak to him."

"Couldn't you just write him a letter?"

"I don't have his address."

"I see." Wade pointed at the book in my hands. "And you thought perhaps the address is in *there*?"

"The thought crossed my mind."

"You won't find it. Still want to buy the book?"

"Absolutely. I love history, and when I meet an author, I'm always curious to see how he writes."

"Not with the brilliance of R. J. Wentworth, I regret to say. We used to get people asking about him all the time. Thirty years ago, my father had a thriving business, selling Wentworth's books to people who asked about him. In fact, without Wentworth, he wouldn't have made a living. Nor would anybody else in town, for that matter. Tipton would have dried up if not for the tourists Wentworth attracted."

"But not anymore?"

"His fans got old, I guess, and people don't read much these days."

"So a waitress across the street told me."

"This town owes him a lot, even if he didn't mean to do us a favor. In these parts, if you're not born here, you're always an outsider. But after more than forty years of living here, he's definitely one of us. You won't find anybody who'll tell you where he is. I wouldn't be able to look him in the eyes if I violated his privacy."

"In the eyes?" I asked in amazement. "You mean you've spoken with him?"

"Despite Bob's reputation for being a hermit, he isn't antisocial."

"Bob?" I asked in greater amazement. The familiarity sounded almost profane.

"His first name is Robert, after all. He insists on being called Bob. He comes into town on occasion. Buys books. Eats at the Pantry. Gets a haircut. Watches a baseball game at the tavern down the street."

I continued to be astounded.

"Not often and certainly never on a weekend during peak tourist season," Wade said. "He picks times when he knows he can move around without being bothered."

"Even at his age?"

"You'd be surprised."

"But what's he like?"

"Polite. Considerate. He doesn't make assumptions about himself. What I mostly notice is how clear his eyes are. You've read his work?"

"Many times."

"Then you know how much it's influenced by transcendentalism. He's like Thoreau. Calm. Still. Reflective. It's soothing to be around him."

"But you won't help me meet him?"

"Definitely not."

"Could you at least phone him and try to arrange a meeting?"

"Can't."

"I understand."

"I'm not sure you do. I literally can't. Bob doesn't have a telephone. And I'm not about to knock on his door. Why do you need to talk to him?"

I told Wade about the manuscript. "I think it's his work, but it doesn't have his name on it." I added the detail that I hoped would make Wade cooperate. "It was addressed to his editor. But unfortunately, his editor died recently. They were friends. I wonder if he's been told."

"I only have your word that you're an editor."

"Here's my business card."

"Twenty years ago, a man showed me a business card, claiming he worked in the White House. He said the president wanted to give Bob an award, but he turned out to be an assistant to a Hollywood producer who wanted the movie rights for *The Sand Castle*."

"What harm would it do to put a note in his mailbox?"

"I've never intruded on him. I'm not about to start now."

Outside, a pickup truck rattled past. A few more locals appeared on the sidewalk. Another rumpled guy came out of an alley. A half block to my right, a Jeep was parked outside an office marked *TIPTON REALTY*. I walked over and pretended to admire a display of properties for sale: farms, cabins, and historic-looking homes.

When I stepped inside, the hardwood floor creaked. The smell of furniture polish reminded me of my grandmother's house.

At an antique desk, an attractive red-haired woman looked up from a computer screen. "May I help you?" Her voice was pleasant.

"I was wondering if you had a map of the roads around here. My Vermont map doesn't provide much detail."

"Looking for property?"

"Don't know yet. As you can probably tell, I'm not from around here. But the scenery's so magnificent I thought I might drive around and see if anything appeals to me."

"A weekend place to live?"

"Something like that."

"You're from New York, right?"

"It's that obvious?"

"I meet a lot of people passing through. I'm a good judge of accents. New York's a little far to have a weekend place here."

"I'm not sure it would be just for weekends. I'm a book editor. But I've given some thought to writing a novel."

This attracted her interest.

"I hear the location has inspired other writers," I said. "Doesn't John Irving live in Vermont?"

"And David Mamet and Grace Paley."

"And R. J. Wentworth," I said. "Doesn't he live around here?"

Her expression became guarded.

"Great writer," I said.

Her tone was now curt. "You'll find maps on that table."

As I walked to my car, I thought that the CIA or the Mafia ought to send their recruits for training in Tipton. The townspeople knew how to keep secrets. I chose north, driving along brilliantly wooded back roads. The fragrance of the falling leaves was powerful, reminding me of my boyhood on Long Island, of helping my father rake the yard. He burned the leaves in a fallow vegetable garden behind our house. He always let me strike the match. He died from a heart attack when I was twelve.

I turned up a dirt road, passed a cabin, reached a wall of trees, and went back to the main road. Farther along, I turned up another dirt road, passed *two* cabins, reached a stream that blocked the road, and again went back.

My search wasn't as futile as it seemed. After all, I knew what I was looking for: a high fence that enclosed a couple of acres. The female student who'd been fortunate enough to get an interview with Wentworth years earlier described the property. The high gate was almost indistinguishable from the fence, she wrote. The mailbox was embedded in the fence and had a hatch on the opposite side so that Wentworth didn't need to leave the compound to get his mail. A sign warned *NO SOLICITORS.*

But nothing in the north sector matched that description. Of course, the student's interview was two decades old. Wentworth might have changed things since then, in which case I was wasting my time. How far away from town would he have wanted to live? I arbitrarily decided that fifteen miles was too far and switched my search to the side roads in the west. More farms and cabins, more falling leaves and wood smoke. By the time I finished the western sector and headed south, the afternoon light was fading.

My cell phone rang.

"Have you found him yet?" my boss demanded.

The reception was so poor I could barely hear him. When I explained the problems I was having, he interrupted, "Just get it done. If Wentworth wrote this book, remind him his last contract with March & Sons gives us the option on it. There's no way I'm going to let anybody else publish it. Do you have the agreement with you?"

"In my jacket."

"Make sure you get him to sign it."

"He'll want to talk to an agent."

"You told me his agent's dead. Anyway, why does he need an agent? We'll give him whatever he wants. Within reason." The transmission crackled. "This'll go a long way toward proving you're a necessary part of the team." The crackle worsened. "Don't disappoint . . . call . . . soon . . . find . . . "

With renewed motivation, I searched the southern sector, not giving up until dark.

In town, I refilled the gas tank, ready for an early start the next morning. Then I walked along the shadowy main street, noticing *FOR SALE* signs on a lot of doors. The financial troubles gave me an idea.

Tipton Realty had its lights on. I knocked.

"Come in," a woman's voice said.

As I entered, I couldn't help noticing my haggard reflection on the door's window. Again the hardwood floor creaked.

"Busy day?" The same woman sat at the desk. She was about thirty-five. Her lush red hair hung past her shoulders. Her bright-green eyes were hard to look away from.

"I saw a lot of beautiful country."

"Did you find him?"

"Find . . . ?"

"Bob Wentworth. Everybody in town knows you're looking for him."

I glanced down. "I guess I'd make a poor spy. No, I didn't find him." I held out my hand. "Tom Neal."

She shook it. "Becky Shafer."

"I can't get used to people calling him Bob. I gather you've met him."

"Not as much as other people in Tipton. I'm new."

"Oh?"

"Yeah, I came here only twelve years ago."

I chuckled.

"I drove into town with my artist boyfriend," she said. "We loved the quiet and the scenery. We decided to stay. The boyfriend's long gone. But I'm still a newcomer."

"Sorry about the boyfriend." I noticed she didn't wear a wedding ring.

"No need to be sorry. He turned out to be a creep."

"A lot of that going around." I thought of my CEO.

She gave me a look that made me think she'd applied the word to me.

"I do have an important reason to see him," I said.

After I told her about the manuscript, she thought a moment. "But why would he use a pseudonym?"

"That's one of many things I'd like to ask him." Thinking of the *FOR SALE* signs, I took my chance to propose my idea. "To hear the old-timers tell it, things got crazy here with so many fans wanting to talk to him. You can imagine the effect a new book would create. The publicity. The pent-up demand. This town would attract a lot of fans again. It would be like the excitement of thirty years ago."

I let the temptation sink in.

Becky didn't respond for several moments. Her gaze hardened. "So all I need to do is show you where Bob lives, and in exchange, next year I'll have more business than I can handle?"

"When you put it that way, I guess that's right," I said.

"Gosh, I didn't realize it was so late." She angrily pulled her car keys from her purse. "You'll have to excuse me. I need to go home."

The weathered, old Tipton Tavern was presumably the place Wade told me about, where Wentworth sometimes watched a baseball game. But now the season was over, and it turned out I was the main interest, patrons setting down their drinks and looking at me. As much as I could tell from recalling the photograph on Wentworth's books (a dark-haired man with soulful eyes), he wasn't in the room.

Heading back to the motel, I didn't go far before I heard wary footsteps behind me. A cold breeze made me shiver as I glanced back toward the shadowy street. The footsteps ended. I resumed walking and again heard stealthy footsteps. My Manhattan instincts took charge. Not quite running, I passed my car and reached the motel. My cold hands fumbled with the room key.

In the night, glass broke outside my room. I phoned the front desk, but no one answered. In the morning, not having slept well, I went out to my car and found the driver's window shattered. A rock lay on the seat. The radio was gone.

The surprised desk clerk told me, "The town constable runs the barbershop."

But the barbershop wasn't open yet. Nor was it open after a quick cup of coffee at Meg's Pantry. Determined not to waste time, I swept the broken glass from the seat and drove to the hills east of town. But after a painstaking search, I found nothing that resembled Wentworth's compound.

By then, it was noon. When I got back to town, the barbershop was open. It smelled of aftershave.

"Yes, we've been having incidents lately." The heavyset barber trimmed an elderly man's spindly hair. "A bicycle was stolen. A cabin was broken into."

I took a close look at the man in the chair and decided he wasn't Wentworth.

"Town's changing. Outsiders are hanging around," the barber continued.

I recalled the two druggies I'd seen emerge from an alley the previous day. "What are you going to do about it?"

"Contact the state police. I hoped the problem would go away as the weather got colder."

"Please remember I reported the stolen radio. The rental-car agency will contact you." Hoping to catch him off guard, I added, "Where does Bob Wentworth live?"

The barber almost responded. Then he caught himself. "Can't say."

But like a bad poker player, he couldn't repress a glance past me toward the right side of the street.

"Thanks anyway," I said.

I went to the left to avoid suspicion. Then I walked around the block and returned to the main street, out of sight of the barbershop. As I stepped from an alley, I again had the sense that someone followed, but when I looked behind me, I seemed alone.

More people were on the sidewalk, many dressed like outsiders, the town finally attracting business as the weekend approached. But the locals paid attention only to me. Trying to look casual, I went into a quilt shop, then continued down the street. Wentworth didn't live on a country road, I now realized with growing excitement. He was in town. But I'd checked all the side streets. In fact, I'd used some of those streets to drive north, west, south, and east. Where was he hiding?

Then I saw it. On my left, a gate blocked a lane between an empty store and a cookie shop. The gate had the same white color as the adjacent buildings. It blended so well that I hadn't noticed it, despite having driven past it several times. The blocked lane went past buildings toward the edge of town.

I walked to the end of the street. In a park of brilliant maples, dead leaves crunched under my shoes as I followed a stream. I soon reached a tall fence.

My cell phone rang.

"I hope you've found him," a stern voice said.

"I'm making progress."

"I want more than progress. The Gladstone executives phoned to remind me they expect a better profit picture when I report on Monday. I hinted I'd have major news. Don't let me down. Get Wentworth, or don't come back."

Another gate blocked a lane. It was as high as my shoulders, but I managed to climb over, tearing a button off my sports jacket.

Sunlight cast the shadows of branches. To my left were the backyards of houses. But on my right, the fence stretched on. A crow cawed. Leaves rattled as I came to a door that blended with the fence. A sign warned NO SOLICITORS. A mailbox was recessed into the fence.

When I knocked on the door, the crow stopped cawing. The door shook. I waited, then knocked again, this time harder. The noise echoed in the lane. I knocked a third time.

"Mr. Wentworth?"

Leaves fell.

"Mr. Wentworth? My name's Tom Neal. I work for March & Sons. I need to talk to you about a manuscript we think you sent."

A breeze chilled my face.

I knocked a fourth time, hurting my knuckles. *"Mr. Wentworth?"*

Finally, I took out a pen and a notepad. I thought about writing that Carver was dead, but that seemed a harsh way for Wentworth to get the news. So I gave him the name of the motel and left my cell phone number. Then I remembered that Wentworth didn't have a phone. But if he sometimes left his compound, he could use a phone in town, I concluded. Or he could walk to the motel.

"I'm shoving a note under the gate!"

Back in the park, I sat on a bench and tried to enjoy the view, but the breeze got cooler. After an hour, I climbed back into the lane and returned to Wentworth's gate. A corner of my note remained visible under it.

"Mr. Wentworth, *please*, I need to talk to you! It's important!"

*Maybe he's gone for a walk in the woods,* I thought. *Or maybe he isn't even in town. Hell, he might be in a hospital somewhere.*

"Did you find him?"

In the tavern, I looked up from a glass of beer. "No." Strictly speaking, it wasn't a lie.

Becky Shafer stood next to me at the bar. Her green eyes were as hypnotic as on the previous evening. "I saw you walk in here," she said.

"You and everybody else in town."

"I thought about our conversation last night. I came to apologize for being abrupt."

"Hey, I'm from New York, remember? It's impossible to be abrupt to me. Anyway, I can't blame you for trying to protect someone who lives here."

"May I sit down?"

"I welcome the company. Can I buy you a beer?"

"Rye and Diet Coke."

"Rye?" I mock shuddered. "I admire an honest drinker."

She laughed as the bartender took my order. "Maybe it *would* be good for the town if Bob published another book. Who knows? It's just that I don't like to feel manipulated."

"I'm so used to being manipulated it feels normal."

She gave me a questioning look.

"When I first became an editor, all I needed to worry about was helping an author write a good book. But now conglomerates own just about every publisher. They think of books as commodities, like laundry detergent. If authors don't sell a quarter-million copies, the head office doesn't care about them, and editors who don't find the next blockbuster are taking up space. Every morning, I go to March & Sons, wondering if I still work there. What's that line from Joseph Heller? 'Closed doors give me the willies.' Damned right."

"I know what you mean." Becky sipped her drink. "I'm also an attorney." My surprised look made her nod. "Yep. Harvard Law School."

"I'm impressed."

"So was the Boston law firm that hired me. But I couldn't bear how the senior partners pitted us against each other to see who generated the most fees. That's why I ended here. I don't earn much money, but I sure enjoy waking up each morning."

"I don't hear many people say *that*."

"Stay here longer. Maybe *you'll* be able to say it."

Walking back to the motel, I again heard footsteps. As on the previous night, they stopped when I turned toward the shadows. Their echo resumed when I moved on. Thinking of my broken car window, I increased speed. My cell phone rang, but I didn't have time to answer it. Only after I entered my room and locked the door did I listen to the message, hoping it was from Wentworth.

But the voice belonged to my CEO. "You're taking too long," he told me.

"Mr. Wentworth?" At nine the next morning, amid a strong breeze, I pounded on his gate. "It's really important that I talk to you about your manuscript! And Sam Carver! I need to talk to you about *him*!"

I stared at the bottom of the gate. Part of my note still remained visible. A thought from yesterday struck me. Maybe he isn't home. Maybe he's in a hospital somewhere. Or maybe—a new thought struck harder—maybe he *is* home. Maybe he's sick. Too sick to come to the gate.

"Mr. Wentworth?" I hammered the gate. "Are you all right?" I tried the knob, but it didn't turn. "Mr. Wentworth, can you hear me? Is anything wrong? *Do you need help?*"

Perhaps there was another way in. Chilled by the strengthening breeze, I returned the way I had come and climbed back into the park. I followed the fence to a corner, then continued along the back, struggling through dense trees and undergrowth.

Indeed, there *was* another way in. Hidden among bushes, a gate shuddered as I pounded. "Mr. Wentworth?" I shoved a branch away and tried the knob, but it too wouldn't turn. I rammed my shoulder against the gate, but it held firm. A tree grew next to the fence. I grabbed a branch and pulled myself up. Higher branches acted as steps. Buffeted by the wind, I straddled the fence, squirmed over, dangled, and dropped to a pile of soft leaves.

Immediately, I felt a difference. The wind stopped. Sounds were muted. The air became cushioned, as if a bubble enclosed the property. A buffer of some kind. No doubt, the effect was caused by the tall fence. Or maybe it was because I'd entered sacred territory. As far as I knew, I was one of the few ever to set foot there. Although I breathed quickly, I felt a hush.

Apples hung on trees or lay on the ground amid leaves. A few raspberries remained on bushes. A vegetable garden contained the frost-browned remnants of tomato plants. Pumpkins and acorn squash bulged from vines. Continuing to be enveloped in a hush, I walked along a stone path bordered by rose bushes. Ahead were a gazebo, a cottage, and a smaller building, the latter two made from white clapboard.

"Mr. Wentworth?"

When I rounded the gazebo and headed toward the cottage, I heard a door creak open. A man stepped out. He wore sneakers, jeans, and a sweater. He was slender, with slightly graying hair. He had dark, intense eyes.

But what I noticed most was the pistol in his hand.

"Wait." I jerked up my hands, thinking, *My God, he's been living alone for so long he's lost his mind. He's going to shoot me.*

"Walk to the front gate."

"This isn't what it looks like." My chest cramped. "I thought you were ill. I came to see if I can help."

"Stay ahead of me."

"My name's Tom Neal. I knocked on the gate."

*"Move."*

"I left a note. I'm an editor for March & Sons. Please," I blurted, "I need to talk to you about a manuscript I think you sent us. It was addressed to Sam Carver. He's dead. I took over his duties. That's why—"

"Stop," the man said.

His command made the air feel stiller. Crows cawing, squirrels scampering along branches, leaves falling—everything seemed to halt.

"Sam's dead?" The man frowned as if the notion was unthinkable.

"A week ago Monday."

Slowly, he lowered the gun. He had Wentworth's sensitive features and soulful eyes. But Wentworth would be in his late seventies, and this man looked twenty years younger, his cheeks aglow.

"Who *are* you?" I asked.

The man rubbed his forehead in shock. "What? Who . . . ? Nobody. Bob's son. He's out of town. I'm watching the house for him."

Bob's son? But that didn't make sense. The child would have been born when Wentworth was around twenty, before he got married, before *The Sand Castle* was published. Later, the furor of interest in Wentworth was so great that it would have been impossible to keep an illegitimate child a secret.

The man continued to look shocked. "What happened to Sam?"

I explained about the firm's new owner and how Carver was fired.

"The way you talk about the bus, are you suggesting . . . "

"I don't think Sam had much to live for. The look on his face when he carried his belongings from the office . . . "

The man seemed to peer at something far away. "Too late."

"What?"

Despondent, he shook his head from side to side. "The gate self-locks. Let yourself out."

As he turned toward the cottage, he limped.

"You're not Wentworth's son."

He paused.

"The limp's from your accident. You're R. J. Wentworth. You look twenty years younger. I don't know how that's possible, but that's who you are."

I've never been looked at so deeply. "Sam was your friend?"

"I admired him."

His dark eyes assessed me. "Wait here."

When he limped from the house, he held a teapot and two cups. He looked so awkward that I reached to help.

We sat in the gazebo. The air felt more cushioned and soothing. My sense of reality was tested. R. J. Wentworth. Could I actually be talking to him?

"How can you look twenty years younger than you are?"

Wentworth ignored the question and poured the tea.

He stared at the steaming fluid. His voice was tight. "I met Sam Carver in 1958 after he found *The Sand Castle* in a stack of unsolicited manuscripts. At the time, I was a teacher in a grade school in Connecticut. My wife taught there also. I didn't know about agents and how publishing worked. All I knew about was children and the sadness of watching them grow up. *The Sand Castle* was rejected by twenty publishers. If Sam hadn't found it, I'd probably have remained a teacher, which in the long run would have been better for me and certainly for my family. Sam understood that. After the accident, he was as regretful as I that *The Sand Castle* gained the attention it did." He raised his cup. "To Sam."

"To Sam." I sipped, tasting a hint of cinnamon and cloves.

"He and his wife visited me each summer. He was a true friend. Perhaps my only one. After his wife died, he didn't come here again, however."

"You sent him *The Architecture of Snow?*"

Wentworth nodded. "Sam wrote me a letter that explained what was happening at March & Sons. You described his stunned look when he was fired. Well, he may have been stunned, but he wasn't surprised. He saw it coming. I sent the manuscript so he could pretend to make one last discovery and buy himself more time at the company."

"But why didn't you use your real name?"

"Because I wanted the manuscript to stand on its own. I didn't want the novel to be published because of the mystique that developed after I disappeared. The deaths of my wife and two sons caused that mystique. I couldn't bear using it to get the book published."

"The manuscript's brilliant."

He hesitated. "Thank you." I've never heard anyone speak more humbly.

"You've been writing all these years?"

"All these years."

He sipped his tea. After a thoughtful silence, he stood and motioned for me to follow. We left the gazebo. Limping, he took me to the small building next to the cottage. He unlocked its door and led me inside.

His writing studio. For a moment, my heart beat faster. Then the hush of the room spread through me. The place had the calm of a sanctuary. I noticed a fireplace, a desk, a chair, and a manual typewriter.

"I have five more machines just like it—in case I need parts," Wentworth said.

I imagined the typewriter's bell sounding when Wentworth reached the end of each line. A ream of paper lay next to the typewriter, along with a package of carbon paper. A window directed light from behind the desk.

And in front of the desk? I approached shelves upon which were arranged twenty-one manuscripts. I counted them. *Twenty-one.* They sent a shiver through me. "All these years," I repeated.

"Writing can be a form of meditation."

"And you never felt the urge to have them published?"

"To satisfy an ego I worked hard to eliminate? No."

"But isn't an unread book the equivalent of one hand clapping?"

He shrugged. "It would mean returning to the world."

"But you did send a manuscript to Sam."

"As Peter Thomas. As a favor to my friend. But I had doubts that the ploy would work. In his final letter, Sam said the changes in publishing were too grim to be described."

"True. In the old days, an editor read a manuscript, liked it, and bought it. But now the manuscript goes to the marketing department first. Then the marketing department takes the manuscript to the book chains and asks them, 'If we publish this, how many copies do you think you'll order?' If the number isn't high enough, the book doesn't have a chance."

Wentworth was appalled. "How can a book with an original vision get published? After a while, everything will be the same. The strain on your face. Now I understand. You hate the business."

"The way it's become."

"Then why do you stay?"

"Because, God help me, I remember how excited I felt when I discovered a wonderful new book and found readers for it. I keep hoping corporations will realize books aren't potato chips."

Wentworth's searching eyes were amazingly clear. I felt self-conscious, as if he saw into me, sensing my frustration.

"It's a pleasant day. Why don't we go back to the gazebo?" he asked. "I have some things I need to do. But perhaps you could pass the time by reading one of these manuscripts. I'd like your opinion."

For a moment, I was too surprised to respond. "You're serious?"

"An editor's perspective would be helpful."

"The last thing you need is my help." I couldn't believe my good fortune. "But I'd love to read something else you've written."

The things Wentworth had to do turned out to be raking leaves, putting them in a compost bin, and cleaning his gardens for winter. Surrounded by the calming air, I sat in the gazebo and watched him, reminded of my father. Amid the muted sounds of crows, squirrels, and leaves, I finished my cup of tea, poured another, and started the manuscript, *A Cloud of Witnesses*.

In a slum in Boston, a five-year-old boy named Eddie lived with his mother, who was seldom at home. The implication was that she haunted bars, prostituting herself in exchange for alcohol. Because Eddie was forbidden to leave the crummy apartment (the even worse hallways were filled with drug dealers and perverts), he didn't have any friends. The TV was broken. He resorted to the radio and, by trial and error, found a station that had an afternoon call-in program, *You Get It Straight from Jake*, hosted by a comedian named Jake Barton. Jake had an irreverent way of relating to the day's events, and even though Eddie didn't understand most of the events referred to, he loved the way Jake talked. Jake made Eddie laugh.

As I turned the pages, the sounds of crows, squirrels, and leaves became muffled. I heard Wentworth raking but as if from a great distance, farther and fainter. My vision narrowed until I was conscious only of the page in front of me, Eddie looking forward to each day's broadcast of *You Get It Straight from Jake*, Eddie laughing at Jake's tone, Eddie wishing he had a father like Jake, Eddie . . .

A hand nudged my shoulder, the touch so gentle I barely felt it.

"Tom," a voice whispered.

"Uh."

"Tom, wake up."

My eyelids flickered. Wentworth stood before me. It was difficult to see him; everything was so shadowy. I was flat on my back on the bench. I jerked upright.

"My God, I fell asleep," I said.

"You certainly did." Wentworth looked amused.

I glanced around. It was dusk. "All day? I slept all day? I'm so sorry."

"Why?"

"Well, I barge in on you, but you're generous enough to let me read a manuscript, and then I fall asleep reading it, and—"

"You needed the rest. Otherwise, you wouldn't have dozed."

"Dozed? I haven't slept that soundly in years. It had nothing to do with . . . Your book's wonderful. It's moving and painful and yet funny and . . . I just got to the part where Jake announces he's been fired from the radio station and Eddie can't bear losing the only thing in his life he enjoys."

"There's plenty of time. Read more after we eat."

"Eat?"

"I made soup and a salad."

"But I can't impose."

"I insist."

Except for a stove and refrigerator, the kitchen might have looked the same two hundred years earlier. The floor, the cabinets, and the walls were aged wood with a golden hue that made me think they were maple. The table and chairs were dark, perhaps oak, with dents here and there from a lifetime of use. Flaming logs crackled in a fireplace.

I smelled freshly baked bread and, for the first time in a long while, felt hungry. The soup was vegetable. I ate three servings and two helpings of salad, not to mention a half loaf of bread.

"The potatoes, tomatoes, onions, and carrots, everything in the soup comes from my garden," Wentworth said. "The growing season is brief here. I need to be resourceful. For example, the lettuce comes from a late summer planting that I keep in a glass frame so I can harvest it in the winter."

The fresh taste was powerful, warming my stomach. Somehow, I had room for two slices of apple pie, which was also homemade, the fruit from Wentworth's trees. And tea. Two cups of tea.

Helping to clean the dishes, I yawned. Embarrassed, I covered my mouth. "Sorry."

"Don't be. It's natural to feel sleepy after we eat. That's what mammals do. After they eat, they sleep."

"But I slept all day."

"A sign of how much rest you need. Lie down on the sofa in the living room. Read more of my book."

"But I ought to go back to my motel room."

"Nonsense." Limping, Wentworth guided me into the living room. The furnishings reminded me of those I had seen long ago in my grandmother's house. The sofa was covered with a blanket.

"I won't be an imposition?"

"I welcome your reaction to my manuscript. I won't let you take it with you to the motel, so if you want to read it, you need to do it here."

I suppressed another yawn, so tired that I wondered if I'd fall asleep on the way to the motel. I wouldn't be alert enough to deal with anyone following me. "Thank you."

"You're more than welcome." Wentworth brought me the rest of the manuscript, and again I felt amazed that I was in his company.

The fireplace warmed me. On the sofa, I sat against a cushion and turned the pages, once more absorbed in the story.

Jake was fired from the radio station. He announced that he had only two more broadcasts and then would leave Boston for a talk show in Cincinnati. The upcoming loss devastated Eddie. He hadn't seen his mother in two days. All he had to eat was peanut butter and crackers. He put them in a pillow case. He added a change of clothes, then went to the door and listened. He heard footsteps. Somebody cursed. Then the sounds became distant, and Eddie did the forbidden—he unlocked and opened the door. The lights were broken in most of the hallway. Garbage was stacked in corners. The smell of urine and cabbage made Eddie sick. Shadows threatened, but the sounds were more distant, just as the crackling in the fireplace came from farther away, mimicking the even farther, fainter tap of a typewriter.

The hand on my shoulder was again so gentle I barely felt it. When I opened my eyes, Wentworth stood over me, but this time he was silhouetted by light.

"Good morning." He smiled.

"Morning?"

"It's eleven o'clock."

"I slept thirteen hours?" I asked in shock.

"You're more tired than I imagined. Would you like some breakfast?"

My stomach rumbled. I couldn't recall waking up with so strong an appetite. "Starved. Just give me a moment to . . . "

"There's an extra toothbrush and razor in the bathroom."

As I washed my face, I was puzzled by my reflection in the mirror. My cheeks were no longer drawn. Wrinkles on my brow and around my eyes were less distinct. My eyes looked bright, my skin healthy.

At the kitchen table, I ate a fruit salad Wentworth had prepared—oranges, bananas, pears, and apples (the latter two from his trees, he reminded me). I refilled my bowl three times. As always, there was tea.

"Is it drugged? Is that why I'm sleeping so much?"

Wentworth almost smiled. "We both drank from the same pot. Wouldn't I have been sleepy, also?"

I studied him as hard as he had studied me. Despite his age, his cheeks glowed. His eyes were clear. His hair was gray instead of white. "You're seventy-eight, correct?"

"Correct."

"But you look twenty years younger. I don't understand."

"Perhaps you do."

I glanced around the old kitchen. I peered toward the trees and bushes outside. The sun shone on falling leaves. "This place?"

"A similar compound in another area would have produced the same effect. But yes, this place. Over the years, I acquired a natural rhythm. I lived with the land. I blended with the passage of the sun and moon and seasons. After a while, I noticed a change in my appearance, or rather the *lack* of change in my appearance. I wasn't aging at the rate that I should have. I came to savor the delight of waking each day and enjoying what my small version of the universe had in store for me."

"That doesn't seem compatible with your gun."

"I brought that with me when I first retreated here. The loss of my family . . . Each morning was a struggle not to shoot myself."

I looked away, self-conscious.

"But one day crept into another. Somehow, I persisted. I read Thoreau again and again, trying to empty myself of my not-so-quiet desperation. Along with these infinite two acres, Thoreau saved my life. I came to feel my family through the flowers and trees and . . . Nothing dies. It's only transformed. I know what you're thinking—that I found a sentimental way to compensate. Perhaps I did. But compare your life to mine. When you came here, when you snuck onto my property, you had so desperate a look that for the first time in many years I was frightened. Your scuffed shoes. The button missing from your jacket. The dirt on your slacks. I knew that homes had been broken into. I got the gun from a drawer. I hoped I wouldn't need to defend myself."

Shame burned my cheeks. "Perhaps I'd better go."

"Then I realized you were truly desperate, not because of drugs or greed, but because of a profound unhappiness. I invited you to stay because I hoped this place would save *you*."

As so often with Wentworth, I couldn't speak. Finally, I managed to say, "Thank you," and was reminded of how humbly he'd used those words when I told him how brilliant *The Architecture of Snow* was.

"I have some coveralls that might fit you," he said. "Would you like to help me clean my gardens?"

It was one of the finest afternoons of my life, raking leaves, trimming frost-killed flowers, putting them in the compost bin. We harvested squash and apples. The only day I can compare it to was my final afternoon with my father so long ago, a comparably lovely autumn day when we raked leaves, when my father bent over and died.

A sound jolted me: my cell phone. I looked at the caller ID display. Finally, the ringing stopped.

Wentworth gave me a questioning look.

"My boss," I explained.

"You don't want to talk to him?"

"He's meeting the company's directors on Monday. He's under orders to squeeze out more profits. He wants to announce that *The Architecture of Snow* is on our list."

Wentworth glanced at the falling leaves. "Would the announcement help you?"

"My instructions are not to come back if I don't return with a signed contract."

Wentworth looked as if I'd told a slight joke. "That explains what drove you to climb over my fence."

"I really did worry that you were ill."

"Of course." Wentworth studied more falling leaves. "Monday?"

"Yes."

"You'll lose sleep again."

"Somebody's got to fight them."

"Maybe we need to save ourselves before we save anything else. How would you like to help me split firewood?"

For supper, we ate the rest of the soup, the bread, and the apple pie. They tasted as fresh as on the previous night. Again, I felt sleepy, but this time from unaccustomed physical exertion. My skin glowed from the sun and the breeze.

I finished my tea and yawned. "I'd better get back to the motel."

"No. Lie on the sofa. Finish my manuscript."

The logs crackled. I might have heard the distant clatter of a typewriter as I turned the pages.

Eddie braved the dangers of the rat-infested apartment building. He needed all his cleverness to escape perverts and drug dealers. Outside, on a dark, rainy street, he faced greater dangers. Every shadow was a threat. Meanwhile, the reader learned about Jake, who turned out to be nasty when he wasn't on the air. The station's owner was glad for the chance to fire him when Jake insulted one of the sponsors during the program. The novel switched back and forth between Jake's deterioration (a failed marriage and a gambling problem) and Eddie's quest to find him.

This time, Wentworth didn't need to touch me. I sensed his presence and opened my eyes to the glorious morning.

"Did you sleep well?"

"Very. But I'm afraid I didn't finish—"

"Next time," Wentworth said.

"Next time?"

"When you come back, you can finish it."

"You'd like me to come back?"

Instead of answering, Wentworth said, "I've given your problem a great deal of thought. Before I tell you my decision, I want *you* to tell *me* what you think of my manuscript so far."

"I love it."

"And? If I were your author, is that all you'd say to me as an editor? Is there nothing you want changed?"

"The sentences work perfectly. Given your style, it would be difficult to change anything without causing problems in other places."

"Does that imply a few things *would* benefit from changes?"

"Just a few cuts."

"A few? Why so hesitant? Are you overwhelmed by the great man's talent? Do you know how Sam and I worked as editor and author? We fought over every page. He wasn't satisfied until he made me justify every word in every sentence. Some authors wouldn't have put up with it. But I loved the experience. He challenged me. He made me try harder and reach deeper. If *you* were my editor, what would you say to challenge me?"

"You really want an answer?" I took a breath. "I meant what I said. This is a terrific book. It's moving and dramatic and funny when it needs to be and . . . I love it."

"But . . . "

"The boy in *The Architecture of Snow* struggles through a blizzard to save his father. Eddie in *this* novel struggles to get out of a slum and find a father. You're running variations on a theme. An important theme, granted. But the same one as in *The Sand Castle*."

"Continue."

"That may be why the critics turned against your last book. Because *it* was a variation on *The Sand Castle*, also."

"Maybe some writers only have one theme."

"Perhaps that's true. But if I were your editor, I'd push you to learn if that were the case."

Wentworth considered me with those clear, probing eyes. "My father molested me when I was eight."

I felt as if I'd been hit.

"My mother found out and divorced him. We moved to another city. I never saw my father again. She never remarried. Fathers and sons. A powerful need when a boy's growing up. That's why I became a grade-school teacher: to be a surrogate father for the children who needed one. It's the reason I became a writer: to understand the hollowness in me. I lied to you. I told you that when I heard you coming across the yard, when I saw your desperate features, I pulled my gun from a drawer to protect myself. In fact, the gun was already in my hand. Friday. The day you crawled over the fence. Do you know what date it was?"

"No."

"October 15."

"October 15?" The date sounded vaguely familiar. Then it hit me. "Oh . . . the day your family died in the accident."

For the first time, Wentworth started to look his true age, his cheeks shrinking, his eyes clouding. "I deceive myself by blaming my work. I trick myself into thinking that if I hadn't sold 'The Fortune Teller' to Hollywood, we wouldn't have driven to New York to see the damned movie. But the movie didn't kill my family. The movie wasn't driving the car when it flipped."

"The weather turned bad. It was an accident."

"So I tell myself. But every time I write another novel about a father and a son, I think about my two boys crushed in a heap of steel. Each year, it seems easier to handle. But some anniversaries . . . even after all these years . . . "

"The gun was in your hand?"

"In my mouth. I want to save *you* because you saved *me*. I'll sign a contract for *The Architecture of Snow*."

Throughout the long drive back to Manhattan, I felt a familiar heaviness creep over me. I reached my apartment around midnight, but as Wentworth predicted, I slept poorly.

"Terrific!" My boss slapped my back when I gave him the news Monday morning. "Outstanding! I won't forget this!"

After the magic of the compound, the office was depressing. "But Wentworth has three conditions," I said.

"Fine, fine. Just give me the contract you took up there to get signed."

"He didn't sign it."

"*What?* But you said—"

"That contract's made out to R. J. Wentworth. He wants *another* contract, one made out to Peter Thomas."

"The pseudonym on the manuscript?"

"That's the first condition. The second is that the book has to be published with the name Peter Thomas on the cover."

The head of marketing gasped.

"The third condition is that Wentworth won't do interviews."

Now the head of marketing turned red, as if choking on something. "We'll lose the *Today* show and the magazine covers and—"

"No interviews? That makes it worthless," my CEO said. "Who the hell's going to buy a book about a kid in a snowstorm when its author's a nobody?"

"Those are his conditions."

*"Couldn't you talk him out of that?"*

"He wants the book to speak for itself. He says part of the reason he's famous is that his family died. He won't capitalize on that, and he won't allow himself to be asked about it."

"Worthless," my boss moaned. "How can I tell the Gladstone executives we won't have a million seller? I'll lose my job. You've already lost *yours*."

"There's a way to get around Wentworth's conditions," a voice said.

Everyone looked in that direction, toward the person next to me: my assistant, who wore his usual black turtleneck and black sports jacket.

"Make out the contract to Peter Thomas," my assistant continued. "Put in clauses guaranteeing that the book will be published under that name and that there won't be any interviews."

"Weren't you listening? An unknown author. No interviews. No serial killer or global conspiracy in the plot. We'll be lucky to sell ten copies."

"A million. You'll get the million," my assistant promised.

"Will you *please* start making sense."

"The Internet will take care of everything. As soon as the book's close to publication, I'll leak rumors to hundreds of chat groups. I'll put up a fan website. I'll spread the word that Wentworth's the actual author. I'll point out parallels between his early work and this one. I'll talk about the mysterious arrival of the manuscript just as his editor died. I'll mention that a March & Sons editor, Thomas Neal, had a weekend conference at Wentworth's home in October, something that can be verified by checking with the motel where Mr. Neal stayed. I'll juice it up until everyone buys the rumor. Believe me, the Internet thrives on gossip. It'll get out of control damned fast. Since what passes for news these days is half speculation, reporters and TV commentators will do pieces about the rumors. After a week, it'll be taken for granted that Peter Thomas is R. J. Wentworth. People will want to be the first to buy the book to see what all the fuss is about. Believe me, you'll sell a million copies."

I was too stunned to say anything.

So were the others.

Finally my boss opened his mouth. "I love the way this guy thinks." He gave me a dismissive glance. "Take the new contract back to Wentworth. Tell him he'll get everything he wants."

So, on Tuesday, I drove back to Tipton. Because I was now familiar with the route, I made excellent time and arrived at four in the afternoon. Indeed, I often broke the speed limit, eager to see Wentworth again and warn him how March & Sons intended to betray him.

I saw the smoke before I got to town. As I approached the main street, I found it deserted. With a terrible premonition, I stopped at the park. The smoke shrouded Wentworth's compound. His fence was down. A fire engine rumbled next to it. Running through the leaves, I saw townspeople gathered in shock. I saw the waitress from Meg's Pantry, the waiter from the Tipton Tavern, Jonathan Wade from the bookstore, the barber who was the town constable, and Becky. I raced toward her.

"What happened?"

The constable turned from speaking to three state policemen. "The two outsiders who've been hanging around town—they broke into Bob's place. The state police found fresh cigarette butts at the back fence. Next to a locked gate, there's a tree so close to the fence it's almost a ladder."

My knees weakened when I realized he was talking about the tree I'd climbed to get over the fence. I showed them the way, I thought, sickened. I taught them how to get into the compound.

"Some of the neighbors thought they heard a shot," the constable said, "but since this is hunting season, the shot didn't seem unusual, except that it was close to town. Then the neighbors noticed smoke rising from the compound. Seems that after the outsiders stole what they could, they set fire to the place—to make Bob's death look like an accident."

"Death?" I could barely say the word.

"The county fire department found his body in the embers."

My legs were so unsteady that I feared I'd collapse. I reached for something to support me. Becky's shoulder. She held me up.

"The police caught the two guys who did it," the constable said.

I wanted to get my hands on them and—

"Bob came to see me after you drove back to New York," Becky said. "As you know, he needed an attorney."

"What are you talking about?"

Becky looked puzzled. "You aren't aware he changed his will?"

*"His will?"*

"He said you were the kind of man he hoped that his sons would have grown up to be. He made you his heir, his literary executor, everything. This place is yours now."

Tears rolled down my cheeks. They rolled even harder an hour later when the firemen let Becky and me onto the property and showed us where they'd found Wentworth's body in the charred kitchen. The corpse was gone now, but the outline in the ashes was vivid. I stared at the blackened timbers of the gazebo. I walked toward Wentworth's gutted writing studio. A fireman stopped me from getting too close. But even from twenty feet away, I saw the clump of twisted metal that was once a typewriter. And the piles of ashes that had once been twenty-one manuscripts.

Now you know the background. I spend a lot of time trying to rebuild the compound, although I doubt I'll ever regain its magic. Becky often comes to help me. I couldn't do it without her.

But *The Architecture of Snow* is what I mostly think about. I told March & Sons to go to hell, with a special invitation to my assistant, my boss, and the head of marketing. I arranged for the novel to be privately printed under the name Peter Thomas. A Tipton artist designed a cover that shows the hint of a farmhouse within gusting snow, almost as if the snow is constructing the house. There's no author's biography. Exactly as Wentworth intended.

I keep boxes of the novel in my car. I drive from bookstore to bookstore throughout New England, but only a few will take the chance on an unknown author. I tell them it's an absolutely wonderful book, and they look blank as if "wonderful" isn't what customers want these days. Is there a serial killer or a global conspiracy?

Wade has dozens of copies in his store. His front window's filled with them. He tries to convince visitors to buy it, but his tourist customers want books that have photographs of ski slopes and covered bridges. He hasn't sold even one. The townspeople? The waitress at Meg's Pantry spoke the truth. She isn't much of a reader. Nor is anybody else. I've tried until I don't know what else to do. I'm so desperate I finally betrayed Wentworth's trust and told you who wrote it. Take my word—it's wonderful. Buy it, will you? Please. Buy this book.

# About the Contributors

**Rebecca Allred** lives in the Pacific Northwest, working by day as a doctor of pathology, but after hours, she transforms into a practitioner of macabre fiction, infecting readers with her malign prose. Her work has appeared in several anthologies including *Vignettes from the End of the World*, *A Lonely and Curious Country: Tales from the Lands of Lovecraft*, and *Gothic Fantasy: Chilling Horror Short Stories*. When she isn't busy rendering diagnoses or writing, Rebecca enjoys reading, drawing, laughing at RiffTrax, and spending time with her husband, Zach, and their kitty, Bug. You can keep up with Rebecca on Twitter @LadyHazmat.

**David Annandale** writes *Horus Heresy* and *Warhammer 40,000* fiction for the Black Library, most recently *The Unburdened* and *Yarrick: The Pyres of Armageddon*. He is also the author of the horror novel *Gethsemane Hall* and the Jen Blaylock thriller series. He teaches English literature and film at the University of Manitoba, and is a co-host of the *Skiffy and Fanty Show* and *Totally Pretentious* podcasts. Find him at www.davidannandale. com and on Twitter at @David_Annandale

**Michael Bailey** is a multi-award-winning author, editor, and publisher, and the recipient of over two dozen literary accolades, including the Benjamin Franklin Awards, Eric Hoffer Book Awards, Independent Publisher Book Awards, and the Indie Book Awards. His nonlinear novels include *Palindrome Hannah*, *Phoenix Rose*, and *Psychotropic Dragon*, and he has published two short story and poetry collections: *Scales and Petals* and *Inkblots and Bloodspots* (illustrated by Daniele Serra and introduced by Douglas E. Winter). Through Written Backwards, an imprint of Dark Regions Press, he is responsible for *Pellucid Lunacy*, the Bram Stoker Award-nominated *Qualia Nous*, *The Library of the Dead* (illustrated by GAK), three *Chiral Mad* anthologies (the last illustrated by Glenn Chadbourne), and a series of illustrated novellas. In his spare time he is also the Managing

Editor of Science Fiction for Dark Regions Press, where he is hard at work on a few novels and an anthology called *You, Human.* "Michael Bailey's become one great editor. Rock-solid."—Jack Ketchum

On a cold winter's day in 1970, **John Boden** was born. The years since have been filled with *Star Wars* action figures, cartoons, books, family, life, and love. He currently resides in Pennsylvania, between the capital and Three Mile Island. A bakery worker by day, his evenings are spent with his beautiful wife and sons and working with Shock Totem Publications. He writes when he can and reads all the time, working sleep in wherever.

His work has appeared in *52 Stitches, Metazen, Black Ink Horror 7,* Weirdyear, Necon E-Books, Shock Totem, *Blight Digest,* Splatterpunk, the John Skipp-edited *Psychos, Once Upon an Apocalypse, Robbed of Sleep,* and most recently *Lamplight.* His "not-really-for-children-even-though-it-looks-like-it" book, *Dominoes,* is a thing that's out there and people seem to dig it.

**Gary Braunbeck**'s work has garnered seven Bram Stoker Awards, as well as an International Horror Guild Award, three Shocklines Shocker Awards, a Black Quill Award, and a World Fantasy Award nomination. He is the author of the critically acclaimed *Cedar Hill* series, which includes *In Silent Graves, Keepers,* and the forthcoming *A Cracked and Broken Path.* This marks his third appearance in a *Borderlands* anthology. He lives in Worthington, Ohio, with his wife, four-time Bram Stoker Award-winner Lucy A. Snyder who, despite having lived with him for nearly fifteen years, has yet to smother him in his sleep. Find out more about him at www.facebook.com/groups/4988614289

**Sean Davis** wields a drill by day and writes scary stories by night. His stories have appeared in the anthologies *Silent Screams* and *Amanda's Recurring Nightmares;* and in *The Best of Dark Eclipse* and *Bete Noire #10.* He's a member of the Great Lakes Association of Horror Writers and the Horror Writers Association. He lives in Detroit with his partner, Kate, and a growing number of animals. Visit him at seanmdavis.wordpress.com.

**Louis Dixon** is an author and an artist. His fiction has appeared in Maynard and Sims's *Darkness Rising 2005, Horror Library Anthologies 1* and *2,* and Cemetery Dance's *Bad Dreams, New Screams.* He was once the editor-in-chief for *Dark Recesses* magazine, as well as its art director and contributor. He currently resides in Austin, Texas, with his wife and two children. From nine to five, he is a technology infrastructure architect. You can reach him at his website: www.mlouisdixon.com

**Darren Godfrey**, a former explosive ordnance disposal technician in the air force, now frays his nerves through the exploration of bizarre human behavior. He has published a collection of his short fiction, *Apathetic Flesh*, published by Books of the Dead Press, with an introduction by Kealan Patrick Burke

**Daniel Gunn** is the author of *Destroyer of Worlds* and the novella *Nightmare in Greasepaint* (with L.L. Soares). He's also the pseudonym for Daniel G. Keohane, Bram Stoker-nominated author of *Solomon's Grave*, *Margaret's Ark*, and *Plague of Darkness*. His short fiction has appeared in *Cemetery Dance*, *Shroud* magazine, *Fantastic Stories of the Imagination*, and many more. He and his family live in Massachusetts.

**Carol Pierson Holding** writes as a lapsed capitalist about the tension between business and the environment. Her commentary appears on the Huffington Post and 200 news websites and publications; her essays have been published in *Stratus*, *San Francisco Chronicle*, and the Carnegie Council's *Policy Innovations*. Previously, she ran a brand consulting firm in New York and San Francisco, where she developed the first measurement of corporate social responsibility's impact on brand value, and wrote and spoke about it extensively.

Carol spent her early childhood on a Missouri cattle farm with a frustrated writer father. Her family moved to Los Angeles, where, at Marlborough School for girls, she met her first writing mentor and the first teacher who didn't tell her she was "wasting her potential". Encouraged to go to Smith College to study English, Carol's writing career was derailed when she experienced the joy of lucrative employment and pursued more of it with an MBA from Harvard. The market crash of 2008 flattened her consulting firm and her faith in the capitalistic system, rekindled her drive to write full-time and gave her great material for her novel in progress. She currently lives in Seattle and Camano Island.

**Jack Ketchum** is the recipient of four Bram Stoker Awards and three additional nominations. Many of his novels have been adapted to film, including *The Girl Next Door* and *Red*. In 2011, Ketchum received the World Horror Convention's Grand Master Award for outstanding contribution to the horror genre

**Brian Knight** lives in Washington State with his family and the voices in his head. He has published over a dozen novels and novellas and two short story collections in the horror, dark fantasy, and crime genres. His works include *Feral, Broken Angel, Sex, Death & Honey*, and *The Phoenix Girls Trilogy*. Several of his short stories have received honorable mentions in *Year's Best Fantasy and Horror*.

**Anya Martin** has always rooted for the monster and regrets abandoning her earliest career aspiration——paleontology. She's also half-Finnish, still likes punk rock, though now with a heavy side of blues and experimental jazz, has a bachelor's degree in anthropology, cooks dangerously hot curries, earns her living as a journalist, and abides in Atlanta. Her fiction has appeared in such anthologies and magazines as *Cthulhu Fhtagn!, Giallo Fantastique, Cassilda's Song, Xnoybis #2, Resonator: New Lovecraftian Tales From Beyond*, and *Womanthology: Heroic*.

**David Morrell** is the author of *First Blood*, the award-winning novel in which Rambo was created. He holds a PhD in American literature from Penn State and was a professor in the English Department at the University of Iowa. His numerous *New York Times* bestsellers include the classic espionage novel, *The Brotherhood of the Rose*, the basis for the only television miniseries to be broadcast after a Super Bowl. An Edgar finalist, an Anthony, Inkpot, Macavity, and Nero recipient, Morrell has a Thriller Master award from International Thriller Writers. He received three Stoker awards and was a finalist for two others, as well as for two World Fantasy awards. His latest works are a series of Victorian mystery/thrillers, beginning with *Murder as a Fine Art*. Visit him at www.davidmorrell. net.

**John McIlveen** is the author of the paranormal suspense novel *Hannahwhere* and two story collections, *Inflictions* and *Jerks and Other Tales from a Perfect Man*. He is the father of five daughters, works at MIT's Lincoln Laboratory, and lives in Haverhill, MA, with his fiancée Roberta Colasanti. John has an affinity for black licorice, whoopie pies, and good tequila www.johnmcilveen.com

**Bob Pastorella** is the author of the zombie/western short story "To Watch Is Madness" and is featured in *Warmed and Bound: A Velvet Anthology*, the Booked anthology, *In Search of a City: Los Angeles in 1000 Words*, and numerous publications online and in print. Bob is a columnist, podcast host, and reviewer for *This Is Horror*. He lives in Southeast Texas and is working on a weird-crime series.

**Peter Salomon** is a member of the Society of Children's Book Writers and Illustrators, the Horror Writers Association, the Science Fiction and Fantasy Writers of America, the Science Fiction Poetry Association, the International Thriller Writers, and the Authors Guild, and is represented by the Erin Murphy Literary Agency.

His debut novel, *Henry Franks*, was published by Flux in 2012. His second novel, *All Those Broken Angels*, published by Flux in 2014, was nominated for the Bram Stoker Award for Superior Achievement in Young Adult Fiction. Both novels have been named a "Book All Young Georgians Should Read" by The Georgia Center for the Book.

His short fiction has appeared in the *Demonic Visions* series and he was the featured author for *Gothic Blue Book III: The Graveyard Edition*. He was also selected as one of the Ladies and Gentlemen of Horror for 2014. His poem "Electricity and Language and Me" appeared on BBC Radio 6 performed by the Radiophonic Workshop in December 2013. Eldritch Press published his first collection of poetry, *Prophets*, in 2014. He is the editor for the first books of poetry released by the Horror Writers Association, *Horror Poetry Showcase Volumes I and II*.

He was a judge for the 2006 Savannah Children's Book Festival Young Writer's Contest and served on the jury for the poetry category of the 2013 Bram Stoker Awards. He served as a judge for the Royal Palm Literary Awards of the Florida Writers Association. He was also a judge for the first two Horror Poetry Showcases of the Horror Writers Association and has served as chair on multiple juries for the Bram Stoker Awards.

**Steve Rasnic Tem**'s last novel, *Blood Kin* (Solaris)—a Southern gothic/horror blend of snake handling, ghosts, granny women, kudzu, and Melungeons—won the Bram Stoker Award for 2014. PS Publishing recently released his novella "In the Lovecraft Museum" and Centipede Press has scheduled *Out of the Dark: A Storybook of Horrors*, 225 thousand words of the best of his uncollected horror tales, for early 2016. In spring of 2017 Solaris will publish his new novel, *Ubo*, a dark SF meditation on violence, as seen through the eyes of some of history's most dangerous figures.

**Paul Tremblay** is the author of six novels, including *A Head Full of Ghosts*, *The Little Sleep*, and *Disappearance at Devil's Rock*. His short fiction has appeared in numerous "year's best" anthologies. He is a member of the board of directors for the Shirley Jackson Awards. He is tall, hates pickles, and has no uvula. www.paultremblay.net

Shirley Jackson Award-finalist **Tim Waggoner** has published over thirty novels and three short story collections of dark fiction. He teaches creative writing at Sinclair College and in Seton Hill University's MFA in Writing Popular Fiction program. You can find him on the web at www.timwaggoner.com.

**Daniel Waters** is the author of the *Generation Dead* series (*Generation Dead*, *Kiss of Life*, *Passing Strange*, and *Stitches*). He also wrote *Break My Heart 1,000 Times*, the film adaptation of which is scheduled to be released May 2017 from Lionsgate/Gold Circle. He lives in Connecticut with his family.

**Gordon White** lives in New York with his wife and their dog. He sleeps on the side of the bed farthest from the closet, just in case. His work has appeared in the *Wrapped in Black* anthology from Sekhmet Press, as well as in venues such as *Halloween Forevermore*, *DarkFuse*, *Cease*, *Cows!*, *Punchnel's*, and others. When not writing, he also reads for Kraken Press.

**Trent Zelazny** is the author of several novels, novellas, and short stories in numerous genres including, but not limited to, horror, crime, thriller, science fiction, erotica, and humor. He is also a bestselling international playwright, editor of two anthologies, and has written for both television and film.
Son of the late science fiction author Roger Zelazny, Trent was born in Santa Fe, New Mexico. He has lived in California, Oregon, and Florida, but currently lives with his wife, Laurel, and their two dogs, Banjo and Holly, back in Santa Fe.

**Bradley Zerbe** has published stories in print anthologies such as *Read by Dawn II* and *Best of House of Horror 2009*. His story "Fishing with the Devil" was an honorable mention for the Year's Best Fantasy and Horror 2008. He works for N. F. String & Son, Inc. in Harrisburg, Pennsylvania.

# About the Editors

Olivia F. Monteleone was born under a lucky star (thank God for nepotism). Having graduated from University of Maryland in 2013,with a degree in English, she became quickly certain she wanted no parts of teaching (shout out to teachers: *thank you!*). After attending law school for a semester and several weeks, she dropped out even though she acquired some valuable knowledge—for example, the Socratic method is useless if no one is thinking beyond what society has already constructed. Some would say she landed on her feet; but she often feels she's probably balancing on one foot (but life is more thrilling that way). She is working on a graphic novel, a screenplay, typesets and designs books for Borderlands Press while living in Baltimore with her dog, Bean. She is a glamour troll.

Thomas F. Monteleone has published more than one hundred short stories, five collections, eight anthologies and thirty novels, including the bestseller, *New York Times* Notable Book of the Year, *The Blood of the Lamb*. A four-time winner of the Bram Stoker Award, he's also written scripts for stage, screen, and TV, as well as the bestselling *The Complete Idiot's Guide to Writing a Novel* (now in a second edition). His latest novel is a global thriller, *Submerged*. He lives in Maryland, near Baltimore, and loves the Ravens. With his daughter Olivia, he co-edits the award-winning anthology series of imaginative fiction—*Borderlands*. He is well-known as a great reader of his work and routinely draws SRO at conventions. Despite being dragged kicking and screaming into his late sixties and losing most of his hair, he still thinks he is dashingly handsome—humor him.

It's all about the story...

# Romance

# HORROR

www.samhainpublishing.com

CPSIA information can be obtained at www.ICGtesting.com
Printed in the USA
LVOW11s0232300816

502334LV00005B/230/P